Glass Chimera

a novel by

L. Carey Rowland

http://www.careyrowland.com

Carey Rowland

March 22, 2012

Published by L. Carey Rowland
Cover photography by Kim Rowland
Sketch of Mick by Nora Halsey
printed by CreateSpace.com
ISBN 1452897565
EAN-13 9781452897561
Library of Congress Control Number 2010907933.

Beginnings

1

'T'wasn't a good situation, there in 1927.

To hear the story from ole Wash (Great-Grampa Beau had said) the captain had ordered the boat to be steered too close to a breach in the levee. And so, while the pilot spun the wheel in frantic dismay, the *Leda Mae* gradually got sucked out of the main channel, and then suddenly found herself sliding on a torrent of river water right through a flood-forced levee crevasse.

"She quivered like a bridesmaid in a Yazoo wedding, then slid on down, twirling and rockin' like a sycamore leaf through a sluice gate, until Ole Miss finally dropped her on Beau Rivage ridge," ole Wash had said.

It had happened on this very spot seventy-three years ago.

The "ridge," by Louisiana standards constituted a mere rise of a few feet in several hundred of distance. And this is where William was now sitting, recalling the story that had been told to him of the demise of the *Leda Mae*. He was eating a pastrami sandwich, while taking a break from his work in the microbiology lab.

But even before that unfortunate incident, William's great grandfather, Beauregard Theseus, had quite possibly sat in this same spot back in, oh, 1907 or so, as he took a break from running one of the largest cotton plantations this side of New Orleans.

But now, in 2001, a pickle slice slid from the sandwich onto William's lap. He gingerly recovered it from his jean-clad thigh and slipped it into his mouth. A thought about his work in the nearby lab asserted itself. *Nuclear transfer from cell to cell should be so easy.* Maybe it would be, after a few times. But his mind wasn't ready to go there yet, so it started wandering again. He began to whistle an old melody that just drifted into his head, *"and every stitch was love. . She made my coat of many colors that I was so proud of."*

It was Dolly that called that tune—not Dolly the sheep, which pertained to his work in the lab—but Dolly the singer.

Oh, she had a crystal-clear voice that could whir in your mind like pure white sugar spun into cotton candy. And yet it weren't so sweet that it wouldn't just absolutely pierce your heart, as if the belle herself, *Elise*, were splitting a wet Mississippi watermelon, and you could see its black-seeded, wounded-memory pith spillin' out so redly onto picnic-table recollections of afternoons long gone. Yes, for some reason or other the sound of her voice was plucking at William's insides as if he were still ramblin' along every dusty mile of foothill roads somewhere just north of the Ohio, beyond Kentucky, probably runnin' dang near empty.

Near Athens, William thought it was. Here's the thing: her voice weren't a Mississippi voice; t'weren't a Ohio voice neither. It was a Tennessee voice, resonating high and clear, as the wind on Rocky Top, comin' through the old Chevy radio in a breeze; it was the long flappin' tail of a coat of many colors, somehow soothing his urge to just be somewhere other than where he had started out.

Because this was America; you didn't necessarily end up where you started out.

As William sat munching, a flying blur beneath the nearby oak tree caught his eye. About twenty yards away from his rocking chair position, a black squirrel had leapt from a branch to the ground, and begun clawing for an acorn. Why the squirrel had leaped so dramatically God only knows, for the branch from which it had propelled itself extended all the way to the ground. The creature was frolicking—having a grand time, it seemed—jumping from limb to limb, then to the earth, then back up into its leafy haven again. *It's celebrating squirrelness, doing what squirrels do, actualizing some built-in rodentary genetic inclinations, gathering nuts for winter's approaching dearth.*

The animal's energetic tail began performing a repetitive motion—a back and forth motion slowly whipping the air. As William watched, almost thoughtlessly now, a breeze stirred the uppermost branches of the tree. His vision wandered from the squirrel low to the branches high. The enormous mass of this two-centuried oak organism suddenly struck William full of wonder. *Such a wide occupation of space (and time!).*

The professor's curious gaze meandered to the ground again; he noticed an acorn on the ground beside his rocking chair. *It had all started with a little acorn such as this.* The old arbor, a massive proliferation of steadfast cellulose, was as wide as it was tall. *Surely,* this acorn on the ground had dropped, or been blown from, the big one—the *mother* tree, as it were. Then he remembered the story his daddy had told him about "mama oak" and its nearby offspring. William turned to his left to catch a view of the smaller, younger tree. Standing about thirty yards to his left, and sixty or so yards from the "mama oak," was the one his father had called "baby" oak.

He was at a midpoint between the two. In front of him in the near distance, beyond a grassy pasture, was the cluster of agricultural buildings that included his lab. To his left and behind was a dilapidated gazebo, from which he had retrieved the weathered rocker. He swayed lazily in the warm October sunshine. After estimating the diameter of *baby oak's* trunk— probably three feet at eye level—he judged *mama's* to be about five feet at the same elevation.

The account of "baby" oak's sprouting had been passed to William's grandfather, Thaddeus, by Washington Jones, sharecropper and former owner of this 20-acre plot where William now daydreamed and upon which the two trees so generously cast their life-protecting shade. The legend extended by ole' Wash's telling was that *baby* oak's acorn had been thrust into its loamy home by the hull of the wrecked *Leda Mae* riverboat during the great flood of 1927. He was remembering the tale. A cool breeze stirred. The long, Louisiana summer was beginning, at last, to moderate.

William stood up, set his empty lunch bag down on the rocker, slurped the last swig of iced tea, and walked over to the base of *baby oak.* Standing on the tree's barky-dark, gnarly roots (if you could call them roots, for they were fully above ground), he examined its trunk closely, noting the grey-brown rivulets of space between each chunky ridge. He turned slowly around, balancing on *baby's* knobby knees, and looked back toward *mama.*

Yes, it was about a riverboat's length between the two trees. Ole Wash had said that the *Leda Mae's* paddlewheel had come to its final resting place at the base of *mama oak.* William gazed across the pastured expanse at the twice-centegenarian tree. Even at this distance, her voluptuous roots could be plainly seen, extending radially and forming a bumpy regal platform beneath the wizened trunk.

While gazing at the ancient one, William walked over to her.

As he entered her still, protective enclosure, it seemed she whispered with breezy boasts of having captured, or *rescued,* long ago the faltering riverboat queen. William's nose flared with some musty imagined awareness of shipwrecked lives that had found their watery end at *mama's* submerged roots. Their souls must have flown, like startled birds, from beneath this sylvan anchorage. Now a drooping cloak of low-arcing limbs, moss-laden, proclaimed *mama's* guardianship over the memory of faded Mississippi riverboat glory. But her quirky roots had no comment. 'Twere the leaves and branches who cast their symphony of earthen sorrow.

And there *is* a large cleft in *mama's* trunk. Could it be the gash inflicted by the *Leda Mae's* careening sternwheel?

Up above, a sparrow was chirping.

But good events had happened here too. Perhaps the stately wooden witness preserved some protoplasmic memory of sharecropper Washington Jones. Surely he had rested here, wiping the sweat from his brow during midday respite from daylong gathering of cotton. Surely he had taken a lunch of salted side meat and cornbread here beneath *mama's* merciful shade, in lieu of walking all the way back to the house.

Ole Wash's tale had further informed three successive generations that the two oaken growths, posted as they were on each end of what was for many years the *Leda Mae's* carcass, marked an identifiable site of wrecked-riverboat booty. For years afterward, local folks would visit the site regularly to retrieve blades, beams and planks from the midst of the forlorn boat's dilapidating frame.

Many a plow or hoe blade had been crafted from the *Leda Mae's* forsaken sternwheel. Many a shotgun home had been assembled by sharecroppers who had yanked, pulled and cut wooden treasure from her fashionably slick decks and her formerly sturdy hull. Such was the best and final use of her finely-crafted body parts, which had been, after all, not nearly worn out; for the regal *lady* had met her demise, alas, on her maiden trip down and up the river.

William turned around and surveyed once again the *baby* oak. Standing now on the spot where *Leda Mae's* paddles had spun their last spin, William peered beyond his rocking chair and the weathered gazebo at the younger tree that legend says had germinated beneath *Leda Mae's* rotting bow. She had paddled down from Pittsburgh only once, unloaded her cargo of Americans and cotton in New Orleans, then returned only 57 miles upriver. Her legacy: a scattered bunch of tenant farmers' houses and two live oak trees.

"Honk!. . .honk!" came a startling call from overhead.

For an instant the microbiologist glimpsed overhead a flock of migrating geese, veering in the whisper-blue sky. Then they disappeared beyond the expansive limbs. Noisily declaring a terminus of their annual flyway, they descended onto nearby Lake Mendelle. As William watched geese disappear beyond the gnarled majesty of the old tree, a flock of starlings took flight from its hundreds-year-old branches and headed into the direction from which the geese had flown.

And again his mind took to the air.

Oh, but Dolly had a voice that could break your heart, or put it back together. Thinking back on it, he must have been hightailin' it away from the memory of a certain belle, with the smell of her perfume still waftin' through his wincin' heart like the magnolia blossom on Aunt Charlotte's dinner table, where a childhood picture of the queen of England in blue velvet perpetually surveyed the room from above a sumptuous buffet. Elise's perfume was as pungent in his mind as that magnolia, the only thing that made scents of her absence. The two of them had sat there beneath the queen's benevolent gaze while Aunt Charlotte entertained. But then Elise had disappeared into southern air as thick as her perfume, and William had headed for Ohio and college. The memory, accompanied by Dolly's altous voice on the radio, had fanned out wider in his vacant life than that magnolia blossom in its doilied elegance.

But that was then, and this is now. He waved the distractions away like swamp gnats and turned to walk back to his lab and the task that he had set for himself.

It was time to get back to work. The dutifull left brain knew better than to chase those thumping right-brain rabbit trails, and he understood there's no productivity in permitting brain paths to be trodden by frivolous musings, wherein he might wander into oblivion along Ohio backroads that he had traversed almost forty years ago. At this moment he should be busily engaged in an important procedure beneath the microscope. *Better get back to it.*

It was Dolly that got him back on track. He had thought about Dolly—not the singer with a voice like spun sugar. Dolly, the sheep.

William was, at this time of his life—this juncture in his quest for knowledge, excellence, and proficiency—attempting to reproduce the Roslin nucleus-transfer procedure, which successfully engendered the world's first cloned mammal.

William's project would produce, however, not a new ewe, but a copied cow. Having shaken his mind from the distractions of oak trees, mamas, babies, belles and wrecked boats, he ambled all the way back to the low cluster of university outpost buildings, entered his laboratory and resumed the delicate procedure that he hoped would generate a cloned bovine.

With lunch and those unplanned thoughts safely set behind him in a designated place in the space/time continuum, the microbiologist found himself a few minutes later, back in the lab, gazing intently through oculars into the fertile Petri-dish home of *Elsie*, the calf-to-be, whose nomenclature, if not her primogeniture, would be a subtly anagramic variant of the name *Elise.*

Meanwhile, back at the ranch. A nucleus will not fight back. It will just sit there, being manipulated, allowing any bullish surrogate to penetrate her private space. William pressed the pipette, sucking the coy nucleus out of her cellular home.

You will be replaced, little nucleus, thought William, watching through his microscope as the miniscule blob disappeared into a glass tube. *You are expendable; your place in the universe will be taken by someone else, a nucleus who is better equipped than you for this embryonic mission.*

"Go on, little nukie, and make room for a genetically favorable substitute. Out with the old, in with the new," spoke William softly to his little beast, his little bovine oocyte. Now he squeezed the rejected nucleus out of the pipette, and into Petri-dish obscurity. It became a non-entity, like the fading memory of Dolly's voice on that Ohio backroad and the useless recalling of Elise's perfume.

Carefully, he obtained by similar procedure, the preferred nucleus from a different dish. Then, transporting it from one microscope-enabled workstation to another, he lowered his hand toward the glass container that would become Elsie's embryonic home for a while.

"Whoops!" He dropped it. William had pressed the pipette prematurely, squirting its special chromosomal cargo into cytoplasmic oblivion. Now he would never find it. He'd have to start over.

But not today. Gently setting all instruments aside, the patient scientist rested from his rudimentary opus of genetic engineering, exited the laboratory, and returned to the rocker in the sunshine to reconsider his strategies. He would need help.

All was well, in spite of his dropping the preferred nucleus. The Roslin people in Scotland must have had similar mishaps while assembling the first cloned zygote. Surely, William's project would be simpler. At least he had the benefit of knowing that the procedure *could* work; the Roslin team had published their results just a few years ago. So it was just a matter of bringing together the right combination of cellular components, in conditions that were conducive to embryonic growth. By now it had been done hundreds, perhaps thousands of times, in various species.

Theseus' aim was to produce useful pharmaceuticals from cloned animals, utilizing the predictable cloning method; it would surely prove more efficient than using the cumbersome gene-injection method.

So William Theseus, Doctor of microbiology, President of Theseus University, had thought he'd take his shot at cloning; medical facilities at Theseus were in need of hormones that could be produced by cows in their milk, if their genes were engineered accordingly. Might as well venture into the frontier of recombinant DNA, and do mankind a favor or two, since his financial security was a given. He still had, maybe, a good third of a life of research ahead of him. Starting with the clone procedure was a bit like learning the fundamentals, so that he and mankind could go on to greater, and possibly more profitable, exploits. And if he could get a handle on the necessary procedures, his students at the University would follow.

Couplings

2

"That upstart banty rooster is chasing hens around the barnyard again, Mother," said Noah to his wife. "And in the middle of the night. It ain't natural. What's got a hold of him? I've a mind to take the shotgun after him, so's I can get some sleep."

"Oh, plug your ears, dear. We've got no need for a dead rooster. Besides, he'll calm down in a minute, as soon as he finds what he's looking for. Come on over here, honey. I'll give you somethin' that'll put you to sleep." Then, deciding not to wait for her agitated husband, Becky Davis walked over to the bedroom window where he was peering out at the barn. Standing behind the man with whom she'd spent these thirty years, she wrapped her arms around his brawny back and spoke softly, fetchingly: "Come on, hon. Let's go to bed. He'll shut up in a minute."

And so they did.

The next morning, Noah was drinking coffee while Becky made scrambled eggs. Sitting at the kitchen table, he could see, out the window, the whitened tip of Aradne Ridge about three miles away through the crisp blue Carolina October morning. "We've got a little snowcap on Aradne, mother. The front came through last night, and we're looking at..." He squinted at the thermometer hanging outside on the glass. "We're looking at, oh, thirty degrees. It's about time. This is the latest I can remember, getting' the first freeze. I guess maybe Al Gore's on to somethin."

"You mean the global warming thing?" She looked quizzically at him over little bifocals, and across the stovetop, which was in an island cabinet between the kitchen and breakfast table.

"Yes."

"How can you think about global warming on a morning like this, when it's thirty degrees out?"

"I mean, it should have happened a few weeks ago. Why, when I was a boy, we would have had two or three of these below-30 nights by now."

Becky let out a little laugh. "This warming business doesn't bother me much, since now it's me out there at sunup gathering the eggs, instead of Robby and Roberta."

She cracked another egg, allowing yolk and albumen to slide down into the frying pan. "I suppose the earth really is warming, Noah, but it's probably too late to do much about it, as much stuff as we've already dumped into the atmosphere."

"Well, don't say that to Roberta. She doesn't think much of any defeatist attitude when it comes to global warming. And she wrote in that email last week something about everybody's 'carbon footprint' should get smaller." Noah slurped coffee and looked out the window again. "Speakin' of which, are they coming home for Thanksgiving?"

"Roberta will be driving up here Wednesday night. But Robby won't make it here. He said there's too much going on at the research station. Dr. Theseus will be cloning a cow or some such thing, and he doesn't want to miss it."

"Well I hope if they come up with something productive he can help us get a piece of that action. It would be nice to keep a few more milkers on the side and sell at top dollar to the drug companies. Robby had said maybe we could raise some cows that would produce, right in their milk, proteins for busting blood clots, or insulin for diabetics, or some other drug-kind of substances."

"Oh, let's do it with chickens, honey. They're a lot more manageable, and don't cost as much to feed. Besides, we already know all about chickens." She held up an egg. "See. There's your self-contained natural package for those enzymes, or whatever genetically-engineered stuff it is they're wanting to produce, right there. Wouldn't that be easier to work with than milking cows? Especially in winter time."

"I was thinking of the cows because that's what Robby says they're working with at the research station. What makes you think it would work with chickens? "

"Oh, I read about it somewhere, *Nature* or *Farm Journal*, or, I don't remember where."

"Ah, it's all just pipe dreams, mother. We can do with it, or we can do without it. We'll see if Robby and that gang come up with anything. Meanwhile, back at the ranch, I'm headed out to feed the herd. Thanks for breakfast." Noah rose from the table, retrieving plate and cup, and brought them over to the sink. He kissed his wife on the cheek and offered a stupid little smile. "Some things are best done the old fashion way."

The phone rang as she leaned toward him to receive the little peck. Then she stepped away to answer it, and Noah was headed for the door.

"*Honk, honk.*" As he stepped slowly down the back-porch stairs into brisk mountain morning air, Noah turned his head upward toward the brightening sky to see a flock of Canada geese veering their way toward northeast. Occasionally he would see this, but could never understand why the birds would be headed in any direction but south this time of year. Maybe they were taking a side trip, a pit stop at Aunt Gertie's house.

There were two barns on the Davis property: the old one and the new one. The new one had a lot to do with mechanical implements and gas-powered vehicles. The green metal building smelled of oil and hay, and it was much warmer than the old barn. Noah hopped inside his Dodge Ram, opened the garage door by remote control, and backed the big gray truck out of the building, drove the thirty-odd yards across the back yard to the old barn. He stopped the truck just outside of it, and stepped out. Sparky, his yellow Labrador retriever was at his heels, leisurely wagging his tail, expecting affection. Noah reached down, rubbed the dog's hairy head lovingly. "Hey, boy," said the farmer.

The old barn was a large wooden structure. A cold breeze was whistling through its exterior planks—gray, checked boards that had been nailed to a post-and-beam frame some seventy years ago. Noah took the few steps over to the door, fingered the wrought-iron latch open and slid the weathered planks open. A while back, he had taken the old hinges off it, and mounted metal tracks on the inside of the wall so that the door could be opened without swinging. Sparky followed Noah's every step with fond interest, tail wagging continuously, although this routine was the same every morning at about this time, and had been for many a year. The dog thrived on this regularity, and so did his master.

Noah hefted the big door along its track with a rumbling metallic sound. It was only a month ago that he had converted it from the old hinged arrangement. The project had taken a few days, but he was immensely pleased with the result, even though the benefit gained by it was nothing more than a few saved steps every morning. A life conducted with such routine tasks as his farm required was a life that seemed sublimely improved every time one chore was simplified or improved. He could have automated the old barn door so that it operated like the garage door on the new barn, but he hadn't done it. Didn't know exactly why. Maybe it was because of Sparky. Somehow that first greeting every morning with the faithful canine required movements that were closer to the ground, perhaps closer to the very motion of the earth itself with all its slow rhythms and cycles, than just sitting in a new truck while a septugenarian barn door opened automatically. It just hadn't seemed in keeping with the music of the universe to totally automate this small leg of the journey that would end in visiting cattle that would be fed for yet another winter day.

The wheels could use a little grease though, he noticed.

Noah hopped back in the truck, drove into the barn. Sparky followed. The farmer got out of his truck. The air wasn't really warm in here, but there was far less wind. The contrast of stillness was appreciable. The place smelled, as usual, of hay, manure, and corn. Noah loved it. He had always loved it, since the time long ago when he had accompanied his father on this same chore, fetching hay bales from this whistly old barn to take to cows in the fields nearby.

The ghost of Noah's father seemed to whisper in every little breeze that cooed through the checked gray planks of this place, seemed to move across every wisp or remnant of straw or spider's web that moved with invisible, spritely drafts. Not really. *Swish. Swish.* In the stall, the horse's tail, swish. His huge equine lips blithering a soft blubby mumble seemed to declare that all was at peace with the world. Would that it were true. These were the insignificant, soulful sounds that had accompanied a man's interaction with the animal world from time immemorial. *Mmmmmm,* in rising intensity and decrescendoing cadence crooned Betsy, the milk cow.

So Noah had followed in his father's footsteps of farming. But his son was taking a quite different path.

hddq://riverroad.loc

Robby Davis was driving his muddy little red Nissan pickup along the river road. Wind rustled through the half-open window, loud, but not loud enough to overpower Alison's songbird voice on the radio.

It was a winding little two-lane road that curved along the levee of the Mississippi, about fifty miles upstream of New Orleans. Back among the hardwoods and occasional live oaks, he saw in bright sunshine a decayed landmark coming up on the right: eight ghostly white Doric columns, all that remained of the old Theseus plantation home. The sight bespoke his proximity to the agricultural research station of Theseus University, about a mile further ahead. On Robby's left, just beyond the road, the continuous, grassy slope of the levee rose to its consistently predictable height, thirty-odd feet above the surrounding pastureland. On his right, a brambly barbed wire fence stretched along the road, ten or so feet from it. In the distance, brown, white and black cows grazed contentedly. Above it all arced the infinite blue sky, punctuated with a few puffy white clouds.

The short drive along the river road may have been Robby's twentieth journey to the research complex, situated on a few hundred acres of what had been the thousand acres of delta land upon which Beauregard Theseus had built his cotton and sugar fortune, more than a century ago. Robby's graduate assistantship afforded him access to the modest, remote facility where Dr. William Theseus, great-grandson of Beauregard, spent much of his time scoping the frontiers of microbiology as it applied to numerous agricultural practices. Both professor and assistant alternated between this station and the Biological Sciences department on the main campus in the heart of New Orleans.

This bend on the river road always kindled Robby's imagination. The lonely antebellum columns, man-formed as they were and so starkly incongruent in the overgrowing wildness, remained as silent, stubborn monoliths, superfluous sentries guarding the lost opulence of a plantation culture that had turned to ashes generations ago. Honeysuckle, ivy and scrubby saplings now ruled the spot from whence Colonel Theseus had commanded his legion of slaves and later sharecroppers. Surrounding the old mansion's skeletal array were hundreds of acres: dark, delta loam fermenting microbial memory of black feet whose calloused heels and toes traversed row upon thousandth row of King Cotton's scurrilous servitude.

About a mile past the fallen home site, Robby turned his truck into the familiar driveway of Theseus University Agricultural Research Station. A quarter-mile into the site he passed the oval-shaped "palace" on the right, a large, clean masonry building where selected animals were kept in controlled conditions. To his right were three smaller buildings of the same golden masonry hue. These were labs where most of the experimental work was done. He parked between the second and third building, and stepped out of the little truck. As he approached the door of the middle building, which housed an office, he heard his name called from somewhere out in the field.

"Hey!" yelled William Theseus to his assistant.

Robby stopped, took a few steps backward so he could see beyond building # 3. He saw, standing between the gazebo and *mama* oak, his mentor and boss, Dr. William Theseus. The lanky, sandy-haired professor gave a little wave, smiled. Robby strode into the field, toward the gazebo, a favorite spot for the doc and his associates to occasionally grab a bite and talk about what-all was going on. "How's it going, doc?"

"I dropped the nucleus from the gap-zero donor cell, and decided I was too hungry to continue," said the wry scientist. "Just had lunch. How 'bout you?"

"Yeah, I had lunch. So you haven't cloned Elsie yet?"

"Nope. As a matter of fact, maybe I won't do her." He put on a look of feigned worry.

"Why not? Is there a problem?"

"No. But I think maybe you want to do it. Don't you?"

"Me? Why?"

The middle-aged professor started to take a little stroll toward *mama* oak. "Oh, you're younger...got a steadier hand. It takes a very steady hand, you know. The whole procedure is so incredibly, uh, small."

Robby began following as Theseus ambled toward the old oak. "Well, sure, anything I can do to help."

The professor was looking curiously at the big tree. "Robby, do you see that gash in the trunk of *mama* oak?"

"Yes."

"My dad told me it was inflicted by a riverboat that went through a breach in the levee during the big flood of 1927."

"The flood water brought the boat from the river all the way over here?"

"Yes. And when the paddlewheel, which had long metal tines on it like a fan, struck the tree, they peeled the epithelial layer, or bark, off. And, look at this." He walked over to the tree and put his hand in the crevasse at about eye-level on the trunk. "See. This part of the trunk never regenerated bark. It's just exposed wood. But it was in this crevasse. You see how the surrounding bark continued to grow outward as part of the rings, but inside the gash there, in the wounded part, the tree sort of refused to grow, refused to cover itself with new bark. The cells in that area must have been in a kind of shock, or something."

Robby was obliged to respond to the professor's prompting observations. "Well, immediately after the injury was inflicted, of course there was no crevasse, no protective adaptation. The wound was just a naked gash on the exterior, with high exposure to the elements. The exposed part retreated, while the undamaged bark tissue around it continued to grow outwardly."

"You think so? I think there probably *was* that crevasse there, pretty much in the shape we see here, after the boat struck it. The boat's impact changed the shape of the tree. The tree retained the new shape as part of its continuing development. Correct 'oak' trunk shape became a lower priority than protecting exposed tissue."

"Not really. The tree never put bark back over the wound."

"The boat killed some cells, so those cells didn't send the message to the outside to produce bark there."

"The boat killed some cells? Maybe it just damaged them. Maybe the trauma knocked out part of their genes, those genes responsible for sending bark messages."

"Well, look at those wood cells. Do they look dead?"

Robby walked over to the tree, reached in the crevasse, scratched the exposed wood with his fingernail. "It looks like living cellulose to me."

"So those traumatized cells apparently continued to live. But they stopped making bark."

"They might not have anything to do with making bark. It may be that the surrounding bark cells are responsible for 'expanding' their own influence." Robby laughed.

"Yeah, well anyway, somebody dropped the ball, and the organism ended up unprotected in that spot."

"Didn't make any difference, doc. The tree has survived seventy-three years with that vulnerability."

"But the tree will die one day. Will that day come sooner as a result of this unprotected spot?" The professor raised his eyebrows and formed a funny expression---half grin, half grimace.

"God only knows, doc. I don't think anybody can answer that question. And I know nobody has the time to try and figure it out."

"What we're looking for is the genes that can make those corrections."

"In the tree?"

"In the cattle that we're working on. We want to locate the genes to make those corrections, then replace faulty genes with better ones, and then insert the improved DNA into egg cells. If we can do that for a bull, and for a cow, then mate them, we've got ourselves a herd of perfect bovines, Robby." The professor laughed out loud.

"We'll probably have to improve our own genes first, by inserting some longevity, so we can stay on the project for the next, oh, hundred years or so."

"I don't mean 'we' in the sense of you and me. I'm talking about the collective efforts of all biologists working together."

Robby's cell phone jangled in his pocket. He pulled the thing out and opened it. He looked quizzically at the screen, not recognizing the number. "Hello. . . oh, hi, Marie." A big smile leapt onto his face. "Just fine. How are you? . . . Oh, Florence. Cool. . . Sure. He's right here. . . Yeah. It's good to hear from you." He looked at the professor, who was looking up into *mama* oak at a squirrel, but listening intently to their phone greetings. "Here, doc." He handed the phone to his mentor. "It's your daughter."

"*Buon giorno, mia figlia.*"

"You're not going to believe what happened here last night."

The doc laughed, still watching the squirrel as it worked busily in the tree branches far above them. "I'd believe anything coming from you. The Pope quit his job?"

"No, silly. Vandals overturned a statue in the *Piazza Signoria*. I'm standing here now looking at it, *Hercules Slays the Centaur*, by Giambologna. The statue was overturned; it's down on the steps. Hercules' arm broke off."

"You're kidding, *mia figlia.*"

"I'm serious, dad. The *caribinieri* have the area blocked off.

"How in the hell could anybody do a thing like that?"

"It happened about four o'clock in the morning. We've heard that the perpetrators managed to somehow get a truck into the piazza. They tossed a cable lasso around Hercules and pulled the whole statue over with the truck. Then they hightailed it out of here."

"And the police couldn't catch them?"

"It seems the whole incident took less than a minute to perform. And, at four in the morning, who could have expected such a thing to happen? The police were taken by surprise."

"I'll bet the cop who was watching the piazza entrances is in big trouble."

"Well, actually, he was mugged. We've heard that the vandals tied him up and drugged him."

"Who told you that?"

"Just a woman in the crowd here. There's probably a thousand people here right now, gawking at Hercules with his arm knocked off." Marie laughed. "It's really kind of funny, especially the way the police are handling it. This one inspector, who seems to be the main one--I swear he looks and acts like an Italian version of Inspector Clousseau."

"So, Marie, what would be the motive for such a crime as that?"

"Ha. God only knows. Maybe somebody out there wants to help the centaur obtain vengeance against his slayer. "

"Right. What was depicted in that sculpture? I'm trying to picture it."

"The biggest, baddest hero of Greek mythology is locked in a kind of death embrace with a centaur, whose head is bent back in a quite helpless position. Hercules definitely has the upper hand. The story goes that he was furious because the centaur tried to rape his wife."

"Now, since Hercules gets his arm knocked off in this episode with the vandals, Hercules loses the upper hand," quipped the doc.

"Ha, ha, dad. That's pretty good. But hey, I've got to go. We're going to a concert, and it's about to start."

"Okay, Marie. Thanks for calling. It's good to hear you're still alive every now and then. And stay away from those Italian loverboy types. . .Yes. . .love you too. *Ciao.*"

"Sounds like the epicenter of Renaissance Art has some serious art theives, " quipped Robby, as the doc snapped the phone shut.

Dr. Theseus laughed. "Or vandals. They overturned a statue of Hercules fighting a centaur in the middle of the night."

"Hercules fought a centaur in the middle of the night?"

"No, wise guy." The doc punched him playfully on the arm. "They pulled the statue, a famous statue, over in the middle of the night, with a cable attached to a truck." He chuckled. "Man, it never ceases to amaze me—the strange things that people do."

For a moment, there was an odd silence while he was thinking. Then Robby asked, "The centaur is the one that's half man and half horse, right?"

"Right, in some Greek myths."

"Hey doc, I was just wondering about your clone procedure. If, instead of inserting the selected bovine nucleus into our enucleated oocyte, uh...if you were to slip a nucleus from a human stem cell into it instead, what would we have then? Maybe a *cowtaur?*"

The doc laughed again, this time loudly. "You really are a wise guy, Robby. But no, the new cell would be essentially human, uh, 99% human in its characteristics, because of the human chromosomes in the human nucleus. Only the cytoplasm outside the nucleus would be bovine. But that's a funny thought. Maybe that's how the centaur came to be, and maybe that's why Hercules wanted to kill him. Hercules might have had prejudice against a chimeric centaur—a creature neither fully human, nor fully horse—a creature caught between the world of humans and animal existence."

"Well, we know the Greeks didn't have nucleus-transplant procedures." He smiled. It was a facetious hypothetical remark.

"No, but they must have had *something* like that going on...something a little more primitive, more basic to human urges."

Tails

3

A fat rope went flying through the air like a tossed serpent. Dockhand Dree caught the end, and wrapped it around a flange on the end of the Decatur Street dock. *The Whodoo Queen* was arriving at New Orleans, having sailed from Grand Cayman a few days ago.

The cruise ship had a load of passengers who had cavorted their way through carefree Caribbean venues and were now returning to that port city which funnels water, people and products like a great aortic spout from our North American heartland. It also has the dubious distinction of having become the mother of all North American party towns. From this confluence point the travelers, weary of their revelries, would disperse to all points west, north and east and resume their semiglamourous lives.

The ninety-ninth person to disembark was Simon Lafraneer--a fifties-something entrepeneur whose partly-hungover but dapperly-threaded girth wobbled slightly as he stepped from the gangplank. Simon's rotund face contorted into an uninhibited glower as he collided with Dockhand Dree. The dazed cruiser stepped aside and squinted at his obstacle. The rope-handler's attire of horizontally-striped shirt and gondolier hat clashed incongruously with these roughshod American surroundings, as if this port-of-call didn't quite attain its coveted status as a Venice on the Mississippi.

"That's the biggest damn gondola *I've* ever seen, matey," he cracked to the dockhand.

"*Buongiornio*, you idiot," said Dree. "Watch where you're goin'."

Simon's brief disorientation resolved into a slowly wayward stroll over the levee walkway, accompanied by the jostlings of his talkative fellow passengers. *So much talk. What the hell was there so much to talk about?* His hesitant, hungover countenance this morning belied the raw intelligence hidden within; he knew himself to be smarter than he must appear. Unlike this menagerie of frivolous tourists who skittered around him, Simon had business to take care of in the city of Big Easy.

Oh, it was a party! just to be near this place.

Merging into a giddy sidewalk crowd at Jackson Square, our traveler found himself startled by the tip of a swishing horse's tail across his face, as if he were being welcomed with beastly caresses into King Creole's carnival of curious delights. The ticklish wisp of horsetail in his oncoming path arrested Simon's forward progress; he looked sideways at the animal's black mane, brown neck and then up at the white-shocked face. From beneath a polka-dot banded straw hat, high, whiskery ears protruded. The nervous creature shuffled its feet. With no turning of the head it cast large brown eyes, encumbered by blinders, toward our wayward visitor, as if to say with maybe a little embarrassment: *I did not choose this hat.* Simon thought: *I dreamed of that horse with the hat on. Was it last night?*

Bizarre barkers, fortune tellers, caricature painters and sleight-of-hand buccaneers surrounded the disembarker's path with a gilt drapery of jaded nonchalance that hung upon the humid air like a shroud of unbelief. A sequined jester walked by with flopping hat, fake smile, and alcohol breath at eleven in the morning. A contrived medieval merriment hung upon all this disheveled modernity like day-after Mardi Gras beads on a blinking traffic light.

"Déjà vu, to you too," said Simon to the horse. *Riders on the storm; into this world we're born...*

The wanderer ventured farther; he *was* going somewhere. Across the sedated, Sunday-morning square, then beyond the cathedral spire, an oddly iconic bastion of propriety amid so much frivolous aimlessness. Simon entered the narrow-streeted labyrinth of the *Vieux Carre*, a netherworldly region of wafting enticements: garish sights, exotic sounds and decidedly earthly smells. He was accompanied by a straggle of other strangers who, like himself, were looking for something unusual.

He walked into the *Mephisto Lounge* on Bourbon Street. Peering through the smoky darkness, Simon saw the unusual person he was looking for, a thin, slick blond man drinking coffee at a wooden table in the back of the joint. Next to the table, a neonic juke box blared *Honky-tonk Women.*

Simon sat in a chair opposite him.

"Any luck?"

"Lots of luck, Simon. And it's all yours."

"So you've got something for me?"

"Yeah, man."

"Which is it?"

"O'Nessus."

"No kiddin'?" Simon raised his eyebrows. "Spawn from O'Nessus?"

"The very same." Heinrich smiled.

"And how do I know?"

A waitress in a satin bathrobe approached the two men. "What can I get you?" said she as she refilled Heinrich's cup.

"Coffee and beignets for me, please Madam." replied Simon.

"No beignets here, sir. What do you think this is? The frickin' French Market?"

"Okay, sweetheart. Well, what have you got then, that's, you know, like that?"

"I got Danish. You want it hot, or not?" She chuckled.

"That'll be fine."

"Hot, or not, sweetie?"

"Yeah, yeah, hot."

"And how do you want the coffee?"

"Black, but throw me a shot of Jack Daniels in it."

"Back in a minute, sweetie."

The men didn't speak for a minute or so. Heinrich was looking at the *National Enquirer*. The jukebox provided a convenient cover of noise. Then Simon restated his question: "How do I know what the hell I'm getting here?"

"Certified."

"Oh, is it now? Who's certifying? The owner?"

"The trainer."

"The trainer." Simon said, cynically. He paused. "That's not very convincing , Heinrich."

"The racing association has a DNA record. You can match it if you want."

"That's a little risky, isn't it?

"It's more than risky. It's downright stupid. Just trust me."

"Like a hole in the head. We're back to the starting gate, then."

"Call Rizzo. He'll vouch for me."

"Oh, you think so?"

"You know his winner, *Bullish?*"

"Sure."

"*Bullish* came from the same source."

"from O'Nessus?"

"Uh, no. Same trainer. Squeaky Robinson."

Simon turned the prospect over in his mind for a minute. The waitress brought his coffee and sweet roll. He slurped the coffee. Then he looked at Heinrich and said, "Supposin' I was interested, how much would it be?"

"Uh, ten thousand."

"You deliver?"

"That depends on where."

"My client is near Asheville."

"Nashville?"

"Asheville, North Carolina."

"I guess that could be arranged. It's a little out of the ordinary, out of the beaten path, you know."

"Well, for that price, a few hundred miles one way or the other—what's the difference?"

"Yeah, yeah. We gotta keep it colder than 200 below, you know." Heinrich waved the question aside.

" In frozen nitrogen?"

"Yeah."

"How long is it good for?"

"Longer than you'll be around to think about it—years, as long as you don't let it thaw out like an idiot."

"I'll think about it."

"Aw, c'mon Simon," complained Heinrich, "I didn't come all the way down here for my health."

"Hey, my friend, I've got a deal for you that would be more profitable for both of us." Simon paused, and looked into Heinrich's eyes, to read them. His headache had gone away.

"Yeah, yeah, whatever." Heinrich, exasperated, looked across the room at the waitress,"

"Serious. You could turn this into big bucks."

Heinrich sighed. He was thinking that his last few days of traveling from Chicago might have been a waste of time. Resignedly, he asked, "What is it?"

"Angus embryos, hundreds of them, from South America. We can trade."

Heinrich looked at Simon incredulously, then over at the waitress again. He mumbled, "She must have been pretty easy on the eyes, back in the day."

"Huh?"

"What'ya think? I'm Ben Cartwright?"

Simon bent over and assumed a more serious, conspiratorial tone. "I know you've got buyers for this on your list. "It's top of the line beef."

"Hey! I'm in horse-racin', Simon. I ain't no cowboy. I don't even know any ranchers. What you're talking about has nothing to do with me." For a few seconds, Heinrich halted his little rant. "No. I can see this whole thing has been a big friggin' waste of my time."

"Don't get bent out 'a shape. I'm just checking out the territory. It's no big deal. I just thought you might want to expand your horizons a little bit."

"No. It's outa my league. Fuhgedabahdit."

Simon leaned back in his chair, relaxed a little. "Okay, then. When can I get the other stuff?"

Heinrich let out a sigh of relief. The waitress was passing nearby. He spoke to her, "Can you bring me another coffee, dahlin'?"

She stopped at the table. "Sure, honey."

"And I'll take it with the shot, like my partner here."

"Comin' right up, honey. Anything else?"

"I'll have one of them Danishes too."

"Okay." She looked at Heinrich, and a slow smile crept onto her worn, but attractive middle-aged face. She was a redhead. "You look like a man who could use a good joke. You wanna hear one?"

Heinrich returned her smile, involuntarily. With a little wave of his hand, he said, "Sure, dahlin', let's hear what ya got."

"It's a dirty joke. You still wanna hear it."

"Comin' from a nice gal like you, couldn't be too bad."

She watched him, expectantly. "White horse fell in the mud." Then she let fly a big cackling laugh, and turned around. "Back in a minute," said the waitress as she disappeared into a back room.

Tales

4

Sunday afternoon, October 22, 2000, Robby Davis sat in the student Union coffee shop, drinking coffee and reading the *Times Picayune*. He was reading an article reporting a discussion in the City Council meeting about levees in New Orleans, and whether they were being properly constructed. He looked up. Outside the large window, rain was falling in a steady downpour.

And then a torrent of memory filled his mind. He was back at the home place in North Carolina, watching from the kitchen window, as his father led their two horses, Milo and Mila, out of a gulley-washing rain into the old barn. Robby was about twelve at the time. Just now, he could see vividly in his mind, the shocks of white on both horses' faces. For some reason those white spots, plainly visible to him through the pouring rain, shone brightly in his memory. Three days later and it was still raining; Mila had delivered a foal. His father had let him name the little horse. Although Robby had named it *Red*, he always called it *Reddy*.

"Hello, Robby." A stack of books landed on the table next to his coffee cup, and the beautiful, dark face of Rosa Cyprana suddenly supplanted his little musing with an infilling awareness of the here and now. "Is this seat taken?" Her black eyes and full lips registered an honest, though weary, smile. The question was rhetorical. She sat down.

"Hi, Rosa. How's biology treating you?" Robby couldn't think of anything better to say. Charm was not his forte. But he was smart, and Rosa knew it.

"Reynaud's really piling the work on."

"She's a demanding teacher, all right. But well worth the effort."

"I'm just trying to get out of here."

Robby, a little puzzled, commented, "Uh, I've got an umbrella here. You can use it if you like."

She reached over and lifted a wisp of hair that hung over his forehead, and looked directly into his eyes with a smile. "No, silly. I'm trying to graduate. I'm not going anywhere *right now*."

"Oh, right, Rosa." He smiled back at her. "I feel for ya." There was a little silence. Sensitivity was not Robby's strong suit. Then he thought, and spoke, "Is there anything I can help you with?"

"Well, Robby, since you mentioned it, yes."

"Go ahead. Shoot."

"Cell biology."

"Sure."

"The DNA's all wrapped up in chromosomes, in the nucleus, right?"

"Uh, basically, yes, but not entirely."

"There is DNA outside the nucleus?"

"Yes, in the mitochondria."

"Those are organelles in the cytoplasm."

"Right. They are like power plants, making energy for the cell to use in all its internal functions."

"And they have their own DNA?"

"I wouldn't say they have *their own* DNA. They do have some of the cell's DNA. But it's circular, not presented in helical strands like it is in the nucleus." He thought for a moment. "Actually, Rosa, maybe the mitochondria do have something like their own DNA. That's a matter for discussion. Biologists hypothesize that they existed as independent organisms during earlier stages of life development. It's thought that they were taken in symbiotically by larger, more advanced molecular life forms."

"Taken in?"

"Yes. It's called endosymbiosis. The larger molecule needed ATP, which a mitochondrion produces; the mitochondrion needed, uh..." Robby was searching for an analogy. "a home, a sort of comfortable home."

"I see. And this ATP substance is, er, something phosphate."

"Adenosine triphosphate. Complex life forms need **a lot** of it. Mitochondria produce it very efficiently and prolifically, so the bigger cells took them on."

"As partners." She smiled.

"Right. Endosymbiosis."

"Cool."

"God thought so too." He took a gulp of coffee, and smiled awkwardly while Rosa was writing. The expansive, high-ceilinged room echoed with the sounds of numerous voices, and rain pouring outside.

"It's unique to the mother," he said.

"What?"

"The mitochondrial DNA is unique to the mother. Unlike that in the nucleus, which is formed in the zygote by male and female chromosomes together, the mitochondrial DNA comes only from the mother."

"Really?" She finished notetaking, and looked up at him.

"Yes. Kind of like the virgin birth thing."

"How's that?"

"God wanted to do a new thing in the human race, so he suspended the rules for one particular birth; he cut the male side off, and the whole chromosomal package was from a woman."

Rosa thought for a moment. "Was Jesus a clone of Mary, then?"

Robby guffawed. "Well, I wouldn't say that, I guess you could say God supplied the other half of the helix. At any rate Jesus was unlike any other man ever born."

"I think he was kind of like you."

"I hope so. I'd like to think that I'm a little like him."

"You are, Robby. You are so kind to help me figure this out."

"Any time. What other questions do you have?"

"Enzymes and proteins. What do they do? Oh, look." Rosa noticed someone on the other side of the room. Stretching her arm up excitedly, silver bracelet sliding down to the elbow; she waved to a tall woman and called out, "Hey, Salli. I'm over here." Rosa was obviously glad to see the other woman, who had a small child at her side. "Excuse us, Robby."

As the mother and child approached, Robby could see that Salli was a woman in her early thirties, of similar Mediterranean, maybe Moroccan? ethnicity as Rosa. She was elegantly dressed. Her child was a boy of about four years old.

Rosa leaped up and hugged Salli; they exchanged fond greetings. Then she turned to Robby for introductions. "Salli, this is Robby Davis. He's a graduate assistant here in the biology department." He stood to shake her extended hand.

"Robby, this is my friend, Salli Cretani."

As the lovely woman shook Robby's hand, she said, "This is my son, Alex."

"Hi, Alex." Robby directed a large grin at the boy, who stood shyly at his mother's side, holding her dress for security.

Salli looked at Rosa and said, "Are you ready?"

"As ready as I'll ever be."

"You're sure. He..." The elegant, dark-haired woman arrested whatever statement she was about to make. She had an unusually confident presence. In a kind, yet quite commanding feminine voice Salli looked into his eyes and spoke to him: "Robby would you excuse us for a minute?"

"Oh, sure." He grinned, and lifted his arms from the table with a shrug.

The two women started to walk away. Alex did not move, but stood looking at them, suddenly very content to be where he was. Salli had a sudden thought, turned around. Picking up Alex, she set him in the chair next to Robby. "Now, Alex, you sit here with Mr. Davis while I talk to Rosa. Mama will be back in a few minutes."

"Okay, mama." He didn't seem to mind being left with a stranger.

Salli reached into a large carry-back that was strapped to her shoulder, and produced a colorful book. Handing it to Robby, she advised, "He might like to hear you read this, if you care to, page 40."

It was a dog-eared old copy of Harris' *Tales from Uncle Remus*. Robby felt himself being amused as he flipped through the pages, lingering on the old line illustrations. He looked at the copyright page—1933 edition. *I remember this.*

Salli and Rosa walked over to a large glass panel that afforded a wide view of the grassy commons area outside. Just outside the window were camellias that still had white blooms. The rain had diminished.

Robby stopped turning pages at page 40. He looked at Alex, who was waiting expectantly. *I sure didn't think I'd be doing this today.* He read aloud:

"Then Brer Rabbit talked mighty humble: 'I don't care what you do wi' me, Brer Fox, just so you don't fling me in dat

brier-patch. Roast me, Brer Fox, but don' fling me in dat brier-patch!'

'It's so much trouble fer to kindle a fire,' says Brer Fox. 'dat I 'spect I'll have to hang you.'

'Hang me jez as high as you please, Brer Fox,' says Brer Rabbit, 'but fer the Lord's sake don' fling me in dat brier-patch.'

'I ain' got no string,' says Brer Fox, ' en now I 'spect I'll have to drown you.'

'Drown me jez as deep as you please, Brer Fox,' says Brer Rabbit, 'but don' fling me in dat brier-patch.'"

Robby turned a page and looked at Alex, who was rapt with attention. Robby was getting into it too. *What a good kid.*

" 'Day ain' no water nigh,' says Brer Fox, 'en now I 'spect I'll have to skin you.'

'Skin me, Brer Fox,' says Brer Rabbit, 'snatch out my eyeballs. Tear out my ears by de roots, en cut off my legs, but do please, Brer Fox, don' fling me in dat brier-patch.'"

"Cuz Brer Fox wanna hurt Brer Rabbit bad as he can, so he caught him by de behind legs en slung him right in de middle er de brier-patch. Dar was a considerable flutter where Brer Rabbit struck the bushes, en Brer Fox sorta hung 'roun fer to see what was gonna happen. By n by he heard somebody call him, en way up de hill he see Brer Rabbit settin' crosslegged on a chinkapin log combin' the pitch outa his hair wid a chip. Den Brer Fox know dat he been swop off mighty bad. Brer Rabbit was bleedsed fer to fling back some er his sass, en he holler out:"

" 'Bred n' bown in a brier-patch, Brer Fox—bred n' bown in a brier-patch.' En wid dat, he skip out jez as lively as a cricket in de embers!"

Hmm, thought Robby, *whoever said the fox was the craftiest of critters?*

It almost seemed as if the women had timed their exchange to fit this little episode. They sauntered back across the room, around tables filled with people who were talking, reading, eating. Salli was happy about something. Rosa—he really didn't know her very well, but—she had an undercurrent of worry beneath a slight smile.

"Thank you, Mr. Davis, for helping us in this way."

"Oh, the pleasure is mine. I assure you. You have a fine young man here.

"Perhaps we'll see you again some time. My husband, Kemal, owns the *BookCell* bookshop on Napolean Avenue.

"Oh, yes, I know Kemal. Would you like a cup of coffee, or, anything?"

"Thank you, but we must be going. It was very nice to meet you."

Robby stood as mother and child slowly walked away. Alex offered a wave and smile that seemed to include both Robby and Rosa.

Robby had noticed, with glances between Brer Fox and Brer Rabbit, that Rosa had retained a serious expression on her face throughout her conversation with Salli. "Are you okay?" Her eyes seemed a little red, as if she may have shed tears.

Rosa released a pent-up little laugh, as if something had yearned to burst from her soul. Then he saw a faint smile steal her lips, as she said: "Things are a lot better now than they were just a few days ago. They've offered me a room in their house. I'll be moving in with them tomorrow."

"Oh." He didn't know what to say. His cup was empty. "You want some coffee or something? I'm going for a refill."

"Sure. I'll go with you."

As they approached the coffee line, he asked her: "So you're moving. Where have you been living?"

"I've been in a small house a few blocks off St. Charles, but it's a bad situation."

After an awkward silence, made tolerable by the busyness of filling coffee cups, he inquired further: "Do you care to tell me about it?"

"It's a long story."

"I like stories. Have you heard the one about Brer Fox and Brer Rabbit?" Now he was handing the cashier a few bills.

"Actually, Robby, it's a little bit like that."

"Oh, yeah? How so?" He smiled at the cashier. "Keep the change."

"I'm like Brer Rabbit, hoping somehow to get tossed into a brier-patch. It would be better than the tarbaby I'm stuck with now."

"And what tarbaby is that?"

"Not really any kind of baby...a man I've been living with."

"Ooh. I see. Hey, let's move over there where you were a few minutes ago."

"Sure." They gathered their goods and walked across the room, now less crowded than it had been an hour ago when she had sat next to him. When they arrived at a table by the big glass looking over the commons, he decided not to be *too* inquisitive. So he sat opposite her at the table, and just looked into her eyes. She was grateful to have a friend to listen. He didn't say anything, just looked out the window, and then back at her. What trouble there could be behind those beautiful dark eyes, he could not fathom. Nor could he imagine a man who, having access to the person behind them, would violate that trust. But he knew he was about to hear only one side of a complicated story. Any broken-up love affair could not be a simple story.

"I never should have moved in with Mick. But there's something going on that he's not telling me about." She was wiping tears away.

Robby had the feeling that the hearing of what she was about to say would place him in some kind of risk. But he didn't care. *You only go 'round once. Live life to the fullest. Damn the torpedoes. We're going in..* Furthermore, she was becoming, minute by minute, irresistible to him.

"Something going on. Is it another woman?"

"I don't think so."

There was a very long silence, two or three minutes. He looked out the window. The sky was clearing. He thought of his father, Noah, and the two horses Milo and Mila, and Reddy their foal. *That had been seventeen years ago.* Similarly, it seemed a long time ago that he had followed that memory trail, although It had been only an hour ago. It seemed a long time ago that he had explained mitochondria to Rosa, a casual acquaintance. Now, she was confiding in him. How had she judged him worthy to fulfill some trustworthy role? He couldn't fathom it. *Doesn't she know I'm the dorky kid who blew the curve for everybody else in chemistry class?*

"I moved into his place about a year ago. It was fine for a few months. But as time went by he spent more and more time at the riverboat casino, and I know he was drinking a lot...getting drunk every weekend." She looked at Robby for signs of impending judgment, or rejection.

He said nothing, did nothing, wanted to take her hand, but would not. This was not the time to make gestures that could be easily misinterpreted. He looked out the window at the camellias, then at her again. He wanted to be a mirror for her.

"He took me with him a few times. But I'm not into it. Then he continued asking me for awhile even though I had no interest. By summer, he quit asking me, but he kept going. We've been living like strangers since about the time school started."

"What does Mick do?"

"He's a loan officer at a bank uptown."

"Is he going to make any trouble about you moving out?"

"I hope not. And I don't know why he would. I'm just an albatross around his neck now."

"You're a party pooper." Robby thought he'd inject a little levity into the curtain of solemnity that surrounded them. It worked.

"Right!" she blurted, almost laughing with relief. "That's what I am. I've had it with the party scene, even if it is with all the important people. Well, they're not really important people, although they *think* they are. In fact, they seem pretty low-life to me."

A sudden curiosity filled Robby. "Where are you from, Rosa?"

"Tarpon Springs, Florida. My father, Stephanos, was a sponge-diver and entrepreneur in the Greek community there."

"And your mother?"

"A good woman, Cressida. She passed away two years ago." Rosa looked out the window. Geese were flying by overhead. The sky was almost clear now. She gazed up at it for a few seconds, then down at the camellias just outside the window.

"When are you going to move?"

"As soon as I can get motivated to do it." She was still looking at the flowers.

"I can help you if you like."

"Oh, no." She looked up at him. "No, you don't want to get involved."

"I've got a little truck. If I can help, it needs to be today, because tomorrow I'll be back to teaching and grading tests for Dr. Theseus."

"No, Robby. You don't want to get involved."

"You know, Rosa, there was a time a few years back when someone helped me. I was in a similar situation. And it made a huge difference. After that ordeal, everything got easier."

"What happened?"

"It was pretty much the same situation, except there was no love affair going on. It was just a bad situation with two roommates who didn't like me, and I didn't like them."

"And someone helped you out?"

"Yeah, my buddy Rashad. He's gone back to Nigeria now. Graduated cum laude. He took me into a dorm room in the middle of my second semester, junior year. What a difference his intervention made! In the new living situation, I was able to turn what would have been a disastrous semester into a good one."

Rosa was being very quiet; her expression was changing from relief back to worry. "I don't know, Robby. What would you do if Mick came in while we were moving stuff out?"

He laughed confidently, perhaps a little arrogantly. He was beginning to warm up to this prince-in-shining-armor role. "Well, there wouldn't be any reason to do anything, except...keep moving your stuff."

"Right, Indiana Jones." She nodded her head facetiously. "I could see him decking you."

"Nah. The Lord is my shepherd. He prepares a table for me in the presence of my enemies."

"Yeah, well, I've seen Mick throw tables, when he was drunk."

"I'll tell ya what, Rosa. In a few hours it will be Sunday night. He'll probably go out for one more fling before the work week starts. We'll wait till it's dark, after supper. Then we'll ease on over there while he's gone, grab your essentials, and bingo! you're home free. We'll get you into Salli's place. And if you've got some furniture to be moved...ah," He fluttered his hand with a little gesture to indicate improvisation. "We'll get it some other time."

Risks

5

There was nothing terribly unusual about Mick's place, except the two-headed dog.

Or, rather, the picture of a dog, mascot for a beer company, digitally manipulated to appear as double-headed. Tacked on the inside of the front door, its absurdity jumped out at Robby as he closed the door, as if some hellishly virtual guard dog were growling to abort his entrance. Black spots surrounded the outer eyes on each white head, cartoonishly grotesque, He felt the hair stand up on the back of his neck. The poster's caption read: *Cerbereza—twice the bite of any other beer.*

It was inappropriate for such an elegant little abode. The streetlamp-illuminated front yard, with prolific, sculpted shrubbery and wafting scents of bougainvillea, had possessed no warning of such a sinister sentry within. Robby turned to view an ornate, though compactly quaint, living room, well-appointed with French Provincial furniture of lime green and burgundy. Richly valenced draperies of silk guarded the windows. A little old-fashioned, but tastefully assembled, it appeared to be the home of some older person or couple. An indefinite hint of cedar, or mothballs, masked an undersmell of musty stillness, as if this room's loving caretaker had died or gone away. Robby's eyes wandered back to the two-headed dog. *It just didn't fit.*

In fact, it didn't fit. The bizarre poster had been thumbtacked to the door by Mick Basker, heir of this formerly-sedate domicile, during the Mardi Gras celebration earlier in the year. A client , Ed Chesterfield, had given the poster to Mick as part of an ad campaign, and dared him to display it. The college-dormish *in your face* incongruity of the picture's creepy effect clashed so obviously with Mick's new (but old) digs. His spontaneous placement of the image behind the front door had produced howls of laughter from his inebriated guests. After their uproarious revelries, the picture had remained. as if a claim to his absentee parents' carefully-decorated estate. Mick and Rosa rarely used the house's main entrance.

Which is why Rosa and Robby were now walking in through that same door, guarded as it was by the thought of a preposterous creature. Neither of them knew what to expect, although the prospect for an uneventful relocation was good, since Mick's Jaguar was nowhere to be seen. They walked through the strangely-silent, museum-like room, ornamented with a Grecian urn on a marble coffee table, illuminated by a dimmed crystal chandelier.

Through a dark hallway with a small telephone table and a nightlight, they continued until they arrived in a luxurious kitchen of white marble tops and gold fixtures. But it was a mess. A fried-chicken box was open on the island counter, empty except for battered parts of bones and skin and a greasy napkin. An empty *Cerebeza* beer can next to the box had been overturned, its chimeric mascot gazing mutely, once again, upward at Robby as he walked slowly by. A lonely striped yellow cat caressed Rosa's legs, begging for attention and food with loud meows. Old gray dishwater stood in the sink with half-submerged greasy pots and pans. Scattered across the counters were a chaotic cornucopia of predictably-kitchen articles: peanut butter, crackers, crumbs, forks, knives with dried egg-yolk, an oily, empty smoked-oyster tin, spotty wine glasses. From behind a white ceramic sugar urn, a red crawfish head protruded lamely, remnant of an earlier Cajun-style feast, as if he had crawled forth from the ancient floor of some misplaced Atchafalaya spillway.

"Meow," said the yellow cat.

Rosa paid no attention to it. She was looking for something. There was a dark buffet piece against the wall, near the back door. She opened a drawer in it and removed some papers and envelopes. She wrote a note on a little pad, slid it back into the drawer and shut it. Robby interrupted his indiscriminate survey of the kitchen and looked at her. Rosa's movement's were deliberate and concise, as if she were working through a checklist in her head. *Who is she anyway?* He never would have guessed, as he filled a cup in the Union coffee shop earlier today, that all this would have happened. *I hardly know this beautiful woman, and yet she is allowing me to be an accomplice to this unsettling of her life.* The experience is so. . .*intimate*, as if he were seeing more of her than she realized, as if he were viewing her naked.

But he didn't want to think about that. He had offered to assist her in an hour of need. A noble knight would not entertain such fantasies.

"Let's go this way," she said, glancing at him, with just a hint of appreciative smile turning up the edges of her wide mouth. The dark eyes flashed with purpose. She was on a mission of some kind. Robby had the feeling that there could even be life/death issues stalking her from beneath shadows of this unfamiliar little mansion. *"For my mind misgives some consequence, yet hanging in the stars, shall bitterly begin with this night's".* . .revelations.

She hurried back into the hallway.

She flicked on the light in a small bedroom. Opening an ornate armoire, Rosa began retrieving hangered clothes. She draped a handful of them across Robby's arm. "Can you put these in your truck?"

"Sure. I'll pull the truck around to the back."

"Please don't do that, Robby. I know it seems a little awkward dragging this stuff across the front yard, but we don't want to be hemmed in the driveway if he shows up."

"Oh, right." He obediently arranged the mothballish clothes selection over his arm and prepared to leave the room with them.

"And this. Would you mind taking this?" She placed the papers in a black carry-bag and lifted it onto his shoulder. She looked up at his eyes, interrupting her agenda for a few seconds. "Thank you for doing this."

You can kiss me now, thought he, as their eyes met. *But no. Knight in shining armor.* Even as intimate as his little glimpse into her life was becoming, they were still obviously in different universes. She turned abruptly toward a bureau, began collecting shirts and socks from an open drawer.

This was the scary part. He had to walk back out the front door, past the *"guard dog,"* then across the manicured lawn of this man whom he didn't know, had never seen before, delivering the entrusted goods safely into his own truck. He felt like a criminal. *Actually, it was just such noble deeds as these, undertaken by bold men (such as himself) in the midst of life-changing points of crisis that delivered the world and its vulnerable residents from nefarious dominance by cruel usurpers such as this "Mick" guy must certainly be.*

Thinking of which. . .*he must be that guy who just drove into the driveway.*

A pair of bright headlights turned into the driveway and slid quietly to the separate garage in the back. Robby heard the garage door roll up. He peered cautiously beyond the side shrubbery, heard the low engine sound cease, watched the garage interior turn to darkness as the Jag's lights went out and the door dropped shut. Then silence.

What now? He could barely hear Mick's footsteps in the dark, across the back sidewalk and into the house. Robby looked up at the elegant streetlamp. He felt vulnerable standing at the passenger door of his truck, wondering if Mick had noticed that there was someone loading stuff into an unfamiliar truck right in front of the house. *It was good foresight on Rosa's part— not allowing me to move the truck to the back.* Robby imagined what the situation might be if he were now facing Mick Basker at his own back door in the dark. He shuddered at the thought. *It might have gotten ugly real fast. What have I gotten myself into?* Suddenly, he wanted to get into his truck and drive away, as if nothing had ever happened. *Nah. Knight in shining armor.*

Back to the business at hand. He unlocked the truck door. *These clothes are nice. They should be laid out in the bed of the truck, on top of a blanket or something like that.* But he didn't have a blanket. After lowering the passenger seatback, he tossed the carry-bag behind the seat, then put the seatback upright again and carefully draped the clothes on the seat. He reclosed the door and relocked it. Turning around, he leaned against the truck in a semi-relaxed position. *Now what?*

Robby gazed up at the streetlight. It had an attractive, old world shape and a bulb that made it resemble an old gas light. Perched on top of it was a gilded *fleur-de-lis*, a symbol of New Orleans. *Nice neighborhood. Quiet.* He could barely hear the sound of traffic on distant St. Charles Avenue. *Now what? Somebody has put a lot of time and money into this yard. It wasn't a yard, though; it was a garden.* A birdbath with baby angels stood nearby. He started to walk over to it, decided not to. *What's going on inside?* A night bird was singing quietly, casting with its tune a *faux* sense of serenity. *What's happening inside? Maybe I should go inside and see.* A car drove by. A strange guilt was hanging in his mind, like a spider web that wavered in an invisible breeze in his dad's barn. *I wish I was back there now, back in the beloved Blue Ridge, where all of life was simple and innocent, cold and clear, unlike this present situation, humid and paranoid, in this wild city that never sleeps, waiting outside this guy's house. Whose house? As if I were the criminal here, putting an armload of what could probably be proven to be stolen stuff in my vehicle and cringing at the brightness of every set of headlights that approaches.*

Another car drove by. Of course, it had nothing to do with anything. Robby felt like Buckwheat in the dark. He started whistling a tune. He thought of its words: *"With a shine in my shoes, and a melody in my heart..."*

The bird became suddenly silent. *Yeah, right. Dad's neighbor was just busted for manufacturing methamphetamines. The whole world is suspect.* Something rustled in the bushes nearby, a small animal. *Including me. I could be a suspect now. They could be in there right now, making up, maybe kissing and making up. And here I am out here...not a good situation for a country boy in the city.* The squirrel, or whatever it was, moved again. Then he heard the sound of its little feet landing on a tree trunk. He knew the sound, from hunting when he was a kid, back in North Carolina. *Back in the days of innocence, the days of children, when we didn't even know girls who shacked up with party animals.*

It's not likely they were reconciling. They're probably arguing, maybe even fighting. Maybe he has pulled a gun on her, or a knife! Hell, I better get out of here. It's none of my business.

But what is going on in there Maybe I should go in. Knight in shining armor

Rosa answered his question with a flick of the porch lights and an open door. Then he could see her face, dimly lit beneath the two lamps. "Robby, thank you for being patient. I've got some more stuff here. Can you help me with it?"

"Yes, ma'am." *So much for unfounded paranoia.* A scientist should have known better than to get so subjective over a little broken up love affair. *It happens all the time.* Good women get fed up with their errant men and leave them. He thought of the old song:" *A good hearted woman in love with a good-timin' man. She loves him in spite of his wicked ways she don't understand.*"

"She loves him in spite of...? I hope she doesn't. She deserves better. But you don't know that. Maybe she made the whole thing up. Maybe she's using you, the naïve, geeky grad student to make him jealous. *I could never provide for a woman like this guy does. She might have brought me along just to sucker him into some...*

"Hey, Robby!"

"Uh, yeah. I'll be right in." He turned around and pretended to adjust something on his little pickup.

"Come on in and meet Mick."

Reluctantly, he walked toward the house. The baby angels on the birdbath were laughing at him. He could see it in their eyes, even in the dim light of the streetlamp.

The two-headed dog was laughing at him too, as the cruel enchantress Rosa shut the door behind him.

Back in the house, the formal living room, he was received by Rosa and her former lover. The first thing he noticed about Mick was his tense smile. He was a good-looking fellow, with a ruddy face, sandy hair, and a faint scar across his cheek that made him look like a fallen hero, *like Bruce Willis when he just fell off the wagon, or. . . there was the moustache. . .Sgt. Pepper. He was Sgt. Pepper, without the glasses, but with something to hide. One thing for sure—he's nervous.*

Mick extended his hand. Still with the fakey smile, he said, "Hi. I'm Mick Basker."

He's a dork, just like me. Robby felt his confidence returning. Robby shook, but only said, "Hello." He was a scientist, not accustomed to passion-streaked love triangles.

"So, Robby, she's leaving me, and you're helping her get away." Their eyes met for a second; then Mick's turned away. He glanced at Rosa, then looked down at some magazines, *Southern Living* and *Smithsonian*, that were arranged neatly on an end table. His blue eyes were a little bloodshot.

Rosa left the room. She was still working on a list.

"I, uh, have a small truck. We happened to meet up this afternoon, on campus. She said she would be moving. I offered to help. That's all."

"What did she tell you, Robby?" Mick was looking up again, briefly.

"Not much." But then Robby felt that he should be a little more forthcoming. "She said you don't like to spend much time at home."

"She probably told you I drink too much." His antagonism was mounting.

Robby was slow to reply. He looked down at the magazine cover, which seemed to be a sort of escape focal point for Mick's eyes. The *Smithsonian* cover featured a photo of the Egyptian Sphinx. "Uh, yes, she said that, Mick."

Rosa breezed through with another armload of clothes on hangers, as if she didn't want to get involved with whatever conversation might ensue. Robby, realizing her task-oriented persistence, extended his hand, which held a key-ring. " Here. You might need these."

"Thank you." Their eyes met. He could see her gratitude.

"I think you'll need a blanket, or something to cover the truck-bed."

"Got it right here." She lifted her right arm slightly so he could see a sheet beneath the clothes.

Robby looked back at Mick, who was standing as if he had nowhere to go, looking quite downcast. Robby had a sudden memory, of his friend Donnie who'd been caught writing cuss words on the bathroom wall in fourth grade. *He looks like Donnie.* And Robby felt like a principal as he pondered what he would say next. "Well, do you?"

"Do I what?"

"Do you drink too much?"

"That's none of your fucking business." Mick seemed to be back-and-forth between melancholy and belligerence.

Robby lifted his hands in a gesture of concession. "Hey, man, it doesn't mean a thing to me. I'm just here to help out."

"When I need your help I'll ask for it."

"Hey, Rosa asked for help, okay?"

She came back through. "Another fifteen minutes and we'll be out of here." Then she was gone again, through the hall.

Then Mick changed his tune. "You want a beer or somethin'?"

"Oh, no, thanks." Robby felt himself relaxing a little.

"I've got some good wine, chardonnay. It was my mother's stash."

"I appreciate that, Mick, but, uh, Rosa has got things she wants to do."

"The hell with Rosa." He let out a little chuckle, as if it were funny.

"That might be part of your problem."

"Say what?"

He wanted to advise Mick to ditch the arrogance, the rotten attitude. But he thought about it. *I am, after all, a guest in his home, an uninvited intruder upon his private—*

Suddenly, Robby was vaguely aware of a blur moving directly toward his face. Mick's roundhouse punch caught him on the chin, and Robby felt himself reeling backward. There was pain, and the strange, bloody smell of something gone wrong inside his mouth. Instinctively, he stepped back, recovering balance. Looking directly into Mick's eyes, he repeated, "That might be part of your problem," as he raised his hand up to the jaw to check for damage. "You've screwed up bad; you've no one to blame but yourself for your present condition, Mick."

Mick stood openmouthed, dumbfounded that his fist had provoked no reaction in kind.

Strypes

6

"Jabber, jabber, jabber," said Nao to Gladys, as he set down his wok. He walked around to, then through, the swinging door into the dining room so he could speak to his waitress face to face. "Don't you ever get tired of talking? I'm trying to find out if the peppers & onions order is for a low-sodium person." And her high voice had been running in overdrive yappity-yap-yap-yap talking to one of her codependent old admirers seated at the counter.

"No MSG," said Gladys, smiling. She meant well. Her continuous commentary was, in fact, one of the great selling points of Nao's restaurant, because people love Gladys. They would come from all over the city just to have her take their order. And the food was excellent. So Gladys' waitsmanship and Nao's culinary prowess combined to make *Louie's* one of New Orleans' most popular diner destinations. Nao had bought the place from Louie a few years back, before he passed on. Gladys was part of the deal.

Some people were just made for certain niches in life. Gladys had been peering over those narrow black horn-rims for thirty-seven years, gathering food orders from neighborhood patrons and world travelers with such ease and finesse that you could just about *papier-mache* an entire Mardi Gras float with the ten-dollar tips her ministry had generated.

Oh, but she does have a mouth. She knows how to use it though: "I'll never forget my first day at work, honey—the day Kennedy was shot. Louie went out and bought a TV. He hadn't had one in the place before that, didn't like people getting too interested in anything but the food. I think that was the day he resigned himself to being a diner operator instead of a chef uptown. People were coming in here in droves to watch the TV, drink coffee. And most of them just ended up eating here even though they wouldn't usually, because they just, well, I guess they just wanted to be someplace where other people were. You know what I mean, dahlin', " she had said to Nao the first time he spoke to her, ten years ago when he first started cooking for Louie.

"Oh, gawd, he never shoulda gone to Dallas. somebody shoulda told him that; somebody shoulda convinced Jackie not to let him go," she had been saying to Nao through the kitchen window, even as Nao had been trying to keep up with orders. He was not yet near proficient in English at that time, 1990, when he had just come over from Taiwan.

"Nobody knows what's going to happen from one day to the next," Nao had tried to say to her, in between orders for gumbo and oyster poboys.

"Oh, somebody shoulda known, dahlin'. Somebody probably did know," she had insisted, raising eyebrows behind the horn-rims. He had looked at her blue eyes behind those glasses and thought the specs were so out-of-style for an American to be wearing. Now the dorky frame style was coming back, so maybe Gladys had been on to something all along—so far behind the crowd that she was ahead.

Things hadn't changed much in ten years, as far as communicating with Gladys goes. He still had trouble getting her to silence long enough to get the orders straight. Both Louie, and now Nao, had resisted the convenience of touch-button food-ordering. "We're not serving fast food here," Louie had said, authoritatively. Nao agreed, and had persisted in the time-tested method of spoken (yelled) communication between wait staff and cooks, although his comprehensive challenges were larger than Louie's had been, Nao having no benefit of English as a native language. In fact, though, he had probably learned more English from Gladys than any other person.

The phone rang. "Don't answer it. I'll get it." He walked back into the kitchen, wiping his hands on a towel, then picked the phone up.

"Louie's"

"Hey, it's Robby. Are you busy?"

"Never too busy for you. What's up?"

"Can you whip up some of that etoufee? I've got someone with me. We're hungry, but don't have a whole lot of time, so I thought I'd call ahead."

"You got it. Etoufee for two. What else?"

"Uh, salads, but I'll see Gladys about that when we get in."

"Coming right up. We'll see you in a few then."

"Right,, bye." He hung up the phone, looked out the kitchen window. Ten p.m, the place is starting to thin out a bit. A middle-aged man whom Nao had never seen before walked into the diner.

Simon Lafraneer looked around for an empty seat. He definitely didn't want one at the counter. It was too late for that. He wanted to slouch a little bit. Gladys, reading his mind, said, "I can get this booth ready for you in just a second, sir, if you'd like."

"That would be nice. Can I sit there?"

"You sure can, honey, if you don't mind watchin' an old gal clean it up right in front of you." She was noticing his impressive pinstripe suit and now-loosened tie. As she swabbed the table clean with a deft turn of the wrist, she reached into a front pocket of her apron, retrieving a silverware set wrapped in a paper napkin. She set it in front of Simon as he settled into the vacant booth. "What can I get you to drink?"

"How 'bout a Bud?" said he, opening a menu he had retrieved from behind the napkin dispenser.

"Coming right up, sir."

He watched her start to scuttle away. But she paused at the next booth, where an elderly couple was finishing a meal. Gladys spoke softly, with an air of confidentiality, to the sixtyish woman, whose makeup and red lips seemed a little overdone in the glare of this all-night diner. But Simon, whose prolific snooping skills were habitual, could hear snippets of Glady's veiled yapping:

"The doctor said it could never happen, and it was Frank's. . . but he found something that somehow didn't fit in. . . maybe cattin' around. . . and the next thing ya know she turns up. . ."

The other woman pulled a hand up to her mouth, rounded her lips in an O position, "No! When?"

"July." Gladys stepped back, with a self-satisfied smile, having inserted some timely grafting into the neighborhood grapevine. She resumed a path to the back room, while the amused news-recipient turned toward her husband. "Didn't I tell you. . ." but hubby wasn't looking at her, wasn't listening either. Instead, his attention was riveted upon an event happening on the other side of Napolean Avenue.

hddq://thezoo.loc

A bright security light cast its beacon of safety through misty rustling darkness, and across the domesticated wilderness of Audubon Park. Its glinting wavelengths flickered upon the ripple of a black zoo-pond. And that reflecting light shone across the untamed eye of an unexpected night wanderer, one whose goings forth were unaccounted for and certainly unauthorized. Meanwhile, while somewhere in the world at that very instant an errant author or wild-eyed reader was fixing their refined, so sublime *homo sapien* attention upon some worn-out, quaint and curious volume of forgotten lore, which being surely squandered and nearly nappingly pondered, did boldly pose their question to the restless beast,

> "Tyger, tyger, burning bright,
> in the forests of the night,
> what immortal hand or eye
> could frame thy fearful symmetry,"

why, why, the very tiger did creep and creep, then leap and leap, o'er its very irksome cagey keep and pounce upon the earthen floor, its captive status to endure. . . nevermore!

hddq://louiesdiner.loc

And so Harry Clerval, while his wife Clarissa was hearing Gladys' gossipy tale, did squint through the *Louie's* window toward the tall oak tree across the street in the churchyard. For, as he carefully yet blinkingly observed, he thought he saw a tiger, a **striped** Bengal tiger, crouching among the branches, perched above, no doubt ready to pounce upon, unsuspecting passersby below.

"What the hell?" His voice escalating, Harry jumped up, and was kneeling in the booth with his nose pressed against the glass. "Clarissa, look! It's a frickin' tiger, up there in the tree."

And so it was.

Clarissa was squinting. "You've got to be kidding, Harry. It's just-- oh, my gosh, Harry!"

"Gladys! Look at this. You gotta call the cops. There's a goddam tiger up in the tree!"

Gladys and Nao, both hearing, ran out from their customary stations to see what was happening. Simon Lafraneer got up and walked out the diner door to get a better look, as if the glass were obstructing or obscuring his view. But sure enough, there was a tiger in the tree. It seemed a little like an apparition in the night. His first impulse was to cross Napolean Avenue to get a better look, but of course his cautionary instincts made better sense of that impulse. He stood in front of *Louie's*, but near the door just in case.

Cars were passing, unaware. A bus puttered by. The animal was surveying the scene, apparently not interested in mauling anyone.

Gladys peered through the glass at the tiger. "Oh, poor kitty! He just wants someone to love him." She cackled with uninhibited laughter. Nao had phone in hand, talking to the 911 people,

Simon shouted to some pedestrians across the street. He had to yell twice before they noticed him. "Hey! Hey! Stop walking. Look. There's a tiger up in that tree!" Across the street, a group of three young men halted in their tracks when the message registered with them. Gazing upward, then visually confirming the unlikely warning, they slowly walked backward away from the creature's area of potential striking.

It just so happened that, at that moment, Robby stopped his little red pickup right in front of *Louie's* diner, feeling lucky that he'd been able to get a place right in front of it, because the back of the truck was full of Rosa's stuff. Unaware of any feline danger, he undertook a very precise parallel parking procedure. When he was done with it, Nao cautiously exited the diner and tapped on the passenger glass of Robby's truck, all the while keeping one eye on the tiger across the street. He knew that the big cat could leap down and be anywhere within a large striking range within a matter of seconds.

He crouched. Rosa lowered the truck window. Looking past Rosa at Robby, Nao warned, "Listen carefully, Robby. You need to look over to the left, across the steet, up in that big oak tree." He waited for a moment.

"Holy cow!" Robby knitted his eyebrows when he caught sight of the unlikely creature. "What the hell is going on here?" Rosa craned her neck to catch a glimpse of whatever it was. Her long hair fell across Robby's arm. The unexpected mingling of danger and Rosa's sudden hairful caress catapulted his senses into hyper-awareness.

"Omigod!" she blurted.

Nao chuckled. *What a strange situation.* "I've got your crawfish etoufee ready, brother."

Robby was in no mood for levity. The encounter with Mick had put him into a nervous state, and the surreal quality of the present situation was about to push him over the edge, although he was revealing no hint of such desperation. His eyes were obsessively fixed upon the big cat across the street. "What the hell is going on, Nao?"

"I don't know. We just noticed it a minute ago. It must have escaped from the zoo."

"Right." Robby nodded his head in slow agreement.

"But you might want to go ahead and get out of the truck, and come inside."

"Sure." The young scientist continued his visual analysis of the feline. *How in the world...?* Traffic had ceased from passing in front of the church. There was no visible crowd of gawkers gathering, for every person in the vicinity had slinked away into the nearby businesses. The drug store on the corner hosted a huddle of curious viewers, straining around one another to catch a glimpse of *Calcutta* the cat. That was her name. She was, in reality, a very perfect, gentle cat, although she had not been beyond the confines of a cage since being shipped from Calcutta five years, or more, ago.

"Why would I want to get out of the truck? I feel pretty safe right here." Robby was squinting at the tiger. "How in the hell could that animal have gotten way over here? There's only one place it could have come from."

"Audubon Zoo," added Rosa, still leaning toward him so she could see through the driver window.

"I think the police have stopped traffic now," said Nao, still crouching beneath the passenger door.

"Hmmm. Why couldn't they have stopped the tiger before it traipsed through a of mile of neighborhoods?" asked Robby, still watching the tiger, now with keen interest. *This is a rare event. The animal didn't have any instincts for this circumstance; it seemed to be stranded in the tree.* He chuckled. "This is classic, cat stranded in a tree."

Rosa picked up on Robby's mood change, which was moving from fear to amusement, not too hard a transition if you're behind safety glass and sheet metal in a truck enclosure. "Where's the fire department?" she asked, with a humorous inflection.

He turned away from the tiger and looked at her, smiling. "Right."

"Well," offered Nao, "the authorities can't just '*stop a tiger*.'"

"They could have shot it by now," said Robby, looking back at it.

"That's probably a million-dollar tiger there." said Nao, somewhat facetiously.

"Huh, that's probably a million-dollar lawsuit if it mauls somebody."

"People were surely giving her a wide berth, and that's how she wandered so far from the zoo," opined Rosa.

"She?" asked Robby.

"That's undoubtedly *Calcutta*, the only tiger at the zoo right now."

"She doesn't seem to have much interest in mauling anybody, seems remarkably docile."

"She must be domesticated by now."

"Right. Should we make a run down to the drugstore for some kitty litter?" joked Robby.

"You go. I'll stay here to make sure you don't get a parking ticket." They laughed. It was such an unlikely situation that it was turning out funny to them.

There was silence for a few seconds while they gazed at the strange sight. Calcutta opened her big mouth and let out a howl. *I am somebody*, she said. Robby thought of the MGM lion, and imagined the little musical flourish that accompanied that longstanding movie signature. Below her was a monumental sign lit up, with black letters on brown stone: **St. Aloyisius Catholic Church.** The big cat had chosen for its perch a very large oak tree. There was another one of similar size nearby. Together the two trees formed an architectural symmetry, now dramatized by night's shadows, with the church doors as a focal point. The feline was lounged in a conjunction of two branches, about eight feet from the ground, blinking, directly above the church sign, and apparently content. It seems that, in the unprecedented jaunt from her cage through a mile of New Orleans streets, no one had riled her. Residents knew who she was. *How could it be **any** tiger but Calcutta?* they must have wondered.

Behind and to the right of the sign, concrete steps ascended to a gargantuan pair of wooden, ellipse-topped doors that formed a grand, though appropriately sedate, entry. Not much of the stately church building's façade was visible, its upper reaches being shrouded behind the canopy formed by the two large oaks in front.

"She's seeking sanctuary," cracked Rosa.

"Ha. She's having second thoughts about the escape, wondering if it was the right decision." They chuckled.

"She's definitely out of her comfort zone," said Nao.

"And yet she seems so utterly comfortable," Robby observed. "What's strange is. . .she could make one hell of a ruckus if she wanted to. She could turn this place upside down with confusion if she chose to." He thought for a moment. "I wonder what her genetic inclinations are. I wonder if the years of captivity have conditioned her beyond her wild, natural response to what could be a dangerous setting."

"The human world, a dangerous setting," said Rosa, with a hint of irony.

"Definitely dangerous for her, if she's not in a cage."

Case in point.

The sedated, somewhat surreal stillness of Napolean Avenue at that moment was interrupted by the sudden, though stealthy, approach of a stalker, skilled in this sort of thing. Gray/white/black camouflage occluded his purposed arrival upon the scene. He had a rifle in his arms, and it was poised in the ready position. Not yet aiming, but ready. The hunter, whoever he was, was looking steadily at the cat. He was speaking to her in his mind. He knew her mind. He had hunted her in the far reaches of the savannah, in Africa. *Not her, however.* But one like her. He knew about wild animals. He knew what they were capable of.

He knew about wild animals.

Calcutta took notice of her stalker's arrival by rising from the position of rest that she had assumed, rousing from her uninvited survey of the boulevard below, with its manufactured menagerie of streetlight-streaked mechanical beasts having paws of rubber and snouts of chrome.

She growled. She is, after all, a tiger. And she didn't like this one bit. Her instinct was demanding a response. She howled. She's savage, not tech-savvy, not aware of the power of projectiles and triggers.

She leaped.

He shot.

She died. It didn't take long. The hunter knew what he was doing.

"Omigod!" said Rosa.

The hunter walked slowly to his prey. Standing beside Calcutta, he paused for a few seconds. Then he crouched, took her lifeless head in his right hand, and turned the beastly face up to get a better view of it.

A beautiful, striped animal.

A blue-light started spinning nearby. The next thing Robby saw was a police car stopping in the middle of the street, directly in front of the scene. Two cops and a large dog were instantly out. Their egress from the cruiser, however, was immediately followed by a stance. The lead officer addressed the shooter directly through a bullhorn, "Lower your weapon to the ground. I repeat. Lower your weapon to the ground."

The hunter slowly complied.

"Turn around with your hands up."

The hunter slowly complied. He knew the drill. In fact, he half-expected as much. He knew the world would be slow to accept his bold contribution toward the safety and security of New Orleans' residents: one killer cat threat—neutralized. A second police cruiser pulled up. The whole scene was swimming in blue flashes.

One cop who emerged from the second vehicle walked slowly to Robby's truck. Stopping just short of it, he motioned for Robby to lower the window.

"Sir, did you see what happened here?"

"Yes, sir."

He took a few steps closer and leaned down, peering into the vehicle. "I'll need you to remain here for a few minutes to make a statement."

"Yes, sir."

"You can get out of the truck now, sir."

Robby gingerly opened his door and emerged. The previously motionless street was becoming a beehive of activity. One officer was establishing a perimeter for investigation by suspending a wide yellow plastic strip from tree to parked cars, to more cars, to tree , to church stair-rail to tree.

Crowds of people were gathering on the sidewalk. They seemed to have come from nowhere, like flies. Above the church, the Lord of the flies monitored their situation.

Robby assumed a position on the sidewalk. He was standing beside Rosa and Nao. Grinning at Nao, he said, "I guess I shouldn't have preordered that etoufee, *n'est ce pas?*"   Nao said nothing, just returned the grin and turned backward to see his restaurant. Gladys was at the door with a notepad in her hand. The red scarf on her head was a little flame of color in the middle of *Louie's* blandish diner storefront. She stepped aside as several customers eased out the door to watch the proceedings.

Simon Lafraneer took a few steps toward the street, and stopped at the curb just a few feet from Robby. "That's a helluvah thing to happen to such a nice tiger, eh?"

Robby looked over at the stranger. "That guy, whoever he is, is a damned good shot. If he had missed, he'd have been in real trouble."

Simon, eyes steady on the event across the street, spoke knowingly, in his British accent. "That's probably an automatic rifle. I daresay if he'd missed he could have taken the animal down several times before it actually pounced on him."

Gladys opened the door and called to her boss, "Nao, I just got an order for catfish."

"Call Julian and tell him to come in as soon as he can get here, and Anna too, if you can find her. We might be doing business all night. I'll be in in a minute." He turned back toward the street.

Gladys stood in the entry, holding the door open, with a sullen expression, as if registering a passive-aggressive statement that this is not supposed to be happening right now and don't we have better things to do.

Nao glanced back at Gladys and was disappointed that she hadn't closed the door. "Go ahead, Gladys. This is going to be like one of those special times, like, like—when Kennedy was shot."

The reluctant waitress stepped backward, allowing the diner door to shut. *"Calcutta ain't no Kennedy,"* she mumbled.

Kingdoms

7

"You are what you emulate," said Robby." He looked at Rosa as she plopped beside him in the booth; now they were inside *Louie's*, and hungry, finally getting around to the crawfish ettoufee. It was past midnight.

The hubbub over Calcutta's demise had passed like a lit-up river queen on a dark night. The cops were gone; the animal control officers had carefully removed the tiger's carcass, while a large crowd and numerous camera crews looked on. The very courteous police lieutenant had interviewed Robby, Rosa and Nao, and several other witnesses. The hunter had been escorted away in the first patrol car that had arrived upon the scene. But a lot of people were still milling about.

As Robby and Rosa had resumed their hours-delayed expedition to the restaurant, conversation had somehow rambled around to a discussion of the differences between *homo sapiens* and other mammal species. The curious British onlooker, now known to them as Simon, had contributed to their discussion, interjecting with appreciable interest thoughtful questions and comments along the way. As Simon was seating himself opposite the couple, in the booth that Nao had reserved for them, he opined that people were just like animals, only smarter.

Robby responded to that: "You are what you emulate; you are what you aspire to be. Obsess with the animal kingdom, and you'll become like an animal. Imagine yourself with a soul, something beyond the animal kingdom, and you'll become..."

"An angel," quipped Rosa.

"Or something like that. Believe me, I spend a lot of time looking at the animal kingdom, through a microscope. We don't want to be like them.

We don't want to be like *E.Coli*, or sheep or cows, or chimpanzees, or even dolphins. We want to be..."

"Human," continued Rosa.

"Thank you."

Simon smiled wisely like a sophist. "Human, like the hunter who so efficiently and accurately brought Calcutta's life to an untimely end."

Gladys stopped at their booth, notepad and pencil in hand. "Congratulations," she said. "You're my fiftieth booth today. I've been here twelve hours straight now." She looked nonchalantly at Simon as if to say *aren't you impressed.*

"We're gonna give you a medal, sweetheart," Simon said drily.

She looked at him over the horn-rims, almost with a smile. She was convincing herself that this whole thing was just dragging on for too long. Then Gladys' blue eyes suddenly followed someone walking through the front door. "Thank Gawd, honey. You took your sweet time getting here," she remarked to a young man with slick black hair, Julian, her replacement. He threw her a poutish smile. Without stopping, he raised his arms and simulated violin-playing. "I feel your pain, dahlin'."

"He's gonna be a **hero** tonight," said she, sassily, " because Nao asked him to come in early, instead of 4 a.m. when he usually starts. Like Bungalow Bill there, the hero," she continued loudly as Julian disappeared into the back room, still playing the violin.

"What inscription should we put on her medal, Rosa?" Simon asked, with *faux* seriousness.

"Purple heart, nothing less," agreed Rosa.

"Yeah, yeah, whatevah." She flashed a glare at Simon, but still tinged with an almost-smile. Gladys could not allow herself to have *too* good a time this far past her bedtime.

"Well, Gladys, I ordered crawfish ettoufe about four hours ago. Is it ready yet?" said Robby, with a melodramatic flair.

"Honey, I hate to tell ya, he served it to somebody else while you were out there talking to the cops. But he's got another batch going. It'll be a few minutes though. What about you, dahlin?" She looked over the horn-rims at Rosa.

"I'll have the broiled red snapper, and a Caesar salad."

"Okay." She wrote it. "What about you, Mr. Hitchcock?" tossing her stare toward him with a quick movement of the head."

Simon met her eyes directly. "You're awfully feisty for an old gal this time of night, sweetheart."

Finally, she cracked a smile. "I been doing this awhile now."

The Brit chuckled and looked out the window quickly, then back at her. They were all having a good time now. In spite of Calcutta's demise, there was an atmosphere of special amusement pervading in *Louie's* tonight. "Bring me a T-bone steak, medium, with baked potato. But before that, get me a Guinness."

"For *you*, I can get one. You want a salad too?"

"I'll take one, like the lady's."

"Caesar."

"Righto."

Rosa was pointing to the TV. "Look, they're reporting on the tiger."

A blonde woman reporter was speaking. They had seen her covering the incident earlier across the street, but had been unable to hear her report. "...The shooter has been identified as Bill Hathaway of New Orleans, long time proprietor of *Safari Now! Expeditions*, a travel agency on Ursulines Street."

"Oh, the guy's a professional." said Robby. "No wonder he took the tiger down so expertly." Gladys brought their beers.

The TV report continued: "Since the safari-man's self-directed shooting of the tiger was not authorized by any law enforcement or animal control agency, he may face criminal charges. Our interviews of passersby and witnesses on Napolean Avenue reveal a wide range of opinions about Mr. Hathaway's deed."

"It's despicable," came the voice of a dark-haired, wire-rimmed woman on the tube. "This man took it upon himself to kill a well-known and well-loved pet of this city. The children of New Orleans will grieve for Calcutta. I myself will feel the loss of her, having fed her many times as an Audubon volunteer. She will be greatly missed. And we would expect that a full criminal investigation will be conducted."

And another, a young fellow of about thirty with spiky hair: "An escaped tiger is a menace, and cannot be allowed to roam the streets like an alley cat. The guy has done us all a great service. That tiger could have killed someone very easily. No, I do not think he should be prosecuted. We should take up a collection for his reward. I live just one block away from St. Aloysius, and I'm lucky he got to the tiger before the tiger got to me, or my two children."

"What do you think?" asked Simon, looking at Robby.

"Hey, you saw where we were. We had a perfect view of the whole thing.   If I hadn't been inside the truck, I could've used the guy's intervention. How else would they have recaptured him?"

"The animal control department is specially equipped to deal with the threat," said Rosa. "They probably would have used a tranquilizer dart, or at least wounded it in a way that would enable a capture."

"Those things take a while to work. The tiger might have gotten pretty upset about the dart before it took effect. That's the dangerous part. I wouldn't want to be the one to have to pull off that maneuver. A big cat like that one moves quicker than you can blink. No, once a dangerous animal is out, I don't care how much it costs, it should be written off. It's not worth sacrificing a human life," said Robby.

Gladys brought salads. As soon as she had scuttled away, Simon assumed a curiously new demeanor. He smiled. "Well, let's consider something else besides a dead tiger for a moment, shall we?"

"Sure. What's on your mind?"

"I have what may prove to be a lucrative business proposition. Would you like to hear about it?"

Robby looked carefully at this gentleman he'd met, randomly, less than two hours before. Life on a college campus did not often present opportunities to conduct business with persons so nattily attired, especially during the midnight hour. *What a wild night: a two-headed dog, then a belligerent banker, an executed tiger, and now a business proposition.* He shrugged his soldiers. "Okay."

Simon began his explanation slowly: "I represent a biomedical firm, Parthenonics, LTD, founded in 1988, by myself and several investors."

"In Britain?"

"Established in Georgetown, Grand Cayman Island." He paused. "Our firm has invested generously in technology for acquiring, preserving, and distributing unique biological specimens to biomedical laboratories."

"What kind of specimens?"

"Excess embryos, oocyte and sperm samples of all kinds, genetically engineered cells, recombinant cell lines, stem-cell lines."

"Animal, or human?"

"Both."

"Human embryos?"

"We have assisted in those types of services, yes."

"Cloned zygotes?"

"We've had experience with those too."

"Cloned human embryos?"

Simon laughed. "We haven't encountered one of those yet. As far as I know, there has not been one produced yet."

Gladys was upon them with the long-awaited, belated dinner.

Robby wasted no time, dug right in, as did Rosa. Simon judiciously held any further presentation while activity level was high at the table.

"Gladys, this Tabasco is about empty. How about another? And a glass of water?"

"Please, water for me too," added Rosa. "And another slice of lemon."

"Gotcha. Your steak's coming, Dr. Watson," said the waitress. "Let's get everything now, because I'm outa here. Julian will finish you up."

"What about your tip, my dear? inquired Simon, with an expression of feigned concern.

"You can give it to Julian, sweetheart. I've already made a bundle today. He's gotta do the hard part anyway, the cleanup."

"And where do we send your medal, Gladys?" asked the Brit.

She laughed, but turned around and headed to the back again.

"So why are you telling me this? asked Robby.

"You work in a biomedical lab don't you?"

"A research lab, not the same as a working biomed lab. How'd you know?" Robby looked Simon in the eye.

"I overheard your interview with the policeman. I was actually listening quite closely. I hope you don't mind."

"I don't mind. But you've got the wrong guy. I'm a nobody. You'll have to see Dr. Theseus about all that."

"Oh, absolutely, my boy. But you do most of the procedures around the lab, don't you?"

"Nah."   Robby was emptying the last of the Tabasco onto his crawfish ettoufee. "Gladys, give me some help here."

Julian brought a new bottle of the hot sauce.

"What is it, exactly, that you're looking for, Mr. Lafraneer?"

Depths

8

"We are anchored," said Noah to his friend Robin. "But if you think we're gonna catch fish here this time of year, I think you're nuts."

"We've gotta go deep," countered Robin. "Cast out toward the middle. There's a shelf over there, probably sixty feet deep on the other side of it."

Noah followed instructions. His lure sank for several seconds before he started retrieving it. Sure enough, he got a hit.

"What'd I tell ya?"

"I never would've thought it." He began the reeling-in. Reel in; let out; reel in; let out. Whatever it was, it was big.

"One of them stripers," announced Robin. "They go deep this time of year, I tell ya. But they're still down there."

"I guess they gotta keep eatin' something," said Noah, continuing his pulls.

"Yeah, but not as much in winter. I think they go into a semi-hibernation down there."

"This one's not hibernatin'."

"You woke him up. Now he's mad."

Noah pulled the fish in—a twelve-pound striped bass. It took seven minutes. He pulled the creature off his lure, tossed it in the cooler, and cast again. "It's amazing to me that anything can live down there where it's fifty-five degrees all the time."

"Shoot, that's nothing. Think about cod in the North Atlantic, or king crabs off Alaska."

"With the crabs, it kind of makes sense that they could stand low temperatures."

"Why is that, Noah?"

"Oh, I don't know, the shell just seems to be better equipment for a cold-blooded animal. It's just—"

"Because it's an exoskeleton? You think it keeps the cold out better than skin?" Robin laughed. "It's probably the other way around, actually. A shell has less insulative quality than skin does."

"Yeah. I'm gonna ask Robby about that some time."

"Think about polar bears. That's what's amazing to me. They're mammals, like us." Robin made another long cast into the deep water of Lake Maxwell. "And yet, they jump in and out of arctic waters like it was nothin'. And they're walking around on ice all the time."

"Without shoes," enjoined Noah, while retrieving his line slowly. "Surely there's another one down there."

"Surely there is, hopefully a school."

It was about 8 a.m. now. The sun on their faces was heavenly warmth. The wind, now receding, propelled a mild, but steady succession of ripples that lapped against the fiberglass boat hull. It was a calming sound, a sleepy little slapping. *Oh, but that sun feels so good on my face, after launching out here in the cold dawn.* On the edge of the lake, a hundred or so yards away, a troop of ravens began squawking. The men were quiet for five minutes or more.. This was the peace they had sought in coming here, along with the fish, of course.

"It must not have been a school," said Robin.

"A stray striper."

After a while, Noah said, "Huh, that's a funny thought. A polar bear without shoes, as if they ever needed any."

"They're genetically equipped with feet that can withstand icy cold," Robin explained.

"I guess we humans are equipped with intelligence to make shoes, and wear them."

"God gave us sense enough to come in from the cold."

"Ha, ha. That too—intelligence to build shelter, and wear shoes."

"Yee haw! whammydiddle. There's another one." Noah was reeling in excitedly.

"Looks like you've got the genes for finding fish," cracked Robin.

"I'm wearin' my lucky jeans, that's all." Reel in; let out; reel in, let out, for about four minutes, and he had an eight-pounder in the boat.

After a return to quiet, Robin was thinking about something: "Sense enough to come in from the cold. Hmm. Why do you suppose we even **need** to come in from the cold, when the polar bears, or any other animal for that matter, don't even need to?"

"Hmm. Now that's something to think about Noah." And so they thought for awhile, ripples sleepily lapping beneath the boat, warm sun on the face, whisper breeze every now and then.

"Loch Ness."

"What?"

"My grandpa saw the Loch Ness monster," said Noah.

"You think so?"

"Yeah."

"What did he say about it?"

"It was a long way off; he didn't get a real good look at it."

"Let me guess. It was night, and he'd had a little nip of scotch to ward of the Scottish chill."

"He said it was in the daytime."

"Well, then, what did it look like?"

"He never actually told me."

Robin laughed out loud. "Whoooa! Nelly." I believe it. I think he's on the line now." From the way his rod-tip was going down, it was obvious that something big was being brought in. Robin was struggling, his pink tongue poking out from tight lips and auburn beard. He worked the fish for twenty minutes. Reel in; let out; reel in; let out. When at last they saw the ghostly flash several feet down. Noah said, "Oh, yeah!" and grabbed the net. A few more cranks, and Noah scooped the fish up in the net, a tweny-pounder. *Tha's what I'm talkin' about!* Into the cooler it went, with the other two.

After a return to quiet, Noah was thinking. "I have a picture in my mind of what the Loch Ness monster looks like, but I don't know if it's based on what granpa told me, or some other source, or an image that I just dreamed up in my head."

"Well, what does it look like?" queried Robin.

"Uh, brontosaurus."

Robin chuckled. "Like a. . .*Jurassic Park* brontosaurus?"

"Yeah."

"Hmm, something to think about." Ripples slapping the boat sleepily. Warm sun, whisper breeze every now and then.

"What was it they did in that movie?"

"Cloned dinosaurs," said Robin. He chuckled as he said it. "What a crazy idea. I guess they made a lot of money on the movie, though."

"And the book."

"Yeah."

"What was it. . .some fossil or something, that they used to clone the dinosaur?"

"Uh, it was. . .It could only have been, that they found some preserved soft tissue from a dinosaur."

"Right, from a tar pit or something."

"I don't remember. It's a wild idea though."

"But plausible."

Robin laughed. "Ha, in a kind of science fiction way, it makes sense."

"Hmm, something to think about." Ripples slapping the boat sleepily. Warm sun, whisper breeze every now and then.

"You think Nessie might be a clone?"

"Nessie?"

"The Loch Ness monster."

"Oh, she's been around too long for that."

"How long has she been around?"

"Well, if my grandfather saw her, and he was born in 1902, died in '63, it would have been long before anybody even thought about cloning."

"Some guys cloned frogs in the 50's."

"Yeah, Robby told me that one time. But still—"

"It's more likely that Nessie's been around forever."

"We know **that's** not true."

Something to think about. Ripples, warm sun, breeze.

"There might be a family of 'em down there beneath the cold rippling waters of Loch Ness," Robin speculated.

"That's the most likely explanation."

"Or there might be a family of tall tales coming out of the Scottish imagination."

"**That's a more** likely explanation. My granpa, as I remember, was kind of a strange bird anyway. He used to wear a kilt sometimes and play bagpipes."

"That's not strange. There are guys doing that every summer at the Highland Games up on Grandfather Mountain."

"True. I'm just sayin' he was definitely an old-world kind of guy. You don't see people like that around any more."

"Unless they just got off the boat."

"Yeah, you know what I mean. America has a way of assimilating everybody, making everybody alike. Nobody's really strange after a family has been here a generation or two."

"I wouldn't say that. You haven't watched any TV lately, have you?"

"Well, yeah. That's a good point," Noah agreed. "My granpa Angus might have marched to a different drummer, but he would have surely thought it strange that we'd be breeding sheep and cattle as exact duplicates, without sex, in order to produce milk with drugs in it."

"Pretty amazing, huh? Have you heard any more from Robby about that?"

"He said they're doing it in Scotland. They've cloned sheep that produce specific proteins in their milk, to make drugs that will thin human blood so it doesn't clot."

"I've heard of that—gene pharming: p-h-a-r-m-i-n-g."

"Pretty clever. He says it'll be more economical than producing the drugs in a laboratory. If it works out, Becky and I might buy a few of them and raise 'em. See what happens."

"Ha! Noah Davis, gene pharmer," said Robin, exaggerating the 'pharm.'"

"We couldn't keep Robby down on the farm, but we'll keep him in the 'pharming' business one way or t'other."

Noah's rod-tip took a nose dive. "Oh boy. Here we go again—another hybrid coming up from the depths."

Pursuits

9

"That's tempting," said Vincent. " But let me think about it." At the moment, he was too caught up in *Mudzilla Meets Gorgonzuan* to have interest in a "job," code word between him and buddy Tony to suggest a profitable course of action, usually involving the unauthorized procurement of someone else's property without their knowing it.

"It's a piece of cake, Vinny," pleaded Tony.

"I'm not in any hurry here, okay?" objected Vincent, turning away from the video game long enough to flash a warning with his eyes to his younger partner-in-crime. "It's f---g Monday morning. Talk to me about three o'clock." He looked back at the screen. "Shit. Now look what you've done." *Gorgonzuan*, the three-headed dragon, had inflicted a near-death blow to *Mudzilla*, Vincent's hero. He jerked on the joystick, his thin 19-year-old frame wrenching every twisted possibility of torque upon the monster's defensive thrusts. By Vincent's prompt dexterity, the super-ape was able to recover from Tony's interruption, and the other monster's potentially-fatal jabs, by performing a ***building parry***. A building parry is Mudzilla's super-strength feat in which he picks up an entire building from the cityscape on the video-game screen and thrusts it at his nemesis, Gorgonzuan. The move worked. Mudzilla had successfully warded off death again, for the ninth or tenth time in this session. But it wasn't over yet. Mudzilla's masterful delivery of the building parry had not only afforded him more time on the planet. It had driven Gorgonzuan backward. The multi-headed beast was hanging on to a bridge superstructure for dear life, breathing fire like his life depended on it, and bellowing in frustration. Mudzilla, taking full advantage of his enemy's vulnerable position, leaped high into the air with a double-foot kick so perfectly executed that the stranded monster fell over backwards. Gorgonzuan's three heads were flung around the bridge's suspension cables like ropes on a spool, as his body plummeted over the edge, and clawed feet were left hanging in midair halfway down to the video-blue river.

Game Over.

Vincent pushed the video game with both hands, imposing a slight wobble on the machine as its front legs lifted slightly off the ground and landed back on the mall floor with a scraping sound. "Yes!" He swung his right arm in a quick airbound uppercut in celebration of his achievement.

This was the moment Tony had been waiting for. "Come on. Let's check it out," he said, excitedly."

"Hey, chill man. We got all day. Let's get some coffee."

They began walking down the middle of the mall, Tony chomping little steps in a muted frenzy of hyperism. It was stop-and-go, stop-and-go for him, the sixteen-year-old dropout who made a career of keeping his older companion busy with lucrative expeditions. Tony had the legs. Vincent had the brains. With calculated coolness, he walked slowly down the middle of the wide public space, looking outward, through the high glass walls at a barge puttering down the Mississippi River, and the bridge beyond with tiny tops of a hundred moving cars crawling like ants across its suspended ribbons of steel and concrete. The bridge looked like an antique version of the more streamlined structure upon which Gorgonzuan had just met his fate for the thousandth time. The morning sun, barely discernible through a smoggy lowland haze, illuminated the Crescent City with a dull glow. Vincent was not yet ready for any real action. But the video game had been a good warmup to get his reflexes tuned. He might need them to be in top form later when Tony's prospective "job" would be played out.

Swaggering down the mallway, he sees himself like Julian, his older brother. But there is a large difference between the two brothers: Julian is a working man, while Vincent is a vagrant, and—whenever paired with his sidekick Tony, a thief. Vinnie could not discern that coolness and integrity are not the same. But soon he would be given an opportunity, like all young men and women, to learn the difference.

"Come on, Vinnie. I got somethin' to show you on Tchoupitoulas."

"I told you, Tonto, I gotta get some coffee."

Vincent continued his leisurely stroll down the middle of the great wide concourse of grandiose impulse-buying tourismo. Tony slipped into a confectionary, leaving Vincent to slide by the storefronts unhurriedly practicing his solitary strut, with eyes wide open for whatever feminine attractions may present themselves along the way.   Tony emerged after a couple minutes, with a funnel cake and a feathered mardi gras mask, to rejoin his mentor on their walk toward nowhere.

"What the hell you gonna do with that ya little prick, goin' to a masquerade ball?" He stopped, deftly fingered a hunk of the funnel cake and shoeveled it into his mouth.

"It's for Tessa."

"Ah, that's sweet, Antonio," said Vincent, with mocking tenderness. He resumed the walk.

After a while, *Snazzy's Java* came up on their right. Vincent stopped, and spoke to a guy in white apron and white paper cap behind the counter. "Yo, Johnny, whatya got for me today?"

"Hey, Vinnie." He smiled. " I got cappucino."

"Yeah, tha's what I'm talkin' about."

Johnny dried his hands on a towel and pulled out a demi-tasse cup. "You seen the Jag lately?"

"Nah, you?"

"Yeah."

"Good."

Johnny did the cappuccino. Vincent turned around, leaned against the glass counter, watched a barge passing on the river outside. Tony munched on his funnel cake. "How's the river?"asked Vincent.

"Kinda slow, but it's pickin up."

"You been workin' out?"

"Yeah, man, every night. You oughta drop by."

"I might do that." He peeled off a dollar and fifty cents, laid it on the counter.

Johnny set the cappucino and a white napkin next to the money. "Thanks."

"Da Nada, man. See ya 'round."

"Later, man."

Vincent and his sidekick walked through glass doors and sat at a table outside overlooking the River. Vincent took a sip of his cappucino, then opened the paper napkin. Johnny had written one word and one number on the inside of it: *Esplanade 9*.

hddq://micksgarage.loc

At nine p.m, that Monday night the duo went to an old garage behind a small house on Esplanade Avenue, east side of the *Vieux Carre*. Mick's Jaguar was parked in the short drieveway. When Vincent and Tony walked in, Mick Basker was sitting behind an old worn-out oak desk, nothing on top of it except a few magazines, a chunky glass with ice and watered-down whisky, and the bottle next to it.

"Hello, Vincent. Thanks for coming," said Mick, looking tired.

"Hey, the pleasure's mine. You know my man Tony, don't you?"

"Yeah, Tony, good to see you again." Mick leaned back in his old swivel chair, took a sip of his drink. "You want a drink?"

"Sure."

"Couple glasses over there. Ice is in the little fridge." He paused, watched Vincent sit in the wooden chair opposite the desk, while Tony put ice in their glasses. "That last drop you made for us worked out pretty good for you didn't it?"

"Yes, sir, real good."

"That's great, Vincent. We've got some great opportunities coming up." Their eyes met directly for a second or two. "I thought you might like to know about them."

"Right, Mick. We've looking for opportunities."

"I've got a delivery here that needs to be made, and a pickup."

"Sounds simple enough. Where?"

"Close." He took a gulp. "Close, Vincent. You can take the bus, if you, uh, if you mind your manners." He smiled at his own facetiousness.

"No problem."

"In fact," Mick was thinking aloud, "the bus would be a good idea. Do it in the daytime. Business as usual."

"I'm trackin' wi'cha."

"Take the kid with you to cover your back."

"Okay."

"Anything goes wrong, I don't wanna hear about it anywhere, anyhow except through Johnny. You got that?"

"We'll make it happen without a hitch."

"Huh." Mick smiled. He was a little drunk. "Famous last words." No screw-ups, and there's more where that comes from. There's two bills in this for you."

Vincent shrugged. "Yeah, okay. Where we goin'?"

"You know where the Adonis gym is?"

"Sure."

"That's the delivery. Give this package to Arnie." He opened a low desk drawer, producing a brown papered shoebox, which he set on the desk.

Vincent looked at the package. "Does Arnie have something for you?"

"No. That's been taken care of."

"So that's it? Just hand the package to Arnie?"

"Yeah. Then there's the pickup. You come back over here to the *White Swan* antique shop on Royal Street."

"Right."

"See Mrs. Toulouse."

"She'll have a wooden crate for you, about like a crate of oranges. Strap it on the hand truck that she gives you and bring it here. It's only six blocks from here. Business as usual in the daytime."

"Gotcha."

"And you still have the key from last time, right?"

"I've got it."

"Nobody but you, Vincent, has that key."

"You can be sure of that."

"No offense to the kid, but it's just you, right?"

"Right." Their eyes met intensely again.

"Easy money. Not bad for a couple hours work. That's a hundred an hour."

"Beats the hell outa levee work."

"Right."

"Give Mrs. Toulouse love and kisses for me, will ya?"

"Sounds nice. How's your beautiful woman doin'?"

"Bitch left me."

"Sorry to hear that, Mick. Anyway, it'll be done tomorrow."

hddq://buffplace.loc

"What's in the package?" Vincent asked Arnie.

"What's it to ya?"

"Hey, whateva. I don't give a flip." Vincent knew Arnie from way back.

"Candy. You want some?"

"Gym candy?"

"Yeah. You look like you could use a few,"

"Nah, man. I'm good."

" It's good for attracting the ladies, Vinnie."

"Nah, man, I've got natural talent in that department."

"Sure you do, Vinnie. Think of what you could do it you'd just buff up a little."

"Nah, man, I'm good. Hey, I'll see ya."

"Yeah, right."

hddq://royalstreet.loc

Mrs. Toulouse was a beautiful woman. And she still was. Beneath hair unnaturally black and stylishly coiffed upon her sixtyish countenance, her blue eyes sparkled with alert intelligence. The red lips and low-slung neckline had exactly the effect that she intended on Vincent's attentions, or on the intentions of any other man, for that matter. She's a shrewd businesswoman who knows how to make best use of every asset.

"Can I interest you in some antiques today, young man?"

"I'm uh, I mean, Mr. Mick Basker sent me to pick up something."

"Vincent!"said the woman. with an agreeable smile that could melt a man's heart. "Mr. Basker said you would be coming."

"Uh, yes, ma'am. You got that right." He looked down at his feet, and shuffled them around.

"You and your brother have a look around the place. I'll prepare the package." She cast the smile over in Tony's direction.

She disappeared into a back room.

"Stop slouching around you idiot. Whad'ya think this is, a frickin' mosh pit? Try to be a little more dignified," said Vincent to his younger charge. The older boy, eyebrows knit in warning, approached the younger to intimidate him with his very closeness and taller stature. Their noses almost touching, Vincent gripped Tony's arm with persuasive twisting. "Didn't you hear what Mick said last night? We've left the small change stuff behind. No more runnin' from the cops for a couple of sawzalls and nail-guns. We're doin' *business* now. Try to act like a businessman instead of a snot-nosed kid for a change."

Tony just glared and wrenched his arm away.

An elderly couple, softly speaking German, were admiring a music box nearby. They became instantly rapt into the intricate dream machine, which stood by itself, enclosed in a hatbox-sized bell jar on a small marble-top table. Tony could dimly see pastel blue and pink baroque figures waltzing in a circular pattern amidst the golden mechanisms, while the *Blue Danube* rang out in low glockenspielish clarity through the stillness of the antique shop, as if lulling some long-gone silver-spoon blueblood baby to his afternoon nap.

Surrounded by elegant French Provincial, stately English bookcases, mutedly colorful Italian still-lifes, and the spirit of Strauss' Viennese masterpiece, the young whippersnapper did not know what to make of this 18th century moment of regality suddenly thrust into the frenzied acquisitiveness of just another day on the cusp of 21st century blahblah.

"There you go, young man," she said to Tony, which announcement took the kid by surprise because, for a moment he didn't know where he was. Her sparkling blue eyes whisked him further into the dream.

It seemed a little out of place—the hand truck that she was wheeling toward him. Her china-fine hands, with pronounced blue veins, passed before him, red fingernails flashing in Technicolor, as the fairy queen of Royal Street presented the aforementioned crate to young Tony Alioso.

"Thank you, ma'am," said Vincent. "Is there anything else we can do for you while we're here."

"No. Please tell Mr. Basker that I am dying to know where he intends to put the pieces, and if perhaps he needs a pedestal for their display."

"Yes, ma'am," replied Vincent, trying to smile with debonair suavity. *Whatever the hell she's talking about.* And the two boys were groveling out the door.

Six blocks down on Royal Street to Esplanade, Tony was still in a dream. "I never thought an old lady could be such a class act." declared Vincent. They turned onto Esplanade, went another block toward the River, and crossed the street into the house where they had met with Mick the night before. It was 5:15. Vincent was surprised to see Mick's Jaguar in the squatty little driveway. They wheeled the precious cargo into the entry door of the garage, grinning with self-satisfaction.

"My man, Vincent! You got somethin' good for me."

As they entered, Vincent deftly commandeered the hand-truck from his sidekick's transportive entrustment and presented it to the boss, who was looking more energetic than he had the night before.

Mick produced a roll of bills, peeled off two C-notes and handed them to Vincent like it was nothin'. "Let's lift it up on the desk."

Vincent and his sidekick carefully obliged. "Set it down *easy*," commanded Vincent.

Mick used a screwgun to withdraw screws from the upper side of the wooden-slatted crate. With the top completely removed, he reached into the bedding of fine wooden shavings, looking like a thick layer of dried spaghetti. Further inside he slit two layers of bubble wrap and gently pulled the pieces out. After removing five odd-shaped, bubble-wrapped objects, each one about a foot wide and foot and a half long, he set them on the desk while Vincent set the wrappings aside. Mick carefully removed the bubble-wrap from each one.

When he was done, five golden glass horses stood in magnificence upon the old desktop, their nostrils flaring, tails arching, their necks curving, and attitudes demanding the admiration of any nearby ceremonial persons or entities. Suspended in a time-warp of glass perfection, each beast had been assigned by the artist a prancing posture unique to itself. Yet they were integral in equine agreement, forelegs lifted high in an indomitably confident gait, that all can be declared well wherever they are. Let the horses come forth!

If there glass asses could.

"Well, gentlemen. Thank you for your help. How about—visit Johnny in the next day or two? And we'll see what else is in the works."

"Sure," said Vincent, obsequiously. "We'll be in touch." They left.

Mick locked the door. He walked around the pieces to gain a frontal view. There were two exactly alike, twins in the same position. Mick picked up the clone, turned it gently upside down. After pulling a strip of cellophane tape from its gonadal parts, he was able to remove the small area of glass in which that anatomically male detail was depicted. Now there was an aperture in the sculpture's groin about one inch wide by one and a half inch long. Mick gingerly tipped the horse right-side-up.

From the horse's sexual would-be a small dark object tumbled onto the little bubble-wrap underneath. It was an electronic chip. Mick retrieved it with a plastic tweezer. He placed it in a black velvet ring case and dropped it in his pocket. After turning out the light and locking the garage door behind him, Mick lowered himself into the driver seat of his Jag, turned on the engine and the lights, and headed for his lonely home.

Charges

10

"Electroporation—isn't that what Dr. Frankenstein used to make his monster come to life?" asked the student in the front row. The class laughed.

And Dr. Theseus also laughed. "Hmm. I never thought about it that way, Erik. Frankenstein was...' The professor was considering the problem. "He was a character in Mary Shelley's hypothetical imagination, but for a guy tinkering with biological processes 200 years ago, he didn't do half-bad," He laughed. Their final topic on this particular day was the use of electrical current as one means of fusing cells together in a laboratory. "It seems bizarre to us now, but at the time it might have seemed to Mary Shelley (not that she was a scientist) like the next step in scientific research."

He continued. "That's a funny question, Erik, but actually a very good one. In the early 19th century, electricity was a new frontier for experimentation. In Mary Shelley's non-scientific mind, electricity was more than an area for research. It was a *mysterious* force that nobody understood. So she wrote a fantasy story about what could happen if men were to unite principles of scientific experimentation with their own haphazard attempts to improve life." The professor paused.

"There are bound to be a few mistakes along the way," offered Erik.

"Right. Science is based on hypothesis, trial, and then figuring out what went wrong and forming a better hypothesis."

"In that case, the experiment went *really wrong.*" A murmur of laughter came through the class. Erik was a bit of a showman.

"Not an unusual thing to happen in human endeavors," said the doc. "I think that might have been part of Mary Shelley's point. But now that you raise this question, I'd say that one thing that went wrong (it's only a silly story after all) was his application of electrical current to the entire organism, instead of conducting it on a cellular level. In life, everything starts at the molecular level, and then from there the cellular level. When we speak of **electroporation**, Erik, we're talking about putting two **cells** together—two very small eukaryotes, then applying the electrical charge to disable their membranes so they'll fuse together, becoming one entity."

"So it's like sex, but without the fun," interjected Erik.

Dr. Theseus looked at his smartest student and had to laugh. Then he said: "Boy, you're really charged up today aren't you?"

Hahahaha.

"Anyway, mister wiseguy, the point is this: changing the organism at the cellular level during its inception is **much** more efficient than Dr. Frankenstein's fantastical application of current to the whole specimen, which was like, overkill, like trying to move a little rock with a stick of dynamite. But if we can use **well-controlled** electrical processes to facilitate changing the genetic identity of an animal, then it develops according to the new genetic plan that's been put into it. That one little electrical procedure," He held up his hand with forefinger and thumb only a centimeter apart. "has the ultimate effect of changing the life of the entire organism. It's **much** more efficient, and ultimately more powerful because it's concentrated. But of course," He smiled largely. "There's no way that Mary Shelley, or Dr. Frankenstein, if there ever was such a person, could have known that at the time, much less performed the experiment." The doc looked at his watch. "I've kept you too long. But there may be a lesson in this Frankenstein thing after all—don't get too carried away in the lab. See you on Friday."

The fourteen students in Dr. Theseus' microbiology class left the room in a flurry of animated chitchat. It wasn't often that the class would pursue such a rabbit trail discussion as the one into which this electroporation topic had lead them. *Leave it to Erik to come up with some offbeat application of scientific endeavor.* It wasn't the first time that William had entertained doubts about Erik's inclinations as a young biologist. The kid was brilliant, but he definitely had an inquisitive nature that trod dangerously along the outer limits of scientific propriety. *Could be another Crick or Watson. . .or could be a Frankenstein. Time will tell. Maybe we can keep him here for grad school, keep an eye on him.*

William Theseus, having returned to his office, picked up the phone and called his assistant. "What are you doing?" he asked when Robby answered his cellphone.

"Uh, looking at a platypus in Audubon Park. I'm on a jog."

"Come see me when you get done."

"Okay."

"How long will that be?"

"Thirty or forty minutes."

"Good. I'll see you about 5 o'clock."

"Yes, sir, 5 o'clock at your office."

Robby snapped his cell phone shut and looked down to complete the reading that he had begun before the phone interrupted his rest-stop from jogging. The bronze-cast sign read:

Sporting a duck-bill, beaver tail, and otter feet, this unusual mammal, native of eastern Australia, lays eggs instead of giving birth to live young. Electroreceptors in its sensitive bill enable the platypus to locate its prey by detecting electric fields generated by muscular contractions. And unlike any other mammal, the male carries a venom, which can be inflicted upon any attacker through spurs on the male's hind feet.

Robby took another look at the odd creature, which seemed to manifest a hodgebpodge of mammalian and birdlike features, with perhaps a little reptilian sting thrown in for defensive prowess. *Funny-looking thing. God's got a sense of humor.*

Then feeling refreshed by the short break from running, he resumed his forward progress back to campus.

hddq://theseusoffice.loc

"So who is this guy, Simon Lafraneer? asked Dr. Theseus, as soon as Robby had taken a seat. He mentioned your name."

"I met him the other night at *Louie's Diner*," answered Robby. " I couldn't really ascertain what he was up to. It has something to do with cryonics, though. He said he represents a company that provides services for medical researchers."

"Well, he had some pretty good references. I scheduled an appointment with him tomorrow afternoon. I want you to be here."

"Sure, doc."

"What else did he say?"

Robby laughed. "That was a wild night. It was the same night that Bungalow Bill guy shot the tiger. It happened right across the street from *Louie's*, you know. By a fluke, I just happened to be there, and I met him. I remember he said he's from Grand Cayman Island. His company wants to buy surplus biological samples. He said they have cryogenic capabilities, and they're interested in recombinant specimens—"

"Embryos?"

"Yes. He mentioned frozen embryos."

"Cows, sheep, what kind?"

"Well, I don't know. He seemed to know about our research with cows."

"Did he say anything about clones?"

"It did come up, but I don't remember the context. Like I said, it was a wild night. There was all this talk going on about the dead tiger and Bungalow Bill, and—"

"You just be sure and be here tomorrow afternoon at 3 o'clock, Robby, when he shows up here."

"I'll be here."

"And check out his company for me. See what you can find out about, uh—"

"Parthenonics."

"Yes sir. I'll do a search on it."

"Something tells me this guy is a loose cannon."

hddq://theseusofficeagain.loc

At three o'clock Thursday afternoon, Dr. William Theseus was reading correspondence in his office on the third floor of Arno Hall. The office, larger than a typical professorial hole-in-the-wall due to his stature as grandson of Thaddeus Theseus, was tastefully appointed in an ivory tower sort of disheveled grandeur. Bookshelves lined all the walls. Every horizontal surface presented curiosities of the ages: an ancient brass compass with a barometer of the same motif to accompany it, a spyglass, sextant, antique microscope, a picture of William's grandfather with Jonas Salk, a picture of his great grandfather with President Coolidge, a green felt blotter with an iMac on it. Behind the mahogony desk were two large sash windows, each composed of old-style twelve-grid glass panes, allowing a grand, though rain-darkened, view of the symmetric quad below, which consisted of a long rectangular grass lawn bordered entirely by live oak trees and Spanish-style buildings along its perimeter.

A very impressive office indeed. Although William had long ago been given options to serve as president of the University, he had allowed that honorable task to pass to his older cousin, Romola Beardon. His interests and inclinations had always centered steadfastly on the frontiers of knowledge rather than the intrigues of politics and the burdens of public stewardship.

Robby, seated in a chair opposite the desk, was reading student papers. He stood as, precisely at 3 o'clock, the portly, ruddy, very dapper Brit, whom he had previously met during the unusual events of four nights ago, was ushered in by Linda Valasquez, William's secretary.

"What's on your mind, Mr. Lafraneer?" asked William with a smile, after greetings and seatings were dispensed with.

"First of all, Dr. Theseus, allow me to express my appreciation for this appointment. I know you are a busy man." Robby was impressed with Simon's businesslike, yet very cheerful countenance.

"No matter," said William, with a wave of his hand. He refolded his arms on the desk top in expectation of whatever was to come. "I understand you represent a company that provides services for biological research."

"That's correct. Parthenonics Ltd. We've been collaborating with research facilities around the world since 1992. I'd be happy to tell you more about our work at your discretion. However, it is quite another matter that I'd like to bring to your attention today."

"Oh, and what would that be?" asked William, with eyebrows slightly raised.

"I understand that the Theseus heritage includes an area of land where your ancestor, Thaddeus Theseus, had owned a plantation."

"That's right. He grew cotton and sugar cane."

"And if my information is correct, that plantation was the location of a riverboat that was left stranded after the big flood of 1927."

"The *Leda Mae* did wreck in 1927, and it landed upon a spot that was owned at the time by Washington Jones, a sharecropper who had been born a slave on the plantation. He had purchased the small parcel in 1891 from my great-great-grandfather. But our family repurchased it from his heirs in 1941."

"Ah, yes." Simon paused. He seemed to be considering what had just been said. Then he continued: "Well, isn't inheritance a wonderful thing? I myself have recently acquired some property by that means. My uncle, Paul Lennon, of Liverpool, passed away last year. I, being the only heir, received from him a quaint home in Lancashire to whence he had retired after almost fifty years as a cotton merchant. After I had taken on the place, I was inspecting its contents. In the attic I came upon an old trunk. You've seen the kind, I am sure—an antiquated design with a rounded top, metal exterior and brass trim around its edges."

"Yes. I've seen them."

"In this trunk, and quite a large trunk it was, my uncle Paul discovered a letter that had been written to his grandmother by her brother, a Russian expatriate name Plato Zupoff. They—brother Plato and sister Katerina—had fled Russia in 1917. Being the son and daughter of a noble family, they had forsaken a large estate and barely managed to escape the Bolshevik rabble."

"Oh, where did they flee to?"

"Berlin. They arrived there in January of 1918."

"That was a helluva time to be going into Germany."

"They were well-connected, but didn't stay there long. With a little help from others of nobility, they kept moving, south, and eventually got to Venice, where they caught a steamer to London. In 1923, Katerina married Emile Harthouse, a Liverpool cotton merchant."

The desk phone rang. "Pay no attention. Linda will get it. Go on."
It rang twice and stopped.

"By 1927, Katerina's brother, Plato, was representing the Harthouse interests, and making regular trips to America, buying cotton. In fact, he bought large quantities of it from your great grandfather, Thaddeus. The letter that I have found describes a riverboat journey that Plato undertook from New Orleans to Memphis in 1927."

"But he never made it to Memphis," interrupted William.

"Righto," affirmed Simon, with a voice now gaining momentum, because he knew he had the ear of William Theseus. The visitor sat up excitedly in the chair, his back becoming upright. Robby found himself listening with interest, for the Brit seemed to be quite a storyteller. Simon slowed the pace of his tale: "Plato made it only as far as *Beau Rivage* plantation, because that's where the flooded Mississippi River deposited the *Leda Mae* when the River breached the levee."

"I know the exact spot," blurted William, leaning forward with enthusiasm. "Robby, we talked about it the other day—the gash in the oak tree."

"What a coincidence," Robby remarked.

Simon leaned back in his chair. Having obtained their attention, he was now completely at ease. Quite a storyteller, or businessman, as they would soon discover. "Yes, well," He chuckled, facing slightly upward now. "There is another *exact spot* that you may find some interest in."

"And what spot is that?"

"The spot where he buried his suitcase."

"Well, where's that?" puzzled William.

"I'm hoping to find it. I'm asking your permission to search your property for that suitcase," Simon said, with a level gaze directed squarely at William Theseus.

For a moment, William didn't know what to make of this request. His eyes narrowed as he surveyed the Englishman, dressed very properly in grey gabardine with vest and royal blue tie, the same hue as Theseus University blue.

"Hahahaha," laughed William, now thoroughly amused. *Whatever this guy is up to, he sure knows how to make an interesting proposal. But this is starting to sound a little far-fetched.* "So you want to go digging around for a suitcase that's been in Mississippi River mud for seventy-three years?"

Simon laughed. "Oh heavens no. It's not the suitcase I'm after. I'm sure it's long since rotted away by now." His gaze drifted around the room, as if he were waiting for their curiosity level to rise another notch or two, which it did. His face betrayed an almost indiscernible smile. But the level of William's skepticism was also taking on a little water, perhaps contributing ultimately to a shipwreck of Simon's proposal, whatever that might be. "I realize this seems a bit preposterous, and it may prove to be nothing more than a hare's breath," said he, with ruddy face nodding sideways, "but it is the *contents* of that suitcase that may prove valuable to us."

"Contents?"

"200 gold florins."

"Florins?" William was wondering.

"Original Florentine issue, 1492, solid gold coins."

"Plato was carrying 200 gold florins around in a suitcase?"

"According to the letter he wrote to his sister, yes."

"On a riverboat, where there were probably gamblers and thieves?"

"That's precisely why, according to his letter, he buried the suitcase. He found himself suddenly in a precarious situation in which he thought himself to be surrounded by unscrupulous people."

A knock came on the door. "What, Linda?"

The lovely secretary opened his office door and leaned in. "It's Dr. Yoblinsky, reminding you of the departmental meeting at 3:30."

"Ok. Thank you, Linda. I'll be there. Tell him to start without me if necessary."

She shut the door.

"Where were we?" he muttered.

"Gold florins," said Robby, with curious amusement. Simon sat patiently. He was in no hurry, for he had come all the way from Grand Cayman for this very moment.

"Ah, yes. Buried treasure." William swiveled around slowly and looked out the window. Clouds were hastening the evening. Lamps in the quadrangle had just come on. "And on my property?" He thought for a moment, elbows on the chair-arms, knuckles folded under his chin. "Or, more precisely, on *University* property. So why should I let *you* go searching for it?"

Simon laughed. "Three reasons, my friend: Number one, the suitcase was property belonging to my great uncle, and Number two, you're a proper bloke, and will do the right thing. Number three, I'll donate half to you, or to the University, as you wish, if we can find the gold."

"It's probably a wild goose chase anyway, don't you think, Robby?" asked William, swiveling toward his assistant.

"Or a needle in a haystack," said the young man.

"Oh, not a needle in a haystack," added Simon. "Plato's letter includes a specific description of the spot."

"Really, now?" asked William. How do I even know there *is* a letter›"

"Because I've got it right here," replied Simon. The gentleman reached inside his coat pocket and retrieved a yellowed envelope. Leaning across the desk, he handed it to the professor.

William took the envelope and looked at it. The address was handwritten in a concise, archaic script:

Mrs. Emile Harthouse

17 Blue Jay Way

Blackburn, Lancashire

William turned the envelope over. Mrs. Harthouse had slit its top edge with a letter opener, so that a crimson wax seal remained intact, with double-headed eagle insignia. Carefully, the professor retrieved the four-paged letter, unfolded it, and looked intently at it for several seconds. Then suddenly he laughed. It was written in Russian.

"But it *is* very old. I'll say that. It *looks* like a 73-year old letter." He laughed again. "So, Mr. Lafraneer, what is written here about the location of the gold florins?"

Simon's voice took on a quietly authoritative tone, almost academic, so that he was confirming documented information to the eminent scholar. "What is written here, Dr. Theseus, is a brief account of how the boat became stranded—"

William interrupted. "What does he write about that? How did it happen?"

"The River was very high, spilling over the levee in many places. As they paddled upstream toward Memphis, the crew spotted a very large breach. The wreck occurred simply because the captain allowed the pilot to steer the boat too close to the breach. A fierce current took the pilot by surprise and, before the craft could be properly steered, sucked them right over the failing levee. Plato writes that it was a wild ride. People were screaming, fearing for their lives. The force of the water propelled them like a raft on an upland stream, half a kilometer beyond the levee. The boat finally ran aground against a large oak tree. The passengers were stranded all night, although some brave souls swam to dry ground. The next day a bunch of the locals—mostly blacks they were—came in small, flat-bottomed boats and rescued the passengers. Two people had been lost in the confusion before the boat ran aground; their bodies were later recovered nearby. But of course Plato Zupoff survived.

William was mildly amazed that this account conformed so accurately with what he knew to be true—the telling of the incident as it had been spoken to Beauregard Theseus by Ole Wash, the sharecropper.

"What happened then must have been a bit of a comedy," continued Simon. "Plato had his luggage, very heavy with gold coins, that he didn't want to let go of, because he certainly couldn't trust anyone with it. And yet, there was no way he could be rescued without accepting assistance and risking discovery of his booty."

"A rich man who must pass through the eye of a needle," said Robby.

"Pardon me?" asked Simon with mild confusion.

"Nothing. Sorry for the interruption," said Robby, looking at Dr. Theseus, who knew Robby's mind, and understood the reference to a parable of Jesus. "Anyway, Mr. Lafraneer, so what did he do?"

"Here's where the letter's content becomes quite cryptic. You see, my great uncle ends his prose letter rather abruptly at that point with a poem, which, in Russian seems quite insignificant in its content, but translated into English is (I shall read it.):"

Where rabbits in their slumbery dens are bent,
the fox would chance upon a golden glint
which was the last of many laid so near yon oak
which raging river did provoke.
But young Plato's hopes, ne'er made complete,
would surely surface near yon muddy creek
where fox and hare run by and by
as Plato pens 'in Acadiana doth it lie.'
For the seeker whose Ariadnic thread's not torn
there's a strand of florins yet unshorn,
with whiffle and waffle and bullion yet
for the harey Theseus to by shovel get.

Yeah, 'tis two hundred thence near princely Louisiana shack,
an hundred more near Buncombe's pack, beyond Saluda track.

Simon's final cadence was followed by a brief silence.

Then William, with an attitude of something between impatience and amusement, asked, "You've got to be kidding me. That's it?"

"There are a few more details about the rescue indicating that Plato's suitcase was never recovered."

"He probably carried it out himself."

"Well, he did carry some of it out."

"This is getting ridiculous." Dr. Theseus looked at Robby, his face registering irritation. "So I'm late for a departmental meeting for *this?*' I'll get back to you about this. In the meantime, don't do anything. Robby, please escort Mr. Lafraneer out, and obtain any other information that seems pertinent."   He closed up the laptop, inserted it into a black carrybag, and walked out the door.

Robby turned to look at Simon Lafraneer. The Brit was standing with hand outstretched and a queer smile. On his pink palm lay a bright gold coin, its edges thinned and its *fleur de lis* embossment worn smooth with age. What *an amazing element gold is!* The thought struck upon Robby's mind as its brightness seemed to jump at his senses with preciousness. The unreadable smirk on Simon's face conveyed an eccentricity incongruent with their academic setting. "You see, Mr. Davis. I've already found several of the florins."

"You did? Where?"

" North Carolina."

"What?" Then Robby's cellphone rang. "Hello."

"Hey, I need you at this meeting." Robby heard the voice of his mentor say on the phone. "Get rid of that guy. We'll talk about it later."

"Okay. See you in a minute." He closed the phone. "Mr Lafraneer, Dr. Theseus needs me at the departmental meeting. So we'll have to get back to you on this matter. I'll call you about it, uh, soon."

The Brit extended his hand in a final greeting, his smile having become now a very pleasant picture of normalcy. "Very well, then. Cheerio."

And so Simon Lafraneer exited the office of Dr. William Theseus.

Passages

11

Confusion in the face of despair this is what plato had experienced first hand in 1927 when he threw his suitcase overboard while the mississippi torrent was raging his racing mind a-raving his sunken soul yet praying his precious coinage sinking into the deluge below a slinking and then muddy brown a-slaying his hopes and dreams of ever a-being a rich man sagely grazing upon the grassy glades of heaven on earth where he thought he'd find wealth and health and sobriety steady respectable propriety like his sisters husband back in england was it all about to plummet 'neath a choppy sloppy muddy glumment of mayhem how could it end this way? but wait.

The dark brown hand reached down and grabbed Plato's.

A strong hand.

The muscular arm, accompanied by a large brown face inside a black halo. The bearded mouth opened; then out of it came the voice of rescuous thunder: "Come on up here, suh. You can do it. Just pull hard. Hard!" he yelled the last word. Give it all you got, suh!"

Plato strained to accommodate the life-giving hand vise-gripping his arm. And he did pull hard. And then he was up, up from the sloshing lower deck. Suddenly his wimpish efforts were supplantedd by a strength far greater than his own. He was being lifted. The large arm was propelling him upward. And then he was standing next to the tall man on the upper deck of the *Leda Mae.*

Still Alive. This happened seventy-three years ago.

The great brown hand had pulled Plato to safety on the riverboat queen's deck, which could sink no more, for she was now aground, and awaiting the mighty waters to subside.

But Plato's safety had been unsure. For at the very moment when a pilot's skillful maneuvering had turned to frantic desperation, at that very moment, as *Leda Mae* had begun to drift in perilous draft like nothing more than a twigged bamboo raft, at that dreadful moment, Plato had been looking over his shoulder.

An unknown pursuer had been on to him. A dark assailant had ascertained by keen powers of observation and gambler's intuitive obfuscation—the likely contents of Plato's swarthy bag. And so at that moment of the riverboatman's fateful error, the cotton trader's fortune had already begun to sink, as his elusive strategies did slink into a more careful, calculated mode. Someone was after his florins.

And when the ship's random floating path had been, at last, ended upon the old oak tree, Plato had seen that the assailant's face was still behind him, still watching with hawkish intent his every move. And so, in a moment of unexpected islolation and unplanned desperation, he had flung his precious cargo into the raging waters below, and then skittered, so that the pursuer's awareness of its presence would be scattered. And he himself would be free to elude, unencumbered by his former hidden golden burden, and thus to retrieve, at some later date untold, the cargo onto which he could no longer hold.

He threw it in the water. Its splash was hardly noticeable in the churning flood. But then the fearful, fleeing man found himself unable to maintain a secure position as waters swamped Leda Mae's lower deck like laughing froth upon a tinker's dam. And he thought that surely he was damned.

And then the big brown hand.

Washington Jones had raised him from the flood. And He saw upon the back of young Wash's hand, old blood. But he didn't know where it had come from, and he didn't know how, and he didn't know why. "Thank you," said Plato to his rescuer.

Washington Jones' people had come and taken them to safety, but Plato had been aware of the pursuer's crusty whiskered face, with hollowed cheeks and steely eyes, lurking behind, following, knowing of his secret deposition of the booteous bag , but not knowing its location. So with fear and trembling he had settled in upon the humble straw-stuffed bed that Wash's family had offered him that night. And with trepidation had he stealthily crept out from their shotgun shack, under a slithery half-moon, and to the secret spot where he knew his gold to be. A muddy covering he found upon its buttoned back. Safe and sound he wrested from the mud the soggen sack. Silently he stole beneath the Washington shack, leaving a suitable reward, of fifty florins there for them to find, his appreciation for their saintly work in kind. The rest he buried in such a place, that no man nor beast with sallow face could ever find. There was no trace.

Three days later, having taken a room in a nearby inn. Plato was about to return once again, under cover of night, to the scene of his secret burial, a rabbit hole near a certain muddy bayou. But while checking out from the room, there was again on the edge of his heightened peripheral sight, the man with the sallow face. And so he could do nothing.

This was not good. He must elude the man if he could. He must do something totally unexpected and carefully remove himself from the vicinity until some later date untold to once again obtain his florin gold. Without warning, he jumped upon a horse-drawn stage. A full day's ride in fearful elusion did he glide, until the carriage brought him with his fear and watchful eye to the middle of New Orleans. He could be lost in a throng. His over-running sometimes confidence, sometimes fear, was that a rabbit would have no reason to eject the precious horde, and so therefore it would be safe for many a day and night, even many a moon and year, until he would return in triumphant conclusion of the escapade to recover what was rightfully his without the threat of a sallow-faced man.

But when he emerged from safe seclusion in the wooden horse-drawn swift elusion, there was no peace, no deliverance because he saw—and came to conclusion—that sallow man was still in pursuit, for there he was in a pin-striped suit! Standing beside a placard on Rue Bourbon which read: **For the benefit of Mr. Kite, there will be a show tonight.**

And so once again, in yet another moment of perilous elusion, the hunted bird lit into frantic flight—this time upon a train of perfect iron and steamy might. He escaped away into the night! O'er the long dark trestle and the misty southern dawn, dew was dropping from the roses as he pulled into Birmingham. But that was not yet far enough away to elude the sallow man with whiskers gray, and so he kept on keeping on, through Atlanta, and Valhalla, Greenville and Spartanburg, until finally from the huffing, puffing steel machine he stepped down, made a new connection to an old mountain dream, headed up Saluda creeper grade, along a clear and clean Carolina stream. He hadn't seen the sallow man since New Orleans.

In that morning of 1927 the sun came up over Rooster's ridge, burning off a steamy fog that had lingered in the valley below. As the steel beast defied gravity with uproarious steam and great clattering cams, crawling toward the crested gulch of continental divide, Plato Zupoff felt he had at last eluded the man who was seeking to take away his gold. He had outsmarted the sinister sallow who surely would have slit his throat without thinking to get his 300 florins. He was gazing out upon the turtlish strung-out ridges, as they glowed in backlit magnificence of opalescent dawn, and beheld sunlight's tangent rays struck upon naked trees of brown. Below him, vast forests were rooted in leafen. moldy earth. A wintry hibernation had cast all earth with sovereign dormancy. As the bellowing train crept up Saluda mountain, decelerating as it climbed, a foreboding solemnity bloomed, like lichen on a fallen log, and sedated his fitful mind. It was a cruel awareness: the old train was hauling him up that brown mountain to die.

And who would mourn his passing?

hddq://platogone.rip

41 miles beyond Saluda mountain, and 41 years past Plato's arrival in Asheville, a cluster of pink rhododendron blossoms broke the stillness of a solemn gathering. It landed with a little thump upon his last earthly habitation, an ornate, silvery-gray box six feet under the grassy mountainside called Double-Eagle Bald. Eliza, his wife of 38 years, returned her hand to its folded, prayerful position and watched, with her head hung low, while the soft pink and green bouquet grew higher and wider upon his box. Zelda, Cornelia, Grover, Eugene, MaryBeth, Ashley and Thomas released their last earthly contributions to their father's departing spirit. By Plato's request, a single gold florin was added to the arrangement by his business partner, W. O. Whittington. With a little thud it landed between the woody blossomed twigs, and then a shovel-full of dirt rudely added its earthen weight and swishy declaration of finality upon this last planting of their affections. July 14, 1968.

As the funeral party turned away, Jeffrey Davis gently took the hand of his grieving wife, Cornelia, second daughter of Plato Zupoff. Slowly they walked to a long, black Cadillac hearse. He opened the back door; she got in. On the other side of the hearse, Noah, fifteen-year-old son of Jeffrey and Cornelia, held the door open for his younger sister Catherine as she awkwardly gathered her satin dress and scrunched into the back seat with their mother. As he lowered his head to join them on the back seat, Noah thought he heard something. So he stopped, straightened his lanky frame to a standing position again, and stood there with the door open.

"Come on, Noah, what are you waiting for?" asked his uncle Eugene in the front seat.

"I thought I heard something," replied Noah, raising his eyes to the surrounding hills, and his ears to a sound of whistling nearby.

"What is it?" asked Eugene.

But the answer was blowing in the wind. "Nothing...I guess," answered Noah. A sudden wave of shadow spread across the grassy mountaintops as a cloud covered the sun and the wind gusted. Then the soft faces of angels turned down, watched their leaving of Plato's hole in the stony ground. A harmony of breezes continued round and round, and back to town, lost and found. And yes, there had been a sound.

hddq://louvreceiling.loc

"Oh, what a dream I had last night, Becky," said Noah to his wife.

She lowered her face, looking over the bifocals, across the kitchen island and the breakfast table at her husband drinking coffee. He was looking out the window, as was usual for this hour of the morning. The wind was whipping around outside; she could see that it was going to be a bright day. Branches on the neon-orangey sugar maple beside the barn were swaying up and down. She continued scrambling eggs. "And what dream was that, Noah?" she inquired.

"I saw a burst of pink rhododendron blossom against a blue sky," said Noah. "And then it landed on my chest."

"What landed on your chest?"

"The rhododendron blossoms."

"Okay, and then what?" asked his accommodating wife.

"I was looking up into the blue sky. Then...a man, a strong man, very muscular...He was a black man..." Noah's voice trailed off. He was looking out the window.

"And...?"

"He's *smiling* at me." Noah chuckled. " He's smiling, and then he reaches down to me. He's like, up above me with this blue sky background. He reaches down, smiling, and he's waiting for me to take his hand."

"And...?"

"And he laughs, and says: 'Come on. Come on up. You can do it. This is what you've been waiting for."

Becky spatulated the eggs from the skillet onto a plate. Then she put a biscuit next to it.

A low laugh jumped out of Noah's lips. "So I...I reach up to him. And he grabs my hand. He's got a grip like a winch, pulling me up like a winch. But it doesn't hurt. It's just...."

"Just what?"

"Just, uh, supportive, and he's pulling me up. The next thing I know, I'm sitting up, But he keeps tugging. Not forcefully, though."

"Were you scared?"

"Nah. It wasn't anything like that. He was helping me to get up. Then, all of a sudden I'm going up..." Noah stood up, walked around the little breakfast table, and opened the louvered window shutter so he could get a better view of the back yard. Cows were moving slowly across the hilly pasture in the distance. Then he sat back down. "And I heard whistling."

"Oh? Like a tune? Like the Sound of Music, or—"

"It wasn't a tune. It was just a whistling, like the wind." He didn't say anything for a few moments. Then: "And angels."

"No kidding?" Becky was serious. It wasn't like her husband to see angels, and she didn't quite know what to think "Well, what did they look like?"

Noah chuckled. "I don't know. I just...I couldn't see them. But I knew they were there."

"I believe you, dear. Then what?"

"Well, that was it. I guess I woke up.

Blasts

12

Robby Davis looked at his mentor with utmost curiosity, and rephrased the question. "You want to teach the microbiology class the technique of cloning by nuclear transfer?"

"Yes," affirmed Dr. Theseus. "This is the future. This is where biotechnology is going. If we're going to release graduates into the wide world of experimentation and the wider world of biotech production, they should at least be familiar with these procedures."

"It seems a little half-baked."

"Well, it is, Robby. but in this emergent practice, there are a hundred or more procedures for every verifiable result. At Roslin, they constructed over 500 embryos that ultimately yielded only seven live lambs, in order to produce Polly, the first example of cell-mediated transgenesis in a mammal other than a mouse." The doc paused to look into his huge microscope, as big as a microwave oven with a blender on top of it. "That's an awful lot of nuclear transfers to come up with seven live lambs, and even at that, it's more efficient and manageable than using the procuclear microinjection method."

"So there's going to be a great demand for biologists to do these, uh, multiple procedures?"

"Multiply that number, let's say 500 nuclear transfers by the number of genes—100,000 or so, in the human genome, with all the operations on the horizon—splicings, transplantations, mapping, marking, probing, regulating. The future is wide open, and there is so much work yet to be done. Here, Robby, look at this." He gestured toward the oculars at the top of the microscope.

Robby stepped over to the instrument and looked into it.

"You see that egg cell?"

"Yes. It has a nice round shape."

"It's an oocyte from one of our Holsteins, just a regular cow."

"Okay."

"It can become, instead of just a regular milk cow, a transgenic cow that produces the enzyme AAT—used to treat emphysema and cystic fibrosis—right in its milk. The farmer milks the cow, and, instead of sending the raw milk to the dairy company, he sends it to a pharmaceutical company that isolates the enzyme and processes it for use by people who suffer lung ailments."

"Yeah, I was telling my dad about this a while back. He raises cows, you know."

"I remember you telling me that. Anyway, that oocyte you're looking at is about to become a transgenic embryo that will mature and produce milk with AAT already in it. The genes to produce that enzyme were engineered in a culture of fetal Holstein fibroblasts up the road here at the State Univeristy lab."

"I've talked to Dr. Tudge, who manages that lab," said Robby.

"He and Dr. Ritchie gave me this sample from the thirteenth passage of this fibroblast line. These cultured cells will be the donors, from which we'll obtain the AAT-engineered karyoplasts."

Robby looked into the microscope again. "So we're going to put a nucleus from one of those fibroblasts into this egg cell?"

"After we've removed its own nuclear material from it. The egg cell you're looking at is in metaphase II, so it doesn't really have a nucleus. It has a cluster of chromosomes."

"I see it. It doesn't seem to have any features."

"Right. One disadvantage to working with bovine cells is their opacity. The labs that are doing serious work in this field use cells from other species, mostly mice, for many reasons. But one reason is visibility. Anyway, we're working with cows."

"Okay. Why cows?"

"Cows are what we have. We're not equipped like the front-runners at Roslin, or in Wisconsin, or inJapan, to do the cutting edge research, which largely involves mice. The cows are. . . well, let's just say they're a little closer to the real world of commercial possibility than mice are. Anyway, the egg cell you're looking at has been treated with cytochalasin to soften its cytoskeleton. And I've also treated it with fluorescent dye, so we can track the DNA. Since the bovine cytoplasm is so opaque, the dye will enable us to see if we've actually extracted the chromatin from the host. I learned this from reading Wilmut's article about Polly." The professor gestured vaguely with his hand, as if to wave their inquiry into another phase. "You see the egg cell, then, and it is backed up against an object."

"Yes. That object must be the large pipette with suction to keep it in place."

"Correct. Now, let me take a look." Robby stepped away from the microscope, and the doc peered into the oculars. He turned a few knobs, each adjustment of millimeters controlling microns of actual movement in the cellular world below. After about two minutes, he said, "Now, look at this."

Robby looked.

"That's the polar body that has been separated by the cell's meiosis from the new haploid chromosomes. What you're going to do is thrust the pipette through the cell wall, and through the polar body, and suction out the chromosomes that are beneath. Are you ready?"

"As I'll ever be."

"Okay. Move your right hand to the next knob away from you. That's the pipette control. Turn it gently and see what happens."

Robby spun the knob ever so carefully. In his microscopic field of vision, he saw the pipette advance toward the cell. "Got it."

"Now insert the pipette into the cytoplast about a third of the way, past the polar body. Be careful. Dr. Ritchie says this work is a little like flying a helicopter."

" I can see that. Done."

"Now apply the suction. Do you know which knob it is?" The doc watched Robby carefully move his hand. "Yes. That's it. I think you may have some aptitude for this. Let me have a look." They switched places for a few seconds. "Alright." He moved away, resumed his position of instruction while Robby looked in again. "Now, the knob on your left will move the oocyte out of your view, so you can look at the pipette by itself. See if you can accomplish that."

"Okay," said Robby after a few adjustments.

"Now, tell me what you see," said Dr. Theseus, as he flipped a switch.

"I see a glow inside the pipette."

"I think you got the chromosomes, then. We must have successfully enucleated this egg cell. Let me have a look." He placed his eyes on the two oculars, peering down into the small, small world of molecular manipulation. Robby saw a little smile raising the corner of the doc's lips. "Yep. That's it. We got it. Now watch what I do." He performed a maneuver using several of the knobs. "I'm setting this cytoplast aside, so we can get the donor into place and make a transfer."

The professor opened a door on a stainless steel container, and withdrew a Petri dish, which he set gently on the countertop beside the microscope. Within the glass container was an opaque, colorless gelatinous lump—the fibroblast culture that would provide the genetic identity of their newly-enucleated cow egg. Dr. Theseus withdrew a clean pipette from a drawer below the countertop. After removing its white plastic wrapping, he set the pointed glass end of the gleaming instrument to the surface of cultured living cells in the Petri dish. With a gentle squeeze, he suctioned a small sample of the teeming karyoplasts up into the pipette. After moving his arm in a careful arc across the counter, he deposited the cells onto a slide. He set the pipette down, adjusted the position of the slide, and deftly inserted it into the big microscope. Setting his eyes back to the oculars at the top, he turned knobs generously until he was able to zero in on the specimen that he had just obtained—a batch of undifferentiated, Gap 0, Holstein calf cells that had grown in the Petri dish, having reproduced independently from 30-day-old calf fetal cells that had been obtained three weeks ago.

"Were you watching when I set the cytoplast aside a minute ago?"

"Yes."

"See if you can reposition it so we can get the host and donor, the cytoplast and karyoplast back into the same field of view."

"Robby set his hands gingerly back on the mysterious knobs. Back and forth between several of them for a few minutes and he was able to set the egg cell back into the path of the pipette containing the new chromosomes. "I can see why Dr. Ritchie compares this to flying a helicopter. The three-dimensional aspects of putting these two together are tricky."

"Right," agreed Dr. Theseus. "It requires some skill. You're doing *real* work in three-dimensional space. It's not oversimplified, like in a video game."

The room was silent for a moment while Robby continued his maneuverings.

"But it's not nearly as creative as the real thing," mused the doc.

"The real thing?" asked Robby.

"The bull and cow actually do a much better job at this than we do, and probably enjoy it a lot more."

Robby laughed. "You mean—a better job at making an embryo?"

"Yeah." The professor chuckled.

"But their efforts produce a result that is not nearly as manageable."

"That's true. And I can see that you're catching on to what this is all about. It's all about animal husbandry that is *smart*, instead of just random and instinctual."

"That;'s the difference between us and them, doc."

"Say what, Robby?"

"As humans, we want to master everything. We maximize, optimize every circumstance as much as we can. We *subdue* the earth and every living thing in it, converting every species' natural processes to our own purposes," the young assistant opined.

"As if we really knew what our own purposes are," mused the doc.

"Well, our purposes here are to obtain AAT enzyme so that people with lung problems can breathe better. Am I right about that?"

"That would be the objective in a real biotech company. Yes. What we're doing here is just experimenting with procedures so that students can know what the hell they're doing when they're out there in the laboratories of the world, being called upon to engineer the sought-after, hypothesized 'high-expressing' founder animal that can engender a whole herd of transgenic cattle. Then the gene manipulation to produce a desired protein or enzyme is complete. The animals are fixed so they do most of the work. And the lab people are freed up to go onto bigger and better quests."

"I've got the cytoplast back into position now; it's up against the big pipette."

"Let me have a look." Rain started outside; they could hear its dull pounding on the windows of the outer room. "What you need to do is rotate that cell around until you can see the hole from which you. . ." The professor habitually grabbed a knob and started making the adjustment he was talking about. "There it is. I've got it visibly located. You rotate it so that it's in the polar position and the karyoplast can be inserted right back through that same hole. There's no sense in wounding the cell twice." He stepped back.

Robby reassumed his position at the helm. He could see the wound, but it wasn't quite lined up, so he made adjustments with his fingertips so that the egg cell, its hole, and the pipette containing the new DNA were lined up in an axis.

"Whenever you get it properly lined up, go for it," urged the doc.

And then Robby did. With the egg and its karyoplast in opportune position, he slowly thrust the micropipette, with its precious genetic cargo, into its new cellular residence. "That's all she wrote, I guess," he announced. "Check it out."

As Dr. Theseus confirmed that the nuclear transfer phase was complete, he said, drily, "Now we've got this calf ready for a little surrogate gestation. All that's left is to jump-start the little Taurus and then park it inside one of the cows."

"Jump-start?"

"With electrofusion."

hddq://stcharlesave.loc

Saturday afternoon, Robby and Rosa took the old trolley downtown so they could walk around a bit. They went up on the levee to watch the boats passing on the river, the parenting tourists with their young charges, the late afternoon sun moving in its westward arc toward a hazy horizon. Being two souls swept along the great confluence of human strivings and wanderings, their young hearts beat the same as billions, yet with uniquity that spiraled around tiny messengers harkening to every fiber of their existence.

She had a negative view of life at the present, its fascination having been dulled somewhat by sensuous choices that had accelerated hotly and heavily for a while. But her inebriation with Mick and his fast lifestyle had faded, like embers after a fire, during the last year or so. She wasn't yet on a rebound, but idling along on a valence that daily revolved around a dull core of finishing school.

Robby's perspective, on the other hand, had wound itself around a perpetual scaffold of human enquiry that sought to unravel the coded mysteries of life itself. His involvement in mapping of the microbiological world and coveted mastery over its enigmatic processes had required of him a geekily positive approach to every little challenge that the great laboratory of life presented.

Together this perfectly cool October afternoon, they sat on the levee in a grassy spot, two chromatic specks amidst the noise and haste, drawing closer to each other, leisurely gravitating into an axial attraction that could possibly exclude the destructive and distractive forces that diminish and dilute the noblest urges of people in this world.

Cars, trucks buzzed across the Mississippi River bridge a mile away, but in full hazy view, looking like ants in the distance, with only their tops, their little domes and upper appendages, visible behind the superstructure of gargantuan bridge. As the sun pulled its dusky curtain downward toward a perfectly flat delta horizon, a menagerie of twinkling lights made themselves known within that matrix of quasi-industrial commercial metropolis, punctuated with neighborhood layers and avenue strips, criss-crossed with boulevard boundaries and bounteous urban amenities. Leviathan, alluvial brown waterway slid through the very aorta and soul of it all, with microcosmic wavelets lapping gently against concrete bulkheads a stone's throw below the two young viewers.

There was no sound in it worth considering really, just a dull hum of human wanting and wasting, striving and stopping, heaving, like a low 60-cycle-per-second buzz in an old fluorescent. No sound worth considering really—until a winging seabird screeched, startling the pair from behind, or one of the boat behemoths let forth its preposterously-loud fog-horn bellow.

It was a man-made environment that could, at the drop of any old mad hat or fat cat, drown out sensitivity, squelch individuality and neuter passion.

"Life is incredibly complicated," said Rosa as she watched, across the river, the West Bank shimmering from daytime browns and grays into nightly jeweled darkness. Then she turned, looked at her new friend. Reflections from the cityscape were like sparks in her eyes. A breeze whispered.

Ever the dork, Robby downshifted his own musings into a credible follow-up: "You know how complex a computer is?" It was half question, half answer.

"Yes."

"As incredible as it all is—what people can do with computers—its all based on memory systems of only two characters: zero and one."

"Uh-huh. They make up bits and bytes." She pulled the band off her pony-tailed hair, and it cascaded gloriously upon her shoulders.

"As seemingly infinite as all those combinations are, based on only two characters—the composition of the biological world is based on *four* characters."

"Oh yeah?"

"Yeah. G, A, T, and C."

"The T is thymine. I remember that one."

"Thymine, cytosine, guanine, and adenine: building blocks of DNA. So, while artificial intelligence is constructed upon a base of two, *original* intelligence of the natural world is built upon a base of four."

"As if the possibilities of a two-based system were not great enough to do everything that needed doing."

"Yeah. Whatever multiplicity of permutations can be assembled, *or even conceived*, with the two-base system is then squared and *cubed* exponentially by the expansion into a system built upon four. It's mind-blowing, isn't it?"

"Like I said, life is complicated," Rosa affirmed, smiling at him. They laughed. "Robby, I had a funny thought when we were walking by that graffiti wall a while ago. Some budding artist had drawn those bionical creatures."

"I noticed them. The silvery ones that look kinda like droids or something."

"They were incredibly detailed. Somebody had put a *lot* of time into those artworks. I was wondering why an artist of such ability would spend all that time on a graffiti, something that's just *free*."

"Maybe he's got no worldy success in it, so he's got nothing to lose. It's pure art."

"It made me think of cave-man paintings."

"Ha. Right. That's a cool idea. 21st century urban dwellers practicing self-expression just like Neanderthals. Maybe humans don't change as much as we think."

"Painting images on walls must be pretty basic human endeavor."

"Art is a primal urge." Robby simplified.

The evening was still warm, but getting just chilly enough to require a cozier location. "Hey, let's go down to the Café du Monde and get some coffee and beignets," said Robby.

"How 'bout we do that after getting some real food somewhere?"

"Yeah, let's do it. I could go for an oyster poboy." They walked eastward along the top of the levee; all of New Orleans twinkled on a flat delta 30-feet below. Behind them, just a hint of Saturday's daylight faded into the west. *What a beautiful night. "Honey, could we ask for more?"* "Whenever I think of those cave paintings, Rosa, I recall seeing animals in them."

"Oh, yeah." She laughed. "Mastadons."

"Mammoths and sabre-toothed tigers. I think it was a big event when they killed a big animal. Their killing a buffalo or whatever was a triumph over death, because they had meat for another week, or month, or whatever. The hunters would go out and slay the terrible beasts, protecting their women and the rest of the tribe from certain death, while hanging up some serious protein in the process."

They laughed. She nudged him with her body, like a tamed football block. "Are you a cave-man at heart?"

"Maybe down in my genes somewhere."

"Down in your jeans?" She stopped walking. And there was a silly smile on her lovely face.

"Uh." He could feel himself blushing. "I didn't mean—"

"It's okay, silly." She poked him playfully in the abdomen, then continued to walk. "Or maybe you're like the guy who commemorated the event by painting the animal pictures on the walls."

"Nah, I'm the guy that cuts the meat up so everybody can eat it. Like yesterday, I had to do surgery on a live cow, in order to implant an embryo in her uterus."

"Wow. Is that part of your work out at the river research station?"

" Yes. I was helping Dr. Theseus complete a cloning procedure."

"No kidding? You cloned a cow?"

Robby had a sheepish grin. "I guess you could call it that. The doc masterminded it. I did the grunt work."

"What kind of cow was so lucky as to rate cloning?"

He chuckled. "A very special cow."

"Yes, well . . . how so?"

"This cow produces medicine in its milk."

"What kind of medicine?"

"Not really medicine, but an enzyme called AAT, alpha-1-antitrypsin. It's the basis for drugs to treat lung ailments, like emphysema."

"How on earth do you do that?"

"Genetic engineering. It's patching genes together at the cellular level, to create new species."

"Oh, how creative."

"Yes, it is creative. Microbiologists are taking the beneficial characteristics of various animals and assembling them to make ideal breeds of cows, sheep, horses."

"Humans?"

"I'm sure, eventually someone will get around to that."

"What about you? Would you clone a human?"

"Nah." He paused for a moment. They were entering the crowded Jackson Square now. "Go to the left, and around the square. We'll get something to eat at Ralph & Kakoo's." They skirted around a group of people who were mounting a horse-drawn carriage.

"Robby?"

"What?"

"Can you make a horse that doesn't poop in the street?"

"Hahahaha. It'll never happen. Some things *cannot* change." They turned into a wider area, where artists had their work set up for sale, and there was more space between pedestrians. "Maybe they could engineer a sac, like a kangaroo has, but strategically, uh, *genetically* placed so that it would catch the stuff as it comes out of the horse's rear end."

Rosa laughed out loud at this. Her eyes were bright with reflection of streetlamps. She raised a hand to cover her wide mouth, although Robby thought there was no need to hide such beautiful lips with coy gesture.

He looked at her with surprised amusement. "You think that's funny, do you?" She stopped. He moved closer to her.

She was still laughing, couldn't answer. Instinctively, he grabbed her hands and raised them together into a sort of prayerful position. She couldn't cover her mouth, so she lowered her head, still laughing. And he was so utterly fascinated at her mirth. It was so unlike him. After a few seconds of gazing into her merriment, not knowing what to do, he raised one hand and stroked her black hair. An old song jumped into his head, and he knew why. *Black, black, black is the color…of my true love's hair.*

She took his hand gently; they resumed the walk. The laughter was slowly replaced with a smile that wouldn't go away. *May it never go away.* Robby thought that maintaining a smile like that on a woman's face could make a man's life worthwhile. They didn't say much until they were seated at the restaurant. They ordered wine. He had his oyster poboy. She got a bowl of gumbo and a big slice of French bread that she hadn't ordered. She cut the bread in half and put a piece on his plate, then sipped the wine.

Finally, she resumed. "So, you wouldn't clone a human?" The corners of her mouth were still turned up with levity. She looked directly into his eyes.

"Why bother? The old-fashioned way is better." And they enjoyed his little joke for a minute. They could dwell on this theme forever, but it was too soon for that. "But seriously, Rosa, I've been thinking about the pictures thing."

"The pictures? You mean the graffiti?"

"The graffiti, the caveman paintings, and. . ." He we was trying to think of something. "And everything in between. People have been making images throughout the history of the human race. I guess that when cavemen drew pictures of their conquest over animals, they were, in a way, sort of *retaining* the event, like, making the memory of it last."

"Like hunter's today taking pictures of their trophy kills."

"Yeah, but it's more than that, it's. . ."

"Religious."

"Yes. Not only were they retaining the moment of victory over the animals that threatened them, but they were somehow raising its significance to a higher level."

"They were asserting their mastery over the natural world."

"Yes, something like that. Primitive humans contended with a natural environment that had fierce forces—not just wild animals, that could trample and kill them. The elemental forces of nature, like lightning and volcanoes, could wipe them out in a heartbeat. And of course they feared those mysterious elements over which they had no control. Ultimately though, I think that fear sort of metamorphosed into a fearful *respect*, in the same way that warriors respect each other's ability to end the life of the other. And then, strangely, men came to *revere* what they feared. I think that as generations passed, in some cases their reverence evolved into a *worship* of those mysterious entities that could sovereignly control their destiny."

"They worshipped those things that—if not subdued—would kill them."

"Yes. and to appease those forces, they sacrificed to them. I think those cave paintings were a primitive kind of sacrifice, and probably accompanied by bloodletting of some kind."

"The pictures were religion, then, not art?"

"What's the difference?" asked Robby. "Anyway, it's beyond our power to speculate. People in the modern age are so far removed from that primitive, survival mindset that we cannot relate to it authentically. Art for us is just a pastime that arises from an abundance of leisure. Religion is just ritual that we hold in common to remind ourselves that we are dependent upon something greater than ourselves. Having conquered the animal kingdom, we turn our sights upon that realm which we cannot control— ourselves. The beasts that threaten us now come from within us."

"Robby." She was looking at him intensely.

"What?"

"You've thought about this a lot."

"Yes." He laughed a little. "I guess I got a little carried away with it."

"That's fine." She smiled. "For some reason, when you mentioned worshipping entities in the natural world, I was reminded of the golden calf."

"Yes! That's exactly what I'm talking about—when Moses came down from the mountain with the laws. That was the precise moment in history when one man announced a true revelation that there was, in the world, a greater power than just elemental forces contending with each other."

"You mean God?"

"You're damn right I mean God! The Creator—the One who wrote the code."

At that moment, the diners in Ralph & Kakoo's, and the diners in every other restaurant in the city of New Orleans, and the residents and tourists who were walking through the streets, finishing tasks at work, beginning tasks at home, cooking dinner, watching television, making love and whatever else humans in a great city do—they all heard, or felt, a low rumble. But it wasn't a *real low* rumble. It shook the walls of their buildings and they felt the vibrations in their feet, and it, whatever it was, provoked them all to ask, or at least wonder: *What the hell was that?*

What it was was an explosion at a chemical plant on the West Bank.

hddq://bourbonstreet.loc

Simon Lafraneer walked out of a strip club on Bourbon Street, feeling terribly frustrated. A crowd of curious and drunken strangers made him feel no better. He was wandering in a world that had no care for him, a world that he sought to use, but it was using him. His cell phone rang.

"Hello."

"Hello, Simon."

"Hello, luv."

"What are you doing?"

"Trying to shake up some bloody business. I've been meeting with some new clients."

"When are you coming home?"

"It'll be soon, luv. . .next week." He was walking through the raucous crowd. *People are strange, when you are lonely.*

"What's the noise? Where are you?"

"Just had dinner, going back to the hotel room."

"You've gotten scads of calls, dear. Do you want me to tell you about them?"

"Did Reginald call?"

"Yes. He said the GenUm account is about ready."

"Well, that's good. I'll email him."

"And the Bloomball man called. He said he has surplus embryos, and he wants to talk to you. Do you want me to give him your number?"

"No, I haven't found a buyer for them yet."

"What about—"

"Just send me an email with the important stuff, luv. I've got a headache now. I'm going back to the hotel to get some sleep. Good night, Gladys."

"Bye, Simon. Come home when—"

Simon snapped the phone shut. He slinked back to his hotel room, ever a salesman powerless to come in from the cold. Treading the sharp cryogenic edge of *homo geniture*, he knew himself to be precarious upon a bed of loneliness. But he was bound to keep prospecting until paydirt was struck. He knew intimately well the hollow enticements of solitude, but was fear-frozen in the face of them. The spectre of failure incessantly shadowed his pursuits. He must not lose the game.

In the midst of his striving, a chimeric presence had snuck its goatish head upon his once-blissful union with Gladys. Bit by bit, he had fallen beneath the spell of its pervasive imagery. Offering no warmth, no love, it nevertheless constricted his wanting life with serpentine agility. Half-drunk, he fell into an empty bed to embrace the many-colored beast. And in his bed, and in the wayward street beneath, *the people bowed and prayed to the neon god they made.*

Codons

13

Sunday afternoon, Mick Basker slept until 1:30, then got out of bed, made some coffee, and sat down at his computer to take a look at the chip that he had retrieved from the glass horse's gonads four nights ago. He reached down to open the bottom drawer of his desk. Then he noticed a scrap of printed paper, about the size of a small index card, on the floor nearby. Recognizing it as a slip that he had found within the figurines' crate, Mick picked it up to get a closer look. This is what was printed on the little paper:

> Congratulazioni! Lei ha comprato uno degli articoli di vetro più belli nel mondo. Quest'edizione a bassa tiratura della "*Quadriga Marciana*" ha soffiato degli artigiani specializzati della Società del Vetro Leoni di Venezia, Italia. Gli articoli di vetro sono i riproduzioni squisite delle sculture di bronzo che fa la guardia di sopra del vestibolo occidentale della Basilica di San Marco in Venezia. I cavalli originali sono giungi a Venezia con il ricco bottino di guerra dai Veneziani dopo la conquista di Constantinopoli al termine della IV Crociata nel 1204 A.D. Dopo cinque secoli, nel 1797, Napoleone li fa trasferire a Parigi, ma i cavalli erano ritornati alla Basilica di San Marco nel 1815.

But Mick knew no Italiano, so he set the little paper aside, and reached down again to the bottom drawer, from which he produced a yellow pharmaceutical container, a pill box. Inside it was a was a patch of plastic foam which concealed a little green circuit board about the size of thumb. Carefully, he inserted his chip, looking like a little black crab with metallic legs, into the device, then pushed the assemblage into a USB port on the computer. He typed and moused his way to the chip's data, and when he found it this is what he saw:

OAT, GHN-1:17q22-q24, DTNBP-1:6p22.3, IGF-2:3q28.

But he didn't know what it was. He hadn't known what it meant when he first viewed it four nights ago; now looking at the codes, or whatever they were, still held absolutely no meaning for him. He would have to talk to Franz about this. He would have to make a call.

So he went in the kitchen, still a big mess now that Rosa was no longer around, poured another cup of coffee. This time he sloshed a shot of whiskey into the cup. He grabbed a hunk of French bread, and a slice of cheese from the fridge. Returning to the small paper-strewn office room, he again sat at the computer, and was looking with puzzlement at the numbers and letters on the screen, as if another peering and the shot of whiskey might enlighten him to its hidden message. No clue. He set the coffee and bread down on the desk, reopened the lower drawer to get Franz' number from the address book. He dialed the number on his cellphone. This required some concentration, since it was an international call, with country code, etc. and now it was ringing on the other end, somewhere probably near Venice.

"Yah?" said the voice.

"Franz?"

"Yah."

"This is Mick Basker, calling from the United States."

"Yah. You got the package," came the affirmation, in German accent.

"I did. Thank you. It arrived a few days ago, just as I expected."

"And you've looked at it?"

"Yes." Mick paused, expecting another question. But none came. So he continued, "I don't know what to make of it, though."

"I am not surprised. Your pieces must be paired up with some others in order to get the full effect."

"Oh, I'm glad to hear that." Again he paused, expectant. But there was only an awkward silence, exacerbated by the delay of intercontinental electrons. "So. . . what do you recommend?"

"Talk to Simon. See what he says."

"Simon?"

"Simon Lafraneer, my associate."

"Okay. Where would I find him?"

"At the Monteleone Hotel, in your city. Do you know it?"

"Oh, yes. . .Is that all?"

"Yah."

"What room?"

"What room? Do you think I am the *concierge*, my friend? I do not know the room. I think you have all that you need to know now."

"How do you spell that name?"

"Lafraneer, with and 'f,' as in my name, after the 'La,' and then. . ." Franz spelled it for him. Is there anything else I can do for you, Herr Basker? I was right in the middle of something."

"No, thank you. I am sorry for the disturbance. I had forgotten—"

"It is no matter. It is pleasure to do business with you. Simon can tell you whatever you need to know, okay?"

"Yes."

"Keep in touch, Herr Basker. Perhaps our collaboration will lead to greater things, yah?"

"Sure. Thanks."

"Ciao." And Franz hung up.

Mick's call to the Monteleone afforded him only the knowledge that Mr. Lafraneer was registered in room 1204. Later, in the evening, Simon returned his call, and they met at a place called the *Crab's Dream*, near Jackson Square.

Mick was sitting by a shuttered window in the place, nursing a drink, when Simon walked in. It was eight o'clock. Mick had been watching, as instructed by Simon, for a man with a gray herring-bone hat that had a feather in it. Mick gestured to him, and stood.

"Mr. Basker?" said the Brit, as he set an umbrella against the wall beside the chair. They shook hands. "Pleased to meet you."

"Mr. Lafraneer. Thank you for coming."

"My pleasure, my boy." He sat, as the waiter, a goateed man of middle age, clad in black pants and white shirt, arrived at the table.

"Can I get you something sir?" as he set down menus and napkins with silverware.

"Please bring me a Jack Daniels with water, with one ice cube." Simon said.

"And for you, Mr. Basker?"

"Let's start off with a large shrimp cocktail, Nick."

"Coming right up," and he hurried away.

Simon smiled at his new acquaintance, and studied him for a moment. "Franz had told me to expect a call from someone, but I didn't know who it would be. Whom do you represent, Mr. Basker?"

"I facilitate loans and other instruments for Banc*Cher*, which is one of the oldest banks in New Orleans."

"How old is it, sir?"

"1907. It's still a family business."

"Ah, that is rare these days. And how long have you been with the bank?"

"Not long. A little more than two years."

"I see. . .And what family is it?"

"The Champlains."

"Yes. I know of them. I live on Grand Cayman, you know."

"Oh, a favorite place of mine. It's a hell of a nice place, actually."

"You've been to hell, then?" asked Simon.

"Pardon me?"

Simon's face registered something between comedy and authentic inquiry. "Surely you've been to hell, if you've been to Grand Cayman."

Mick was confused for a few seconds, but then remembered something about the island. "Oh. . .yes." He let out a little laugh. "On the north end, hell, with the rock formations."

Simon laughed out loud. "It's a bit overrated—the lower end of Seven Mile Beach is, of course, much more enjoyable than hell."

"Right." Mick was amused with the Brit's gregarious levity. Mick, being a younger man, was not quite as relaxed as Simon, the seasoned businessman world-traveler. Unsure of the 'hell' connection, he decided to get back to business."And who do you represent, Simon?"

"Parthenonics. LTD, founded in 1988 by myself and several investors."

"Franz Hallfrich is one of the founders?"

"No. He is not a partner, though we have been working in cooperation with him since 1997. Franz is a quite independent, and remarkable, entrepreneur." Simon had a twinkle in his eye, beneath bushy eyebrows. "You could say we have a symbiotic relationship with him. He is very knowledgeable about what is happening on the Continent. And he, ah, he referred you to me?"

"Yes. He said you could help me to make good use of a shipment that he recently sent to me."

"A shipment? And what was that?" asked the Brit, smiling curiously.

The waiter brought Simon's drink. "Would you like some dinner, gentlemen?" He set the shrimp cocktail on the table, and a small bowl of remoulade sauce.

Mick replied, "I'll have a house salad and crawfish bisque."

"And for you, sir?"

"What do you recommend, Mick?"

"Do you like seafood?"

"I love fish and chips."

Mick laughed, starting to relax. "How about the red snapper, then?"

"If you recommend it, my boy."

"Yeah, that's it, Nick. Red snapper, fried, with hush puppies." He looked up at Simon. "You don't come to New Orleans and not order seafood."

"And a salad, sir?"

"Caesar salad, please, a small one."

"And a bottle of the house red, please Nick."

"Yes, Mr. Basker."

With that taken care of, Mick resumed. "I received a shipment of Venetian glass this week." He paused, expectant.

Simon was listening carefully. "A shipment. . .a large shipment, as in, you will retail the glass here in New Orleans?"

"Uh, no. It's just a work of art. Actually, four figurines, horses cast in glass."

"Ah, yes, from the Leoni works?"

"That's right."

"The Leonis do absolutely marvelous works in glass."

"Yes. I thought so too." Mick was waiting for a certain response from the cheery Brit.

"And?" said Simon, with a hint of suggestion.

Mick was unsure about what to say. This type of business was new to him. He dipped a shrimp in the red sauce and ate it.

"And, was there something else with the glass?"

"Yes."

"Well, out with it, my boy." Simon laughed good-naturedly. "Was there, ah, a message, something special?"

"A, uh, computer chip."

Simon's eyes narrowed. He was amused. "Very small, eh?"

"Right. Very small."

"And were you able to read the contents of it?" asked Simon, as if this happened every day.

"I did read it."

"And what did it say?"

"Hell if I know," blurted Mick, and looked out the window, taking the last gulp of his drink.

Simon laughed, totally at ease. "The chip contained, perhaps, a message that you don't know how to interpret?"

Mick looked back at the spiffy Brit, and laughed, relaxing again. "That's right. That's exactly right."

"Well, my boy, what did it say *exactly*? Maybe I can help you understand the meaning of it. I've done this before you know."

Mick sighed. He didn't want to repeat the message, with its mysterious numbers and letters. Reaching in his shirt pocket, he produced the little paper with Italian printed on it. On the back he had written the message that had been retrieved from a glass horse's gonads. He slid it across the table to Simon, who picked it up and looked at it, with an expression of mock seriousness on his face, an expression which then metamorphosed into a faint smile. "These are genetic codes."

"Genetic codes?"

"Locations on the human genome, in the DNA chain." Simon smiled, as if this is common knowledge that people sent through glass horse sculptures every day of the week.

"Okay. . .and?"

"The second one refers to human growth hormone. The other three, I'll have to look up." Simon looked directly into Mick's puzzled eyes. "Does this mean anything to you?"

"Uh, no, not really."

Nick brought them a bottle of wine and popped the cork. Mick took a gulp, appreciatively. "Nah. Whatever the hell it means, I don't know." He laughed. "And I *paid* for this information."

"Now just wait a minute, Mick. If you're dealing with Franz Hallfrich, I can assure that this is important, and, probably in the long run, *valuable* information." The older man's eyes studied those of the younger. "Let me ask you a question or two."

"Sure." Mick shrugged, clueless, but willing to be instructed.

"Did you know, for instance, Mick, that certain people, people with great athletic aspirations, are willing to pay generously for this substance?"

"The growth. . .you mean the growth hormone?"

"Right."

"So it's like. . . steroids?"

Simon leaned back and smiled. Then he inclined forward again, so that his face was close over the table. His voice lowered. "This hormone is far superior to steroids. It's works better for building muscles. And it, get this, Mick. . .it burns fat. It strengthens ligaments and tendons. It's absolutely safe, and on top of all that it's not detectable."

"Oh, yeah? Not detectable. What the hell difference would that make?" Somehow, Mick didn't understand how he should be impressed with this information. "So maybe I'll just go down to the K&B and buy me a bottle of it."

"The K&B?"

"The drug store."

"You can't get HGH at a drug store, Mick."

hddq://circentral.loc

It's pumping through you.

Henry Globin looked up at the bright, white LED sign overhead. Its digitally updated letters were flashing: **Stand by for**

Next Compression. Next Compression in .50 seconds. Henry nudged his buddy, Luke O'Site.

"You ready?"

"As I'll ever be."

The line of passengers was becoming shorter every second. The wait was not long. The Mickey was running along like a well-circulated machine. Henry's group assumed their places in line, stepped nimbly past the mitral gate, through the aortic valve at just the right moment, and were pumped along with their fellow passengers into the Cerebral Avenue line. It was an intense ride, something like a Jamaican bobsled run with a twist of absolute upside down roller-coaster vertigo thrown in that made for a nice discombobulation and transportational fear-factor rush. "Wheeeee-ha!" Hands up in the air. Swshsh. Uh-oh Better calm down. The platelets were looking at him funny. Better act your age. You are working after all, can't have too good a time. Shshsshshsssh glrgleshwshgrgleslippingslipsliding gliding careening through arterial slickeriness with minimal obstruction fast and faster and careening and up *and down and over and out and I know one thing each time I find myself flat in my pace I pick myself up and get back in the race that's life.*

"Here's where I get off," said Luke. "Airway Drive. We've got some unauthorized bacteria infestation on the Alimentary Canal."

"God be with you!" shouted Henry to his friend, as Luke jumped off the train.

Henry was headed for the Pit, the glandular station right in the middle of Grand Central Neuronic Headquarters. Today he was working as a driver/guide for a group of Corpuscles. It was an important, though quite routine, mission. A few more millimetres of arterial rush, then deceleration in the hypophyseal line, and they were pulling into the station at the Pit Stop.

Pituitary Station. Disembark in .20 seconds, said the sign, and Henry did, at the appropriate time, seasoned traveler that he was. His clients disembarked as well, and dispersed to various points.

"Thanks for the help," a few of them said.

"Da Nada, man. Any time. I'll be going back the other way in a little bit if any you guys want some expert company."

The station attendant, seated behind a sign that said **Mitey Kindria**, casually asked him, without looking up: "Destination?"

"I've got an O^2 dropoff here. Then I'll be catching the return to CircCentral."

"Step to the right, please. You can discharge your Oxen with ATP for transport to the Energy Department. Then pick up a load of CO^2 for delivery to CircCentral. Take the Vena Cava for your return trip. That gate is just beyond ATP on your left."

"Hey, thanks," said Henry.

"No problem. Be careful going through ATP, though. There's heavy activity there. We've got a code yellow for acidosis in sector 17."

"Sure. I'll keep my eyes open."

Arriving at ATP, he encountered a long line of Oxen and their handlers waiting to be dispatched. Henry snapped open the leash, releasing the two Oxen he'd brought along, O^1 and O^2. He petted the both of them; they were good little critters, wagging their tails, a protein's best friend. Having completed his mission, Henry then made his way through the crowded terminal to the Vena Cava gate.

O^1 and O^2 sat obediently, looking out the membrane at an ocean of cytoplasm. Soon, a trainer would come along and put them to good use. After walking 40 or so yards down the concourse, Henry looked back at the two creatures. They were sitting patiently as Oxen do, protein's best friend. Above them at the ceiling was a lit-up sign:

**Neuropsin II Convention passengers, take Tram B to Sector 23.
16S-type RNA delegates take Tram C to Sector 18.**

When Henry arrived, five minutes later, Vena Cava gate, he had a few minutes to chill out. He sat on the floor, gazing out the membrane, beyond the crowded concourses of Mitey Kindria, at an ocean of cytoplasm stretching as far as the eye could see. On the horizon, barely visible in the distance were the Golgi Islands. And far beyond that, Henry knew, was the great Continent of Nucleus, the deep interior of which drew the brightest chromatins and the most talented sugars, movers and shakers who climbed that great double-spiraled ladder of success, making decisions, wonking policies that extended far beyond the nucleopolis itself, to every reticulum in the great hinterland and every centriole between here and the next universe. He aspired to go there himself one day.

But not today, just another day in the life of a specialized protein. He did like his job though. Henry considered himself fortunate to be a guide, and he usually enjoyed the commutes between all his assignments and CircCentral.

But as he watched the great open cytoplasm, his heart was pierced with a pang of desire, for looming up from the horizon was a magnificent sailing ship, with brilliant sails rippling in the breeze, and azure-white sprays jettisoning from both sides of its bow. Henry couldn't keep his eyes off it. He stood and watched it for a long time, until it came quite close, and he forgot where he was, and he missed the next Vena Cava push. When at last the golden galleon passed straightway in front of him, he saw the RiboNucleic flag flapping atop the mast, royal blue background with a red orb in the center, and white border. And he saw written upon the bow in gold letters the name of the ship:

HMS RuNAbout.

Oh, that he were on that great ship! Oh, that he might climb to its apex, and survey from its crow's nest cytoplasmic grandeur and the boisterous cellular wind in his wings! Such adventure! Such freedom! Where is it going?

The ship is so close. But for this window, I could throw a stone and hit it. I can see the white's of their eyes. The boat must be docking nearby. I shall meet it at the dock!

Henry started to run down the concourse in the direction that the **RuNA**bout was moving. But he checked himself. *No need to risk running into someone.* The ship would obviously be docking somewhere nearby. So he restrained himself, continued in the direction, east it was, for a good half kilometer. Then he saw it—the sign, in large, archaic wooden letters: HMS **RuNA**bout, On Time, bound for the Ribosome Islands, and returning to DeeNay, Nucleus.

hddq://miteykindovue.loc

A few minutes after docking, Captain Dean Gene was sitting in the *Mitey Kindovue Restaurant* having dinner with his core crew. Turning to the first mate, he asked the question, "How are we fixed for ATP, Tom?"

"It's going on board as we speak, cap'n. The stocking crew is right on it."

"Good. Where do we stand on aminos supply, Dick?" He looked at the chief angler.

"We're at about 85% now, cap'n. Based on our projected course, I anticipate no problems in hitting 100% of capacity by the time we reach the Ribosomes. If we get as far as the Canary Centrioles and haven't caught schools yet, a five degree adjustment to east should take us through the Tuna Lysosomes where we'll surely catch all the aminos we'll need for this trip."

"Sounds good, Dick. I want us to be absolutely as efficient as possible. That means having enough aminos to use the entire stock of ATP, and keep those enzymes busy. You know what I mean?"

"I'm with you, cap'n. My brother Jimmy is one of those enzymes, and I know he's looking forward to a full load, what with Christmas coming and he wants to get some overtime."

"Well, yes, mateys. Let's try and make it a prosperous Christmas for all the folks on the Ribosome Islands. Plus. . ." The captain raised his bushy gray eyebrows for emphasis. "There is a shortage of peptides in the Cell now, ever since August. And shiver me timbers, mateys, let us not forget the bottom line—Proteins! Let's hear it for the Proteins!

The five seasoned sailors joined together in spontaneous song, while the two wives who were present, somewhat embarrassed, witnessed along with the other two dozen diners in *Captain Nance's Seafood,* their jolly, customized rendition of an old sea song:

We sail about on the Roundabout.

And we're all about what they sing about.

And they sing all around 'bout the Roundabout,

which nobody can deny!

The uninhibited sailors celebrated, and thus extended, their notoriety by raising their mugs on the last note of the song, clinking them all together, then completing their cadence with large swigs all 'round. There was no eye nor ear in the place not upon them. Just as the boastful cheer subsided and the restaurant's air of quiet normalcy returned, a woman's operatic voice rang like a ship's bell across the restaurant, "Yoooooooohoo. Dean!"

"Dorothy!" answered the captain.

The redheaded woman moved without hesitation toward the captain with a big smile on her face. They hugged. "Matey's, ya gotta meet my sister Dorothy." Though three of them already knew her quite well. "Dorothy, you know Tom, Dick, Harry. Over there's Rufus and Murray. and Rufus' wife, Maggie, and Harry's wife, JoAnne."

The first mate, Tom, stood up to allow a seat for Dorothy. She sat in the middle of the jolly eight, making them a jolly nine. "What have you been doing, my brother?"

"What have I been doing? What have we been doing, mateys?" A rhetorical question, which the lively captain answered himself. "What we've always done—sailing the noblest damn ship that ever skimmed o'er seven-seas' cytoplasm." Then noticing a waitress nearby, he summoned her with a gesture. "Elsa, how 'bout a grog for my sister here? Have you eaten, Dorothy? Tell the girl what we've been doing, mateys."

As the lovely redhead (though she might have been a grayhead) sat beside her brother, Tom stood beside the crowded table and addressed the assembly, but most especially the fair lady Dorothy, as he recounted, "We started out by acquiring the finest (every voyage's cargo being of course finer than the one before it) collection of single- strand RNAs that ever replicated from   an unzipped DeeNay. You shoulda seen those bases! The pollies could hardly keep up with 'em. As fine as any I've ever seen. And the nucleotides, just a-swellin'!" The exuberant ole salty-dog sailor burst into a scrap of ancient melody:

'Twas in the merry month of May,
when the nucleotides, they were swellin!

Young Mickey on his DeeNay lay,
all for the love of Barbry Ellen.'

Dorothy offered a little applause. "Oh, Tom! That is so sweet."

Tom continued. "We loaded 'em up at the dock in Chromostown and set sail on the great swan's road, our course set for Mitey Kindrea and the Ribosome Islands. Now here we are, two thirds of the way there. We stop at a pub and glory be! who walks in but the prettiest lady I ever did see!

"Oh, Tom!"

The Captain laughed. "Ain't you ever gonna give up, matey? How many years have you been saying that to my sister?"

"I figure it might stick in her mind one o' these years."

Their reverie was suddenly calmed by the approach of a ruddy young fellow with curly red hair and a bold step. The gregarious captain turned to address him. "Well, hullo there, matey. Shiver me timbers. Who might you be, young sailsnapper?"

"The name's Henry, sir. Henry Globin. I saw your ship come in. I was wondering if you might need another hand on board."

"Captain Dean Gene raised his head quizzically and, with one hairy eyebrow raised, surveyed the young man. He didn't say anything for about 12 seconds. Then he asked the boy, "You got your sea legs, boy?"

"My what?"

Hahahahaha! Much to the amusement of the salty dogs.

"Ah, go on now boy.   Ya better get back to yer. . . whatisityasay you do?"

"I'm a driver and guide in the CircSystem. I run regularly between CircCentral and here, and, well, all over the body."

"The body?"

"Yeah, you know, the body. Mick Basker's body. The guy that we're doing all this work for.

"Mick Basher," repeated the Captain, tentatively.

"Basker. Mick Basker."

"We're working for the Nucleus, boy. We have been for, oh, thirty years now."

"Twenty-nine, cap'n," Tom corrected.

"Twenty-nine."

"Yes, sir. With all due respect, Cap'n Gene, you gentlemen have been doing a fine job all these years. . . I mean, you're flat out famous around here—"

"*Roundabout* here," inserted the captain.

"Absolutely, sir. All these years, making it possible for The Cell to crank out GH1 Protein."

"Protein.! You hear that, mateys?"

"Yeah, yeah!" The mateys agreed, with gusto. They love their work. They're good at it, and they know it.

"I know your Cell-wide records for catching aminos, both for size and for weight, have been unmatched for as long as anyone roundabout here can remember. And so, since you represent the highest standards in your profession, and I've reached the top of my line, I thought I could—"

"Your line, my boy," interrupted the captain. "And what might that be?"

"I am, sir, a driver, a *good* driver for the Circ, and a guide, too. I've won excellence awards for two years now. And just now I saw your ship, and I just know that what I do on the Circsystem I could do for you as well."

"A driver," the captain repeated skeptically, as if he didn't know what a driver was. He looked around at his crew, gathering their attention. Then, with a mischievous grin, he said, "A landlubber is what you are."

"With all due respect, sir, I do have sea legs."

"How's that? How can a querky landlubbin driver have sea legs if he's never been on a boat?" The captain knew intuitively that the youngster had not yet sailed.

"A *Circ* driver, sir, in the circulatory system. I deliver Oxen to Mitey Kindria all over Mick's body. And I guide corpuscles and leukocytes."

"You do, huh?" The captain didn't say anything for about twelve seconds.

"He seems like an awfully nice young man, Dean," said Dorothy.

"I do have sea legs, sir. I just know it. Have you ever heard of the Jamaican bobsled runners?"

"Jamaican. . .Hahahahaha"

"With all due respect sir, my body has survived two years of strenuous, high-speed race-type propulsion, at several g's, being pumped through continuously hypertensive compressions along extremely crowded arteries and veins. . . like, uh, well, like a damn astronaut."

"Astronaut?"

"What do you need done, Cap'n?"

"Well, I need knee surgery."

"Sir, I'll give it a shot. Let me see your knee."

"Never mind." The captain laughed, impressed by the boy's bravado, if not his boastful resume. It seemed like about half bullshit anyway. He could detect a bit of his own young indomitable self behind those bright blue eyes, full of impetuosity. The boy's request seemed more a challenge than a question.

"I mean, sir, what do you need done on the boat that isn't currently being done?"

Captain Dean Gene hesitated. "I guess we could use someone to scrub the decks."

"I'm your man."

"And..." Captain Dean Gene looked slyly at Tom. "And we need someone to climb up in the crow's nest twice a day to get the big picture."

"Sir, yes, sir. I can get the big picture for you, sir."

"Well okay then, matey, get those landlubbin' legs moving. I'll see you on the deck in thirty."

hddq://crabsdream.loc

"Better than steroids, you say?" asked Mick.

"It's naturally occurring in the human body. So the nitpicking busybodies can't detect it in their tests," said Simon

"There can't be much market for it, then, if it's used by just a small group of extreme athletes., You're referring to the cyclists, and Olympic track stars and—"

"Body builders, footballers, boxers, wrestlers, soccer players, all over the world will really go for this stuff."

"Well, why don't they then?"

"It's controlled. You can only get it with prescription. And it's damned expensive."

"Hmm. Mick wasn't too impressed. There was something about it that didn't quite jive, as far as profit potential goes. *Too narrow a market.* "It's probably, uh, expensive because it's natural. What, are there a bunch of Mexicans or Cambodians somewhere who have growth hormone drawn out of them every day like, uh, like they're giving blood?

"Oh, no, the hormones are synthesized in labs, in cultures of reproducing cells."

"And that's natural?"

"Oh, yes. It's all by biological processes, except for the gene-splicing. I suppose it would be a stretch to call *that* a natural process. The gene for human growth hormone is spliced into a bacterial plasmid. Then the plasmid is introduced into a bacterial culture. The engineered cells multiply by simple fission. And as they do, these specially-equipped ones produce the growth hormone proteins as a bi-product."

"Like cows, making milk."

"Yes," affirmed Simon. "Very much like that. The bacteria become like domesticated animals, yielding products that we humans need."

"Hmph. A frickin' herd of germs cranking out growth hormones. What the hell will they think of next?" Mick smiled. He was looking across the restaurant at a lady who had just walked in. "What about the other three?"

"The other three?" asked Simon. He could see that Mick was mildly amused, but not actually interested in his developing prospect.

"The other three, uh, hieroglyphics there, or whatever they are—the IGF and the, whatever it is."

"I'll have to look them up, Mick, don't know right off the top of my head what they are."

The waiter brought their salads. "Can I get you anything else right now?"

"I'd like some sliced lemons, please," said Simon.

"Coming right up, sir."

As the waiter turned away, a woman at the next table called him. "Oh, Nick," she said.

"Yes, Mrs Picou." He stopped to hear her.

"I read your poetry in the Hyacinth."

"Oh, thank you. Did you like it?"

"Nick, it was. . .overzealous personification, and . . ."

"And?" Nick smiled at her.

"Blatantly anthropomorphic."

"Well, Meryl," Simon heard Nick say. "We can't please everyone, you know. We. . . We do what we like, and we like what we do."

"Just kidding, Nick. I found it very interesting."

"Thank you," said the polite waiter. Would you like to see the dessert tray?"

"Just bring me some pineapple sorbet, please."

"Coming right up, Meryl."

Simon, having a thought, summoned the waiter before he could get too far away. "Pardon me, sir," said he, loudly.

"Yes, sir," responded Nick, turning abruptly on his heels.

"You can get me something else, if you don't mind."

"Yes."

"Do you have malt vinegar?"

"Oh, yes. Of course, for the fish."

"Righto. Thank you." And he was off again.

Simon reached into his inner coat pocket and withdrew a folded paper. Opening it up, he set it on the table and appeared to be analyzing its contents very closely, and comparing it to the small slip that Mick had produced earlier. He studied the two papers intently for a few moments, intermittently taking a bite of salad. Mick's fascination with the woman who sat at the bar was growing, and so he contented himself to muse upon her presence and eat his salad. After a while, his curiosity broke the silence.

"What are you doing there? Interpreting the 'genetic codes'?"

"Not exactly. I'm afraid I will not be able to do that until I can get to the hotel room. But I *am* interpreting them in a different sort of way than what I had expected."

"That's good. It's all Greek to me."

Simon laughed, still looking intently at his page, whatever it was. "Not Greek," said he. "But it does pertain to Greek. Plato, actually." A curious smile crept upon his lips. He leaned back slightly, raised his head and looked directly into Mick's eyes. As he did so, he turned his paper around and set it on the table in plain view for Mick to see. And this is what it said:

> From the **OAK** , the **ANCIENT TREE** you see, **GO** to the **HARE'S** nest, which is **NORTH** as far as 'q' determines it should be, each step being   positive 'q' beneath your knee, and not a negative as your genetic map would seem to be. In other words, add your 'q's and you shall see how far that it may be, beyond the tree.

> Then, within the hole to which you're sent, *where rabbits in their **DENS** are bent,* you'll find the Ariadnic **THREAD** is rent, until you find it far away again, '*NEATH BUNCOMBE'S PACK, beyond Saluda track,* where 'p's are miles, as 'q's are steps, not east not east, but west, yes west..

> **IN** both these destinations **GOLD FLORINS** you shall see, if you but follow these directions from the tree.

For several minutes Mick gazed at the cryptic print, clueless. Then he looked up at his strange new acquaintance and said, "What in the hell is this?"

Simon chuckled. "This, my friend, is the email that I received from our associate, Franz. He sent it at the same time as he requested that I meet you here. I do believe it is the key to interpreting your 'genetic code.'"

Nick arrived; with effortless flair he set their dinner on the table. The exquisite seafood aroma was irresistible. Simon was dousing his fish with malt vinegar; Mick was sprinkling fil'e on his bisque. Before he took the first bite, he declared, " Like I said, it's Greek to me." Then he honed in on the crawfish.

"It is a three-part puzzle," explained Simon. He took a fork-full of red snapper. "Ah, this is good. A creole twist on fish and chips."

"I, uh, see two parts." Mick nodded his head toward the two mysterious messages, which Simon had set aside, next to the wine bottle. "Where's the third?"

"I've got it, but not here. It's back at the hotel. But there is quite enough here, with these two components, for us to gain some understanding of the message."

"So, there is a message here?"

"Yes. I believe that, when we combine the code that you have received with this other little thing, we'll have. . ." Simon didn't quite know what to describe what they would have.

"We'll have bullshit. I've paid good money for some meaningless information."

"Oh no, my boy. I am certain we have something quite valuable here. You may not know Franz Hallfrich. But I do. How much did you pay him for this information? "

"I can't really say, Mr. Lafraneer, but it was about five times the value of the artwork that it came in."

"I see," said Simon, having some knowledge of Franz's unique methods of doing business, which often involved artworks of obscure origin. "Let me reassure you. We certainly have something valuable here. We just need to figure what the message says, so we can find it. And that's why I'm here, you see. I've got the key to your information, which will lead us to something very valuable." Simon dabbed his chin with the white napkin and leaned back.

" Well, okay, then. What the hell is it?"

"Solid gold," said Simon. Then he sipped wine from the glass.

Auricles

14

"Solid gold?" asked Mick, peering across his glass at Simon Lafraneer. "Where?"

"That's what we're going to find out." Simon nibbled on a hush puppy at the end of his fork. "Actually, I know where it is. I just don't know *exactly* where it is."

"Where?"

"About fifty miles upriver from here, near the levee, buried in the ground."

Mick put his glass down. "Why are you telling me this? If there is gold," He laughed skeptically. "If there is this *buried treasure*, as you say, in the ground near here, and you've known approximately where it is, why haven't you searched for it?"

"First of all, Mick, understand that you have provided, I hope, the missing link here, without which I would have had no clue as to where to begin digging. You see, your genetic code here, which is, look at it, precise information, with numbers and so forth."

"Why the hell did this Franz guy send that to me?"

"I don't know, my boy. You made some kind of deal with him, didn't you?"

"I purchased some Venetian glass sculptures from him."

"Is that all?" Simon put his arms on the table and lowered his voice. "Wasn't there something *else* that accompanied the glass?"

"Uh, yeah, these f....g hieroglyphics. I didn't ask for what he sent."

"What had you asked for?"

"I just, uh, billed him for some money that he owed me. He said he'd send me a surprise package that would exceed the value of what he owed me."

"I see. Well, my boy, little did you know it at the time, but you were buying into a very special arrangement. This is a once-in-a-lifetime opportunity."

"Oh yeah? Just how much 'gold' are we talking about here?"

"Two or three hundred gold florins, original Florentine issue, minted for the deMedicis in 1492."

Mick, being a banker, knew something of the history of money. "Surely you jest," he responded, incredulous. Suddenly, Simon was watching the younger man flail arms in the air and shake his head vigorously. "Wait, wait. You're bullshittin' me here," Mick protested.

"No, no. Calm down. This is delicate business. Don't call attention to yourself." Simon detected, for the first time, something like mental instability in his new associate's countenance. The Brit's voice lowered to a whisper. "You've got to be rational, Mick. This truly is a once-in-a-lifetime situation. And now, I've got as much stake in this venture as you do. Let's not blow it here."

The younger man, having calmed down, though with a redder complexion, responded with new interest. "Okay." He looked around the restaurant. "Then show me how these pieces of your puzzle fit together."

"Righto. Now, as I was saying, Franz has included you, for whatever reason I don't know. . .that's between you and him, in this project. Perhaps he brought us together with this information because we happen to be in the same locale. Or, and this is what I was about to say, Franz probably knew I'd need some assistance to recover the goods, because the recovery of it will be a *delicate* maneuver."

Mick laughed nervously. Now he seemed as if he were on something. He lowered his voice. "Don't tell me we have to, uh, *steal* the stuff."

"Absolutely not. This resource was property of my great uncle, Plato Zupoff, and I am the only heir."

"Plato?" Mick chuckled, a little inebriated. Whether it was the wine, or the prospect of riches, or both, Simon did not know. "Still sounds like Greek to me. Haha."

"He was actually a Russian who came to the U.S. in 1927. He had converted all the fortune he had into these gold florins. He was, you know, liquidating, because he had decided to become an American and he wanted to start over. So he brought it in coin to the U.S. He came in on a transatlantic from Liverpool to New Orleans."

"With that much specie on him? That was risky."

"You're damn right it was risky, but even more so when he got on a riverboat headed for Memphis, because the boat got caught in a flood and shipwrecked just south of Baton Rouge."

"I've heard about that incident. Yes."

"The riverboat was named Leda Mae, and when it happened, the best that Plato could do for himself was to bury the goods somewhere near the wreck, because it seems some unsavory characters had figured out what he was carrying."

Mick's expression changed to dismay. "Ah, if he did bury it, somebody has probably recovered it by now. This might be a wild goose chase."

"Could be. But it's worth a try."

"Maybe. Whose land do you think it's on?"

"The owner is Theseus University."

"Ha!" Mick was lol. "You're talking about the old Theseus Plantation."

"That's right."

"Hmmm. Well, Simon, what have you figured out?"

"We need to take a close look at these documents, mine and yours."

"Yes. And you say there's another one."

"That's right."

"How 'bout? we finish up here, go to your hotel and get the other thing. Then we can go to a little warehouse office that I have nearby."

"Sounds good to me."

hddq://frenchquarter.loc

A few minutes later, the middle-aged entrepeneur and his foolish young accomplice were whipping through the narrow streets of the *Vieux Carre* in Mick's Jaguar. Night was coming, and the gas streetlamps were flickering, as Sunday night revelers roamed the wild streets looking for they knew-not-what, or comfort, or just plain liquor and sensual druggery, to numb their drudgery. *And the people bowed and prayed to the neon god they made.* Even as early as it was, some had taken to carousing in drunken nirvana with imagined chandeliers on their heads and mardi gras beads strung like glittering nooses round their necks. On many occasions our treasure-seeking duo might have joined them in the stuporing of America. But tonight, Simon and Mick had better things to do. They were on to something, or they, at least, *hoped* that they were. The Jag whipped right past them all, headed for Mick's garage on Esplanade.

Having arrived at the place, Mick provided a seat for Simon at the plunky little desk, and together, accompanied by a half-empty bottle of whisky, they went over their cryptic findings with a fine tooth comb.

Simon took off his coat and rolled up his sleeves. "You see these letters on your code—O,A,T,etc. They correspond to these words that Franz capitalized in the email that he sent to me: OAK, ANCIENT, and TREE, etc."

"But why all the mumbo-jumbo?"

"Mumbo-jumble?"

"Why did he go to this elaborate scheme, with coding to two people?"

"I don't know. Maybe he wanted to make sure that, if this information came into the wrong hands, it would most assuredly be gibberish."

"Well, your part there, with the oak tree, and going north and all— looks like you could have had a pretty good shot at finding the gold with just that information."

"Ah, but the numbers, you see. . ." Simon pointed at the numbers on Mick's little paper. "See the 1, the 17, the 22. That data is not found on my copy. It gives, I should think, the precise information for locating the stuff, without which I would have been wandering around in the dark aimlessly."

"In the dark? You don't think we can find this secret place at night, do you?"

"We might have to."

"Maybe, maybe not. Have you talked to somebody at Theseus?"

"As a matter of fact, I have. I talked to William Theseus himself, and he doesn't believe me, or at least, he doesn't seem to. When I explained the prospect to him, he became very skeptical."

"Ah, hah. He didn't take the bait, but you figured I would, huh?"

"Well, my friend, he didn't have the specific information that's been given to you."

"The numbers, you mean?"

"The numbers, and the lining up of the letters, which reinforces the validity of the two codes as they fit together."

"And the third piece in the puzzle, which you mentioned."

"Yes. I've got it right here." Simon pulled the paper from his briefcase, laid it on the old desk for Mick to inspect:

Where rabbits in their slumbery dens are bent,
the fox would chance upon a golden glint
which was the last of many laid so near yon oak
which raging river did provoke.
But young Plato's hopes, ne'er made complete,
would surely surface near yon muddy creek
where fox and hare run by and by
as Plato pens 'in Acadiana doth it lie.'
For the seeker whose Ariadnic thread's not torn
there's a strand of florins yet unshorn,
with whiffle and waffle and bullion yet
for the harey Theseus to by shovel get.

Yeah, 'tis two hundred thence near princely Louisiana shack,
an hundred more near Buncombe's pack, beyond Saluda track.

Mick was silent for a few minutes while he read it. When finally he looked up, Simon pointed out to him: "Now, notice that certain phrases in this poem, which was written by my great uncle Plato Zupoff, are also included in this other composition, which Franz sent to me."

Mick looked at the second paper, searching for clues:

From the **OAK** , the **ANCIENT TREE** you see, **GO** to the **HARE'S** nest, which is **NORTH** as far as 'q' determines it should be, each step being   positive 'q' beneath your knee, and not a negative as your genetic map would seem to be. In other words, add your 'q's and you shall see how far that it may be, beyond the tree.

Then, within the hole to which you're sent, *where rabbits in their* **DENS** *are bent,* you'll find the Ariadnic **THREAD** is rent, until you find it far away again, '*NEATH BUNCOMBE'S PACK, beyond Saluda track,* where 'p's are miles, as 'q's are steps, not east not east, but west, yes west..

IN both these destinations **GOLD FLORINS** you shall see, if you but follow these directions from the tree.

"Oh, okay. I see: 'where rabbits in their dens are bent.' It's italicized," said Mick."

"Correct. And the other one is 'neath Buncombe's pack, beyond Saluda track," added Simon.

"Hmm. Buncombe's pack. What the hell is that?"

"Pack Square, in Buncombe County, North Carolina, which is to say, Asheville."

Mick looked up at his newfound treasure-hunting mentor with what amounted to a crude form of admiration. "No kidding. How do you know that?"

"I've been there. In fact, my friend," Simon straightened up, reached into his pants' pocket. "I've already recovered some of this gold." Raising his hand from the pocket, he opened it for Mick to view the gold florin that lay, like a brilliant apparition, upon his flattened palm, with *fleur de lis* side up, which would be an impressive omen for a New Orleans resident.

"God almighty!" exclaimed Mick, wide-eyed. "You're legit!"

"Oh, absolutely, my boy. I wouldn't steer you wrong. Here. Have a look at it." As Mick inspected the golden coin, Simon set down the small slip with the genetic code:

OAT, GHN-1:17q22-q24, DTNBP-1:6p22.3, IGF-2:3q28.

When Simon discerned that the gold florin had provoked its optimum magnetism upon the young banker, he continued his lesson in deciphering coded treasure messages. "Now, let me show you how I acquired that piece."

"How many did you get?"

"Only twenty-two of them. But according to the poem," He pointed to the poem's last line. "there should be a hundred of them in the North Carolina location. I couldn't get them all because, well, there were circumstances. . . long story short, I couldn't get them all."

"Are you going back for them?"

"I plan to, eventually. But this location will prove twice as lucrative. See the second-to-last line: 'Yeah, two hundred thence near princely Louisiana shack.' That's what we're after."

"So, how did you find that location without these numbers?"

"That situation in North Carolina is quite different from this one. Plato settled there, had a large family. The florins that he had managed to carry with him, were, I think, the beginnings of his business in Asheville, a mercantile establishment, which later became quite prosperous. And, although I didn't have these numbers, I did have some advantages, being a relative and so forth. And I managed to find this much of what was left."

Mick gazed at the florin with longing, rubbing it gently between thumb and forefinger. "Do you have some more of these here? I'd like to see them."

"No. I carry that one for. . ."

"For good luck," quipped Mick. He was very relaxed with Simon now. He leaned back in the old swivel chair, his eyes still adoring the coin. "Where do you keep the others?"

"At home, in Grand Cayman."

"You know, these are probably worth a lot more than just their simple weight, or face value."

"'Tis true. And there are more, if we can only decipher this puzzle."

They were silent for a minute, thinking. Mick returned his attention to the three papers. This email one here—who wrote it?"

"That's a good question," observed Simon. "I was wondering about that myself. It appears to have been composed by our associate, Franz Hallfrich, based on some document that Plato had left behind."

"Right, because it says 'your genetic map.' That doesn't sound like something that Plato would have written."

"You're right about that. Plato died in '68. That's a little too early for anyone, even the best scientists, to have used these numbers in referring to the genome."

"As far as that goes, Simon, uh, who wrote the poem?"

"That poem I found in a trunk in my grandmother's attic in England. I'm sure it was penned by Plato himself. Here it is, if you'd like to have a look at it." Simon handed the yellowed envelope to Mick.

The young man studied it intensely, and suddenly: "Hahahaha!" lol. "It's in Russian!" Cool." Mick's gaze did not linger long on the letter, for his neurons were beginning to wrap around the possibilities that had been opened in this caper. As the synapses started firing, he had a thought which brought his consideration back to the three papers that lay on the desk before him. These three together were the key to unlock the earthen safe-deposit-box, wherever it might be on Theseus University grounds. Looking down at his little paper—**his** little paper, which had been sent to **him,** he suddenly saw it for what it was—**his** share in the prospect of 200 gold florins! "So Simon," says he. "What do these numbers mean?"

"Let's take a look at them. First, notice here the reference to 'the oak tree.' That's undoubtedly the oak tree upon which the Leda Mae grounded as the flood receded. And it, in fact, still stands. I've been to the site, and seen it."

"You've been to the site?"

"I've viewed the tree from a distance. We'll have to formulate a plan for obtaining access to the site. As I said before, when I approached Theseus about it, he dismissed me. I guess he thought I was a crackpot. Can't really blame him. It seems a rather preposterous tale. Anyhow, perhaps that's where you can be of service. You're local. We'll have to devise a plan."

"A *stealthy* plan, or something more, uh, legitimate?"

"I honestly don't know, Mick. But, you see, according to this, we'll go to the oak tree, then proceed north, 'as far as the q determines it should be.' That is surely a reference to your genetic code sheet there. Let's have a look at it."

"Here are the numbers," offered Mick: "1, 17, but they're *before* the 'q.' The others are after the 'q.': 22, 24. Do you think they're all together? Or two different sets of numbers?"

"Good question. We'll have to figure it both ways, and work by trial and error when we get there, unless we find another clue to clarify it. Let's add them all up, for starters."

"And they are all positive numbers, according to this: 'each step being positive q beneath your knee.'"

"Righto. And they're all steps, as a man would take, we assume. Let's add them."

"One, and seventeen, 22 and 24," Mick read. " which totals sixty-four. Sixty-four steps north from the oak tree."

"That's a quaint number," observed Simon, and he sang the little tune: *When I get older, losing my head, many years from now...*" Simon thought of his wife back home in Cayman, and had a pang of guilt, a stabbing of his empty heart.

"Then there's a, uh, a *rabbit hole!* Is that where the gold is? In a rabbit hole? How the hell did your buddy Franz come up with these directions?"

"Now, that I do not know. I can say only that, when I investigated the second location, near 'Buncombe's pack,' the effort paid off handsomely."

"This is going to be a wild hare if I ever saw one!" proclaimed Mick.

"You got any ideas about how to pull this off?"

"Actually, I do, Simon. I do have an idea," Mick mused.

Generations

15

Half a city away, Dr. William Theseus sat in the baggage claim area of the New Orleans airport. Bustling people were going every whichaway; the air was thick with rising humidity and dropping temperature. The season's first cool front had blown in, so the lazy southern autumn was now descending with barometric grayness of intensity, dropping camellia petals on shrubby quaking medians along ramps and boulevards where traffic whined, and rain glistened on the chrome and wheels of cars as they slid up to their huddled passengers beneath concrete caverns of thoroughfare, while inside the airport a random clamour of thickening crowds, clattering in confined fluorescent space, fermented the dank Dixie air with cacophonic jazz of just intense life and sweat, all of these folks having some place to go and some place they've just been, the wetness and coolness of early evening compelling so many of them to traverse beyond the terminal hubbub toward some streetlamp glow of evening promise, while others trudged inexorably, the tyranny of the moment burdening their bodies with raincoated solemnity and the dripping urgency of umbrellas. William watched them while he waited for Ophelia to arrive.

"I hope all will be well," William heard a nearby woman softly speak. This odd lady, not the one he was waiting for, stood apart from the gaggle of travelers who sought their bags at the conveyors as they rolled with irksome mechanical slowness. Alone amidst the crowd, garbed in black, with her words plopping like insignificant raindrops among the teeming mundanity of voices and bodies, she addressed the air itself, as if it were cousin to her:

"We must be patient. But I cannot choose but weep, to think that they should lay him . . ." Long jet-black hair, curling down upon her shoulders past blackness of turtleneck cashmere, framed her masqueradish goth of blood-red lips, pale white skin and whiter-still stark string of pearls. ". . . in the cold ground," she moaned.

William saw her, heard her plainly speaking, but could identify no companion. *Was she pleading? Was she praying? Was she through these words displaying grief, or pain, or some profundity?. . .She seemed so smitten to the core.*

"I'll tell my brother about this. Thank you for your good advice." Then her painted eyes flashed with recognition, and the darkened lady stepped toward the busy baggage carousel. With a deft snap of the wrist, she retrieved a stylish black leather bag, then extended the handle and turned to exit from the baggage area. "I'll get a taxi. Never mind! Tell them to ignore the signs. And tell the ladies all goodnight. Tell them all put out the light." Wielding her wheeled bag across the crowded floor, her black-clad bod went directly for the door. And as she turned her face away, William saw the part 'twas missing from this play: a receiver wrapped upon her ear, and mouthpiece so that someone might hear. "Good night, ladies. Goodnight," she said. William watched her wheel it through the door, and thought there must be something more.

But before he turned his head again, his friend Ophelia came up beside him. "Hello, William. Thank you for coming." She was standing erect, and smiling broadly.

William hugged his old friend.

"Where have you been all my life?" quipped William, smiling impishly.

"Chasing rainbows," came Ophelia's quick retort. It was an old joke among them.

He looked at her carefully. It had been twelve years ago that he last saw her, at a conference in Boston. Her anthropological sojourns had encompassed a wide range of interests, including a lively vigilance of developments in the world of biology. Those dark brown eyes, sparkling as ever, connected instantly with his. The wrinkles around them projected a quiet affirmation of the universal maturing that has taken place among boomers, who, like all generations, had managed to outgrow the impetuous believing that nothing could ever impede their youth and flexibility.

And she was, of course, a little plumper than he remembered her. The casually elegant maroon cotton dress, with colorful embroidery along a gathered neckline, suggested an allegiance to traditional feminine sensibilities. But above the stitched design, adorning Ophelia's swannish ruddy neck, a bold display of coral-hued and gray-streaked agates hung upon her strong scapulae. The round stones were set in polished silver, and seemed to declare a hand-wrought identification with raw, native American notions of beauty, while complementing her pale Anglo face with elemental simplicity. Though she was older, she looked fresh. He could see a blue vein in her temple. Yes, he remembered that. "Rainbows?" said he. " Have you found the pot of gold yet?" he joked.

She laughed. Then those welcoming eyes turned aside as she caught site of her bag approaching on the carousel. "As a matter of fact, William, yes." She retrieved the small carpetbag, which had an antiquish floral pattern in maroon that matched her dress.

"Can I get that for you?" he asked, not knowing how to interpret the affirmative answer to his question about the pot of gold.

"I've got another one coming. You can carry it, if you don't mind."

"Sure, Ophelia. It's great to see you."

"Likewise, Theseus." Grinning, she looked back up at him. She used to call him by his last name, back in the day, when they were at Bowling Green together, and she, being Elise's best friend, had counseled him on her ebullient ways. But Elise had married someone else. Three years ago, the news of her death in a plane crash had pierced his fading memory of her with yet another pang of sorrow, as if he had at last lost her, even though the losing had happened long before. After recovering precariously from the college love affair, William had later married Rosalind, his wife of seventeen years, before she died of ovarian cancer.

Ophelia Doss, during all those years, had been married only to her work as an anthropologist, pertaining mostly to Cherokee culture. Her diligence in the field had resulted, two years ago, in an appointment as chairperson of the Department of Anthropology, Bellel College in Asheville, North Carolina. But the flight from which she was now disembarking had come from Washington, DC, where she had convened with colleagues at the Smithsonian.

Ophelia's second bag came, a large brown leather one. William grabbed it, extended its handle and prepared to wheel it in the direction of the exit. "Hold on a second, Theseus. I need to get something out of there."

William wielded the luggage item onto a nearby seat. Ophelia unzipped an outer compartment. "I should have done this this morning," she said, while retrieving a pair of running shoes from the pocket. She then sat in the next seat, removed the low-heeled pumps she had been wearing, and promptly slid the gray and black running shoes over her nyloned feet. "I'm breaking these new shoes in." She held up the dressy pair that had just been taken off. Then, putting them in the same outer pocket where the running shoes had been, she continued. "But the breaking-in is just a little bit more than I want to endure right now. Ahhh, there now, I'm ready to go." She wiggled her feet to signal the relief in having donned comfortable shoes. "Where are we going? I hope it's a long way off. I'm ready to walk."

"Not far, Ophelia. My car is in the parking garage just outside."

"Well, good then. I'll find a place to walk, near wherever you accomodate me, William. I've yet to complete my five miles for today, especially after that cramped flight. The walking gets blood circulating, keeps the muscles responsive, and the brain constantly engaged. Keeps the neuropsin up, you know."

"Neuropsin?" quizzed William, raising his eyebrows.

" It's a protein that enhances memory and learning in the nervous system."

"Yes. I've heard of it. The Chinese are researching it." They were walking out of the automatic door now. "And so, you think exercise generates a higher level of neuropsin in the nervous system?"

"Oh, heavens, exercise generates higher levels of everything, William."

"Except fat."

"Right. But all the good stuff. Exercise elevates all the good stuff." They paused at the crosswalk.

"Sure," agreed William. They continued toward the parking garage, as cabbies stopped courteously.

"I'm just kidding. William." She waved her hand flippantly. "I don't know much about neuropsin. But I was just reading about it in *The Post.* It is a hormone that's only present in humans, not any other mammals. It may have something to do with why we're human, and chimpanzees are not."

"Hmmm, right." agreed William, amused. *Same Ophelia I remember. There's not another one like her in the world.* "I think you're talking about neurotrophic factor, a protein that..."

"Yes, that's it, Theseus. It helps the brain do its job better. The article was about exercise increasing the production of that protein. The hypotheses were based on a study at Harvard. But the point is, William, that, at our age, it's all about exercise, don't ya know."

"From the looks of it, Ophelia, you must be attending to that regimen pretty consistently."

"Well thanks, honey, for noticing. I've got a personal campaign going on the Bellel campus to get people away from the indolent lifestyle that seems to have captured us 21st century humans."

"Oh,that's good."

"If people these days (me included) had to contend with forces of nature like the Cherokee did a mere hundred years ago, we'd all be..." She paused as they crossed the street, with traffic backed up. The concrete ramp overhead amplified that ominous reverberating and guffawing of idling engines mingled with acrid smell of auto exhaust and diesel fumes, which universally occludes all passengers everywhere who have just disembarked from silver bird-machines, then are wandering, airstruck and ear-struck through generic concourses of psychology gray and madding-crowded terminals of blue and gold traverse and then recovering their belongings from buzzing conveyors, all the while dialing their cells. Then, egressing through whispering automatic doors to ground transportation that whisks them to New Orleans or New Delhi or Venezia or Valhalla or wherever it is that they have landed, they find themselves recovering from the displacement of place and time while talking to a relative or some old friend.

"That reminds me, Ophelia. I read your article in the Journal several months ago, the one about the Cherokee woman—"

"Nanye-hi, a Ghighua of the Cherokee," said Ophelia, pronouncing the name clearly and with volume suitable to overcome the din of traffic.

"Yes. Nancy Ward,"

"Funny, you remember the Anglicized form of her name. That's typical."

"Typical? Typical of what?"

"Oh, you know, William, the whole Anglo-Saxon hegemony thing where we think we have to classify all the world by our own English taxonomy and then put everything in boxes so we can tuck it away to gather dust and make us feel better about ourselves."

"Say what?"

She laughed goodnaturedly. "Oh, never mind. Don't get me started."

"No...hey, you're an academic, right? The world for us is all about categorizing and identifying, isn't it?" Suddenly, as they were walking through the relatively quiet parking garage, William noticed how loud he had been speaking. So he dropped it down a few decibels. "Our whole ivory tower of research and theory and ideas and numbers—it's all founded upon classifying and—well, I guess it is an Anglophile kind of thing."

"The Greeks, the Greeks started it. We can blame them, especially Plato." She laughed again. "But no, William, it's not all about naming and identifying. It's really about discovering the wonderful world that we've inherited from our forebears, and then using what we have learned to make the world a better place."

"Well that's well-said, my dear."

"Anyway, old pal, the point of my article was that Nanye-hi, or Nancy as you call her, was a person who changed the world. She found herself in a certain time and place in history. She knew where her people had come from, where they had been for untold generations. But she saw, clearly, the writing on the wall, of what changes would come as a result of the imposition of 'civilized' white culture on their primitive lifestyle. And as a result of her foresight, *and her determination to act*, she was able to develop skill in weaving, and in domesticating animals, and then teach these newly-acquired knowledge bases to the young Cherokee women, and their world has not been the same since."

"Wow. That's a mouthful." He was opening the car-trunk now."

"You're damned right. The breakneck pace of Western civilization was moving over the Cherokee nation like a freight train over a box turtle—"

"Oh come on, now. It wasn't *that* bad. And it's always been that way. Like the old song says: *Take your place on the great Mandela, as it moves through your brief moment of time.*"

Ophelia hoisted her bag into the trunk of William's old BMW. After he closed it, she looked at him carefully, and paused for a moment, with a sad smile on her face. "History is a trail of tears, William. Everything that happens demands a *dear* price from its participants." She was watching him. They were both realizing, in the silence of the garage, just how much water had passed beneath the bridges of time since their last visit. "Something's lost and something's gained in living every day."

William laughed. He was challenged and inspired by the exuberant presence of this old friend. "I've heard that somewhere. Where have I heard that?"

"Joni Mitchell."

"Ah, yes. *Both Sides Now*. It all comes back to me now."

"It's good to see you, William." With no inhibition, and no formality, she hugged him. And it was a good one; he was already enjoying her, although he could now discern the ruffled feathers beneath this (what he knew to be) strange bird's wings of fire. They got in the car.

"Where do you want to go?"

"Ha. This is your town, Theseus. I don't know the first thing about it. Don't you have something you need to do, or some place you need to be? Don't let me detain you. I'll just be a fly on the wall, appreciating your hospitality, or your chauffership, or whatever this turns out to be."

"Oh, nonsense. You're hungry, right? It's dinnertime."

"Well, yes, I could go for some dinner, now that you mention it."

"Okay. We'll go to Arnaud's."

"Sounds good to me, whatever it is."

"It won't be Cherokee food, though."

She just laughed, looking out the window at the mundane, dusky freeway torrent of traffic and rain. "Whatever."

"And I doubt it will be lo-cal."

"That's okay. I'll relax my standards for an hour or so. Maybe not *lo-cal*, but definitely *local*."

"Precisely, local color," agreed William.

They rode along the freeway for a few minutes, zipping toward downtown New Orleans. As they veered to right, she could see the skyline in the distance.

"So, Ophelia. Refresh my memory. Why did you come here?"

"I have something important to show you."

"What is it?"

"Just wait a little while. I've got to think about how to present it."

"Oh."

Her cellphone rang. "Hello. . ."

How to present it? He was wondering.

She was speaking into the phone. "Yes, child's games, like they play in Tanzania, or Somoa, or. . .that's okay. . .I think so. It sounds like a good project. . .I did, yes. . .I'm in New Orleans now, about to have dinner with William Theseus. . . well, okay then. . . Oh, Margaret. . .tell Reo to write up his proposal in the next week or so. . .good.. .bye."

"How to present it?" queried William. "As if, it's a dissertation or something."

Ophelia was confused for a moment. "Oh, it's not a dissertation. We're just a college. It's just a research paper on children's games in primitive cultures, if there is such a thing as a primitive culture still in the world."

"No, I mean the 'something you want to show me.' Hello, this is like, what you just said to Margaret, you're in New Orleans now, and you said you have something that you want me to see."

"Right, well, this is not just any old thing. I've got to preface it."

"Okay, go ahead."

She laughed. "I'm not ready yet. Wait until we get to Arny's."

"Arnaud's"

"Oh, excuse me, now we've gone from being Anglophiles to being Francophiles." She looked out the window, then pointed. "Ah, I see there, one of your famous cemeteries, with all the crypts above ground."

"You're dead right, Ophelia."

"Ha ha."

"That's not a Francophile thing, though, for you anthropologists. It's just a. . . a below-sea-level thing.

"I see."

"A very practical custom, actually. The early French discovered pretty quickly that if they didn't put their deceased above ground, they might see them floating around when the next spring flood or fall hurricane rolled into town."

"I see. Don't get me started on the multiplicity of ways that diverse cultures allow their dead to influence the here and now. I need to hear about you, William Theseus. What have *you* been up to? Running a university?"

"No. My cousin, Romola, takes that role. I stay close to the microbiology department."

"Okay. And, do you just manage all the microbiology professors, or, are you teaching—"

"I am teaching two undergrad microbiology classes. I prefer to leave the graduates up to the faculty. I *am* doing some research. It's my favorite pursuit, actually."

"And that is, what?"

"SCNT." He looked at her to read her face. *Speaking of child's games, guessing games.*

"SCNT?"

"Yes."

"And I'm supposed to know what that is? Uh, let me see. **Something Called Newts and Toads, SCNT.**"

"That's close, but you'll have to wait until we're having dinner to find out what it is—"

"Wise guy—"

"I've got to think about how to present it," he said, repeating her phrase as jest.

"Oh, I get it. Two can play this game. This is no problem. I'm an expert guesser, and very proficient with acronyms."

"Go on."

"South Carolina. . .uh, New Testament."

William just laughed.

"Somatic Cell Nuclear Transfer"

William's jaw dropped. "You're kidding. How'd you know?"

She was laughing too. "Cherokee secret. The raven told me."

Now it was William's turn to be confused. "The raven?"

"Yeah, the raven," said she, smugly, looking out the window. She was playing the game. "White man chases raven from the corn field because he doesn't want the bird to steal corn. But what he doesn't know is, farmer will lose *more* corn when deer and coons come and rob cornfield. If raven is allowed, however, his share, he will make such a ruckus when the other critters trespass, the farmer will hear the commotion and be able to chase the intruders away."

"So, who's got time to go chasing wild animals from the corn field? The farmer's probably too busy working on his truck to be bothered with checking up on a bunch of crows every time they decide to make noise."

"Wise guy. See, That's the trouble with you civilized types. The raven is the farmer's friend, and he's due his share. He earns it by serving as an alarm."

William's lol. "Sure," he agreed, conceding.

"The raven is man's friend, woman's friend, and he told me about Somatic Cell Nuclear Transfer."

William's still lol. "Nah, Ophelia."

And they were mutually amused by the ridiculous path of their banter. After a while, she said, "Actually, William, I've been watching you."

"Watching me?"

"Like the raven, I have an advantageous perspective."

"Oh, yes. I can see that now," he said, in mock seriousness.

"A bird's eye view of fox and the hare in the field."

"Do you?" He could play the game too.

" William, you're like the hare, in his den, bent in slumber."

 William paused. " Bent in slumber?" A furry memory was nudging his consciousness. But before he could think of the reference, it slipped into a hole somewhere in his head. *What is she talking about? Methinks these words are the evidence of the strange bird's mystical character. I remember this aspect of her now. It was why I chose Rosalind instead of her.*

" Bent in the slumber of your comfortable, ivory tower existence."

He had to think about that one for a second. "Dear Ophelia, isn't that a little like the pot calling the kettle black? . . . or, white?"

" 'Tis nothing, my dear William. It's not that I've been watching you, literally. But you should remember that your profile in the game is much higher than mine. So it's easier for me to monitor your impact on the world. I saw your letter to the Journal about the new cloning procedures, and how important you consider them to be, what with Dolly and all that. What I really mean is, I've been watching these developments in molecular biology, and your public response to them was duly noted, from my perspective."

"Well okay then. Thank you for looking out for me."

"I also saw, dear Theseus, your article about directed molecular evolution."

"Oh yeah?" William was surprised. "Aren't you right on top of the eight ball."

"Yes. Thanks to you, I now have a better understanding of how you guys shuffle mutations in test tubes to create new gene sequences." She reached into a small pocket on the front of her dress, just above the hip, and withdrew the cellphone again. Flipping it open, she looked at its face to check the time. "Oh dear, oh dear, I shall be too late."

"Too late for what?"

Suddenly Ophelia was caught up in some thought. She was gently biting her lower lip. "Ah, nothing. I was supposed to call somebody about half an hour ago."

"You'd better do it then. Don't you think?" He was exiting at St. Charles Avenue.

Whatever it was that distressed her, it suddenly passed. She looked at him with a quite curious smile. "Oh, it's nothing. It can wait." She set the phone on her lap, then put her hand back into the little pocket and withdrew something small from it. "Oh, by the way, William, here's what I came here to show you." Turning her hand over palm upward, a bright gold spot shone from it suddenly, surreally, like some power pill in a kid's video game, "Look what I found."

William was steering the BMW suavely, with one hand, curving down the ramp toward a stop light, but when he saw the coin glinting at him like an apparition, William instinctively touched the brakes, a little too zealously.

"Whoa, boy. Maybe I *should* have waited until we got to Arny's," she declared.

Migrations

16

"Where did you get that?" asked William.

"An old woman gave it to me."

"She *gave* it to you?" William was looking at the coin intently, until the light changed and he had to drive onto St. Charles Avenue.

"Uh, it's not actually mine. She placed it in my care."

William was trying to remember where he had *just* recently seen one exactly like it. Could this be a coincidence? *Whatever is happening here, I know I have seen two incidents of the same coin.*. Then he remembered—the British guy who had come to his office with the wild story about a rabbit hole. William's mind was racing, trying to make sense of it, as the Beemer settled into a noiseless idle. The light turned green.

"Watch where you're going, William. You almost rearended that car, " Ophelia warned.

He was gazing at the florin.

"You can go now, William."

"Who was this old woman that gave it to you?" He eased onto St. Charles Avenue.

" She entrusted it to me. She's the grandmother of a student of mine."

"And there are how many of these coins?"

"Thirty-eight."

"Where?"

"In a safe-deposit box in Asheville."

William drove on for a few minutes, speechless. On the grassy median to their left, the old trolley rumbled by headed the opposite way. Rain was falling. "Can you tell me what this woman's name was?"

"Zelda Fitzsimmons."

"Zelda," mused William. They turned onto Canal Street, went a few blocks, turned into the *Vieux Carre,* all the while riding silently, as William was perplexed at these developments. Ophelia silently took in the sights as dusk turned to night, and gaslamps in the Quarter flickered bright. He parked the old BMW. But before they got out, William turned to his old friend and said, "And who the hell is Zelda?"

Ophelia looked at him steadily, greatly amused at the labyrinth of puzzlement she was weaving in his head. She did have a raven-like intensity about her. Reflected lamplights flickered in her eyes. Ophelia answered slowly, " Zelda Fitzsimmons is the grandmother of my anthropology student, Alice Pack. Alice is the daughter of Lamar and Lucy Pack. Alice' father, Lamar, was a descendent of Skipping Canoe."

"A descendent of what?"

"Skipping Canoe, a militant of the Cherokee back in Andrew Jackson's time."

William leaned back in the leather seat and released a long sigh. "Our restaurant is just up the street here. We'll walk to it." He got out of the car, Ophelia following suit. He locked it with the remote, and they unfurled umbrellas. They strolled along the hundreds-years-old *Rue Royale,* a street first trod by French traders, later sold to President Jefferson as part of the city of New Orleans in the Louisiana Purchase, and later defended by Andy Jackson against the British in the battle of New Orleans, 1812. The avenue was dark, but sedately illumined with flickering gaslamps. A story above, intermittent railings of ornate ironwork portrayed the filigreed formality of a former age, backlit by the subtly lit hues of private residences. A sparse wandering of people out for the evening brought passersby, speaking, laughing, stepping high, or cruising low, to and fro, just for show. On a corner beneath an overhang, a nurse was selling poppies from a tray. Our pair stepped across a dirty curb. A young man's voice passed them in the evenening's turbidity: "N'Awlins has that at the Seventeenth Street canal..." They walked on slowly.

"Ophelia, how many of those gold pieces did you say you have?"

"Thirty-eight. They constitute Zelda Fitzsimmons' endowment to Bellel College. She turned them over to me during an interview just before she died."

"Interview? About what?"

"About her life, and her interest in the Cherokee heritage, which she felt was threatened."

William raised his eyebrows. "Yeah, to put it mildly. How did you meet her?"

"Her granddaughter, Alice Pack, a student of mine, brought me to Zelda's home, which is very near the Cherokee reservation in North Carolina. Alice and I conducted a very long interview with her. It lasted all day, and then she cooked dinner for us."

They were quiet for a few moments, still ambling. "Woohoooo!" came a yelp from a reveler approaching from the Bourbon Street direction.

" So, was, uh, Zelda a Cherokee?"

"No, but her daughter Lucy married Lamar Pack, who was a descendent of Skipping Canoe."

Arriving at Arnaud's, they stepped inside, folded the umbrellas. A tuxedoed *maitre 'de* with large, dark eyes and slick, black hair greeted them. "Good evening, Dr. Theseus. Your table is ready."

"Thank you, Antoine. And this is Ms. Doss, who will be dining with me."

The man gave a curt bow, then turned on his heel and lead them to a table by a window. The place was dark and candlelit, and smelled of seafood and fresh bread. A low, comfortable presence of diners populated the room. Snippets of mild conversation could be heard as they walked through the tables. Soft strains of music wafted through the ambiance—Albinoni's *Adagio*. After they were seated, William continued his inquiry. "Okay, Zelda's son-in-law was a descendent of Jumping Canoe."

"Skipping Canoe." Ophelia laughed and looked at him with strange appreciation. The table's candle was reflecting in her hazel eyes.

"Yes."

"Zelda told me that, over the years, she had become quite close to Lamar. And through his influence, she developed a fervent empathy for the Cherokee."

"Hence the endowment of gold, entrusted to the sensitive anthropology professor," quipped William.

"Well, yes, but that came at the very end."

"Where did Zelda get the gold?"

"I'm getting to that." Ophelia knew how to maximize the effect of her intricate tales and drawn-out yarns as she spun them into a colleague's ear.

William rolled his eyes. "I can tell you this, Ms. Doss," in a mildly jocular tone, "you anthropologists better not get too far out in your theories about the differences between sexes being culturally acquired, because there are definitely some intrinsic differences between the way men think and the way women think."

"Whoa, lone ranger. Where did that come from?" She was actually thrilling to his reaction. The mischievous smile crept across her lips, exacerbated with a crow's feet of wrinkled merriment around her eyes. This is what she lived for—provoking reactions.

"Women," he teased. "and their circuitous logic."

"I'll get around to it. Be patient." She held him by a thread.

"Right, Dr. Doss. Excuse the intrusion upon your windup."

"Windup?"

"Like a pitcher winding up, in baseball, before he throws the pitch to the batter."

"What's that got to do with the plight of the Cherokee, William?" She was an ace up curiosity's sleeve.

"Nothing." He laughed in feigned frustration. He knew full well his predicament. He was at her mercy, and destined to pay the tab too.

A waiter, looking like a twenty-year-younger version of Antoine, visited their table and initiated the evening's fare. The interruption gave this odd couple a moment to adjust to the two complementary world-views presently engaged across candlelight and glinting silverware.

"As I was saying," she lingered.

He waited, demonstrating how patient he could be. This really was kind of fun.

"You see, William, the Cherokee people, and really *all* native Americans, for that matter, were blindsided by the onslaught of European culture."

Tell me something I don't already know.

"The thing is, they had absolutely *no idea* of the immensity of it—the sheer, prolonged relentless profusion of whites, from the time of those first gentle encounters back in the seventeenth century, all the way through the Dawes Commission effects of the 1890s. Their accommodating attempts at reconciliation with the Anglo-Saxon hordes became more and more—"

"Futile," said he.

"That's right," as she climbed on the soap box. "They had no concept of private property, no sense of deeds and property lines and plats at the courthouse, no comprehension of legal procedures, which had taken millennia to evolve in Europe. In fact, one of the principal conclusions of the Dawes Commission was that native peoples could never be assimilated to American life until they learned to accept and make use of property development according to the laws of 'civilized' society. Their existence from time immemorial had evolved according to the awareness that all Nature was an inheritance of the tribe, collectively."

Jeeves brought the wine, and poured it for them. William was thankful for Ophelia's opportunity to catch her breath.

"It's natural selection, as applied to whole cultures," observed William, curtly.

"I suppose it is," she agreed, somewhat reluctantly. She remembered him this way, always cutting to the chase with his darty little, oversimplified comments. "That doesn't excuse it, though."

"No, it doesn't. But it's the history of the human race. When you get right down to it, it's the history of life on this planet. And yes, Ophelia, it is sad—all that sensitivity and awareness of the natural world—it is muted by the roar of mechanized, legalized—"

"Traumatized," she inserted.

"Well, yes, I am sure the Cherokee were traumatized by it all."

"We ourselves are traumatized by it, William. As a civilization, we are one big, walking schizophrenic basket case."

William chuckled. "Ah, it's not that bad. Some of us are not incapacitated with Kafkaesque alienation."

"We have lost touch with the Earth itself," she insisted. "There is no way we can appreciate its magnificence, and its *exquisite, delicate* fragility, with the roar of bulldozers and diesel engines filling our ears, drowning out our awareness of the *Gaia*."

"Ophelia?"

"What?"

"You flew here today on a jet, didn't you?"

She sat back in the chair, sighing, having talked herself into a tizzy. Resignedly, she said, "Yes, I did William. And that's the dilemma I'm telling you about. That's the alienation—"

"The angst, yes," he added, sweetly, "but it's not a problem for *me*. I have no issue with the way things have turned out."

"You're part of the problem, William."

He chuckled. "And you're not? Who got on the airplane in Washington today and exited here in New Orleans? Who benefited from the combustion of those thousand-odd gallons of jet fuel, with their accompanying hydrocarbon emissions into the stratosphere? It wasn't me, dear friend, except—" He paused thoughtfully. "Except insofar as I now have the exquisite pleasure of your company here tonight."

She gazed at him with a sad smile. "I just don't know how the world can go on this way."

"Well, you've actually got a very good point, Ophelia. I don't really mean to make light of it. But I think the pendulum does swing the other way though. It's like Hegel's dialectic, the thesis being primitive life as the native tribes lived it, and the antithesis being the march of destructive, *and also constructive...*" He raised his finger to emphasize. "Civilization. The **synthesis** of those opposing forces is, perhaps, our gradual adoption of the revisionist, environmentalist sensitivity with its proactive adjustments that lead to healing and correction."

"But we'll never again inhabit the Earth in the way the indigenous peoples did," she said, pensively.

"No, Virginia, we will not. It is gone forever." He paused. She was not responding. Reevaluating this last conclusion as a little too blunt, he added, "Although we do have, uh, national parks and city parks and such places. . ."

The sad smile reappeared, and he thought a tear glistened her eye. "I know that's not really a consolation, Ophelia. It is sad what the world has come to. But we have to find the silver lining somewhere. Otherwise. . ."

Jeeves came and they ordered dinner.

Then quietly, he continued, "Otherwise, what do we have. Is all lost? I think not. We've got to view the world like we see your glass there."

She looked at the crystal goblet for a moment. "Half-full?"

"Yes, my dear. That's it exactly." He offered her a reassuring smile.

"But I'm drinking it. It will soon be empty," she observed, and sipped. "And I suppose you have a bottomless wine bottle."

"The earth itself is a bottomless vintage," he proclaimed, flippantly.

"I doubt it."

"I'll refill it when you need it," said he, softly. They were quiet for a minute; she was caught up in thought. "Here," said William, raising his glass. I propose a toast. *La chaim!*" They clinked the glasses and sipped white wine.

Jeeves brought salads.

After a few minutes of raw food and Roquefort, he dropped another challenge. "Are you going to tell me now where Zelda got the gold?"

"You fox," she exclaimed, newly amused at his finesse in the game.

"You said, when we were riding here," He had to pause, and get his recollections straight. "I was the hare, *bent in slumber*."

She shrugged, having a good time. "You have some fox attributes."

"Don't we all?"

"Yes, Theseus. I think the indigenous peoples are the hare, and the civilized world is the fox."

"I suppose that's true, in an oversimplified way."

"It was in a rabbit hole."

"What?" William was startled by the obtuse statement.

"In a rabbit hole," she repeated, as if assuming that he understood her elliptical references.

"*What* was in a rabbit hole?" He was continually entertained by her artfully eccentric pronouncements. *She wouldn't make much of a wife, but she's a very interesting date.*

"The gold florins," she said quietly. "Zelda found them in a rabbit hole."

"You're kidding."

"Well, it wasn't actually a rabbit hole. It was a cave, but rabbits were living in it."

William paused, with a tomato wedge halfway to his mouth. "And did she just *happen to find* this cave?"

"Her father had left it for her. He was on his deathbed when he described its location to her."

"And what location was that?"

"He had a large tract of land, over a thousand acres, in Haywood County, North Carolina. It bordered the Qualla lands. And he had hidden the gold there in the cave. It was his cave, on his property. It was a well-chosen place. Only an informed family member, or a rabbit, could have found its entrance.

"Hmm, interesting. I guess that's what people did before they got in the habit of hiding their booty in banks," observed William. "I wonder how long he had it hidden there."

"Zelda recovered it in 1968 after her father died. She said that he had found the cave in 1929 and stashed the horde then."

"Oh, it's kind of funny, how different customs were before modernity changed everything. Hiding gold in a hole in the ground. Who would do such a thing nowadays?"

"You might be surprised. There are plenty of people out there who don't trust the financial system as fully as you do, William."

"Sure. It could happen."

"And after 1929, don't you know there were a lot of people probably stashing gold somewhere," she speculated. "Maybe he hid the gold in November, after the stock market crashed."

"Could be. I don't think there was much gold in circulation then. The Federal Reserve had rounded most of it up. Most folks had been converted to banking, by that time, hadn't they? There wasn't so much, any more, the 'hiding it in the mattress' strategy for retaining wealth."

"Or in caves," she agreed.

"But this fellow, Zelda's father, *did* choose a cave, or rabbit hole as you call it, instead of a bank, for whatever reason."

Several tables away, a group of four men were having dessert, drinking *aperitifs*, but arguing, apparently about some business strategy. They had gradually become quite loud in their disagreements. William glared at them and addressed them loudly across the room with a simple "Excuse me." His bold vocal intervention produced an immediate acquiescence. "So sorry," came the repentant response, in a British accent, and their disturbance was thereafter subdued.

His attention having been diverted, it took William a moment to regain his inquisitorial acumen. "Who was he, anyway? Zelda's father—what was his name?"

"Plato Zupoff."

A perplexed expression swept across William's face, as if he couldn't remember something. Ophelia was finishing her salad. She took a sip of wine. "Excuse me," he said, and extracted a cell phone from his shirt pocket. He punched a few buttons on the phone and waited. "Ophelia, may I see your gold coin again please?"

She set the treasured object on the white tablecloth beside the glass vase, which contained a pair of red roses. The florin was absolutely a beautiful object. He picked it up, and began rolling its worn edges between his fingers as he studied it, with his elbow resting on the table.

"Hello, Robby.". . ."How are you?". . ."Yes, good. I know Rosa.". . . "Right, uh, molecular anthropology.". . ."It's similar to that, yes—analyzing genetic sequences to". . ." That's correct, using variations among different people groups to reconstruct the history of human colonization."

William removed his elbow from the table as Jeeves arrived with his broiled entrée of mahi-mahi, while Ophelia received her bowl of crawfish bisque with rice. She picked up the silver spoon and gingerly tasted it, lightly blowing the delicacy to cool it before touching her lips with the spoon. *Yes! Creole food, nothing else like it.*

"The Navajo, so they say. . .maybe, oh, 10,000 years ago," said William, still on the phone.

"Or the Incas, in Peru," Ophelia interjected.

William lowered the phone a little and smiled at her perceptive comment. "But listen, Robby. *I* have a few questions for *you* this time." . . . "Who was that fellow we talked to in my office last week?". . ."Uh-huh, and what did he say about those coins?". . ."Plato, uh," He looked at Ophelia. "What was Zelda's father's name?"

"Zupoff. It's a Russian name," she replied.

"Right," said William, into the phone. His eyes widened in sudden surprise. "She was your *what*?"

"My great aunt. Zelda was the sister of my grandma Cornelia," answered Robby. He was sitting in the *BookCell* having a decaf latte with Rosa. "And do you remember? Simon said there were two stashes of gold, one in North Carolina, and the other one here, at the Theseus plantation. And doc, I didn't tell you this, because I was checking out some of the facts. But I think there may be something to Simon's cockamaymy tale, because I've seen one of those coins, and it sure looks authentic to me."

William had squeezed some lemon juice on his mahi-mahi. He took the first delicious bite of it. "So have I," he said into the phone. "At least, I think I have."

Primes

17

"Mr. Watson, come here. I want to see you." said Mr. Bell into his new device.

The phone rang. Sam pointed the remote at his TV and clicked the mute button. In the old movie he was watching, Mr. Watson (Henry Fonda) was making history as he scurried back to the lab where Mr. Bell (Lawrence Olivier) had just spoken that first telephone message ever. So Mr. Watson's elated response to Mr. Bell's electronic command was rendered silent on the TV screen. Sam put the remote down and picked up the phone. "Hello," answered Sam Cricket, who was resident caretaker of the Theseus University biological research station on River Road.

"Hello, Sam."

"Hello, Dr. Theseus."

"How's everything out on the placid end of the Theseus domains?"

"Humming right along. Nothing to report, sir."

"Good. Be sure and keep an eye on the power supply out there. We're having some gusty winds here in the city. Is it windy out there?"

"Yes."

"You know where the emergency generators are."

"I do. I'll make sure they're on if we have an outage."

"If there are any interruptions in the electrical power, please check the nitrogen freezers. They need to be maintained at a temperature lower than minus 196 degrees Celsius."

"Got it."

"You should check that readout now, just to make sure it's okay."

"I'll do it."

"And if there are any power blackouts, keep a close eye on them for me."

"Will do."

"I'm not really expecting an incident, but there have been a few outages here in the city due to limbs on power lines."

"I'll go out now and take a look at the generators and the freezers. Anything else?"

"You can take a look at the little calf that was born yesterday."

"Sure."

"Okay, Sam. Thanks."

"Bye."

Sam put the phone down and donned his shoes. He walked through the kitchen of the little bungalow where many a grad student caretaker before him had lived. Closing the squeaky back door, he stepped out into the blustery night, and what a windy night it indeed was.

Fifty or so meters away, a pair of gnarly, youthful vagabonds had been stealthily treading the thick, wet grass of the open field. Quickly and quietly came the command of one to the other: "Get down!" The pair proned themselves immediately in order to avoid discovery.

At the bungalow, Sam decided to return to the kitchen for his raincoat before venturing any further. And so the door squeak was heard twice, which was no small benefit to the unkown intruders.

"Keep your head down, idiot!" Vinnie warned Tony, in a whisper.

Pulling the raincoat hood over his head, Sam made his way across the shelled parking area to the labs. First he entered the utility room where the generators were, and confirmed that the switches were in their proper position for immediate startup in the event of any power failure. This he did. No problem there.

The vagabonds saw a light go on in the building closest to them. Vinnie looked at his watch, and pressed a button on it. The light was on for two minutes, then went off.

Sam walked out of the utility building, and walked the eighty-odd meters to Lab #1 where the nitrogen freezers were. He entered the building. The vagabonds saw a light go on, on the opposite end of the complex.

"Yep. Hunky-dory," affirmed Sam to himself, as he viewed the digital readout: -196° C. Vinnie saw the light in Lab #1 go out. It had been on for fifty-four seconds.

When Sam got back to the TV, popcorn in hand, Mr. Bell was speaking to a panel of distinguished listeners about the power of electrical impulses to communicate sound.

Out in the blustery night, The elder vagabond waited a full three minutes after the last squeaky closing of the old kitchen door. "Okay, Mudzilla, follow me, and stay down," he commanded in a hoarse whisper.

"We don't need to stay down, Vinnie! We'll be soaked by the time we get there."

"Why do think we wore these zoot suits, idiot?"

"Shit."

"It's worth the 300 just to take this job slow and easy." Vinnie reached over to his sidekick's face and twisted his nose. "Shut up, ya little prick, and do as you're told, or you'll screw this thing up."

"The guy's not watching us now."

"We don't know what he's doing. He may be checking us out right now through the window."

"Aw, like hell he is."

"Mick said these people are pretty smart. We're not taking any chances. Just stay behind me, and do exactly as I do until we get to the big tree."

And so the duo crept fox-like through the night. *Br'er fox, he lay low.* When they reached the old oak, Vinnie slithered around its base to the other side. He stood up. "Now you see, dork, this tree is between us and the complex. We're good to go now. We can even use the flashlights. See." Suddenly a bright beam extended, like a light sabre, from Vinnie's hand to the ground. Tony could see raindrops passing through its laser-like path. "But we still have to be careful. Do exactly as I do until I say different."

Satisfied that at last he had the situation under control, the elder vagabond pulled a flat laminated paper from inside his shirt. He transferred the flashlight to a pocket in his raincoat, then produced from his shirt pocket another flashlight, smaller than the other. He used it to look at his waterproof instruction sheet. "This says we are to take sixty-four steps due north." Reaching down to his belt, he pulled up a small compass which was strung to his belt, and set it on the laminated paper. The small flashlight on the instrument revealed a need for him to pivot a quarter-turn to his right. "There now, I'm facing due north. And this is good—just like Mick said. Going straight in that direction, we'll have the big tree between us and the complex the whole way."

"That's pretty lucky," agreed Tony.

"Yeah. I'll walk in front. You carry this." Deftly, he unbuckled a leather strap on his right leg, then handed Tony a small collapsible shovel, military-issue. Tony accepted the tool, which would most likely be an essential part of their covert operation. He pointed the small flashlight to the glistening grass and began the forward trek. "Stay right behind me. One, two, three. . ."

Sixty-four steps later, he sat on the ground. Tony followed suit. Vinnie looked back at the lab complex. It appeared to be just as it was when they had passed it, quiet and normal. "This is it." He looked around. His urban eyes, unaccustomed to the botanical environs, squinted into the darkness, trying to interpret its contents.

"WOo-hoo-oOh," cooed the low-slowed owl, very near.

"Hhhu!" gasped Tony.

"Shhhh! It's just a frickin' owl," Vinnie whispered.

As luck would have it, the spot in which the duo now found themselves was a low area, so that it seemed they could move about with some freedom without being seen from the complex. Vinnie carefully directed the little flashlight around in a low circumference, searching for any trace of whatever it was he was supposed to be looking for. About twenty feet away was a still, small bayou.

Then he saw them.

Two red eyes were looking back at him through the misty dark.

About ten feet away. He held the light on it steadily. It did not move. "What the hell?" whispered Tony.

"Shh. We're looking for a rabbit hole, right?"

"Yeah."

"We found the rabbit."

Slowly, Vinnie began to steal toward the hare. *Br'er fox, he lay low.* But as soon as he started in that direction, the red eyes vanished. *Br'er rabbit, he lay lower.* "WOo-hoo-oOh," cooed the low-slowed owl, very near.

When Vinnie reached the spot where he thought he saw, he did see, *sho'nuff*, a hole in the ground. It was a muddley little hole, with little rabbit pawprints going into it. *Br'er rabbit, he lay low.* "Tony, bring that shovel over here." The junior vagabond crawled, shovel in hand, over to the secret spot.

"Start digging right here."

"Where?"

"Right here, where the *hole* is, ya hare-brain."

Tony followed his mentor's command. He continued the task for twenty minutes, then removed the rubber rainsuit, and resumed, thirty minutes, forty minutes. Vinnie kept the little light on the task. Neither one said a word. It was kind of fun, really. Tony was covered with mud. City boy had never done anything like this before. *Br'er rabbit, he lay low.* After an hour and twenty minutes of digging, the shovel struck something solid. They were four away, and three feet down from where they had started.

"There! Did you hear that?" Vinnie asked. Tony struck it again. It sounded metallic. The elder vagabond pulled out his switchblade and used it as a digging tool to remove the mud from a small object. After a few minutes, Vinnie knew intuitively it was a man-made object. He picked it up and wiped the mud away. It was a magnifying glass. He held it up, filled with wonder, and wiped the lens as clean as he could get it. "Frickin' A!" exclaimed his young accomplice.

"Keep going!" came the elder's reply. The clackety thump they had heard was from some treasurous thing bigger than a looking glass. There was something beneath it, something more substantial, of which it was merely the harbinger.

Clackety-thump. Clackety-thump. Every time the shovel struck! Clackety-thump. And then there were muddy strips. Vinnie grabbed them with his hands, They fell apart like paper in his fingertips. Strips of something, shreds, muddy shreds, strips, shreds, strips and shreds, strips and shreds, muddy strips and shreds, and then:

The golden glint! Beneath the flashlight's yellow beam, a golden hint! The golden glint! Florins from the hart's house source. They're heaven-sent!

Vinnie attacked the stash with a ferocious rip—gleaming golden in his grip! So slick and smooth and clean and bright—gleaming precious in his sight. More precious, more gleaming than he ever saw! Far better than Mardi Graw.

They had nothing to put the booty in.

hddq://theseusguesthall.loc

At 11:07, while he was escorting Ophelia to her room in the University guest accommodations, William received an urgent phone call. It went like this: "Hello."

"Dr. Theseus!"

"Yes."

"This is Sam, at the research station."

"Yes, Sam. What's up?"

"I just discovered a couple of prowlers out here. There were two men, or boys, running through the pasture lot."

"Where are they now?"

"They're gone. They ran away as soon as I confronted them."

"Did you, uh, get a look at them?"

"No. They were walking through the grass, out there near the old oak. I wasn't sure about what I was seeing at first. But I could hear their feet slogging through the wet grass. When I could see that there were two people, I called out to them. As soon as I did, they started running like hell. I could barely hear their voices; they sounded like a couple of young guys."

"When did this happen?"

"Just two or three minutes ago. Do you want me to call the sheriff, or anybody?"

"Could you see anything on them, like things they may have stolen?"

"No. They were in slick, black rainsuits. That's all I could see—the security lights outside kind of flashing on their wet rain gear. And they were hooded. I never got a look at their faces."

"Sam, you, uh, you don't need to call the sheriff just yet. But go outside and check the labs. They were all locked, right?"

Sam donned his raincoat. "Absolutely, doc. They were locked. But I'm going to check them now." He was hurrying through the parking lot, with the phone to his ear, beneath the hood of his raincoat. "I'm at the utility. It's locked, just the way I left it a couple of hours ago when I checked the generators."

"Good, Sam. You're doing fine. No need to worry. Look at the little window in the utility building. Is it intact?"

Sam walked over to the window, pressed the glass with his hand. "It's okay. I'll check the labs now."

William was seated in a wing chair in the lobby of Bienville Hall, where guests of Theseus University would stay while visiting. Next to him was an identical wing chair, in which Ophelia had made herself comfortable inspecting a large book, *The Lower Mississippi Valley*, which she had discovered on the nearby marble-topped coffee table. She had chosen it from a small collection of similar volumes displayed beside a white china bowl with a bouquet of crimson camellias.

William held the cellphone patiently, listening for Sam's reports on the other end. "Lab #3 appears to be okay."

"Look at the windows."

Sam walked around the building, inspecting the exterior with a flashlight. "Looks okay."

"How about the office? and your place?" asked William.

Having come full circle around the lab building, Sam peered at the the two small buildings on the other side of the parking area. "It's okay."

"Good, Sam. Keep going around the labs."

In short order, the grad student was able to confirm that the other two labs and the office were undisturbed. "I think everything is okay."

"Walk to the back side of the office," the doc instructed.

"Nothing amiss here," Sam confirmed.

William found himself studying Ophelia's pale face, while she was intent upon text and pictures pertaining to *The Lower Mississippi Valley*. He couldn't decide if her strawberry blonde had been enhanced with color, or not. The maroon dress, long and cottony, natural, topped with Indian necklace, presented a curious, though quite fetching, complement to the running shoes she had donned upon arriving at the airport six hours ago.

"Now, Sam. We've established, I think, that there has been no break-in. Am I right?"

"As far as I can see, there has been nothing like that, nothing out of the ordinary, except my seeing these two guys running."

"Think about where you first saw them, and where you last saw them."

"All right. When I noticed them, they were near the old oak tree, about twenty or so yards this side of it."

"Walk to that spot. Go slow. Keep the flashlight trained in front of you."

Sam followed the professor's instructions precisely. As he walked slowly into the dark field, he was remembering. "There was an unusual noise. When I startled them, and they began running, there was a shuffling noise that accompanied their running."

"Like the sound of their raincoats flapping in the wind, and rain?"

"Sure, but there was another noise, a sort of, uh, like gravel? or. . ."

"Or footsteps squishing in mud?"

"Nah, this is all thick grass out here. Maybe it was like, uh, change? Pocket change, jumping up and down in a person's pockets as they're running."

"Hmm."

"I'm at the spot, I think, where I first caught sight of them."

"Look around you. What do you see?" asked William. A couple of faculty members were passing by as he sat in the spacious lobby. They hesitated, as if to greet him. William smiled broadly at them and waved, making it obvious that he was on the phone.

"Nothing special. . .Oh, here's their trail. I can see where they were slogging through the grass. The grass is about due for a cutting."

"Look in both directions, Sam, in the direction from which you think they were moving, then in the other direction, the one they were headed in as they ran away."

Sam could see nothing but wet green grass that had been lightly trampled, and fine raindrops passing through the strong light beam of his flashlight. Intuitively, he turned southward, in the direction of the intruders' hasty retreat, and walked slowly along the trampled grass. He remembered now that their accelerated pace, after he had shouted to them, had seemed quite clumsy, as if they had been trying to move quickly but were unable to do so. Meticulously, he studied every foot of the beaten path upon which the duo had hastened to evade capture. Sam followed the trail carefully, intent upon his mission, for several minutes.

William spoke to his guest. "How are you doing? I bet you're tired."

"I'm good, Theseus. Don't mind me."

"I don't want to deter you from getting some rest, Ophelia."

"I'll go up in a few minutes. This is interesting."

"You're welcome to take the book upstairs with you."

"Thank you. I like hanging out here in the lobby. This is a pretty impressive place you've got here. It's quite a bit swankier than our quarters at Bellel."

William laughed. "What you see is the result of many generous endowments, over almost a hundred years time. It doesn't happen overnight, you know."

"Hmmm." She looked up from the book, at him, with a kooky little smile. That reminds me. We've just gotten a sizable endowment."

"Is that right?"queried William.

"Yes, the one I was telling you about, from Zelda Fitzsimmons."

"Oh, of course." Although it seemed somehow insignificant to William—a stash of gold from a rabbit hole.

"Here's something." exclaimed Sam.

"What is it?" There was a long pause on the other end. William heard a muffled little sound from Sam's mouth. "What, Sam?"

"Incredible! It's, uh, gold—three gold coins."

"Gold?" Dr. Theseus sat upright. Dr. Doss' fascination with *The Lower Mississippi Valley* was suddenly diverted—to the excitement now spreading across his face.

"They look very old, worn around the edges."

"Coins?"

"That's right. Three old, gold coins."

"Can you see the features? What's minted on the face?"

"They're, uh, quite worn, uh, *fleur de lis*. It's a *fleur de lis* motif. Gosh, maybe they're Mardi Gras doubloons."

"I don't think so, Sam. Keep looking. I'm coming out there." William stood up. He turned to Ophelia. "Come on, Ophelia. Let's go. There might be something to this after all."

She didn't have to be convinced. "I never did get my walk in today."

"Bring your raincoat."

"I've got it right here."

"You're coming out here? asked Sam.

"I'll be there in an hour. Keep up the search. Call me if anything unusual happens."

"This is pretty unusual."

"If anything dangerous happens. I mean, don't put yourself in any danger. If you see those prowlers again, don't put yourself at risk."

"They're probably miles away by now."

"Right. I'll see you in a little bit."

"So you don't want me to call the cops?"

"I'll decide that when I get there."

Penetrations

18

Deep in the womb of Salli Cretani something unique was about to happen. Intimate collaboration with her husband was culminating in a great event of Creative proportions. All around them, the excitement was building up. They could just feel it coming.

God had set a great, creative urge deep within them, which would produce a unique work that only they could perform. On this appointed night, the holy place had been prepared, and was ready to receive visitation from the Chosen One.

Salli's husband, Kemal, anticipated the upcoming event with great joy.

For deep within his loins God was orchestrating a great host of dedicated servants to assist in the initiation of their labor of love. The servants had been wandering aimlessly for days and days, but God had appointed a prophet to lead them to the Promised Land. On this special night, the prophet ascended the holy mountain as God's servants watched with great expectation of what was about to take place. When he had found a suitable place on the mountain, the prophet turned around and lifted his staff.

He had been summoned to address those noble ones who had assembled here—a great and mighty company who had made vast deferences and great sacrifices in order to contribute to the sacred mission. As the prophet surveyed the mighty throng of volunteers, teeming to be free, his heart was bursting with inspiration. After a silent prayer to the Great God, he opened his mouth to speak to them, and then all became silent, as they prepared themselves for what lay ahead, and for the words he might speak to them. And this is what he said:

"Four score and seven seconds from now, we will embark upon a great expedition into the long-awaited Promised Land, known to us as Utruss, by the great River Fallopia. I know you have waited many hours and days for this momentous occasion."

The prophet lowered his staff, and the great throng erupted in jubilation and approval. "For he's a a jolly good fellow. For he's a jolly good fellow…" they began to sing. The expectant father, Kemal, could partake of their elation, and he knew somehow they were singing about him.

The prophet turned to resume his message to the mighty horde. As he raised high his staff, they once again hushed themselves in anticipation of his next instruction. "I do believe you are ready to move forward upon this historic occasion." A wide smile shone like the sun upon his face.

Once again the crowd erupted with gleeful approval. And once again, he raised his staff and they fell silent, as they prepared themselves for what lay ahead, and for what he might say to them. And this is what he said:

"Many among you have sought the place of honor in this historic mission, and I commend you for your noble aspirations, but I must tell you this: You will—most of you, in fact—will rise to this great task in a blaze of glory, never to return. Only a very few of you, and most likely only one, will persevere to the very end and bring the sacred mission to fruition. It is a delicate and difficult task that you now set your tails to. Those who must turn back. . ." And there was a pregnant silence. "please do so now."

All were silent. The prophet looked out upon them, and was greatly moved by their collective resolve. "Very well, then. Let it begin," he proclaimed. And a great shout went up from among the gathered horde, yearning to fulfill destiny.

"You have heard from your forefathers how this works. You know the thrust of it, and the great surging power of this great maneuver to bring forth creation. You have been told of it; you have rehearsed it in your fertile imaginations. You have heard their faithful proclamations about the joys that await us in the land of Utruss. You know what our fathers have done. Go now, and do likewise."

The prophet lifted high his staff and waved it broadly toward the vast swift-flowing River Deferens, upon which their rising momentum now began to surge with fervent purpose and ecstasy.

The prophet surveyed that entire scene as the mighty horde passed before him into eternity. He watched them all dive with jubilant abandon into the vast River, and he kept his steadfast eye upon their departure until all had disappeared round the bend of the River—all except one.

He gazed upon that One with a joy that accompanies only those rare events in which true Life is being wrought from raw potential. The One who stayed behind approached the prophet humbly. And when he had come within an arm's length, he kneeled there beneath the prophet's expectant gaze.

"I have expected you," said the prophet. "What is your name, boy?"

"Lance, sir."

"From this time forth you shall be called: Sir Lance."

"Thank you, sir."

"Tell me why you have lingered here, while the others have gone before you to perform their duty."

"I want to obtain your blessing, sir."

"Then you shall have it."

"Thank you, sir."

As Lance turned his head upward, he saw the prophet assume a relaxed demeanor, and then open his mouth to speak: "I have stood in this position for many a year, Lance, waiting for One such as you. The last time I anointed a servant to undertake this sacred mission, your brother Sir Alex came forth, in just such a manner as you have done today. I commend you, as I did him on that day, for your boldness, and for your sensitivity to matters of great purpose and dignity."

"Thank you, Sir."

"And so, Lance, since it is incumbent upon you to overtake your comrades in this expedition and thus fulfill your sacred destiny, I do anoint you, on behalf of our Creator, to go forth in the knowledge and confidence of your holy purpose, and thereby to accomplish its fulfillment in the land of Utruss. Arise, Sir Lance, and go. Do what you have been called to do."

"Thank you, Sir." Now Lance stood erect, knowing that he had received the precious commission for which he had lingered. Without hesitation, the anointed servant turned upon his heel and left the holy mountain. Alone, he dived into the vast River Deferens to make the long journey to Paradise.

The prophet watched until the chosen One disappeared around the bend of the River. "May the Lord go with you, boy," he whispered.

Kemal and Salli sighed with their sweet love's satisfaction. Kemal fell asleep, and Salli got out of bed, went to Alex's bedroom to see how well he was sleeping, since the boy had a bit of a cold. Seeing that all was well, she returned to her husband's bed and joined in his world of dreams.

One floor below the sleeping couple, their family business, the *BookCell*, had just closed for the night. Their tenant and part-time bookstore clerk, Rosa, was shutting the place down. Lingering with her was her friend, Robby, who now assisted her by cleaning the coffee area while she closed out the cash register. While they busily performed these chores, Robby's cellphone rang. "Hello, doc, what's up?"

"Robby, I think there may be something to Simon Lafraneer's cockamamie tale after all."

"Say what?"

"Do you want to hear more about it?"

"Sure."

"Well, that's good Robby. But we can't talk about it on the phone right now. This is a little unusual, I know, and it's late, but you need to come with me right now out to the research station. I need your help out there. Can you do it?"

"Yes."

"Where are you now?"

"At the *BookCell*, on Napolean Avenue."

"That's great. I'm leaving Bienville Hall right now. I'll pick you up in five minutes. Can you handle it?"

"I'm as ready as I'll ever be."

"See you in a few minutes, then. Be out front."

Robby snapped the phone shut and finished cleaning the espresso machine. "Hey, Rosa."

She finished counting five-dollar bills. "Uh-huh."

"I'll see you tomorrow night about seven, right? at the usual place?" Someone had left a bookmark on the counter. He picked it up and read it. *Do not underestimate the power of a man whose purpose is sure.* Robby slid it into his pocket.

"Okay. See you then," she confirmed. He started to leave. "Oh, Robby?"

"What?" he replied, a little nervously.

"Come kiss me, you fool."

He walked over to where she was, watching her carefully, loving her expectant smile. He kissed her slowly. Then a silly old song popped into his head; he spoke the words from it: "Fools rush in where wise men fear to tread."

She rested her steady eyes upon his, rose from the seat and wrapped her arms around his waist. "But wise men never fall in love. . ."

He laughed, but he wanted to offer tears of joy. Instead, he extended the silly song words, "So how are they to know?" He paused, not knowing what to do. This love thing was pretty new to him, dork that he was. "Gotta go. See you tomorrow." And he released himself from Paradise, stumbled toward the door and let himself out. She followed him, and waved goodbye.

Dr. Theseus and Ophelia pulled up in the BMW. Robby looked at his cellphone. It was 12:17 a.m. William stopped the car in front of the bookstore; Robby hopped into the back seat.

" Ophelia, this is my assistant, Robby Davis, a most amazing young scientist." Robby extended his hand across through the open space between the front seats. They shook. William stepped on the gas.

"Pleased to meet you, Robby. I'm Ophelia Doss."

"She has something to show you. Don't you, Ophelia?" The doc was too excited for his own good.

"Hold your horses, Theseus." She squinted at him, feigning disapproval. But the hint of a smile on her lips portrayed a subtle power. Her patient reticence was mildly quelling his peppery impatience. Ophelia was encountering this whole turn of events, ever since stepping into his world at the airport, with a fiercely confident satisfaction, cultivating a quiet revelry whenever she could enjoy the upper hand. Unhurried, she turned to address Robby, and spoke politely, inquisitively. "I understand you're from my neck of the woods."

"Close, Dr. Doss. I'm from Haywood Couny, near Maggie Valley. And you live in Asheville. Is that right?"

"Yes."

"And I know you chair the anthropology department at Bellel."

"Maggie Valley area. Hmm. I was just there about a month ago, for a funeral."

"Oh? Small world, huh?" said Robby.

"Robby, do you know Alice Pack?"

"Yes," said Robby, with rising interest. She's my cousin."

Ophelia turned and looked carefully at Robby. "How's that?"

"Our, uh, grandmothers are sisters."

"Do you mean Zelda and Cornelia?"

"That's right." Robby was a little surprised. "Did you know them?"

"I knew Zelda. One of her last acts was to grant me an interview. Your cousin Alice took me to her."

"Really! That's interesting. I bet she talked about the Cherokee."

"She did. It was a very productive interview. She and Alice and I talked all day. Then Zelda cooked dinner for us."

"When was that?"

"July 9th."

"Ah, and then she passed away in September."

"Yes. Hers was the funeral I went to."

"I see. I didn't make it."

"I know."

"Anyway, Alice is a student at Bellel. Have you taught her?"

"Yes. She is a promising young scholar. . . probably, like you."

"Sure. Ours family is, uh, unusual. We'll see what the scholarly pursuits lead to. I'm happy to hear, though, that you are pleased with Alice's work as a student. Did she take your anthropology class?"

"Ophelia," muttered William as he merged onto the freeway."

She glanced at him with a curious smile. "Yes, Robby. She made A's in both classes that I taught her. But I need to show you what your boss here wants me to show you." Without ceremony or warning, she flipped her gold florin toward Robby in the back seat.

Robby knew only that it was a coin that had bounced from his chest and tumbled between his legs to the car floor. Looking down, he could discern its shape. He picked the precious thing up and began examining it.

William was surprised at how long Robby sat looking at the coin without comment. He was watching him in the rear-view mirror. After thirty seconds or so, he blurted, "Well?"

"John the Baptist."

"How did you know that?" asked Ophelia. "It's just the figure of a man."

Robby laughed. "I've seen one of these before." He glanced up, catching the doc's eyes in the rear-view member. "It was, as a matter of fact, in Dr. Theseus's office. But he didn't seem too interested."

William had to respond to the note of irony in his student's voice. "After I had walked out the office."

"That's right, doc. You were late for a faculty meeting. But I had gotten the impression," Robby looked at Ophelia. They seemed to share, already, an appreciation for the doc's unique mix of personality traits, one of which was impetuosity. ". . .that you were not favorably impressed with Mr. Lafraneer's pitch.

"I'm still not impressed with it. There's something about the guy that doesn't compute."

"I understand. I sensed it too. But hey, there's *something* to it. I mean," He held up the florin. "This is what he was offering. And now there are, apparently, two of them, or *at least* two of them."

"That's why we're doing this right now, Robby. Sam found three more tonight. So there are at least five of them that we know of."

"I have thirty-seven just like that one," offered Ophelia, speaking to Robby.

"Sam picked up those three after he caught two men prowling on the property."

"Two men. Who were they?"

"He didn't actually catch them. He saw them and they ran away."

"What were they doing?"

"We don't what they were up to, but we do know this: they left three gold coins in the grass where they were hightalin' it out of there."

"You mean coins like this one—real florins?"

"That's what we're going to find out right now."

Robby gave a low whistle. They were quiet for a few moments, zipping along now at 70 mph, crossing the spillway on the west end of Lake Ponchartrain. Ophelia was humming a little tune. After a while, Robby said, "Well, doc, what are we going to do when we get there?"

"I don't know."

"Did you call the cops?"

"No, I haven't done that."

"Don't you, uh, don't you think you should?"

"Probably." But the doc made no move to do so.

"They're on your side, you know."

"Yeah. But I think I'll wait until we get there and see what has happened."

Now Robby recognized the old, melancholy tune that Ophelia was humming. *Go to sleep, go to sleep, go to sleep my little baby. When you wake, you shall have all the pretty little horses.* That low, sad lullaby wafting from a woman's throat in the front seat seemed to afford him permission to nod off for a few minutes. It had been a long day. The two professors spoke intermittently in the front seat. . . about gold, and goals, and God only knows. . .

hddq://riverroad.loc

When Dr. Theseus turned the Beemer into the driveway at the research station, Robby was awakening from a short snooze. A police car was parked by the office. On its door was an official seal with the words: **Ascension Parish Sheriff K-9 Unit.** William looked over his shoulder at Robby, and said, "You made a good point about the law being on our side, so I called them." He parked the car. There seemed to be no one near the sheriff's car or the office. Robby noticed, though, that as soon as the doc had closed the car door, he started walking very directly toward the field and the old oak tree. Ophelia rushed to his side, and Robby followed along, a little disoriented from having fallen asleep.

A deputy was inspecting the area around the old oak with a powerful flashlight that he wielded slowly, methodically, in a wide arc. Sam was standing next to him. They were joined by the three newcomers.

"Good morning, Dr. Theseus. Your man here may have interrupted a theft in progress."

"Theft. What did they get?"

Sam held out his hand, illuminating it with his own flashlight. In his palm were seven gold florins. Their brightness seemed surreal. Robby actually wondered for a second if he was dreaming. Sam spoke drily, "These were the ones they didn't get."

"Where are these things coming from?" William blurted.

The deputy looked at him. "You don't know?"

"I've never seen them," the doc replied.

The deputy continued his inquiry. "You didn't know, Dr. Theseus, that you had gold somewhere on this property?" The deputy's expression betrayed a mild amusement as the corners of his mouth turned up, hinting a smile.

"No, sir. I didn't know. Someone had told me that last week, but I thought it was. . .it was ridiculous, what he said."

"Maybe not so ridiculous," intoned the deputy, studying Theseus' face. The deputy rocked on his feet slightly. Out in the field, another flashlight was whipping around, and the low, gentle crooning of two dogs was barely audible. "Who was it that told you there was gold on the property?"

"It was a British fellow. I had never seen him before. Simon, uh, what was his name, Robby?"

"Simon Lafraneer," said Robby.

The deputy looked at Robby. "And who are you?"

"Robby Davis, sir. Graduate assistant. I'm Dr. Theseus' assistant."

"I see. You say you had never seen this man before, Dr. Theseus?"

"That's right."

"How about you, Mr. Davis. Did you know him?"

"Well, I had met him just a few nights before."

"Before what?"

"Before he came to Dr. Theseus' office and told us there was gold on the property."

"He told you there was gold on this property?"

"That's right."

The deputy, silent for a moment, called out to his partner, "Bo, you findin' anything out there?"

"The dogs are onto something," came the reply.

"On what basis did this Mr. Lafraneer state to you that there was gold on the property?"

"It was. . .what the hell was that story he told, Robby?"

"He said that he had inherited a house in England, and he had found, in the attic, a letter from a deceased relative about this gold."

"About *this* gold? here in Louisiana?"

"Well, yes, and some more gold just like it, in North Carolina."

The deputy turned toward Dr. Theseus. "But you didn't believe him?"

"No. I guess I should have taken him a little more seriously." The doc managed a little chuckle. " When he read us a poem in Russian, that's when he lost me."

"In Russian?" The deputy allowed a gentle laugh.

"He read it to us in English. I'm sorry. It had been translated."

"And what, as near as you can remember did this, uh, *poem* say?"

"It said, uh, what the hell did it say, Robby?"

"The poem said that there's a rabbit hole out here somewhere with 200 gold florins in it," Robby replied.

"Yes. That's it. That's what Simon said. Thank you, Robby."

"I see." was the deputy's comment.

From the field came a sudden shout, this time with an urgent tone: "Dale. Come out here. We've got something."

The deputy began walking. He raised his voice slightly to say, "By the way, I'm deputy Dale LaGrange. Why don't ya'll come with me and we see what this is all about."

The trio followed him hurriedly across the field. Ophelia cracked, "I told you I'd get my walk in, Theseus."

"I'm impressed with your persistence, Oph, but this is Monday. You missed Sunday's walk."

"It seems you're dragging me around the countryside now, just like you used to drag Elise around back in Ohio, and in the middle of the night, no less."

"Ha. You asked for it," was William's retort.

"Just kidding, Theseus. This is kind of exciting."

"Yeah. You had to come all the way down here for a little excitement. What do they do up there in the mountains—sit around and watch the grass grow?"

"Right. That's about as interesting as it gets up there. Whereas, here you have your grass strewn about with gold coins."

Robby was lol. *This was ridiculous. Who would have thought it? What time is it anyway?*

"Watch out for rabbit holes, my dear," advised William to Ophelia as he grabbed her hand. She had stumbled.

And then, there they were. Both deputies had their power flashlights trained on a large, muddy hole in the ground. A few feet away, just beyond the loose dirt that the vagabonds had shoveled out, five more florins glinted.

"Yep, looks like a larceny to me," said Officer Dale Lagrange.

"What are those, uh, shreds? asked William.

Robby knew. "Those shreds are the remains of Plato's suitcase." He walked to the hole, squatted close to its sloppy, wet aperture. Strips and torn scraps of decomposed leather and fabric lay in disarray, having been tossed aside only hours before by the frenzied pawing of two N'Awlins street kids who were up to mired up to their waists in a seventy-three-year-old fortune pit. Robby pulled some more dirt out of the hole with his bare hands. Looking up at the deputy, he asked, "Do you mind?"

"No," replied Lagrange. "We should sift through this a little bit for clues about the identity of these midnight diggers. Deputy Ballard will help you." The grad assistant and the deputy combed through dirt for a few minutes, finding nothing of consequence.

"It looks like they got it all, except for those they dropped along the way," said Ballard.

"Bo," said Lagrange. "Can you see further down into the hole?"

Ballard directed his flashlight into the hole. "Ha. There's a rabbit in there." Robby lowered his head to get a view into the hole, and there were two red eyes staring back at him.

"*He* must have been wondering what the hell was going on," mused Dr. Theseus. "This is crazy. I never would have thought. . ."

Br'er Rabbit, he lay low.

Surpluses

19

Monday night descended coldly with flurries and thousands of hurrying footsteps upon the grey sidewalks and streets and fleets and sleek trains of Berlin, ancient Teutonic heart-city and sinew of Prussian Germany. Nine time zones and one ocean west, it might be late enough in the misty Louisiana morning for Franz Hallfrich to rouse his business partner with an intercontinental phone call.

So while most of the good Germans were finding exodus from the great city, Franz was treading crowded sidewalks against the flow, bound for his office three blocks from Friedrickstrasse station. Having just returned from a lucrative trip to Venice, he was returning to the Parthenonics office to tie up a few loose ends and make the phone call. But Simon didn't answer, so Franz set himself to tying up the loose ends and after about thirty minutes he was done, so he called Simon again, with still no answer. Then he reached inside the low desk drawer to refresh his memory of a certain golden opportunity by reading a letter that he had received from his grandfather several years before. And this is what it said:

```
Plato Zupoff, proprietor
Great Star Mercantile Co.
54 Lexington Ave.
Asheville, North Carolina
United States of America
```

Dr. Karl Hallfrich
79 Horsestrasse
Berlin, Germany
September 15, 1929

Dear Karl:

I recently obtained your address from our old
friend, Hans Zoller. As you can see by the above
address, I am now a citizen of the United States. I
am so very grateful now for the opportunity to
thank you, after all these years, for your help in
that perilous summer of 1918 when my sister and I
fled the senseless desecration of our Mother
Russia. Your wise intervention made it possible for
us to escape the Bolshevik rabble that had turned
all order and productivity into madness.

We remember, as I am sure you do, the unholy
anarchy, the treachery and sacrilage, of those days
of war and revolution—when no man knew from one day
to the next who could be counted as trustworthy.
And so many good Russians were executed without
explanation or trial. Had it not been for your
securing our place on the train to Berlin, Katerina
and I would have certainly perished with the others
whose allegiance to the Czar and to Mother Russia
had cost them their lives. Thank you.

You may remember this, perhaps not as well as
I do. I had, by Providence and no small bribery,
managed to obtain three boxcars of wheat that had
been harvested on the land formerly owned by my
parents, Anatoly and Artemis Zupoff. Your superiors
in Berlin had commanded that the shipment be made
immediately, to relieve the hardship of your people
after so many years of sacrifice in time of war.

You obtained a place for Katerina and me and our cargo of wheat, so precious during that time, in that train. We were to leave that same day, September 7, 1918. What you may not have known was this: the Bolshevik goons stopped us in Vyazma and demanded that Katerina and I be removed from the train. Our papers had been satisfactory enough for the zealots in Moscow, but everywhere in Russia someone else was in charge. Once again, Providence and a careful use of our resources preserved our place on that west-bound train that transported us back to the civilized world. Although we later found troubles and shortages in Berlin, these did not compare to the vindictive cruelty and indiscriminate violence we had seen the Bolshevikii inflicting upon their own people in the name of their god Socialism.

Just before our escape, two women had tried to assassinate Lenin. In the aftermath of their failed attempt, all hell broke loose on earth. Under commands from the Commissioner Against the Counter-Revolution, a bloodthirsty man named Peters who signed death warrants en masse as if they were orders for farm animals to be slaughtered, the paranoid secret police expanded their unjustified massacres of the guiltless peasants, and then they hunted down hundreds of intelligencia and executed them without trials or even inquisitions. In the midst of this bloody business, we managed to find an escape from Russia, thanks to you and to our Great God!

Now I can, perhaps, return the favor. Our friend Hans informs me that your son, Helmut, will be coming to the United States soon, or maybe he is already here. And I want you to know that I am here to help him in any way I can. So please

provide my name and this address to him if you
would like to do that. The place where I live
here, in mountains that are very much like our
beloved Urals, is a wonderful town named Asheville.
And God has blessed me with great prosperity here.
No need for socialism here in the United States of
America! No need for a Kaiser! Every man who
chooses to be a king can be the czar of his own
realm here.

Should Helmut choose to visit me here in North
Carolina, U.S.A., he can find a sizable stock of
gold which I deposited in a discreet location near
New Orleans, Louisiana, U.S.A. About 55 miles
northeast of that city. If he is willing to seek
out the gold and bring it to me, I will give him
half! It consists of 200 gold florins, original
Florentine issue 1492, so it would be well worth
his effort. I myself have not recovered the gold,
because I have had no need of it, such has been my
success in the United States of America.

These precious goods can be found on the
property of a Negro named Washington Jones. His
tract adjoins the plantation of Thaddeus Theseus, a
prominent cotton planter who is known by everyone
in that vicinity. If Helmut is able to locate this
property, here is how he will find the gold that I
buried in the ground after a riverboat wreck that
left us stranded. Zuerst soll er den alten Eichenbaum finden, der
die Kleinbauern „Mama Eichenbaum " nennen. Der Baum ist nicht schwierig
zu finden. Er ist der größte, älteste Baum auf dem Land von Washington
Jones, sowie der Baum, darüber Lev Tolstoy in Krieg und Frieden
geschrieben hat. Dann soll Helmut diese Anleitungen folgen:

Von dem Mama Eichenbaum lauf mal 64 Schritte nördlich. Du wirst
da einen Kaninchenbau finden, in der Nähe eines kleinen Bach, der hier ein
„Bayou" heißt. Das Gold ist in diesem Kaninchenbau beerdigteat .

Do not worry about the Negro, Washington Jones. He will remember me. I spent a night at his house, and he showed kindness to me. I left him a rich reward, also in gold.

This deposit was made because I was being pursued by a man who, I know, would have killed me for the gold if given half a chance. It was necessary in that precarious situation that I flee quickly, and that is how I came here to these mountains. I did manage to bring 100 florins with me. It was all I could carry without being encumbered by the weight and the bulk of it. I have used a small number of this hundred to found my mercantile venture here in Asheville. Business to date has been so very lucrative that my first small appropriation of the florins has been sufficient to carry me into prosperity that Russian peasants can only dream of. So I am, as they say here in America, fat and happy. What is even greater is that next month I am to be married to a most beautiful and perfect woman, Eliza Renland!

So please, my dear Karl, send your Helmut to me if he comes to America, and I will assure that he has great opportunity.

Sincerely,

Plato Zupoff

hddq://backtoneworleans.2000.loc

By Monday morning, 10:00, Dr. William Theseus had managed to get back home to New Orleans and get a few hours sleep. While drinking coffee and eating an English muffin at his kitchen table, he made an important phone call.

"Good morning. Thank you for calling the Monteleone Hotel."

"Do you have a Simon Lafraneer registered?" asked William.

"One moment, please. . .yes, I'll connect you to his room if you like."

"Please do."

"Hello."

"Simon Lafraneer?"

"This is he."

"William Theseus here."

Simon answered cheerfully. "Dr. Theseus, it's good to hear from you. What can I do for you?"

William had an intuition that he should handle this communication delicately. "I want you to know that I appreciate your visit last week."

"Certainly. Thank you for taking the time to meet with me."

"I'm sorry I had to leave so suddenly."

"Oh, it's quite all right, Dr. Theseus. I understand."

"Yes, well, have you, uh, any new developments to report?" asked William

"Developments?"

"Pertaining to the, uh, gold florins that you talked about."

"I am, of course, still interested in having a look at your property, to see if my information is correct."

"I see." William paused. He had to think for a moment. This was not the response he had expected. "It was your opinion, if my memory serves me well, that there are authentic Florentine gold florins buried on University property."

"That's right, sir, at your research facility, northwest of the city."

"And you have some specific information about their location?"

"Maybe. You may remember that all I had to offer was the—"

"The poem."

"Yes, the poem," echoed Simon, " and my impression was that you were not convinced of its authenticity, or, of its value as an indicator of the gold's location."

"Well, that's true. But I'm wondering if there is some more specific information."

"Actually, Dr. Theseus, I have learned more about that supposed location since we talked."

"What is it?"

"It is, uh, a little difficult to explain," answered Simon, cautiously. There was an awkward silence.

"Would you like to have lunch, Simon?"

Surprised, the Brit hesitated. "That would be, ah, good. That would be very good."

"I'll pick you up then, about noon?"

"Ah, yes, that would be good."

"I'll see you at noon then, at the Monteleone."

"Jolly good."

After the call ended, Simon immediately called *Bankcher* to talk to Mick. "May I speak to Mick Basker, please?" he asked.

"One moment please."

After a minute of phone music, a woman picked up.

"This is the Commercial Loan department. How may I help you?"

"I'd like to speak to Mick Basker, please."

"Mr. Basker won't be in today. Can I give him a message?"

"No, thank you."

"Would you like to speak to one of our other loan officers?"

"No, thank you."

hddq://canalstreet.loc

"What was it that brought you to New Orleans, Simon?" William asked, as he turned the Beemer onto Canal Street.

"There were two business possibilities, actually. The most important is this one that I had presented to you. The other pertains to my representing a group of South American ranchers who have high-quality Angus embryos for sale to ranchers in this country."

"Those are cryogenically preserved embryos?"

"That's right."

"You have facilities for cryogenic preservation?"

"Yes, at my home base, in Grand Cayman. My firm is also associated with labs in Liverpool, Santiago, and Berlin."

"You provide embryos for research as well?"

"Yes, mice, sheep, amphibians, but also cultures and microorganisms. We have a wide range of biological resources."

"That's an impressive range of services."

"We like to think so." Simon looked at William and smiled. Up to this point, he had felt a little anxious.

"How about human embryos?" asked William.

Simon had not quite expected this line of questioning. "Ah, yes, within the guidelines of propriety, as determined by, ah, international protocols."

"Do you have some now?"

"I, ah, I would have to check with my associates to find out about that."

"If you have human embryos, where would they have come from?"

"Just about anywhere in the world. They are surplus."

"Surplus." echoed William, raising his eyebrows.

"That is to say, ah, from *in vitro fertilization.*, most likely. There have been conditions under which we assumed responsibilities for specimens that had been shelved indefinitely."

"That's interesting. Such as?"

"IVF samples that were retained through divorce situations, or deaths in the families, or legal problems, or questions about genetic deficiencies, or just, ah, space problems."

"Space problems?"

"Shortage of space, you know, in a laboratory, or some such."

"Or demand for stem cells?" inquired William.

"Yes. There is a demand for stem cells.

"Probably worldwide, eh?"

"Yes. They do have the greatest potential for experimental flexibility, and researchers acknowledge this anywhere you go."

"That's very interesting. Are you very hungry, Simon?"

"I could certainly eat," Simon said, with a chuckle.

"Would you like to see our humble frozen nitrogen arrangement? Perhaps you could advise me as to how it might be improved."

"Certainly, I—"

"It's in the same location as our prospective expedition. It's just a little bit of a ride."

"Oh, absolutely, I'm in no hurry. This business is my first priority."

"Good." They were on the freeway now, zipping along at 60 mph. "Did I understand correctly that you have acquired some more information pertaining to the gold location?"

"That is true, Dr. Theseus. I recently received an email from my associate in Berlin. It contained some specific instructions."

"Instructions. That sounds very helpful."

"I should hope so."

"And what are the instructions?"

"I have them right here." Simon produced a slip of paper from his briefcase, and showed it to the professor. "Since you're driving, perhaps it's best I read it to you. You can read it for yourself later."

"That would be good. Thank you."

Simon read it aloud:

"From the **OAK** , the **ANCIENT TREE** you see, **GO** to the **HARE'S** nest, which is **NORTH** as far as 'q' determines it should be, each step being positive 'q' beneath your knee, and not a negative as your genetic map would seem to be. In other words, add your 'q's and you shall see how far that it may be, beyond the tree.

Then, within the hole to which you're sent, *where rabbits in their* **DENS** *are bent*, you'll find the Ariadnic **THREAD** is rent, until you find it far away again, *'NEATH BUNCOMBE'S PACK, beyond Saluda track*, where 'p's are miles, as 'q's are steps, not east not east, but west, yes west..

IN both these destinations **GOLD FLORINS** you shall see, if you but follow these directions from the tree."

William was visibly excited. "That is very specific. It sounds, in fact, precise enough to act upon."

"Absolutely. This is what I had hoped to share with you all along."

"Thank you for your patience with me on this venture," said William.

"Well, it is, after all, your property, Dr. Theseus. I would be powerless to act upon it without your cooperation."

"You're right, Simon." William looked directly at the Brit, who reciprocated with a rather dumb, innocent grin.

They were silent for a minute or so. Then William said, "There's a place out here near the lab where I like to eat—*Broussard's*, where we can get the best oyster poboys. Have you ever had one?"

"No, can't say I have. But it sounds good."

Another silence. Simon had placed the little paper on the console between the two seats. William picked it up to have a look. He skimmed through it, while still driving. "Is there anyone else who has seen this?"

Simon was a little startled by the question. But he obliged William with a reply. "Yes. You notice the 'p' and 'q' references there. Do you?"

"I see them."

"Those are references to another document, which I did not have until just a few days ago. And it was provided to me by a man here in New Orleans."

"Who is that?"

"Mick Basker, a banker, or, I should say, a loan officer at *Bankcher*. He is a young man."

"Hmm. And why was this other information sent to him?"

"Now that I do not know, honestly. My associate in Berlin sent it to him."

"What is it?"

Simon produced another slip of paper from his briefcase, and handed it to William:

OAT, GHN-1:17q22-q24, DTNBP-1:6p22.3, IGF-2:3q28

William studied the odd little nugget of info for a few seconds, while driving. He was perplexed. "These are genes."

"Quite so. Terribly odd, isn't it?"

"Genes for production of human growth hormone, dysbindin, and insulin-like growth factor. And that first one—O, A, T is, hmm, I'm not sure, something to do with eyes, I think."

"Correct. But the significance of this data is, I believe, the numbers. You'll see, when you can read it more carefully, a correlation between certain bits in the first instruction paper and the numbers in these genes. In the case of the human growth hormone gene, for instance, the numbers appear to indicate, according to the other document, a specific number of steps to be taken by the person who is seeking the gold."

"That's incredible!" William was fascinated with the apparent intricacy of these 'instructions'. "How in the hell did all this come together?"

"Oh, God only knows, Dr. Theseus. It all started in the mind of Plato Zupoff, seventy some-odd years ago."

Simon's cellphone rang, emitting strains of the finale of Tchaikovsky's *1812 Overture*. He flipped it open. "Hello." . . . "Mick, I've been trying to call you" . . . "Good news. Dr. Theseus has agreed to take me out to the research station, and we are headed there now." There was a long silence while Simon listened to Mick's reply on the other end. William was listening carefully, but could hear nothing except Simon's breathing, since Simon is a rather large man. "That's not necessary, Mick. We're about to find out once and for all, I think, if there is any validity to this rabbit hole story." There was another long silence. "It doesn't matter, Mick." . . . "Where are you, anyway?"

William inferred that Simon was talking to the person who had provided the genetic list, and so he said to Simon, "Tell your friend he can join us at the research station if he'd like to."

Simon, preoccupied with whatever Mick was saying to him, glanced at William with a polite smile. "I don't think so. Hey, old chap, Dr. Theseus says you can join us out here for the search." . . . "Why not? This could be the big one.". . . "Oh, I wouldn't worry about that." . . . "Absolutely not." . . . " Well, have it your way then." . . . "I hope you'll be feeling better." . . . "Don't forget" . . . "Mick?" He snapped the phone shut and sighed.

William was so very curious. "I take it that was your partner who had received the genes list."

"Yes, although he's not my partner. We were sort of thrown into this together by my associate in Berlin."

"What's his name?"

"Franz Hallfrich."

"The banker, here in New Orleans, is Franz?"

"Oh, sorry. Franz is my associate." This local fellow is Mick Basker. He's a young man, a loan officer with *Bankcher*."

"And I take it Mick will not be accompanying us on the search?"

"No," Simon said.

"Why not?"

"He says he is ill."

"Where is he?"

"I don't know. He never said."

hddq://glasschimera.exp

Mick Basker's avaricious venture to obtain gold that was not his, never was his, and in fact would never be his, except for the few days that he was able to have it in his possession and deceive himself into believing that he had some legal right to the brilliant bullion, simply because some guy in Germany had sent him a coded message about a seventy-three-year-old stash of the precious metal in a rabbit hole somewhere in Louisiana, was nevertheless presumption.   His questionable motives, methods, and downright foolish recruitment of two street kids not yet dry behind the ears to obtain the Zupoff deposit, so hastily abandoned during a time of extreme fear and consequently poor judgement, were about to be exposed in all their stupidity by the long arm of the law to the unmerciful illumination of public exposure and personal crisis and not only that but he was under a lot of stress, not knowing what to do, contemplating a hasty retreat but knowing that you can run but you really cannot hide. He was about to feel like, and he sensed it with impending trepidation, a chimeric plasmid under the glass cover of a Petri dish, being examined by a smarter-than-the-average-bear microbiologist.

It was, in fact, a microbiologist's gold that he had stolen, and not just *any* microbiologist, but one who happened to be emeritus of a hallowed university because his great grandfather had founded it. William Theseus was a merciful man, but he also knew when someone had crossed the line of inappropriate acquisition. And stealing the University's gold was not the way to go, and so William called the law, and this is how it happened:

"He knows about this, doesn't he? asked William.

"Who knows about it?" asked Simon.

"That's what I'm asking you, Simon—who knows about this gold that's hidden in my grandfather's yard? Is it just you and me, or is there someone else who knows it's there?"

"I, I, I, yes, he does, uh, I mean, if it is, indeed there, if there is gold there, in your grandfather's, uh, plantation."

"Dammit!"

"But he wouldn't know for sure, until we, ah—"

"There *was* gold there, just like you said, Simon, but now it is gone!"

"What do you mean?"

"It was stolen last night. We have an eyewitness."

"You think it was Mick?"

"I think it was Mick, yes, Mick, what's his last name?"

"Basker."

"Yeah. Who else could it be but him? This is no coincidence. And *you* gave him the information he needed to find it."

"I tried to tell you last week—"

"Oh, shut up, Simon. It's none of your damn business what might or might not be buried on my grandfather's place—"

"It was *my* great uncle who left it there, Theseus!" countered Simon.

"Doesn't matter now." William opened his cell phone and pushed a few numbers. "May I speak with Deputy LaGrange please?". . ."At 7 p.m?". . "Then I'd like to speak with the sheriff, please." He rolled his eyes and waited for a minute or so. "Good morning, sir. This is William Theseus.". . . "Yes. Thank you. Your people are very helpful. I have some new information for you." . . . "Okay. I have the name of a suspect." . . . "Mick Basker." . . . "No, but he lives in New Orleans. He's a loan officer for *Bankcher*." . . . "Because I have found out that he has some information about the location of the gold, information that no one else could have known.". . . "No, not even me. I just found out about it.". . . "Sure. I'm headed there now.". . . "Thank you, sir. About fifteen minutes.". . . "That's correct. Good bye."

Tricks

20

The van began at ten to six when Mr. B. performed his tricks without a sound. Silently, Mick had turned the key, and the van engine began to purr. "I want you to stay down between those back seats until I tell you to get up," Mick had instructed his two bumbling assistants. *Br'er fox he lay low.*

They had waited as long as possible under cover of darkness and a convenient honeysuckle thicket. At ten minutes to six, it was obvious to Mick that the brightening sky would have soon betrayed their suspect location. He had decided it was time to make a move—time to get out of dodging and get back to the place they once belonged. One nervous banker and two clueless street kids, clutching their risky prize of 157 gold florins, turned as stealthily as a van can onto the River road in pursuit of invisibility.

"I just can't see how you could screw up something as simple as this," Mick had muttered as they turned, a few dreadful minutes later, onto Airline highway to make a beeline for the Crescent City.

That had been eight hours ago, and of course the two young punks had not really screwed up. They had obtained the goods. It was their presumptuous mentor's half-baked booty plans that had rendered their caper imminently discoverable.

Mick was beginning to understand just how discoverable this nocturnal golden opportunity had become when he called Simon later that morning. The Brit's unexpected rendezvous with William Theseus was putting a major crimp on Mick's evasion strategy.

His mind was racing like a fox on the run. *There's no telling what might happen between Simon and Theseus if Simon starts blabbing about the 64 steps from the oak tree, and how he had obtained that piece of the puzzle. If I had included Simon in last night's run, he wouldn't be with Theseus right now. What in the hell's gonna happen now that they've seen that hole in the ground? Simon has no reason to cover for me, unless I somehow get to him and get him divvied into some of the gold. Is it too late for that now? I should have brought Simon with us last night. Now he's going to screw this thing up..*

His cell phone rang for the third time since he had gotten home. Looking at the display, he noticed the time: 1:35 pm, and the caller identity, his secretary. He downed the last nip from his whiskey glass and decided he was feeling brave enough now to answer it. "Hello, Rhonda. Don't forget I'm taking the day off."

"Sorry to disturb you, Mr. Basker. I just thought you might like to know."

"It's okay, honey. What's up?"

"Mr. Duplessis called for you twice, about that industrial site at Elysian Fields. I think he's decided to meet their price."

"Okay, thanks. That's good."

"And you got a call from Sheriff Marchand of Ascension Parish."

"What did he say?"

"He asked for you to call him. You want the number?"

" "Uh, sure." Mick wrote the number as she spoke it.

"And Lt. Moriarty, with the NOPD, called."

"Moriarty, he's . . ."

"the one who's always selling benefit tickets, Last week he called about the benefit for Mrs. Kite, whose husband was killed in the line of duty last month at Bishop's Gate."

"And what did he say?"

" He just asked that you call him."

"Okay, Rhonda, anything else?"

"That's all. Do you want me to call Duplessis and set up a meeting for tomorrow?"

"Duplessis?"

"About the Elysian Fields project."

"Uh, sure."

"What time?"

"Uh, how about . . .doesn't matter, whatever . . ."

"Okay. You don't sound too good, Mr. Basker. Are you feeling any better?"

"I'll make it."

"I'll call you after I've set up the appointment with Mr. Duplessis, then?"

"Just email me."

"Okay."

"See ya, Rhonda." *I should have brought Simon with us. Now he's going to screw this thing up.. . . Marchand. . . Moriarty. . . for the benefit of Mrs. Kite. . .*Mick closed the phone and poured another whiskey.

hddq://jurassic.per

It might have been seventy million years ago that a large asteroid hit the earth somewhere near Cancun. And it might have been that the big space-tossed boulder would have thrown such a cloud of dust and disturbance into the earth's atmosphere that it probably altered the pecking order of biological kingdoms for thousands or even millions of years thereafter.

Earth shaking events. They happen.

It might have been that the severe rearrangement of earth's biomes had put a major crimp on the old dinosaurs. Maybe they became like DOS after Microsoft, just slipping down into the dark hidden recesses of the new program, relegated to subterranean, hydrocarbon pools of potential energy, their giant-generating introns and exons having been unraveled and liquefied like the assets of international corpuses and cartels that would later profit from their demise. It might have been that the superbad, supermad totally-rad reptile kings and queens of the jungle could no longer compete with the smaller, sleeker, smarter, uppity mammals who were in the ascendancy and currently favored by the committee for Natural Selection. It might have happened that way. And maybe the superbad supermad totally rad reptile kings and queens of the jungle found themselves faltering, over the next few eons, losing their command of the playing field, becoming more and more baffled at their waning ability to throw their weight around any more, until finally they just, maybe, gave up the ghost and conceded their diminished reptile role to those miniscule, dust-lickin' mutated cousins who would later distill all that serpentine angst and alienation into a venomous infusion of death—inflictible on those new-kid-on-the-block mammals who were ruining the neighborhood. Equipped with the ugliest, hissingest triangulated head that God ever allowed on a breathin' creature, these slitherin' peabrains could nevertheless still proudly carry on, simply by opening their mouths, the dominance and intimidation of their ancestors. Speak of the devil......

"Watch out for the damn snake!" yelled Simon. He grabbed Robby by the collar as he was about to approach Mick's front door. The animal promptly stuck out his tongue and slithered back beneath the azaleas.

Simon stepped up to the door and knocked. He looked sideways at Robby with a strange grin. "Be careful, young man."

"Thanks," said Robby. "I'll try to do that." He looked around again, remembering the last time he was in this place—the night Rosa had moved out of this house. The place seemed quite different in the daytime, very attractive in spite of the snake,and it was indeed an impressive neighborhood.

Mick opened the front door and peered from his darkness, squinting. "What can I do for you Simon?"

The Brit immediately caught a whiff of the whiskey. "Have you got a few minutes, Mick? I'd like to talk to you."

"Why the hell did you bring him?" queried Mick, a little sloppily.

"Robby's going to help us find that gold we were talking about yesterday. Can we come in?"

"What's he got to do with it?" Mick looked steadily at Simon, having apparently no inclination to allow them into the house.

"He's got essential information,Mick."

"Ha!" said Mick, mockingly. "*I've* got the essential information. You know that."

"Maybe. Maybe not. That's what we need to find out. Let us in and we can figure this thing out."

I should have brought Simon with us. Mick stared at the Brit for half a minute. "Okay, you sumbitch. But you've got to come in the back door."

"Whatever, my boy." said Simon, exasperated but relieved.

Mick closed the front door with a little more force than necessary. The two visitors gingerly treaded the sidewalk over to the driveway and then to the back sidewalk. Robby noticed a little statue placed within the ornate foliage. It was a figure of a little black boy holding a cane pole over a seashell-shaped pool, about the size of a bathtub, but clogged with scum and fallen leaves.

They strolled around to the back, trying to be cool. Robby was wondering what Simon's strategy might be. When they reached the back door, it was open, except for the screen. Simon called to Mick within. "Mick."

"Come on in," came the reply from inside, as if from a a deep well. Simon and Robby walked into the kitchen. Mick was leaning against the counter by a refrigerator. The place was elegantly furnished, but dark. The smell was a little funky. Dishes were stacked in the sink. Robby could see that not much had changed since that unpleasant night, the last time he was here. "You want some coffee?" asked Mick.

"Sure," Simon said. He looked at Robby. "How 'bout you, Robby?"

"No thank you," Robby answered Simon's question, as if Simon were the host.

"This is Robby Davis, Dr. Theseus' assistant," Simon said.

Mick. pretending to prepare to make a pot of coffee, grabbed a plastic cup from the counter and tossed it into the sink. It clashed with the resident silverware alarmingly, as if the resultant clatter were Mick's unspoken protest of their presence.

Simon initiated his strategy of feigned cooperation. "You ought to go to the Theseus place with us and check it out. Maybe we can work together to find what we're looking for."

"Franz sent *me* the numbers, you know," said Mick, resentfully. He looked at Robby, as if suddenly realizing he shouldn't have mentioned such privileged information. He was spooning coffee into a paper filter.

"Precisely, my boy. Let's go see what the numbers lead us to," Simon said, a little too cheerily.

Mick was seeing through Simon's charade. Suddenly, his voice took on a bitter tone. "Don't give me that 'my boy' bullshit. I know you've been out there already. You decided to link up with Theseus without my help. You grabbed the numbers that we figured out and went with them."

Robby could see that two smooth operators were trying to bluff each other. *Wasn't it the other way around? Didn't Mick 'grab the numbers' and act independently on them?* But Robby didn't want to get involved.

Mick continued his tirade. "What the hell did you find when you got there, Simon? Did you find the gold?" Mick was full-blown mad now. His face, already reddened with the whiskey, puffed out more, and veins were protruding on his neck. He threw a spoon on the counter with a loud clatter.

Simon kept his eyes trained on the foolish young man's face. "Mick, where were you last night?"

For two seconds, Mick was totally still. He was facing the counter, with his back turned to his inquisitors. Then, with no warning whatsoever, he was all over Simon, flailing. Robby saw the flash of a silver object in his hand, like a spectre of something terrible. And Robby pounced immediately, instinctively, grabbing the drunken fool who had a knife in his hand. But Robby had no experience in such irrationality and the next thing he knew was an unholy pain in his back—an excruciating point of agony as the sharp edge of Mick's dirty kitchen knife slid across his spine and hip. Simon caught sight of the blade moving through thin air after its merciless swipe, With a sudden Herculean thrust of power he released himself from Mick's drunken grasp, retrieved the small revolver beneath his suit jacket and without hesitation shot Mick in the leg. Mick was immediately groveling on the floor. "Oh shit! Oh shit!" he protested, as he doubled up with pain. Robby had passed out on the floor. Blood was everywhere. Simon pulled out the cellphone and called 911.

hddq://theseusmed.loc

Rosa Cyprana went to the hospital to see the man she admired, who was in dire straits, not her ex-boyfriend. But when she arrived there, Robby had been whisked deep into the inner workings of medical emergency. Now surrounded by doctors, nurses, and God only knows who else, his capacity for self-directed ambulation hung suspended by a thin neuronal thread.

She didn't enter the emergency waiting area to see Mick's sister; nevertheless, Josephine was the first person she recognized. *No. You don't understand. I'm not here for your brother the loser. I'm here for the other guy—the guy Mick stabbed. I could have told you a long time ago that it would come to this—Mick's constant flirting with trouble. I should have told you. It's too late now. The deed is done. You should have known. You should have seen the signs.* Rosa turned her back on Josephine. *I'm not here to see you.*

"Rosa, I'm so sorry," said Mick's sister.

Leave me alone. Rosa whimpered. *You have no clue about what is happening here.* "Go away, Josephine."

William Theseus walked into the waiting room. He looked around, saw Rosa, and approached her. "Hello, Rosa. Robby has talked about you quite a lot lately."

"Dr. Theseus. . ."

Josephine, feeling suddenly very awkward, slinked away. "Excuse me," said she, and took a seat nearby.

"What do you know about this situation?" asked William.

"Robby has been stabbed in the back. His spinal cord may be severed."

"How did it happen?"

Rosa cried again. That was her only answer.

William touched her cheek. "I'm so sorry this has happened, Rosa. I know what good friends you have become." She turned away and sat down. He took the seat next to her. "I'm looking for Simon Lafraneer. You know him, don't you?" She nodded. "Have you seen him here?" She shook her head.

Then Simon walkd in. He walked to their seats, and squatted in front of them.

"What happened?"asked William.

Simon answered in a hushed voice. "We visited Mick at his house, to make an inquiry. He was a little drunk. We were in his kitchen, had just started talking. I asked him where he was last night, and the next thing I know he's all over me, daft, and with a knife in his hand. I figured I could handle him, but then Robby grabbed him from behind. Mick swung around like a madman, and then before I could do anything, Robby's on the floor and there's blood everywhere."

"Oh, God!" Rosa wailed. William put his arm on her shoulder.

"I didn't know what the hell would happen next, so I pulled out my small handgun and fixed Mick real quick so he couldn't do any more damage."

"You shot him?"

"Damn right I did. If you had been there—"

"It's okay. I'd have probably done the same thing."

"It was pathetic, to see him wallowing on that floor, and whining like a baby, while Robby just lay there."

"You called 911?"

"Yes, and I stuffed a dish towel under Robby's back to try and stop the bleeding."

"Thank you, Simon." said Rosa. She looked up at the two men.

"Oh, I'm the one who is thankful, my dear. If Robby hadn't intervened it might have been me on the floor." He looked across the room. "I've not been in a tight spot like that since the Falklands. I'm so sorry it has come to this."

"It's not over yet," said William.

"What are they doing to Robby now?" asked Rosa.

"I do believe, Rosa, they are trying to evaluate the damage to his spinal cord. That's what Ellen, the ER nurse, had told me when she called me about an hour ago," said William.

"Do you think it can be repaired?"

"It's too early to tell, Rosa." He squeezed the back of her neck affectionately, like a father would do. "Based on what Ellen said, the spinal cord has been injured. It could be severed, or just partly severed."

"If it's severed, what then?"

"Let's not speculate about it, young lady. We'll just have to wait for the doctor's diagnosis." William's professorial admonishment replaced the hopeful demeanor. "The situation is bad enough without adding ill-informed assessments." He had a sudden thought. "I've got to call his dad. Excuse me." He pulled out the cellphone and punched a number. "Hi, Linda.". . . "Don't know. We haven't heard anything yet. I need the number for Robby's parents. Can you get it for me? Sure." The doc repeated some numbers as he punched them into his phone. "Thank you. . . No. cancel that. . . . I'll let you know when . . .Bye." Dr. Theseus called the home of Noah and Becky Davis, Robby's parents in North Carolina. He stood up, walked out through the hall and into the cool evening. This would not be pleasant.

Rosa felt as if she were waking up from a bad dream, but then another bad dream awaited her. She looked at the Brit, whom she had not seen since the night she met him, the bizarre night at Louie's restaurant when a man shot the tiger in the church yard across the street. "Thank you for calling me."

"Robby had spoken of you quite fondly. I've seen this kind of thing before. The presence of a good woman can make a big difference in a situation like this."

"If only we could get to him," she worried.

"He's probably under the surgeion's knife now, unable to hear anything we could say to him."

"Unable to hear?"

"Anesthetized. Or at least I hope so." He smiled.

Rosa had no inclination to smile. "What were you guys doing?"

"We had to ask Mick some questions about—"

"About some stupid gold story, or crazy. . ." Rosa shook her head disdainfully. Her beautiful brown eyes rimmed with tears again. "It's just like Mick to get into some harebrained get-rich-quick scheme."

"He was a little drunk."

"No doubt, especially in the second half of the day. Were they arguing about something? These guys didn't even know each other until Robby helped me to move out. I never should have dragged him into this."

"You had nothing to do with what happened, young lady."

She looked into his eyes, searching for answers. "So, it's just a coincidence that Robby gets stabbed by my ex-boyfriend after he helped me move out of that house?"

"This was about money."

"What money? What the hell was going on that I didn't know about?"

"This started long before Mick got involved."

"It's gold, right?"

"That's right."

"Where was it? Where did it come from?"

Simon looked around the room innocently. There were enough players in this tangled web already. With one man on an operating table, possibly near death or paralysis, and another shot, it seemed risky to allow the woman whose favor was coveted by both men to enter into the fray. Simon had seen danger in the lives of people before, but he didn't like inviting it. "I cannot say, dear lady. You will have to get that report from your friend, Robby, when he wakes up."

A woman in green scrubs sauntered up to them. "Hi. I'm Ellen. You're here to see Robby Davis, right?"

"That's right," said Rosa, looking up anxiously at the tired nurse.

"Which of you is next of kin?"

"Is he all right?"she asked, in an urgent tone.

"He's going to make it."

"We are neither of us next of kin." said Simon.

"Where is Dr. Theseus?" Ellen asked.

"He stepped out for a few minutes. He's calling Robby's parents in North Carolina," answered Simon.

"Please tell him to come knock on that door when he gets back in."

"Sure, Ellen. But is that all you can tell us?" asked Rosa, persistently.

"Dr. Selig will tell you about it when Dr. Theseus comes in, okay?" The busy nurse was discreetly making her exit. "Just tell him to knock on that door. He's going to be okay." She faintly waved a farewell to signal that their conversation had ended for now, and disappeared behind the door.

Rosa had a despondent look on her face. "I never should have let Robby help me move stuff out of that house. I never should have exposed him to—"

"Young lady, if you want to assign blame here—it was *I* who never should have taken him to that God-forsaken house. Mick and I had been considering a business venture, and Robby got dragged into it because he offered to help Theseus, but I never should have taken him there. I should have kept the dispute between me and Mick."

"Simon, why did, why did you call me?"

"After it happened, and I had set the dishtowel under Robby's back to stop the bleeding, I saw the lump in his pocket that I thought must be a cellphone. I pulled it out. I had already called 911. I looked through the numbers he had programmed in there. Oh, and I had to slap Mick around a little to get him to shut up. He kept cursing me. In Robby's phone I saw 'Mom & Dad,' but decided against calling them right away, figuring it would be better to have some diagnosis from a doctor first. But when I saw your name, I remembered having met you that night at the diner, when that fellow killed the tiger."

"Oh yes, how could anyone forget such an odd thing as that?"

"Right, well, so I called you."

"That was the night I moved out of Mick's house. Robby brought his little truck and helped me. He was such a saint, hardly knew me at that time."

"Yes, well I daresay, Rosa, you have no problem recruiting help from men whenever you choose to accept it."

"Whatever, Simon. So you called me before you called Theseus?"

"I didn't call Dr. Theseus. I didn't. . .ah, you could say, I didn't want to be the bearer of bad news in this case. He's an important man around here, and I knew he would get news of this crime soon enough."

"Crime?"

"Absolutely, my dear. Probably attempted murder. He'll be doing time for this. You can be sure of that. You won't have to worry about him getting in your way for awhile."

Rosa's face assumed once again an expression of remorse. On the other side of the waiting room, Dr. Theseus came in. He rejoined them. "Any news?"

"The nurse would like to give you an update. She said you could knock on that door to summon her," Simon said.

Without hesitation, the doc went to the door and knocked. He peered through the glass, then settled back on his heels, rocking forward and back slightly as he waited. After a minute or so, Ellen came out, joined by the surgeon, a man of medium height, middle age, and longish grey hair combed back on his head. Brown eyes shone through wire-rimmed glasses.

Theseus knew him. "Dr. Selig, thank you for looking out for my assistant."

"Hello, Dr. Theseus. Robby has suffered serious injury, but we were able to get to him quickly enough to minimize the loss of blood. His condition is relatively stable now. We're working on getting blood out of the abdomen. The wound, right up against his spine at T-10, is a dirty one, so we're still working hard to avert infection, minimize the nerve damage in whatever way we can, and evaluate the condition of his spinal cord. He has suffered what appears to be a partial severing of the spinal card. I think that is a realistic assessment at this point. He is showing signs of nerve function in the left leg, even some movement. So that's good news."

"When can we see him?" asked Rosa, quietly.

Dr. Selig looked at her. "It'll be a while yet, possibly a couple of hours from now when we can get him up to ICU."

"Too early for a prognosis, Dr. Selig?" asked Willliam.

"I'm hoping we can call this one Brown-Sequard's syndrome—a hemisection of the spinal cord, and this would mean a long, slow recovery of some limited functions in the legs."

"And the bladder and bowel functions?" asked William.

"Too early to say anything about that. If we can get him into therapy in a week or so, we should see our way more clearly through that."

"He'll be confined to a wheel chair, doctor?"

"Ah, most likely yes, but maybe not 100%. Maybe 50% recovery of ambulatory function. Individual responses to this injury vary widely." He offered a gentle smile. "A lot of recovery in this type of injury—partial—is determined by the person—their resolve, personality. I just have to say it this way: There is hope for some recovery, but I can also tell you this: His use of legs will be very limited from now on."

"Neurons in the spinal cord don't regenerate," said William.

"That's correct, Dr. Theseus. As you know, nerve cells are tricky. Those axons will regenerate in some parts of the body, but not in others. Unfortunately, the spinal cord is not a bundle where regeneration takes place."

"There is some promising research going on though, Theo," added William.

"True, at UC-San Diego, there's some good work being done with gene therapy, but it's just in laboratory animals now. It will be a while yet before anything workable comes out. Maybe in ten or twenty years." He shrugged.

"What about prayer?" asked Rosa, timidly.

"That's a good place to start." He smiled broadly, and looked at William. "We doctors need all the help we can get. Isn't that right, Dr. Theseus?"

"So true." agreed William.

"Please excuse me. Dr. Batros is still working on our man. I've got another patient coming." He looked at the nurse. "Is there anything else I should cover at this point, Ellen?"

She looked at William, then at Rosa and Simon. "I should be with Robby as long as he is in the ER. We've still got a lot of work to do in there. You'll hear from me again in the next hour or so. ."

"Well, then," said Dr. Selig, extending his hand. "I'll move on to the next one. Dr. Theseus." He shook hands gingerly with Theseus, then disappeared behind the wide wooden door from which he had come.

Axons

21

"What he don't know won't hurt him," said Vinnie to his sidekick.

"He's not gonna like it." said Tony.

"How's he ever gonna know?" Vinnie posed the question rhetorically, laughing. He flipped the gold florin into the air, as if it were a nickel. "Heads I win, tails you lose." Vinnie lowered his arm so Tony could have a look at the flip. The dim figure of a man, ostensibly John the Baptist, was visible in bright gold on the back of his hand. "See, heads. I win."

"You win what?"

"I win the right to keep both of these coins." He stopped and looked out through the large glass at the River, with all the West Bank and the bridge lit up.

"No way! Give me my half, or I'll rat!"

"Chill out, ya little prick. I gotta hold these for safekeeping. You'd probably screw up and lose 'em, or give 'em to some girl just to impress her. These are not Mardi Gras doubloons. They're worth big bucks. When I can cut a deal on them, you'll get your share."

"Yeah, right," said Tony, cynically.

"I'm not shittin' ya, man. Hey, I'll take care of you."

"Mick's gonna find out, and be mad as hell."

"How's he gonna find out if you don't tell him? You just keep your mouth shut about this and it'll pay off big time when I find the right opportunity to leverage these little doubloons. Besides, you still have the C-note, not bad for a night's work, huh. Don't let it burn a hole in your pocket." Vinnie resumed his walking down the mall; Tony dutifully followed his mentor. When they arrived at *Snazzy's Java*, Vinnie greeted their buddy. "Wazzup, Johnny."

"Same old, same old. You?"

"Not much. You got any ideas?"

hddq://northcarolina.loc

Nine hundred miles away, Noah Davis entered the kitchen door of his home in Haywood County, North Carolina. He was later than usual returning from a semi-regular meeting of nearby friends. Something was wrong. He could sense that by the look on Becky's face. "What's the matter, honey?"

"Come in the living room and sit down," she said, then turned abruptly and walked into the other room, When Noah was seated in his favorite chair, she looked into his eyes and said, "Dr. Theseus just called, and he's got some bad news. Robby is in the hospital. He's been stabbed."

"Oh, God! What happened?"

"He said Robby and another man were at some fella's house to ask him some questions about some money. . ." Becky was whimpering.

"Some money? Some what?"

"Not money, no, gold. It was something to do with gold."

"And what happened?"

"The man they were talking to got mad and stabbed Robby."

"Stabbed?" Noah could hardly believe it. "What the hell?" Becky was sobbing loudly. "Where?" asked her husband. "Where did he get stabbed?"

"Dr. Theseus said he was stabbed in the back."

"Damn. This is going from bad to worse. Where, Becky? Where, in the back, was he stabbed?" She was crying. "Oh, give me the phone, woman. I'll call him. I should have known when he took off for that God-forsaken city. . ." Noah called Dr. Theseus' office, but received only voicemail options. It was now past 9 p.m.

"*Where* in the back was he stabbed? Come on and tell me. I've got to know."

She wiped away tears with a handkerchief. "It was in the lower back."

"Where was it in the lower back? Was it in the spine?"

"Yes, Noah, very near the spine."

"Is he going to be paralyzed because of the, uh, crime?"

"They don't know yet. It's too early to know that yet."

"Who's the doctor?"

"I don't know. Dr. Theseus was calling from the emergency room. He had just gotten there. He hadn't even talked to the doctor himself yet."

"That's it. We're going down there. Where's the address book? Get Theseus' cellphone number right now, and get some clothes packed so we can get out of here."

"Honey, it's past nine o'clock at night. We can't just go running off to Louisiana. How are we gonna get there?"

"We'll go to Asheville. If we can fly, we'll do that. If we can't, we'll drive."

"Noah! It's too late. We can go in the morning."

"I won't be sleeping tonight, dear. Put on the coffee."

"Which should I do then? Pack bags, or put the coffee pot on?"

"Get your stuff together. I'm gonna make a pot of coffee. We need to be on the road within half an hour."

hddq://theseusmed.loc

"This is your brain, " came the voice-over on the TV, accompanied by a picture of an egg. "This is your brain on drugs," said the voice, and the image became one of an egg being fried. The sound advice of the public-service television announcement droned on in the waiting room of the Emergency Room of the Theseus University Medical Center. Rosa sat alone, watching it without a thought in the world, her mind perfectly blank. Then the annoying canned laugh-track of some drudge sitcom barged into the room with obnoxiously contrived guffaws. "Oh, puh-leez." She got up, walked to the TV set, reached up to the channel button and changed it. Leonard Nimoy, with funny ears, was on the screen. *I think I can handle that.* Rosa returned to her seat after lowering the volume a few notches.

Back in the inner workings of the ER, Robby was still receiving treatment from doctors, nurses and technicians who were striving valiantly to get his insides cleaned up and his slitted parts put back together again. There was a lot going on behind the scenes:

This just in:

Rob Cerebrum took one look at an urgent feed coming off the wire just now. *I'm not believing this.* But after a second look, and confirmation codes accurately displayed on his screen, he could see it was the real thing, not a drill! He grabbed the microphone at his desk, wrapped his index around the "ON" button, and spoke clearly into the mesh:

"Attention. This is Rob Cerebrum. **Red Alert! Red Alert! Code Red! Code Red!** We are now experiencing a Stage 1 Trauma in Sector T-10. This is not a drill! We are now experiencing a Stage 1 Trauma in Sector T-10. Attention all Oligodendrocytes in the T-10 Sector. We have a breach in the spinal cord. I repeat. We **have** a breach in the spinal cord at T-10. All oligodendrocytes within protocol range of T-10 are ordered to immediately begin production and transfer of **Myelin to T-10 Sector.** All myelin-related proteins and lipids within protocol range of T-10 report immediately to your nearest oligodendrocyte for further instruction.

All bone and blood cells in T-10, you are now under lockdown. Assist in protection and fortification of traumatized neurons in your area. Trauma stage is extreme! Ischemia is critical! Oligodendrocytes, begin immediate construction of myelin sleeve to arrest breach in neurons and defend axons. All neuronal personnel in protocol range of T-10 should remain on your post assisting in fortification and reinforcement of damaged axons.

These orders are effective immediately, until amended by further announcement from central command. All Rob cells keep yourselves vigilant until this crisis is under control. Uphold our highest purpose at all times: One for All, and All for One.

This is Rob Cerebrum signing off. Next announcement in five minutes.

hddq://mickstrouble.sht

"Your goose is cooked." said Simon to Mick, who was now laid up in a hospital bed three floors above and south of the emergency room in Theseus University Medical Center.

"Will you get outta my face? I never asked you to come up here. You and that nerd were trespassing on my property. I have a right to defend myself in my own home. You'll have to talk to my lawyer."

"Who is your lawyer?"

"Jack Gallia."

"What's his number? I'll call him for you."

"What are you talking about? You're the guy that shot me."

"You're the guy that attempted to kill an innocent man for no good reason. You're going to have to cooperate, my friend. You don't have a legal leg to stand on. The sooner you get with the program, the better will be your chances of coming out of this with a minimal prison sentence."

"Shove it, Simon."

"You can start by telling us where you stashed that gold that you stole."

"I don't know what you're talking about. I'm calling the nurse."

"Afraid not, ole boy. I've got the call button right here."

Mick lunged for the call button module. "Shit!" He winced in pain.

"Listen, you spoiled twit! That gold was not yours. You stole it. Just because someone five thousand miles from here sent you some numbers in a horse's ass about treasure in a field doesn't award you ownership of the goods. That gold belongs to me and to Theseus University. The judge, whoever he turns out to be, will put you under the jail unless you start cooperating."

"Belongs to *you* and Theseus? Ha! You've got no claim on that gold. Shit! That hurts." Mick winced again. "Why'd you have to go and shoot me?"

"Why'd you have to go and jump the gun? going out there independently, with no permission from the landowner."

"I don't know what you're talking about."

A gentle knock was heard on the door. Mick's sister walked in with a bouquet of flowers. "Hello, Mick. How are you feeling?"

"Oh, for crisake, Josephine. Can you get this guy out of my room?"

The lovely young lady looked askance at Simon, who put on his best childlike innocence, and addressed her, "I assure you, miss, I mean no harm. I am here to help your brother."

"Help, my ass. This is the guy that shot me, Josephine!"

"After he had nearly killed a man who meant your brother no harm," came Simon's gentle rebuttal. Simon extended his hand and introduced himself. "I'm Simon Lafraneer, miss, and I'm terribly sorry that it has come to this. I came here to apologize to your brother, but he has been too irrational to receive my entreaties."

Josephine, attractive with long, curly brown hair and a tastefully stylish blue dress, inspected Simon with her intense blue eyes, hardly knowing what to think. She declined to accept Simon's hand. But knowing her brother, she looked patiently at him and asked, "Mickey, would you like to explain what has happened?"

"I'm not saying anything until he's outa here." Mick seemed, at last, calm, and somewhat resolute.

The woman looked at her brother carefully, and then at his uninvited guest. "Very well, then. Mr. Lafraneer, I must ask you to leave."

"As you wish," conceded the Brit. "We shall meet again." He made a slight bow in her direction and walked out of the room.

She laid her hand gently on his. The diamond on her ring finger sparkled, even in the antiseptically fluorescent light of the hospital room. "Mickey, what have you gotten yourself into?"

He started to whimper. "Shit!"

Pity had overtaken her expression. She waited.

"Where are mom and dad?"

"They're in Paris, remember? They left a week ago." She set the flowers on a table by the bed.

"I was watching that man down in the emergency room, Mickey. He was with Dr. Theseus. And Rosa was with them. Rosa! dear. Why was Rosa with them, and not up here with you?"

"It's a long story. She left me."

"Why?"

"She's just, damn, stubborn."

"Oh? I know who's stubborn, Mickey. And it's not Rosa."

"She never supported me in anything I wanted to do."

"I wonder why. What was it you wanted to do that she wouldn't support you in?"

"Never mind." He looked away, tears brimming.

After a while, she continued. "I would like to know if my information is correct." She paused. He said nothing. "Is the man you stabbed the same person who helped Rosa move out of your place last week?"

"Yes, that sonofabitch."

"Why did you stab him?"

"Oh, come on!"

"Don't get excited again. "What's his name?"

"It doesn't matter, Josephine. He's a loser."

"He's Dr. Theseus' assistant, Mickey. Now who's the loser?"

"He is. He's a geek."

"Let's look at it this way, Mickey. You've lost the girl. You've lost, from the looks of it, any claim to a legitimate reason for stabbing him. And not only that, but, in the last year or so, you've lost all your friends. Who's the loser, Mickey?"

"I have not lost all my friends."

"Excuse me, all your old friends. The only ones you have now are that bunch of drunks down in the Quarter."

"Don't start, Josephine." He shook his head, then winced with pain.

"You may be right about one thing, Mickey. He has lost one thing." She paused. He said nothing. "He's lost the use of his legs."

"No! Oh, God!"

"That's the best thing I've heard you say. You'd better be crying out to God."

A firm knock was heard on the door. Into the room stepped two police officers. One said, "Mick Basker?"

Mick said nothing. Josephine answered for him. "Yes, officer, this is Mick Basker."

"I have some questions for you."

hddq://callsandiego.loc

William Theseus was worn out. It had been two nights in a row that his day had just kept going, and going, until it had just gone right into the next 24-hour period. Now it was 12:30 Tuesday morning, and this task would be the last thing to do before he would fall into bed. It would be a phone call. Even more conveniently, it would be a call to California, where it was only 10:30. He heard the phone ringing.

"Hello."

"Hello, Eugene."

"Yes."

"William Theseus here."

"Theseus!"

"I hope I haven't wakened you."

"Not at all. I was just catching up on the latest issue of *Nature*. It's good to hear from you."

"What would it take to get you to come to New Orleans?"

"Whoa!" lol "You're talking to a man who lives in the best place on earth."

"Nah, too many people in southern California."

"You can't beat the weather here."

"If you weren't piping in all that water from Colorado or somewhere, the place would be a desert."

"That's probably true, William. but we manage."

"There's plenty of water here in New Orleans."

"And heat. That makes for a very special combination—hot and humid."

"Well, maybe not the most comfortable climate in the world, but, hey, I've been following your research on the Nogo protein, and I really want to get something going here to contribute to the effort. Wouldn't you like to blaze a trail for me?"

"Well, it's like I said, it's hard to beat southern California, and that applies professionally as well as climatically. The department here is absolutely top of the line."

"And that's what we need to do here at Theseus," said William. "Whatever your package is there—I'll add 20% for you to come here and update our department from the ground up."

"That's very generous of you, William. I've been here for ten years now. The kids are in school here."

"Really. Where is Myron?"

"He's at Caltech."

"Good. Chip off the old block. How about Emily?"

"She's a senior in high school here, at Coronado."

"That's wonderful, Eugene." Then William blurted, awkwardly, "I knew this would probably be a shot in the dark. I've got a situation here. . ."

"What's that, William?"

"My assistant, Robby Davis, was the victim, today, of a spinal cord injury, a, I think, he's gotten a partial severing of the spinal cord."

"I'm sorry to hear that, William. That's exactly what we're working on—"

"Yes, I know."

"But in rats. It's still in the laboratory stage. But I think they've initiated some of these procedures in humans at Ligand University."

"I've read about those too. But, uh, with this accident today—or whatever it was—it brings it all very close to home, you know."

"I can imagine. But it's going to take time. You know that." Eugene paused, waiting for a response, but William said nothing. "We've cultured rat skin cells and genetically modified them to produce neurotrophin-three, growth factor."

"Yes."

"When we grafted the modified cells back into the animals, at the injury sites, they have apparently generated axon growth and renewed some walking ability among the animals."

"That's good news."

"Sure, but it's rats." He laughed. You know how this works. It will be a long time before—"

"I understand."

"There's a real trick to solving this myelin problem. Myelin seems to work squarely against neuron fiber regeneration, while on the other hand its loss diminishes nerve transmission signals. So it's 'damned if you do, and damned if you don't retain it. The myelin sheath does its job so well in insulating the axon, that nothing can get past it to regenerate fiber when the nerve has been damaged."

"I guess I'm grasping at straws here. It would be great to have some serious work on this going on here."

"Sure, William. I can. . . I can recommend someone."

"Oh, good. Who is it?"

"Walter Kuralt. He's assisting Stretmayer at Ligand University. They've identified the receptor that mediates the Nogo-66 protein, which has been shown to block axon regeneration after central nervous system injury. They're investigating pharmacological solutions. "

"I see."

"They may be onto something. There's a lot of research going on with this. In Sweden, they're finding that adult stem cells may differentiate themselves into various cell types, according to the cell environment in which they're placed."

"They can switch identities?"

"Possibly. This potential was thought, until recently, to be attributable only to embryonic stem cells."

"So maybe it's possible that neural stem cells in the spinal cord could be assisted in regenerating damaged exons?"

"Could be, if they can overcome the inhibiting effects of the myelin sheath, the Nogo protein, the netrin protein, and whatever other emergency structures the CNS is throwing up in response to trauma. The stem cells, sadly, seem to flee the scene of the accident, and must be convinced to return and render their special services. These researchers are looking for ways to coax them back to the scene of the crime so they'll do their regenerative magic."

"Well, Eugene, do think the answers will be found in pharmaceuticals or stem cells?"

"Whoever gets there first will find use for both, I'm sure. We're working on the pharmacology end of it, although in the long run the stem cells will do the work for us if we can figure out how to control their differentiation. I suspect the stem cells will play a role in virtually every area of regenerative medicine in the future. They enable us to customize each patient's treatment to minimize, or even eliminate, immunological rejections."

"Right,

"But hey, like I said, it's going to be awhile, either way, before they can do anything for your boy there."

"I understand. Who is it you recommend to me?"

"Walter Kuralt, at Ligand. He worked with us for awhile as postdoc, before joining Steltmeyer's team. But I know he's a pioneering kind of guy. If I can think of any capable researcher who might be interested in what you have there at Theseus, Walt would be your man."

"I appreciate it, Eugene. I know it's getting late."

"Thanks for thinking of me, William. I'll send you more about this tomorrow, and I'll include Walter's contact info, too."

"Thanks."

"William, I wish I could offer you more than that, but right now I'm right in the middle of where I'm supposed to be."

"I understand, Eugene."

"'It's your assistant, right? who has been injured?"

"Yes."

"What happened?"

"It's a long story. I won't trouble you with it, but he was stabbed."

"And the spinal cord was severed?"

"We think it's only partially severed."

"That' would be, ah, Brown-Sequard's syndrome, then?"

"Yes. That's what the surgeon called it."

"William, I can't imagine what he must be going through right now, or what you must be thinking and feeling. Your phone call seems a little desperate."

"I guess I'm grasping at straws. I probably knew what your response would be."

"Whatever it is that our research has to offer, I can tell you, is *years* away. There's some earthshaking work going on at Yale, and a few other places. They're closer than we are to clinical experiments. But we've got a long way to go. What's his name?"

"Uh, Robby. Robby Davis."

"I'll be praying for Robby Davis,

"Really?"

"William. It sounds like a cliché, I know, But you know me. We started out together on this biological quest. I've been watching cells and molecules for almost thirty years now, Let me tell you something, William. I'm convinced that deep inside the neurons and the axons, wrapped around the cords and the capillaries of flesh and blood, a divine design governs all that happens there, and everywhere else, for that matter. I've stood back, at times, in awesome wonder at the intricacy, the elaborate complexity— sometimes even the miraculous *simplicity* of this mystery we call life—all of it spiraling within two helices that surround virtually infinite permutations of four—only four—nucleotides."

William had nothing that he could say.

"So when I say, William, that I will pray for your Robby friend, I am not speaking lightly, or tritely. If I could, I'd go into the lab right now and whip up a biological cocktail to coax those axons into regenerating. But I can't. Right now, no scientist or doctor on this earth can do that. One day, we will. But I can do this, William. I can appeal to the great physician—the one who wrote the code and signed the book. That is all I can offer you."

"That's a lot," said William, through tears.

Agonies

22

Tearing across our stubborn sinew, and through our fragile skin, death stalks us each and every one, the enemy within. Surely it will slit our silver cord, but not too soon.

Rosa, seated in the arboretum with morning sunlight that dappled the green canopy of life around her, watched a spider lower itself from a tree limb. It landed on a camellia bloom. In all the wide, wild world, her position was unique. There were not many women in this life whose choice of men demonstrated such blatant extremities. There were not many who would ever find themselves stretched between such disparate poles of men. For the one she harbored such loathing—how could she have clung for so long to his aimless, drunken ways? For the other she carried a precious fascination, like a newly-opened flower in morning drops of dew.

A bumblebee crawled backwards from a nodding fuchsia bloom, nimbly stepping across dark petal-speckles that had lured him into some nectar paradise. He buzzed away in his lazy bumblebee way.

She was thinking about the new thread of life that had been spun out before her, as she had entered into Robby's web of wonder and belief. His universe was so very fragrant with possibility, compared to the raucous sensuality and senseless risk upon which Mick had strung out his chaotic existence.

"Hello, Rosa."

She turned to see behind and to her left, the person whose familiar voice disturbed her unexpected serenity. Approaching upon the bricky path was Mick's sister, Josephine. Rosa had often wondered how such a fine example of womanhood had been blood-linked to the reprobate that Mick had become. "Mind if I join you?"

Rosa slid to her left, as a welcoming gesture, but said not a word. Josephine took the other half of the park bench. Between them was a sweetly awkward silence. A bird was twittering.

After a few moments of quiet repose, so incongruent to the tumult of their disrupted lives, Josephine asked, "Would you care to tell me what happened between you and Mick?"

Rosa shivered. "I should be in class right now. Instead, I'm sitting here wondering what it is I'm supposed to do."

Josephine, who had perched herself, now leaned back into the bench, relaxed. She studied Rosa's face patiently, and sighed, as if that released breath might signal her compassion. "I knew it would come to this—I mean—not this stabbing thing, but, I knew Mick would blow his chance at loving you, unless he could change. . ."

Rosa noticed a sparkle of sunlight in Josephine's diamond ring. "It's unfortunate that whatever you got from the Basker line wasn't passed along to him."

Josephine risked a little smile. "He might pick up on it someday. That's been my hope all along. I had thought that you might contribute to his turning around. You're the first 'good girl' he's ever had."

"If I was good, I'm not now," bemoaned Rosa.

"Oh, it's not as bad as that, Rosa."

"I'm starting to see now why mama told me to wait for a good man."

"I'm so sorry that—"

"Now I've found one—oh, goddam Mick!" Rage suddenly stuck her.

Josephine dared not say anything.

The outburst dwindled to a whimper. "How could this have happened?" She looked askance at the innocent sister. "How in the hell could such a thing as this happen, Josephine?"

Josephine had no words. She only gazed piteously at the girl whose presence she had thought to be her brother's deliverance. She could offer no excuses for her brother or the tragic consequences of his careless life.

"I'm going to shave my head," announced Rosa.

Josephine, startled, felt she would at least comment upon such outlandish reaction. "What would that accomplish, Rosa?"

"I just hate the way things have turned out. I can see no. . .there is no joy for me now. I'll make myself into something that no man would want."

Only her muffled sobs and birds above could be heard.

"Robby was going along just fine in life. He was doing everything right. Right hand to Dr. Theseus, everything going for him—until he agreed to bail *me!*" She was overcome with despair. ". . .out of the pit of Mick's life that I had jumped into, like a damned fool!"

"It's not your fault." Josephine thought her objection sounded so lame in the face of Rosa's raging self-condemnation. She dared not expound.

"How could I have ever let myself be sucked into Mick's bullshitting life! Now a decent man comes along, and Mick has screwed *his* life up beyond repair. I just can't believe this has happened. I feel like going to the River and jumping off the bridge."

Rosa's cellphone rang. "I'm not going to answer that. There's no sense in finding out more about how messed up this can get." The device persisted in its merry little ring tone until it had gone to voicemail. "Oh, what the hell. . ." She flipped it open. "What?". . . "Yes, I'm afraid so." . . . "Whatever". . ."Dr. Theseus?" . . ."Sure. I don't care." . . ." at the arboretum, between the hospital and campus." . . ."Yeah. I'm not going anywhere." . . ."behind the little plaza near the Jefferson statue." She snapped it shut.

Josephine waited a few moments. But with Rosa apparently not inclined to divulge, she finally asked, "Who was that?"

"Some friend of Dr. Theseus. Olivia somethinorother. She's coming over here to talk to me."

"Do you mind if I hang out for a bit?" asked Josephine, thinking of Rosa's precarious reference to the River bridge.

"No. We'll, uh, we'll have a party. That's what Mick would do if he were here."

Rosa's sarcasm suddenly cut into Josephine's sensibility like a knife. A pang of empathy for the errant brother pierced her, as if Rosa's tirade against him should be somehow put to an end, with its excess of bitterness disqualifying any further justification. "Will you ever be able to lighten up on Mick?" she protested.

Rosa just looked at her like *'who are you?'*.

The two women sat in the warm Louisiana morning for what seemed a long time. The birds chirped and whistled their inappropriate celebration of life in the trees overhead. A pleasant breeze stirred upon the cool front that had followed Sunday's rain and the clouding events of fateful Monday. Tuesday's morning was conspiring with birds and sunshine to break the stubborn back of Rosa's oppressive wrath. In spite of all that God's jubilant earth could summon to soothe her, Rosa would not relent. Her disastrous circumstance was, after all, without precedent. It had never happened in the history of the world that one frail woman would find herself caught between two men of such opposable temperaments, who had struggled for one fateful instant to the perilous point of one's near-death and near-paralysis at the cruel hand of the other. It had never happened before, or at least not quite in this way, with the gold, like the woman, caught in the middle between them.

Ophelia, in all her Scottish native-American glory, walked up to them. She extended her hand to Rosa. "Hello. I'm Ophelia Doss." Rosa did not respond in kind. She was insistent that her misery would prevail. But who could blame her? Such a thing as this had never happened before until now.

Josephine, sister of the villain who had inflicted the dire madness upon their sensitive lives, offered her hand to Ophelia instead. "Hi, Ophelia. I'm Josephine Jumonville. Thank you for dropping in."

Ophelia smiled appreciatively. Then she addressed the younger woman. "Dr. Theseus and Robby sent me out here to talk to you."

Rosa's eyes flashed; her head pivoted to catch a better look at the newcomer. "Robby? Is he conscious?"

"Uh, excuse me. Let me rephrase that. Dr. Theseus has sent me, *on behalf of* Robby."

Rosa's wisp of indignation wilted. "So he's still in a coma?"

"He's not in a coma, my dear. He's simply been under the knife a little bit. They had to anesthetize him."

"Have they sewed him back up yet?"

"I don't know what they've done, except that they've done all that they can do to get him cleaned up, the blood out of his gut, and suspend any further damage to his body. Actually, no. They have not sewn him up. The nurse said it's a 'dirty wound.' They can't sew him up until they've dealt sufficiently with the infection, or the potential for infection. The knife was a kitchen knife, you know. It had been in the sink."

"Oh, God!" Rosa's refusal reverted to sobbing.

"Maybe you should spare us the details at this point," said Josephine.

Having never married, Ophelia had not been inoculated against the tactless and crude tendencies of men toward bluntness. Consequently, she had taken some of those characteristics to herself. Not one to mince words, she saw herself *Ghighua*, in the tradition of Nan'yehi. The tragic results of human violence must be assuaged by a skillful blending of truth, provocation, and diplomacy. "I did come here with a specific purpose, you know, Rosa." She was on a mission.

"And what might that be, Olivia?"

"Ophelia, Rosa. I'm here to enlighten you of the events that lead up to this confrontation between your two friends."

Rosa rolled her disgruntled eyes. Ophelia continued. "These guys were not fighting about you. Mick stabbed Robby because he thought that Robby had come to take the gold away."

"Gold." That was an alien concept in this universe of misery. A little green chameleon lizard appeared suddenly on the bench between Rosa and Josephine. Rosa looked down at it. She had grown up with them. They were everywhere in Florida and south Louisiana and everywhere in between. She reached down to pet the reptile, but it promptly scampered away. "Gold? What are you talking about?"

"There was a stash of gold coins buried on university propery—the old Theseus plantation. This Simon fellow, the British guy, had figured out where the gold was, and was trying to get Theseus to let him search for it. But Mick got to it first. Or at least, we *think* Mick got to it first. Somebody stole the gold Sunday night, and all indications are that it was Mick."

"What evidence do you have that it was Mick?" asked Josephine.

"I don't know all the details. You can hear more about it from Theseus, and from the British guy. He kind of put this whole thing together."

"So you don't know what Mick has to do with it?" Josephine asked.

"Mick had some information about the location, that he had gotten from some guy in Germany," answered Ophelia.

"That doesn't surprise me," murmured Josephine.

"What do you mean?" Ophelia asked.

"Mick always has some wacky deals going with people all over the place, all over the world I guess," Josephine answered.

The chameleon skittered out from somewhere behind Rosa, traipsed across her lap, as if her jeans were its personal romping territory . She lowered her hand to the curious creature, expecting that it might crawl onto her finger. But it ran away. "If Mick took that gold," said she, "I bet I know where it is." She did not look up. She was expecting that the lizard might return.

Ophelia looked intently at Rosa's face, which, at last, was portraying no emotion. It was a picture of Medusic stone. Josephine studied the same face, with sudden misgivings about what might be in the offing.

Ophelia penetrated their stunned silence. "Where?"

"Uh, at his house," said the young woman. Her head went up; her eyes met Ophelia's, still without expression.

Ophelia, seasoned by her exposure to Cherokee resolve, wasted no time in her suggestion. "Let's go see."

"Let's go see," agreed Rosa.

Josephine did not know how to interpret Rosa's newfound motivation. "The house is a crime scene, you know," she said. "The police may not let us in."

Rosa looked steadily at Josephine. "It's your house, too."

"My parents' house."

"How's that?" asked Ophelia.

"Josephine is Mick's sister," volunteered Rosa, with a sly tone.

"I see," said the *Ghigua*.

"So, the police may have the place taped off," said Josephine.

"True," agreed Ophelia. "But most likely just the kitchen. That's where the stabbing took place. Anyway, it's your house, too, right? They won't prevent you from entering your own family's house., especially if we can lead them to evidence pertaining to the crime."

"I suppose you're right." agreed Josephine, a little unsurely.

"Let's go this way," said Ophelia, gesturing toward the nearby parking lot. "Dr. Theseus has lent me his BMW."

"Oh, we can take mine," said Josephine. "You can leave his car in case he needs it."

"Okay. Let's get this show on the road, girls," said Ophelia.

They trod the path of sylvan bliss, through the arboretum, with birds serenading and blue sky overhead between the green canopy. It seemed strange to suddenly have found direction in the midst of this odd turn of events. "I love the bougainvillea," said Ophelia, touching one the blossomed vines. "Look at the mimosa," added Josephine.

When they arrived at Josephine's black, like-new Mercedes, Ophelia took the back seat, Rosa the front. When they had gone a few blocks to St. Charles Avenue, Ophelia reached across the console into the front seat area between the driver and passenger. "Have you ever seen one of these?" she asked, and opened her hand to reveal a shiny gold florin that lay on her palm like an apparition.

Rosa looked at the coin, still without expression. Josephine did a doubletake, touching the brakes a little more zealously than required. "What is that?" Her eyes were darting between the coin and the street as she steered the pristine auto.

"It's a gold florin," said Ophelia. "It's what started this whole, sad string of events. You see, Rosa, the altercation between Robby and Mick did not happen because of you. It happened because of this."

They were stopped at a light. "May I see that?" asked Josephine.

"Sure." Ophelia offered the rare coin to her. Josephine took it, rubbed her perfect hand across its smooth surface.

"This looks very old. How old is it?"

"Only five hundred and eight years old," said Ophelia. "These little pieces of metal are what get men into big trouble," she continued. "These little doubloons are why we're riding along this street in New Orleans now instead of Florence or Castille. They're the reason that Columbus and Cortez and all those other explorers came here. They were looking for gold. And when they found it, they'd go to any extreme to get it, then ship it back home where the kings and queens of Europe would have it minted into coins like this."

"Amazing," remarked Josephine.

"And everywhere that gold is found, trouble follows. This is not the first time that blood was shed over gold. Men will do anything to get it, even stab each other in the back.."

"Would you shut up, now?" protested Rosa.

"Pardon me, dear. I know this must be very hard for you. Please forgive me."

After a minute or so, Josephine asked, "How many of those do you think there are in this, uh, deposit?"

"Maybe as many as two hundred."

"How do you know? How did you get involved in this?"

"I've got a bunch of them myself. Or, my school does—Bellel College."

"You teach at Bellel?"

"Yes, I run the anthropology department there."

Josephine handed the coin back to Ophelia, and steered the Mercedes into the Basker driveway. Sure enough, a police car was parked there. The three women got out and walked to the back door, where they were greeted by a policeman. "Good morning, ladies. What can I do for you?"

"Good morning, officer. I'm Josephine Basker Jumonville. I grew up in this house. I'd like to come in."

"You're Mick's sister, then, Mrs. Jumonville?"

"That's right."

"I'll have to ask you to go around to the front door, and please do not enter the kitchen. This is a crime scene, you know. We're still gathering evidence." He pointed to the yellow tape stretched between the back porch columns.

"Of course. What is your name, sir?"

"I'm Lieutenant Pete Vespri. And please excuse me, ma'am. I do need to see your identification."

She pulled out a driver license, then watched the cop's young face as he confirmed her name. "Evidence, huh? So this is not a cut-and-dried case?"

"I can't say, Mrs. Jumonville. This was, however, the scene of a possible attempted murder. So we need to follow procedures strictly."

"I see. Well, thank you." She started to walk around the house.

"Your guests—who are these ladies with you?" He pulled a pen and pad from his shirt pocket. I need to make a record of all visitors until this phase of the investigation is closed."

"Certainly, Lietenant Vestri. This is—"

"Ophelia Doss, from Asheville, North Carolina." She displayed her driver license.

"Thank you, ma'am," said he, writing her name and address. "And you, miss?"

"Rosa Cyprana," said the young woman. *Her laconic attitude is hard to read,* thought Josephine. *I wonder what she's up to. I hope she's not going to get vindictive about this.*

"Thank you, Miss Cyprana," he said, closing the pad. "If you ladies see anything that should be brought to our attention, please call me. I'm just here in the kitchen dusting for fingerprints and such."

They started again to walk to the front. "Oh, Miss Cyprana, you were also a resident of this house. Is that correct?"

"Yes, sir. I moved out a week and a half ago."

"Well, I'm glad you're here. I'll need to ask you to wait just a minute while I get your fingerprints."

"Uh, sure, whatever." She did not appear pleased at the prospect. Rosa had moved from anger to despair to a kind of numb acceptance in the last hour. The next stage of her ordeal seemed to indicate humiliation. She had never been fingerprinted before. The thought of it made her feel like a suspect.

Ophelia, seeming to read her mind, commented, "It's okay, Rosa. It doesn't mean you're culpable. Since you lived here, your fingerprints are all over that kitchen. They need a record of yours so they can tell them from anybody else's."

The policeman stepped into the house, then returned with his paraphenalia and obtained Rosa's fingerprints as they leaned over the hood of his car. The other two women watched. "Are you women looking for anything in particular?"

"Uh, not really, what do you mean?" said Ophelia, a little too brusquely.

He looked at her carefully. She smiled.

"In the house, that is," said the cop, pleasantly. " Is there something in particular that you're looking for in the house?" he asked. He seemed curious, but very relaxed.

"No sir," Josephine volunteered. "I just want to make sure nothing has been stolen, and I, I'd like to gather a few old things from my room. It's the room I had growing up."

He surveyed Josephine's face and smiled. "It's a very attractive home—a great place to grow up, I should think." He was working steadily on Rosa's hands.

"Yes, sir." agreed Josephine.

"Garden district." he observed.

"Yes, we've been very fortunate."

"I'm from Algiers," said the officer.

"That's nice. Our, uh, our maid was from there."

He was a very polite police officer. Looking at Ophelia, he asked, "What brought you down to N'awlins from up there in the mountains. Ms. Doss?"

"I'm visiting Dr. William Theseus. He's an old friend of mine. We went to college together."

"Oh, where was that?"

"Bowling Green University, in Ohio."

"Right. That's a beautiful necklace there. It's, ah, Cherokee?"

"Yes, sir. Thank you for noticing. I do a lot of work with the Cherokee people."

"Good. That should do it, Miss Cyprana. Thank you." He looked at Ophelia again. "North Carolina, huh? I understand that the victim here was a native of that state. Did you know him?"

"Oh, no, no sir. I only just met him a couple of days ago."

"Sunday? Did you meet him Sunday?"

"Yes."

"And then he was stabbed here, yesterday evening."

"That's what we have been told, yes," said Ophelia.

"Do you have any clue why such a thing would happen?" he asked.

"Oh, God only knows, officer. The things that men do to one another—it's, it's tragic," answered Ophelia.

The cop looked at Rosa. Noticing her forlorn countenance, he asked her, "You left this house a week and a half ago. Do you have any thoughts about why Mick Basker might have stabbed Dr. Theseus' assistant?"

Rosa commenced to weeping. She had no answer. Ophelia took her elbow gently and began leading her away. "It's a sad situation, officer. This has been very hard for Rosa. We really need to go now, and, ah, do what we came to do."

"Thank you, Rosa, for your cooperation. And thank you, ladies."

At last they walked around the house to the front door. Josephine opened it with her key, and they entered the house. Ophelia shut the door behind them, making mental note of the poster with a two-headed dog that hung there. *Beer posters, even stranger than their SuperBowl commercials,* she thought.

"Where are we going?" asked Josephine.

"Upstairs, to Mick's old room," answered Rosa.

Josephine led the way. She passed the room that had been hers, paused briefly with her head in the door taking quick inventory. *Nothing amiss there.*

The room at the end of the hall was a large one, although it was cramped with Mick's accumulation of stuff. They entered. The ceilings sloped into a short wall about four feet high on both sides, with a dormer window in the middle of the room on both sides. Walls and ceilings were covered almost entirely with posters of old football stars—New Orleans Saints, Green Bay Packers, and race car drivers—Richard Petty, Mario Andretti. The floor was dusty, and strewn with cardboard boxes in various states of unpacking, as if Mick had visited them occasionally, rummaging for some valued object or another. The bed was piled up with junk, mostly old baseball and football trophies, and plastic model cars—Corvettes and Grand Ams. A thick collection of Mardi Gras beads was draped across each bedpost. Mardi Gras doubloons, gold like florins and silver like dollars, filled two glass mugs on each night table. At the far end of the room was an old roll-top desk with the roll up, revealing a plentiful collection of papers, pencils, pens, Hardy Boys books, ceramic mugs from Germany and Texas.

Rosa walked to the desk. "We need to move this. There are two loose floorboards underneath it. If Mick has the gold, this is where he would have put it."

"I never knew about this," said Josephine, amused at her brother's clandestine strategy.

The three women tugged at the large desk until they had slid it across the floor a few feet beyond the suspect spot. With the floor clear, they were ready to pull up the two floor boards in question. But Rosa stood pointing. She had no intention of penetrating Mick's secret spot. Ophelia crouched, then set one knee on the floor and felt the floor. After a short minute of groping, she inserted two fingernails beneath a board edge. Lifting the wood slightly, she then grabbed, with her left hand, a credit card that happened to be on the floor nearby, and using it to pry, removed a narrow board and set it aside. Then she grabbed another one, and another one, lifted each one and set it aside. Reaching down into the floor cavity, she withdrew a gray metal box. It was very heavy for its size. She set the metal box down. It had an internal lock, which would require a key.

"What do we do now?" asked Josephine.

"Do you have any idea, Rosa, where the key might be?" Ophelia voiced the obvious question that was on everyone's mind. "I mean, you've brought us this far. Think hard. Where would Mick have put it?"

Rosa shrugged. She wasn't into this. "Let's go back to the hospital and see how Robby's doing," she said, sleepily. She sat on the edge of the bed.

"As far as that goes, we could go to the hospital and ask Mick for the key," said Josephine.

"Can I have that for a second?" asked Ophelia.

Josephine, down on her knees, lifted the box with some difficulty, handed it carefully to the older women. "Be careful. It's heavy. It certainly *feels* like gold." She laughed at the idea that she might know what gold inside a metal box would feel like.

Ophelia chuckled as she took the locked box. She shook it. "It *sounds* like gold." They both laughed, amused at the jangly-shuffly noise inside the box as Ophelia, eyes wide open with expectation, moved the mysterious container back and forth. *Could this really be 200 gold florins?* She felt giddy at the thought of what she might be holding.

But Josephine was wondering. "Ophelia, whose gold is this anyway?"

"Ha." She rattled the box one more time, then set it on the desk. "The owner is dead. That was Plato Zupoff, who buried it on the Theseus plantation site in 1927 after the riverboat he was a passenger on wrecked. As to the question of who might the *present* legal owner be, that's a can of worms."

"Let me just ask you this: Does my brother Mick have any claim on this gold?" she asked, standing up and dusting off her bare knees.

Ophelia's lol. "Mick might be, oh, tenth or eleventh on the list of possible claimants for this prize. Let me explain it to you. For starters, when the owner, Plato Zupoff left the gold on Theseus property, it was not actually Theseus property at the time, but was owned by a sharecropper, Washington Jones, who worked for Beauregard Theseus. So that's the first little worm in this can. Did Plato forfeit his right to the gold by leaving it? If he did forfeit , who would the owner be—the sharecropping landowner at that time (1927) or the Theseus heirs? Their family later purchased the land back from Jones' heirs.

"Let's go back to the hospital," complained Rosa.

"Just hold on a minute, honey. We've got to get a strategy here before we do anything," said Ophelia.

"It's not even your gold." objected Rosa.

"You're right there, Rosa. I've already got my share of it in North Carolina, but that's another story."

"*Your* share?" asked Josehpine, somewhat indignantly.

"Uh, some of this was given to Bellel University. I'll explain that later."

Rosa lay back on the bed and sighed, resigned to her role as a passive participant. "Wake me up when you're done."

"Listen up, gal. We need your input here. You're right in the middle of all of this."

"Tell me about it," responded Rosa, with disdain.

"Anyway, there's the question of whether Plato forfeited his ownership by abandoning the gold. He must have been crazy to leave such a fortune in the ground and never come back to recover it. But if he didn't forfeit it, then the question becomes, which of his heirs is the rightful owner?"

"Is Mick one of the heirs?" interrupted Josephine, even though she had never heard the name Zupoff mentioned in her exquisitely documented Anglo-Frankish family lineage.

"No. But Robby Davis is Plato Zupoff's great grandson. Alice Pack, my student at Bellel, is a great grand*daughter* of Plato; and Simon Lafraneer, the man who shot Mick, is Plato's great-nephew.

"That guy—the British guy—he certainly wouldn't have the claim that direct descendents would have," Josephine speculated.

"I suppose not, but he's the one who is responsible for figuring all this out. If it weren't for him, we wouldn't have a box of gold sitting here right now. It would still be out in the mud somewhere."

"If it is gold," Josephine wondered aloud.

Ophelia picked the box up again and shook it. "Does that sound like gold to you?" They chuckled again.

"This is crazy," Josephine remarked.

"It's not crazy, Josephine. It's horrible. Robby being probably paralyzed for the rest of his life is what's crazy." Rosa's bitterness had an edge sharper than a knife.

"I'm so sorry, Rosa." Josephine reached over to Rosa's face and tenderly stroked her hair back. She saw the ubiquitous tears. Thinking to herself about her brother as well as Robby, she suggested, "Maybe it is time we went back to the hospital to see what the prognosis it."

"Who wants to carry this?" asked Ophelia, pointing at the box.

"We can't take that," said Josephine. It was almost a question.

"Why not?"

"It's, it's Mick's box," objected Josephine.

"Sure, honey, but the gold inside it is not Mick's. He stole it."

"We don't *know* what's inside it, remember? It could be Mardi Gras doubloons."

"Ha! Not likely." Ophelia pointed at the two glass mugs full of cheap doubloons. "There's where he keeps the doubloons. Besides, if this box were full of Mardi Gras doubloons, it wouldn't even weigh half this much. Doubloons are made of aluminum, you know. A New Orleans girl like you knows that. No, Josephine, these are not doubloons. There is some serious money in here." She shook the box, exaggerating the strain in her expression and movement to emphasize the point.

"They might be just, his collection of foreign coins."

"True. I tell you what, Josephine. Let's take this box to Mick and ask him what's in it. In fact, we'll ask him to open it."

Josephine was a little dumbfounded at the thought of this. "Whoa, wait a minute. Let me think about this."

"Come on, Josie! Mick's got nothing to lose by answering questions about this box. It may even be evidence of his innocence."

Josephine was thinking hard about it. She wanted to see her brother exonerated, or proven guilty, one way or the other. Confronting him with the box might be an opportunity to force the issue. "Yeah, okay," she said, resignedly.

"Do you want to carry it out, or shall I?" asked Ophelia.

"Go ahead. Knock yourself out. I've got an oversized handbag in my room that will make it easier for you to carry."

"That's a good idea, Josephine."

Ophelia took the locked box. Josephine reached down to Rosa. "Come on, dear. Let's go see how your boy is doing."

If she's thinking that Mick is "my boy," she's sadly mistaken. Rosa allowed herself to be pulled up from the bed, but uttered no appreciation.

Josephine stepped quickly into her old room, took a minute to rummage through the closet, and came out with a "carpet" bag. "This is what the carpetbaggers used to carry their money in when they came down from up north after the war," said Josephine.

"Really?" asked Ophelia.

"Not really," said Josephine, chuckling. "But it looks like what a carpetbagger would have carried, don't you think?"

"Yeah," agreed Ophelia, going along with the joke. " It looks real, uh, nineteenth-century."

"And it *will* do for carrying a bunch of gold!"

"Yeah. It ought to hold it all right." Their amazement at this unprecedented situation was again turning to giddiness.

As they walked down the stairs, Josephine whispered to Ophelia, "Let's ask the cop to open it. He probably knows some trick to get the lock open."

"If he's a New Orleans cop, he does," cracked Rosa.

"Ha! The dead do speak!" said Ophelia.

"Watch out," said Rosa. "I'm not in the mood for this. Let's just get back to the hospital as soon as possible. Please."

"We're right on it."

Then they were out the front door, Ophelia carrying the carpetbag and its presumed-precious cargo as if it were a baby bag, Rosa trailing listlessly, and Josephine plopping in the driver's seat of her flashy Mercedes as she waved to the cop. "Good bye, Lietenant Vestri! Thank you. God bless you."

Mosaics

23

"Yeah, sure I'll open the damn box," said Mick. He had calmed down considerably, with the help of a little valium. He looked at Josephine. "Hand me my keys, please, sis. They're in that drawer over there, the one that looks like a hospital drawer. Oh, I wish I had a drink! Bring me a martini with that please, Josephine."

"No martini for you, Mick." Handing him his ring of keys. She was almost amused at his laxity, but decided to maintain a stiff upper lip to counter the frivolous demands of her semi-alcoholic brother. Mick promptly grabbed the keys and inserted a small, tarnished brass one into the locked box. Flippantly, he swung the top open. "Now there, you see!"

Ophelia and Josephine leaned over for a careful look at the presumed prize. They saw: Blue ceramic tiles, with Arabic script on them.

"What are they?" asked Ophelia.

"They're Cherokee bathroom tiles," said Mick, with a straight face, betraying nothing.

Ophelia studied his face. She was suddenly very serious. Reaching gingerly into the box, she turned one tile over, and then another. The tiles were cobalt blue, about two inches square, with white ceramic mortar stuck to their backs. They looked as if they had been pried loose from a wall somewhere. She studied them intensely for half a minute. "No, they're not!" she said. "Who told you that?"

Mick laughed, derisively. "You still think I'm the guy that stole Plato's gold?" His sanity seemed questionable.

"What are they, Mick?" asked Josephine. "Even I can tell they're not Cherokee anything. That's Arabic."

"If I tell you what they are, will you get off my case?"

"Mick, it's not my case you need to worry about. It's the police, and the judge, and, dammit, you've stabbed someone, and as if that wasn't bad enough they're accusing you of stealing this, this buried treasure."

"Chill out, sis."

"Mick, you don't have a legal leg to stand on. This stabbing is serious, resulting in, possibly, paralysis of Robby's legs for the rest of his life, and. . ." Josephine was near tears.

"Obviously, this is not the gold that you thought it was. So what difference does it make what it is?"

"Come on, Mick. You're evading the question. If you do that in the courtroom, they'll send you up to Angola so fast it'll make your head spin."

"Speaking of head spin, you never brought me that drink." Now he seemed serious.

"These look like tiles from a mosque," observed Ophelia, calmly.

"Yeah, yeah. That's what they are." He looked at her for the first time. "Who are you anyway?"

"Ophelia Doss, Anthropology department, Bellel College." She extended her hand. He took it limply in his and shook, wincing. "I'm guessing Morocco," she said, drily.

"Tunis. Raphe and I were going through there a couple years ago. We came across this mosque that had been busted up by somebody."

"Vandalized?"

"I don't know. It was a mess, though—might have been a little bomb job."

"So you took these?" Ophelia thrived on inquisitions.

"The guide said they'd be valuable, and hell, they look valuable to me, so I brought them home. They've been, uh, ever since, well, you know where they were. You lifted this from my room. *You lifted* this from my room!" His voice was raising, but it went back down. "Hell, Josephine, I didn't think you even knew about this place."

"No comment."

"Yeah, I *bet* there's no comment. You go messin' around in my room, without authorization. Unauthorized entry! Breaking and entering! What else did you lift while you were in there?"

"Nothing, Mick. We're looking for gold. That's all. I'll put the damn tiles back in the floor if it'll make you happy." Josephine was flat-out mad at her brother now, having been provoked to the end of her patience. "Come on, Ophelia. Let's get out of here. My brother wants to rot in his own juices."

"You're damn right. What do you care? Miss friggin' homecoming queen!"

"Calm down, Mick!" she demanded, icily, controlling her voice. "You're making a scene."

"You got that right! I'm making a scene. That's all you ever cared about—not making a scene.! I'm going to make a ruckus like this hospital has never seen. You won't bring me a drink. They'll bring me *something, by damn!* They'll bring me another valium if I need one. I'm in pain here and I need another Demerol."

"Come on, Ophelia. He's insane." She looked at Mick and pointed a finger directly at him. "You can go to hell, little brother! We're outta here."

And so they were. They were outta there. They met the nurse who was running down the hall, but they did not stop.

hddq://icu.loc

Two floors higher and further south, the scene was quite different in ICU. Rosa was looking sadly at Robby, who was connected to all the technology that Theseus Med had to offer. He was sitting up, slightly, but not by his own power. Not much going on here, yet, except severe pain and discomfort, and Rosa's despondent moments punctuated by helpless looks at Robby, who had been robbed of much more than a sack of old gold.

hddq://vinniesdomain.loc

Vinnie eased up to the counter at *Snazzy's*. "How we doing, my main man Mr. Johnny?"

"Not too much. You?"

"Same. I thought I was wrong one time but it turned out I was wrong about it."

"Yeah. I hear ya, man. I had the same problem one time, but then I found out about it."

They laughed. "What can I do ya for?" asked Johnny.

"Mocha Java."

"Comin' right up." Johnny whipped out his stuff and got busy on it. "Hey, y'brotha came by last night with some news. Have you heard it?"

"Nah, man. What's up?"

"It's Mick, man. He's laid up in the hospital."

"Nah, man."

"I'm not shitt'n ya. Some dude shot him last night."

"Who, man? Who would shoot da Mick?"

"I don't know his name—some British guy."

"Where did it happen?"

"At Mick's house, man."

"Nah."

"'S'true, man. I'm not messin' wit'ya."

"What happened?"

"Tha's all I know. Here's your java, man." Johnny slid the fancified coffee across the counter. Vinnie reciprocated with three dollars. "Thanks." Vinnie started to leave. "Oh, here's somethin' Vinnie. Julian said it had somethin' to do with huntin' for rabbits."

"Huntin' for rabbits? Now I know you crazy."

"Tha's what y'brotha said, man. I'm just tellin' ya. I'm tellin' ya like it is."

Vinnie turned it over in his mind. *Hunting for rabbits? Rabbit-hunting. Rabbit h—rabbit hole. Rabbit hole!* "Rabbit hole? Did Julian say something about a rabbit *hole*?"

"Yeah, yeah, tha's it. He said they were arguing about a rabbit hole when the dude shot Mick."

"Nah, man."

"Yeah, man."

"Hey, Johnny."

"Yeah?"

"Thanks, man."

"Da nada, man. Catch ya on the flipflop."

Vinnie got his feet in motion for the other end of the mall section, where Tony was doing the video thing with Gorgonzuan. "Hey, c'mon. We gotta go."

"No."

"Okay, have it your way. I can keep the two—and the other hundred and fifty. I don't need you to help me. See ya." Vinnie was on the move. No doubt about it.

Tony dropped the Gorgonzuan stick like a hot rock and hurried to his mentor's side. "You shit," he protested.

"We got work to do. The cops are onto Mick. And somebody shot him. We gotta get the goods and go, before they figure out what the hell is goin' on."

"Nah."

"Yeah. tha's right."

Five minutes later, they were on the bus for Esplanade. Twenty minutes later, they were at Mick's funky little garage warehouse. Vinnie moved a baby angel sculpture in the back yard, recovered a key, unlocked the door. The place was full of Mick's stuff.

"Must be in here somewhere," said Vinnie.

hddq://trainstation.loc

At 7:33 pm, Tuesday evening, the Amtrak Southern Crescent pulled into the New Orleans train station. Noah and Becky Davis were on it; they disembarked. Dr. William Theseus was there to meet them.

"Hello, Noah. It's good to see you again. Thank you for coming. Hello, Becky." He hugged them. "Robby has been asking about you. He's doing a lot better in the last few hours."

"Thanks for coming to pick us up, Dr. Theseus," said Noah, shaking the doc's hand.

"Please, call me William. And I want you to meet an old friend of mine. This is Ophelia Doss."

Ophelia was smiling and shaking hands with Robby's parents. "I'm just about your neighbor," said she.

"I'm glad to meet you, Ophelia," said Becky. "I know you teach our niece, Alice, at Bellel."

"It's a great pleasure to teach Alice," said Ophelia.

"So you decided to take the train?" asked William.

Becky said, "Noah was pretty antsy right away to hit the road. But in the end we decided to get a few hours rest. We caught the train in Spartanburg, and were able to have a relaxed trip."

"You'd have been worn out after that drive, for sure," said William.

"Right," agreed Noah.

"It's just as well. They just got him into a room of his own a few a few hours ago," said William.

"It was 2:30," Ophelia added.

"He's talking some now," said William.

The four of them began walking through the station to William's car.

"What has he said?" asked Noah.

"I understand he was asking for you, pretty much right away. I think he thought that the wound might have been worse than it actually turned out to be. It' not actually *life-threatening.* It's, ah, debilitating, for sure, but Robby's life wasn't really in question, as it turns out."

"Oh, well, thank the Lord for that," said Becky.

"I am *very* thankful to the Lord that Robby is now sitting up and talking. It could have been a lot worse. If the. . ., well, he's doing a lot better than the first time we saw him."

"Who is with Robby now?" asked Becky.

"There's a young lady that he's been spending some time with lately—Rosa Cyprana. She's been with him continuously since about one o'clock this afternoon. And she was with us last night at the emergency room." said William.

Noah asked, "Who is this guy that stabbed Robby?"

"Uh, his name is Mick Basker."

"Yes. You told me his name earlier. What was happening between them to—they weren't fighting over this girl, were they?"

"I don't think so, Noah, although that might have something to do with why it happened the way it did. The incident took place at Mick's house. Robby and another man had gone to his home to ask him some questions about, uh, another matter."

"Simon Lafraneer It was Simon, right? who was there when it happened."

"Simon called 911, and he didn't waste any time about it."

"I know Simon," said Noah, quietly.

"You know him? How's that?"

"He's a distant relative of mine. He was snooping around in our area for awhile looking for—I never did figure out what he was searching for."

"Gold?" asked William.

"Well, yes, as a matter of fact. Ophelia, you know something about that, don't you?" asked Noah.

"Oh, yes. Thanks to Simon, we were able to find the deposit that your grandfather had stashed in the cave under Aradne Ridge."

"Hmm, maybe so, but I smelled trouble the first time I met that man. What I know is that he was with Robby when this happened, and Robby probably wouldn't have been up to such shenanigans if Simon hadn't come poking around looking for gold. You know, Dr. Theseus, he's a scientist, just like you are. Whatever it was that Simon lead him into is—"

"I do understand your forebodings about Simon, Noah. My first impression of him was the same as yours, and I still haven't made up my mind about him. But I do know this: Because he called 911 immediately, Robby got emergency medical treatment within fifteen minutes of the stabbing. And also, the fact that he shot the stabber shows me that he was acting to protect your son. We have to give him the benefit of the doubt."

"Sure. I'm thankful, like Becky said, to the Lord that Robby is still alive and—not kicking, but he is alive. We'll hear more from him about what happened soon enough. Thank God he can talk about it."

They arrived at William's BMW and got in.

William looked in the rearview mirror at Noah. "You've got unlimited use of this car as long as you're in New Orleans, okay?"

"I appreciate that. What will you do?"

"Don't worry about me. I can use a University vehicle. Would you like to drive right now?"

"No, thanks, William. You can do the honors." Noah smiled for the first time. He looked out at the city of New Orleans, which began to pass by them as William, in no hurry, eased them through the old streets with worn curbs, dim ancient streetlights of ornate cast-iron and opaque glass, abundant foliage between every crevice of human edifice, azaleas, honeysuckle, elephant ears and bamboo between houses that sheltered whole lifetimes of families, whitewashed cypress clapboard with borders of gladiolus , brick columns here and there and then a colonial here and there, worn around the edges, graying and greening at the edges with fine lichen ubiquitous mildew some parts never see the light of day beneath the overstory, and their root-rumpled driveways and sidewalks accompanied by crepe myrtles sentries, with leafy live oak canopy overhead, shadowing vintage cars and bucket of bolts jalopies to transport the humanity dwelling therein—black, white, creole, shuck and jive, jazz in, ease on out, out on the funky street—an old city, musty and decadent with green moss on buildings and on bare dirt between oak roots that protrude radially from their greyed barrel trunks like miniature mountain ranges, limbs overhead twisted curving tributaries of barken oak, squirrels leap, birds chitter, gardenias scent, camellias drop their petals on the moist grass, elephant ears grow high beside arched porches, bungalows, wrought iron now and then, strains of jellyroll music and when the saints go marchin in and humidity, ubiquitous musky undertones and smell of crawfish boil, folks on the street, hole-in-the-wall restaurants with white tablecloths and silverware, iced tea and bourbon inside, Nehi and moon pie, deep south gentility, subdued hostility, liquidity, humidity Carondolet, Canal, St. Charles, Napolean. not stark and clear like the mountains from which Noah and Becky had emerged, but low and slow, big easy, movin' like the big slow river that swept through with lithesome permanence a mile away, depositing its deep dark loam, with hidden smell of mildew graced with overtones of queenly gardenia.

But a vaguely unsettling pathos always came creeping around the corners of Noah's mind whenever he would come here, or, really, to any city. This was because of their mountain. Immense and primordial, it seemed to dispatch its own Paleozoic soul to accompany them, overpowering the shadowy, unsettling influences of hipflip city whoopfiz. Noah would never quite know whether it was the city that was strange, or himself. Maybe it was life itself. Emerging from the mountain's protective shadow, he would once again encounter the terrible, dangerous insecurity of human noise and haste. It was like coming out from under a rock.

And the paranoia was even more intense this time, because of the slashing assault that had ripped open their son's vulnerable spine. Their only son, having at last become a man, was now cut back, by treacherous, literal backstabbing, to unchosen helplessness. It was a crime. It wasn't supposed to happen this way, and it hurt like hell. Now they were arriving at this alien, urban place—this hospital, a place that harbored in its every night-lit nook and sanitized cranny oppressive pain and suffering.

Dr. Theseus parked in front. Noah and Becky got out of the car to enter the immense building, as big as a mountain. They had left a large mountain of peace and serenity to arrive at this little man-made mountain of tribulation. Noah was scared of what damaged personhood he might encounter in Robby's bed, in Robby's eyes, beyond these gleaming lobbies and vast doors. Yes he was scared, he was scared to see his son in this condition, imprisoned here in this alien labyrinth of trouble . They stepped slowly, unsurely, through the sanitary maze of halls, handrails, carts and metallic stands, stations, scrubbed personnel and disinterested strangers, to reach at last the cold, antiseptic room where lay their wounded son.

Robby was in the bed, still. Becky and Noah walked quietly to him. He had been waiting for them; his eyes turned to see them. *Robby's still in there*, seeming like a rabbit in a hole, but he smiled. Thank God. He was a noble son, smiling at them with indomitable Spirit. His eyes were bright with appreciation for their coming. They kissed him on the forehead. Thank God for life that overpowers the force of death. *We can get through this* his eyes seemed to say.

"Oh, Robby," groaned his mama.

"Thank you for coming," he said in a low, unhurried voice, as her hands enveloped his, and she planted another kiss on his cheek.

"How are you, son?" asked Noah.

"I've been better," replied Robby, with a little smile.

"I hear ya," said Noah. "It was a good first step—kisses and cautious smiles. "You want to tell us about it?"

Noah's good attitude was baptized with tears that brimmed his eyelids. "Shit happens."

"You got that right."

"Are you in pain?" Mama asked.

"It's not as bad as it was. They've got it under control with the drip, I think, as far as the wound goes. But there's nothing in my legs."

"No pain in your legs?"

"Uh, nothing."

"No feeling?"

"Right."

"What happened?" asked Noah.

"It's, uh, a long story, dad. I'll ask Simon to tell you about it. He'll be here in a little while."

"Who is Simon, anyway?"

"He's actually a distant relative of ours, you know."

"I wish he had stayed distant."

"This wasn't his fault, dad."

"I understand that." But Noah's tone indicated some doubt. "How is he related to us?"

"It's on your side. Think of your grandfather, Plato."

"Okay."

"His sister, Katerina. They left Russia together after the revolution."

"Right."

"Simon is her grandson."

"How's that?"

"Katerina had a daughter—Marie. She was Simon's mother. Simon grew up in Liverpool."

"You're doing pretty good for a guy who just got stabbed in the back. I don't think I could remember all that if I were in your condition."

"Simon told this to me, this morning. It's actually the second time he has explained it to me."

"Okay, well, we don't want to talk about him, anyway. What about you?"

"What *about me*, dad?"

"I, I don't know, Robby. I'm sorry. I didn't mean to be asking so many questions right off the bat."

"It's okay. As far as the update on what we were doing, I've asked Simon to relate it to you, because it's a lot more talking than I care to do right now. "

"That's fine, son. I'm just glad to see you still kicking—er, not kicking, but, you know what I mean."

"I know, dad." There was the reassuring little smile again.

"You're amazing, boy. Where did you get this patience and forbearance? I don't think it came from me."

"From the Lord, I guess," answered Robby.

"I'd be mad as hell if I was in your shoes now."

"Not much point in that."

"Right."

It was a slow conversation, but they had covered a lot of ground already. Noah pulled a chair closer to the bed and sat in it. Becky kept her hands enfolded over Robby's. "You've got something to be thankful for, don't you, Robby."

"I always have. I always will." He closed his eyes and seemed to retire to slumber for a moment. "It's a good thing I'm becoming a microbiologist."

"Why's that, dear?" asked his mother.

"This whole question of neuron regeneration—it's a hot topic in research now. And now I've got some pretty serious incentive to work on the problem."

"Sure, Robby," said his dad. "I like that. I had thought you'd be working on a way for us to retire to 'pharming' milk cows." Noah raised his hands to indicate the quotes around the word 'pharming.' But now our priorities are different."

"Life has a way of doing that," said Robby.

A gentle knock was heard on the door. Simon walked in. "Hello, Robby, how are you feeling?" Simon looked at Robby, then glanced sideways at his parents.

"I'm getting by. Meet my parents, Noah and Becky."

"I'm Simon Lafraneer, pleased to meet you, although I regret the sad circumstances." He shook hands with Becky, then Noah, who stood up. "Oh no, please don't get up."

Noah returned to his seat. "I understand that you and I are cousins of some sort."

"Yes. Same family tree, but on different sides of the big pond." Simon offered a gentle smile.

Noah was feeling friendly enough, but not ready to smile at anyone yet in this strange situation except his son. "You're Katerina's grandson, then?"

"That's correct. My grandmother, Katerina Zupoff Harthouse, fled Russia with her brother, your grandfather, right in the midst of the Bolshevik uprising and the German army trying to take over Russia at the same time. It was quite a perilous escape, as my mother has told me. Have you ever heard the account of it?"

"I think I have, some time or other. But what about this, uh, gold thing? What the hell has happened with that?"

Simon, no stranger to bluntness, launched right into the explanation. Indeed, he had anticipated an encounter such as this. Dispensing with formalities would simplify the process of getting all concerned parties up to speed, especially these two parents of a seriously injured son. Simon found Noah's reticence to historical elaboration quite sensible. "A sizable deposit of old, rare gold coins was left by your grandfather in two locations. The first is a spot near the Mississippi River about fifty-five miles from here. The second was, as I'm sure you know by now, very near your home in Haywood County, North Carolina."

"Yes, well, that's all well and good, but is it worth my son getting paralyzed over?"

"It's, ah, no. absolutely not. No gold is worth what your Robby is now having to endure."

"But it has happened, dad. Shit happens, I tell ya," interrupted Robby, whose voice had the power of veto over anyone else's opinion in the present situation.

"Okay. I'm sorry. I—"

"Dr. Theseus asked Simon to gather some information, and I chose to go with Simon."

"The man we were talking to was irrational, and drunk. His action against Robby was sudden, and quite unexpected." Simon explained.

"Yeah, dad, and after it happened, Simon shot him in order to put a stop to his insane reaction."

"Well thanks for shooting the sonofabitch. I'm sure that's what he deserves," said Noah, bitterly.

"Oh, he deserves much worse than that," added Simon, vehemently. "They should send him to prison for the rest of his life."

"What would that accomplish?" asked Robby, suddenly managing a strained yell. His veto power was in full effect. The two older men fell silent.

After a while, Noah continued his not-so-subtle inquisition. "Anyway, this guy that stabbed you is the guy that took the gold, right?"

"We don't know that, dad."

"It's pretty likely, though," added Simon.

"What makes you think it was him?"

"He had certain information about its location that no one else had, originally," explained Simon.

"Where did he get this information?" asked Noah, relentlessly pursuing a course to understand why his son had been stabbed. Neither Simon nor Robby answered immediately. "I'm just trying to find out what the hell happened here."

"That's fine, dad. Just keep your voice down."

Simon resumed an explanation with a low voice, "It's complicated, but that information was sent to him by Franz Hallfrich, from Germany."

"Germany?"

"It seems confusing to us now, trying to put the pieces together, but it really gets back to your grandfather, Plato Zupoff, and information that he released to different people through different letters over time. In Franz's case, he found a letter that Plato had sent to *his* grandfather, who had been German ambassador to Russia at the time that Plato fled from there."

"Okay. You can spare me the details. I'm confused enough as it is. What was the information that this guy had from the German fella?"

"Mick Basker, the man who stabbed Robby, had been sent very specific information about how to get to the gold deposit."

"What did it say?"

"The communication that Mick Basker received from Franz Hallfich was basically this: go to a certain oak tree on the Theseus property, take 64 steps due north, and that's the spot where the gold would be found."

"Damn, if that don't beat anything I ever heard," declared Noah, relaxing back in his seat. "Was the gold there? Did he find it?"

A quiet knock was heard. Dr. Theseus and Ophelia walked in, gesturing to all that they didn't wish to disturb the discussion. Simon continued. "Someone went out to the site late Sunday night and dug a big hole in the ground at that spot. Whoever it was—Mick or somebody else—must have found the gold and taken it." Simon looked at Theseus.

"We found five gold florins on the ground that the thief, or thieves, dropped as they were getting away," said William.

Simon handed a florin to Noah. "It was the next day, yesterday, when Robby and I went to Mick's house to question him about it. We found Mick drunk and acting a little crazy, and the next thing you know, he's got a knife in his hand. He was actually going after me, but Robby rushed to my assistance and—"

"Robby, you're too good!" His mother erupted in sobs.

"My son the hero," mumbled Noah, cynically.

William wasn't sure what response should follow Noah's awkward sarcasm, so he said simply, "Your son *is* a hero. He's a brave man."

"Yes, Dr. Theseus," agreed Simon. "I wish that he had not intervened on my behalf, but he decided at that very confusing moment to do so. I am very grateful. Otherwise, it might have been me laid up here."

Noah felt a pang of compassion for Simon, a person who, Noah was now realizing, had gained sufficient respect from Robby that he had chosen to defend him.

A male nurse walked in. Robby addressed the group, "Hey, thanks, friends and family, for dropping in, but I'll be asking you to leave for a few minutes. This is Monty, and he's going to help me take care of some tasks that I used to do by myself. See you in about twenty minutes."

"Look, Robby." His mother held up a cardboard box. "Remember this?" It was a jigsaw puzzle.

"Yes. It's Milo and Mila."

"That's what you called them." Becky noticed that William was looking at the picture on the box, a picture of two horses running. "Robby assembled this puzzle when he was about ten years old. We always called them Milo and Mila, because they look so much like our horses, Milo and Mila. I'm going to put it in this drawer here. We can start on it tomorrow."

"Oh yeah? Aren't you gung-ho for constructive activities, mama!"

"Rehab, son."

"It's the lower parts that need fixing," cracked Robby.

"We'll start with the parts that still work." She touched his hands. "And the neurons up on top." She pointed to his head. "We'll work our way down."

Stems

24

Rosa stepped across blue lettered tiles in the sidewalk—St. Charles—and over the curb, heading north on Napolean Avenue. Up a few blocks, and then she reached her current residence, the spacious second-story apartment-home of Salli and Kemal Cretani. She entered their bookstore, the *BookCell*, and greeted Salli who was sitting behind the cash register. "Ooh! what a wild day!"

"It's a wild world," said Salli. She looked up from something she was writing, and flashed a curiously contented smile.

"Oh, I wish I had it together like you do," said Rosa.

"I'm just about ten years ahead of you. Give it some time."

Rosa looked at her older friend quizzically. Salli just had a certain glow about her.

hddq://procreation.crn

"Lance?"

"That's me. I'm here."

"Oh! I knew you'd come," said Veronica. "Come on. I've been waiting for you."

"You were expecting me?"

"I got word from the man upstairs. Let's go. Time's a wastin'!"

"Okay. It's been a long trip. I don't know what happened to all those other guys."

"Don't worry about them. Come on. We've got a reservation."

Veronica took him by the hand. He'd barely had time to catch his breath. She led him down a primrose path, beneath rose-colored streetlights, until they came to a beautiful river. They continued down the winding path, beside a bridge. Lance caught a glimpse of a blue and white mosaic sign—River Fallopia.

I made it! This is what I had dreamed about. I made it to the River Fallopia! "Veronica, is this the land of Utruss?"

"It's just up ahead, Lance. We'll arrive there by and by. Just come with me." A sleek, black gondola was docked at the edge of the river, with gold letters on its side—Fertile. They stepped in. The gondolier pushed the boat off, and they were drifting blissfully down the River Fallopia, not a care in the world, propelled by a gentle current of love.

Lance was entranced with Veronica's beauty. She looked at him longingly, and said, "I'm yours from now on in life! Are you glad?"

"I, I, I'm very happy about it, yes." He felt lightheaded, dizzy. Up above was another sign, in pink and purple flowers—Tunnel of Love, and yet another sign beyond it—Embrace Life, all ye who enter here!

They were in there for a week! But it seemed like minutes to Lance. He lost all sense of space and time, all self-consciousness. *Where am I?*

Then there was a man, a very gentle man, who pulled their boat aside and tied it with a cord to the dock. "Who are you?" asked Lance, as if in a dream.

"Hi. Welcome to the Land of Utruss. My name is Kemal. I'll be your guide, and not only that, I'm your daddy, too."

He's such a nice guy, kinda funny-lookin', but I like him all right. Then, from the mists, a lovely women appeared. Kemal introduced her, "This is my wife, your mother, Salli. You can see she's, uh, better looking than me. Together, we're going to lead you through this special time. It'll be a great trip, should take about nine months or so. So it'll be a long ride, but you'll enjoy it. All your needs are taken care of. And we've got the map for your journey. The big guy upstairs planned this journey just for you."

"But, where's Veronica?"

"Don't worry about her, Lance. You're a zygote now. It's time for you to step up to the plate and get through this special time, and be born and all. Then when you get out the other side, and grow up you'll, well, you'll find her again somewhere. She'll be like a pleasant kind of longing until you find her. But then when you do find her—hey! look out!"

"Thanks for docking me here. It seems like a good place. What should I do now?"

"Just hang out. Like I said, all your needs are taken care of. You will need to work on your multiplication tables, though."

"My what?"

"Multiplication tables. You'll be multiplying continuously for the next nine months. But don't worry about a thing. We've got your master plan. It's all right here—46 volumes. We'll keep you on track. In a few more days, you'll start differentiating. You'll get the hang of it, and you'll never look back. You ready?"

hddq://coffeeshop.loc

Wednesday morning, two microbiology students were having coffee in the student union. The precocious senior, Erik Wayne, and his grad student buddy Sam Cricket, were discussing the potentials of stem cell technology. But their conversation was interrupted when a group of students paraded through the large dining area with handmade signs—*Stop Child Enslavement. Boycott Niked Sweat Shop Shoes.* The twenty-odd protesters moved noisily through the main thoroughfare proclaiming their message of liberation with exhortations to join their movement. After a few minutes of sweat-shop denunciation rhetoric, their retinue moved outside to the quad where they could broaden their demonstration under a bright blue fall sky.

"You were saying, Erik?"

"Reproductive cloning is for procreation of superior breeding stock, kind of like tweaking natural selection. We're assisting nature, and stepping up the process, to yield progeny that is better-equipped. Therapeutic cloning, on the other hand, is for improving specific genes—replacing defective ones that would lead to disease or disability with normal ones. In therapeutic procedures, the blastocyst is never implanted into a mother. It's dissected so that the totipotent stem cells in its inner mass can be reproduced in large quantities in lab cultures." Erik took a bite from his donut.

"Yeah, in Petri dishes," added Sam.

"Or whatever containers they're using these days," said Erik.

"Are you talking about mouse embryos, or human?"asked Sam.

"You know there's been a lot of this type of work done in the last fifty years or so with frogs and mice and other small species. Now they're starting to refine these procedures so that they can be applied to human development."

"So we're talking about recovering the inner cell mass from human blastocysts?"

"For therapeutic purposes. This type of cloning affords us large quantities of totipotent cells in the laboratory, to identify and replace genes that express as diseases ."

"Right, the congenital diseases like Parkinson's, and cystic fibrosis, sickle cell anemia, muscular dystrophy—"

"Yeah. There are a bunch of them."

"So these guys at Wisconsin and Hopkins and other labs recover the inner cell mass, which is composed, during the cleavage stage in the first few days, of totipotent stem cells."

"The most powerful cells on earth!" exclaimed Sam.

"Almost." Erik laughed. " Geron says the most totipotent—sounds like some tyrant that's stuck on himself, doesn't it? "

"He probably wants to clone himself,"cracked Sam.

"Hahahaha"

Erik continued. "So the *most totipotent*" He lifted his hands in mock adoration". . .are the 'primordial germ cells.'"

"EG cells," affirmed Sam.

"Exactly—the 'key to human immortality' as some have called them. They're the ones that develop in the embryo, after gastrulation, in the testes or ovaries as the fetal sex organs begin to form."

"But anyway, getting back to the blastula stage," Sam prompted.

"Yes, thank you, as I was saying before the *most totipotent microscopic primordial germ cells* reared their germy little heads, hahaha. . .these guys that are doing this type of work, they remove the stem cells from the ICM that has congregated inside the 5-or-6-day old blastocyst—"

"So they're sacrificing the embryo?" Sam wondered.

"I guess you could call it that,"

"What do they do with the outer part?"

"Oh, the trophoblast, God only knows. I suppose they use it for something or other in the lab, or maybe they culture those cells for some other developmental purpose. I don't know. Anyway, they place the totipotent stem cells into culture and propogate them."

"That's what we call a stem cell line," observed Sam.

"Uhhuh, but it's tricky. Those cells have a built-in tendency toward differentiation. If they're kept alive unto themselves, without chemical restraints, they'll start to organize themselves into an embryo again."

"I was reading about this last week in *Cell*. To keep them in the primordial state, they grow them on a feeder layer of mouse cells or something similar that have been irradiated so they won't themselves be dividing."

"Yeah. The feeder layer underneath secretes proteins that nourish the stem cells above."

"And I think there's something about the feeder layer that stimulates the stems to multiply instead of differentiate," Sam added.

"But at *some point*, they want to pull some of the stem cells out and let them differentiate," said Erik. "That's really what it's all about—generating a massive number of pluripotent cells that they can tinker with in order to produce muscle cells, or bone cells, blood cells, whatever is called for in the particular research that they're doing."

"Neurons?" Sam wondered.

" I think they're the hardest ones to reproduce." said Erik.

"The cells of the central nervous system don't take kindly to regenerating. That's what I've read. They're pretty stubborn," agreed Sam.

"The myelin sheath keeps them kind of bundled up, or—"

"I think the lab guys are using neural stem cells to try and get some regeneration going with them."

"Adult stem cells?" asked Erik.

"Yeah, neural stem cells, like those that are found in the brain and spinal cord of any adult," said Sam. ". . .speaking of which, did you hear about Robby Davis, Dr. Theseus' assistant?"

"No, what about him?"

"He got stabbed in the back," said Sam.

"When?"

"Monday night. I heard that the knife grazed his spinal cord, and he might be paralyzed from the waist down."

"Nah! Shit! A nice guy like that. That sucks! Who did it?"

"I don't know. I didn't hear that part."

"Hey, you know what, Sam. We ought to go see him."

"Uh, yeah. Let's do it. He's over at the Med."

"Come on. Let's go see how he's doing—how his neurons are holding up."

hddq://robbys.med.loc

"That's part of the hind leg, isn't it?" said Becky Davis. "You see." She pointed at the picture on the front of the jigsaw puzzle box. "That line between dark brown and blue background, with the curvature. It's that piece."

"Yes. I can see that, mother. But it's meaningless at this point. I've nothing to connect it to. We're working on edge pieces right now. Who taught me to do the edge pieces first?"

"Who? indeed." replied Becky. ". . .the same person who is now pointing out that we don't have a large enough space on this tray to do the entire puzzle. We'll have to do it in sections."

"Okay, then. Get me four trays, and we'll find all the edge pieces and assign them to their quadrants."

"That's a plan, Robby." She looked over at the nurse. "Anita, could we have three more trays like this one brought up, for the jigsaw puzzle."

"Yes, ma'am. They'll be bringing dinner in about thirty minutes. I'll just pull out three more from the cart. They won't mind."

"We'll need to keep them in a safe place, where they can't be knocked around or anything. This is the beginning of his rehabilitation, you know."

"Yes, ma'am. You're the quickest rehabbin' mama I've ever seen, wasting no time. The physical therapist hasn't even seen him yet, and already you've got him working with horses." lol

Through the open door walked Rosa. "Hello, Robby."

"Hi, Rosa."

She took his hand gently. "You're looking pretty chipper."

He saw her eyes sparkling. Then he looked at his mother, who was standing on the other side of the bed. "Mother, this is my good friend, Rosa Cyprana."

Rosa nimbly withdrew her hand from Robby's and extended it across the bed to Becky. "Hello."

"Good morning, Rosa. Robby has told us about you."

"I'm pleased to meet you." Looking at him again, Rosa said "You must be feeling better. You look, uh, more energetic than last time I saw you."

"It's no bed of roses, but I'm already seeing improvement."

"Like what kind of improvement?"

"Well, uh, bowel control is still intact. That's good news." Robby was a little embarrassed to mention it.

"It certainly is, Robby. That's great news!"

"I've still got some working parts down there."

"What about the wound itself? Did they sew it up?"

"No. Dr. Selig says it's a 'dirty wound,' with too much possibility for infection. I guess that, once it's been sufficiently cleaned up, they'll stitch it. A lot of fluid has been draining from it."

"What kind of fluid, Robby?"

"Spinal fluid. They change these blue pads about every hour."

Through the open door walked Erik Wayne and Sam Cricket. "Good morning," said Sam. He walked around the bed to Becky. "I can see by your alert face that you are certainly Robby's mother. I'm Sam Cricket. I'm also a graduate assistant in the microbiology department." He turned to Rosa. "Hello, Rosa." She nodded. "And this is Erik Wayne." Erik smiled and offered a friendly wave.

Erik surveyed Robby's invalid status. Being a joker, he thought of a good wisecrack, but decided not to risk speaking it, since Robby's mother was in the room. So he played it polite and safe. "What's the prognosis, Robby?"

"Well, the latest from the doctors is: it's good news that I've still got bowel control. It's a good sign. You wanna see?"

Hahahaha.

Erik's fair face turned red. The invalid had beaten him to the joke. "I've gotta hand it to you, Robby. I don't think I'd be in such good spirits if I had been through what you've just experienced. You're an inspiration."

"All things work together for the good of those who love the Lord," said Robby.

Rosa wiped tears from her eyes. It still seemed like a cruel joke to her. "How can you say that?" she blurted.

He looked at her carefully, stoically. "Don't get me wrong, Rosa. I'm not trying to put on a front here. I've already had moments of despair. That first night of having no feeling, and no movement in my legs was hell on earth. But what are my choices here? There have been cases of this type in which the victim came out paraplegic. So I'm grateful that my disability doesn't fall into that category. And look. I've got a mother here who loves me, who has dropped everything to come down here and help get through this time." He lifted his hand to touch Becky's face as she moved closer to him. Robby was weeping. "This is harder than. . ."

Rosa put her hands on Robby's face. "I'm sorry, Robby."

"For what?. It's not your fault."

Rosa looked at Robby's mother. "You probably haven't heard this, but your son helped me move out of Mick's house just a week ago. I was living with the guy who stabbed Robby, and then Robby helped me out of that terrible arrangement."

Robby laid his head back on the pillow, and looked at her with disappointment in his eyes. "Rosa, we've already been through this. Quit beating yourself about it!"

Erik, shuffling his feet, nudged Sam. They started to wave goodbye.

"Hey, where you going?" asked Robby, with some urgency in his voice.

"We'll catch ya some other time, bro, maybe tonight."

"Just wait a minute. This will blow over. I want to talk to you."

Becky took Rosa gently by the arm. "Let's take a little walk, dear. I want to get out and see that garden down below. I've been looking at it from this window long enough. I'm wondering what those camellias smell like. Won't you walk down there with me?" She looked over at her son as they walked to the door. Robby lifted his hand as a gesture of departure. "Thanks, mom."

And then there were three young students in the hospital room.

Erik spoke. "So this guy that did this to you was Rosa's boyfriend?"

"He was, at one time."

"What a frickin' low 'life!—stabbing somebody because he took your girlfriend away." Erik said.

"Hey! It wasn't like that. First thing is, I haven't 'taken' Rosa. I just helped her move out of his place. That's all."

"So you're not, like, getting' it on?"

"No, a thousand times no. We've spent some time together lately, but it's nothing like a love thing, or, she's not gonna want a cripple anyway—"

"Hey! interrupted Sam. "Now who's beatin' themselves up?"

"I'm not cultivating illusions, Sam. I'm just telling you. There's a lot more going on here than meets the eye—a lot more than just some stupid love triangle."

"Like what?"

"Oh, I can't really get into it. It involves some, possibly, some stolen property."

Erik looked curiously at Robby. "Well, I know *you* didn't steal anything." His gaze intensified, as he nodded his head slightly. "And I know *Rosa* didn't steal anything. So who does that leave that might have stolen something?" Erik maintained his steady bead on Robby's face. Robby was laid back on the bed, starting to feel worn out. "Are you gonna tell us what this, uh, whathisface?—"

"Erik!" Sam interjected.

"What?"

"Don't you ever know when to stop?" asked Sam. "Always pushing the envelope, always grabbing fruit from the tree of knowledge—"

"What are you talking about, bro?"

"Like that day in class when Theseus was talking about electroporation, and you started rambling about frickin' Frankenstein—you're just—over the top. You're just too much, man," Sam objected.

"What is he talking about, Robby?" asked Erik, playing innocent.

Sam was laughing. "Don't play dummy, Erik. You know what I'm talking about. You're always testing the limits."

Erik allowed a little smile to creep across his face. "What are you guys talking about?"

"Lose the 'stolen property' inquisition, Erik. Can't you see that the injured man here doesn't want to talk about it? You've crossed the line. Learn a little tact, for once in your life, will ya?"

"I'm just—"

"It's none of your business, okay?" said Robby. "This involves legal liabilities, and the University, and you're better off just pretending you never brought it up."

"Okay." Erik lifted his hands in mock surrender. "Okay, so what else is new? Seen any good movies lately?"

"Seriously, Erik," Robby opened his eyes, turned his head lazily, and said, "I need you guys to help me. Can you help me?"

"We can help you, Robby," answered Sam. "What can we do for you?"

"Thanks, Sam. I've got a very real problem here, and I'm going to start working on it right away."

"Okay, bro," agreed Erik.

"The truth is, I have sustained a serious injury—a partial severing of the spinal cord. The official name is Brown-Sequard's syndrome. And since I'm already headed into a career of research in microbiology, I'm going to concentrate my study and focus on this one thing."

"Awesome!" said Erik. "I like it! Hey, I'm with you."

"Thanks, Erik. I knew you'd see it my way. But you can see that, well, I have some constraints here. In spite of that, I'm going to launch right into the research surrounding this neuron regeneration problem."

"I'm trackin' with ya."

"Maybe Theseus will let me work this project into a dissertation."

"Look out! How could he say no to that?"

"First thing I need is a good laptop, one that will detect the campus wireless. There's a lot going on, all over the place—Wisconsin, Hopkins, Yale, UCSF, Stanford, Cambridge. All these labs are working on this problem, or other problems associated with cell regeneration. I need to get online and find out what's happening with it. Can you bring me a laptop? Sam, can you requisition one from the department?"

"I don't think that'll be a problem."

"The other thing is the library. I'll need a lot of resources from there, but, as you can see—"

"Hey, I'll cover it for you. Make a list.," said Erik.

"Actually, I've got a short one right here." He handed over a scrap of paper with names of two books scribbled on it.

"That's quick, Robby. you don't mess around, do you?"

"In fact, Erik, I do mess around. And I'm about to right now. I just rang the call button, and a nurse is coming right now to help me with some special tasks that I used to do without assistance. Right now, though, there's something coming down the pike, and—"

Anita, the nurse, walked into the room. "What now? What am I, the maid?" Robby pointed to his lower extremities. "I'll see you guys later, okay? And, uh, sooner is better than later, because my dear mother is driving me crazy with this jigsaw puzzle."

"It's all part of the plan, Robby," said Sam. "You've got to keep those motor skills and neuron skills at the top of your game."

"See ya. Thanks a lot, guys. Oh, and Erik, any time today on those two books will be fine.

"Got ya covered, bro."

Teratomas

25

Wednesday morning at 11:40, Noah Davis walked into the hospital room where Mick Basker was recovering from a gunshot wound. He entered the room slowly and politely. "Hello. Do you mind if I come in?" said Noah.

"Come in. Who are you?" asked Mick.

"My name's Noah Davis. I came to see how you're doing."

"Have we, uh, have we met?"

"Not until now."

"Well, uh, what can I do for you, Mr. . .?"

"Davis, Noah Davis. I'm visiting here, from North Carolina."

"Are you doing business with someone who banks with us at *BankCher*?"

"No, sir."

"What can I do for you?"

"I just stopped by to chat. I've been visiting my son over in the ICU."

"Your son? How's he doing?"

"He's improving, but he still has a long way to go to recovery. He took a pretty bad hit."

"Uh, who is your son?"

"Robby Davis."

Mick leaned back in the bed and released a sigh. He looked at the ceiling. After a moment, he said, "Why did you come here?"

"To see how you're doing."

"So what are you gonna do? Sue me?"

"Not planning on it. I think the judge, whoever he is, will see that justice is done. You'll be in a criminal court."

"I don't have to talk to you. My lawyer is not here."

"I, uh, I didn't come to talk to your lawyer."

"Good. And you don't want to talk to me either," said Mick, his voice taking a vehement tone.

"Hey, hey," said Noah quietly, raising his hands in a gesture of concession, "Hold your horses. I'm not going to beat you up, or sue you. I'm not even going to cuss you out. I just want to give you an opportunity to talk about, hell, talk about whatever you want to talk about."

"You want me to admit to some crime, don't you?"

"You said that, Mick, not me. You can say whatever you want. I just wanted to, uh, to tell you something."

Mick was fidgeting in the bed. "What's that?"

"What's done is done, Mick. There's nothing we can do or say to change that." Noah walked slowly over to the window, and looked out at the hospital entrance three floors below. Mick's eyes followed him. "And I know my son. He is not a vengeful man. I might be, in some ways, but he is not." Noah looked carefully at Mick, who said nothing, while conveying the most innocent, most perplexed expression that he could muster. "In this life, Mick, success doesn't really come down to who gets the gold, or who gets the girl. There is something much more important than all of that at stake. Do you know what it is?"

"Hell, I suppose you're gonna tell me now about Jesus, or something like that."

Noah raised his eyebrows, and allowed a little smile. "As a matter of fact, yes. I've come to tell you about Jesus Christ, if you're willing to hear it."

"Aw, for chrissake—"

"That's true, Mick, it is for his sake. It's all for his sake."

"Okay. You can go now."

"I will, then. I just want you to know that he forgives, and he's called us to forgive each other."

"Jeez. Are you done yet?"

"Okay. I'm outta here. We're in room 508 if you want to talk some more." Noah raised his hands and eased toward the door, backwards. Then he was gone. The room was quiet except for Mick's breathing.

hddq://research.loc

Sam and Erik were in the library checking out sources for Robby's research.

"What does that look like to you?" asked Erik, as he held a book open for Sam to view. Sam saw a black and white image that he recognized as a photo taken through a powerful microscope, "A fetus," said Sam.

"How old do you think it is?" asked Erik.

"Oh, seven or eight weeks, post ovulation."

"What about this?" Erik indicated a picture in another book.

Sam looked at the second picture. "Hmm. You got me," he said, with a quizzical twisting of his head. "What is it?"

"Teratoma."

"Not very pretty."

"These two are almost the same thing," remarked Erik.

"How so?"

"The fetus developed in the place where it was supposed to be—a uterus. The other was a random tumor in a woman's ovary. But they both started out as stem cells."

"I see," said Sam.

"Stem cells divide rapidly. If they originate in an embryo, they do just fine, multiplying in an organized way as they differentiate into all the cells types of the body."

"Right, in order to form a new organism."

"But if they somehow land outside the uterus, they go crazy."

"They turn cancerous," agreed Sam.

"The same cells—they can go either way, to become a person, or to become a tumor, a useless lump of cells."

"Depending upon the environment that they find themselves in."

"Yeah. Amazing, huh?" mused Sam.

"Yes. Environmental controls, biological signals, in the proper setting—an embryo—mask the genes, or put a rein on them, so they can express themselves in an organized way." Erik moved some magazines around. "And here's something else: an article in *Science* about a strain of mice at the Jackson lab in Maine. The mice grew malignant teratomas that were so deadly they could kill a healthy mouse in a few weeks after experimental implantation. But they could take those *same tumor cells*, inject them into developing mouse embryos, and—"

"They would behave and do what they're supposed to do," said Sam.

"Yeah. It's like the embryo would tame the teratoma."

"Kind of whip it back into line, huh?"

"They'd join in with the embryo's normal development."

"They'd turn back into stem cells, and submit to the embryo's growth plan."

"Yeah, they would return to the DNA plan. Those stem cells, man. I'm tellin' ya what, they're totipotent, if properly directed!"

"It's true, Erik. But you're chasing rabbits, man. We need to get ourselves properly directed. That's what I'm talking about. Let's get Robby hooked up with some sources for neuron regeneration research."

"Sure. That's what I'm talking about. Everything I'm seeing indicates that stem cell research is going to be the key to it," said Erik.

"Erik, Robby's spinal cord has stem cells in it—adult neural stem cells—but they're equipped to generate other new cells according to normal development patterns."

"Sure, not as a response to traumatic conditions. They're progenitors, and as such, they're somewhat advanced in differentiation. They don't have the flexibility—the ready response—to undertake really groundbreaking regeneration tasks in an emergency. That's why the research needs to center around the embryonic ones. They're totipotent!" Erik insisted.

" Where did you learn that?"

"Duh, Theseus University."

"The doc's class hasn't covered progenitor cells yet."

"Independent study, big guy, right here in this library." Erik pointed to his forehead and winked at his friend. "I keep these grey matters cranked up *all* the time, way beyond the demands of the classroom."

Sam laughed. "You nerd."

"Takes one to know one, ya geek."

"Adult stem cells can be reprogrammed by their cell environments. That's what you were saying a while ago, wasn't it?"

"Nah, man, those are the embryonic ones." insisted Erik. "They can be trained to do anything! They're just babies, man. The adult stem cells are too old and set in their ways to be out in the general body parts regenerating. In fact, their misplaced efforts probably have something to do with why cancer happens."

"Listen, Erik. The newest research is indicating that it's stray embryonic stems that go haywire. Adult stem cells, on the other hand, can be reprogrammed if they're set into the right environment. They proved that at Roslin by cloning Dolly from a mammary cell that had been inserted into an enucleated egg."

" Yeah, those Scottish guys put a mature nucleus into a new oocycte. But it wasn't the egg's cytoplasm that set the development clock back to zero. Campbell had previously starved the donor cells into a gap-zero stage that jolted their mature nuclei back to some kind of embryonic programming, or something like that. I know it's confusing. Can you wrap your graduate mind around it? They were turning the fully-differentiated mammary cell back to an embryonic phase."

Erik continued his treatise. "But I'm not talking about reproductive cloning, Sam. What Robby's recovery will require is *therapeutic* cloning, which provides an adult person, i.e. our friend Robby, with his own personal stash of ES cells. And this is how it happens: One. The doctor gets a sample of Robby's cells from his body somewhere, whatever the optimum place is— blood, or cheek, or whatever. Two. They clone Robby by taking his DNA, or the whole nucleus, out of his cell and inserting it into an egg cell."

"Wait a minute." Sam injected. "There are two things wrong with this picture. First off, where do they get an egg cell? And second, think about what you just said. You're talking about cloning a human being. That's illegal, and unethical."

"It won't be implanted in a woman's womb, Sam. That's reproductive cloning. This is therapeutic. The egg will be stimulated, by electroporation or whatever, to respond as if it's been fertilized, and start to multiply cells by cleavage, becoming a blastocyst. The lab guys will let it grow for a few days in the glass, then recover the stem cells from inside it and set them in culture to proliferate. When they get enough of them, they'll treat them a certain way and make them differentiate into progenitor neurons, then inject them into Robby's injured spinal cord and see what happens—"

"Ah, ah, it'll never work. This is the central nervous system of a human being, Erik. You make this treatment sound like a Betty Crocker recipe. Furthermore, here's the real question: What do they do with the rest of the blastocyst after they've taken the stem cells out of its ICM, huh?"

"I don't know." Erik was wearing his own neurons thin.

"Aye, see, there's the rub, Puck. They're sacrificing an embryo. Robby will never go for it. I know Robby, and I can tell you he won't go for it."

"Well it's, uh, Robby. . .it's Robby himself."

"His clone. See. You're asking him to kill himself," said Sam.

"Don't be ridiculous. I'm serious."

"Nah, man."

"As a heart attack."

"You're asking him to kill a little embryonic version of himself, exactly like he was thirty-whatever years ago when he was in his mother's womb. I tell ya, he won't allow it," said Sam.

"No way. How could he be killing himself when he's still alive after the fact?"

"It's probably not a true clone of Robby anyway. The egg cell came from some woman. What woman would it be? Are they gonna go down to Bourbon Street and find a woman to sell her eggs?"

"Don't be ridiculous, Sam. The IVF clinics have egg samples that women have donated for research. But the woman's identity doesn't matter anyway, because the DNA is 100% Robby's. In this cloning strategy, the egg chromosomes have nothing to do with the zygote's genetic identity"

"What about the mitochondrial DNA? There is some DNA in the egg cytoplasm, you know," said Sam.

"Negligible."

"Ha! How would you feel if you were a woman and your mitochondrial DNA was called 'negligible.'?"

"Feeling has nothing to do with it. Whatever DNA is in the egg cytoplasm is statistically non-existent, infinitesimally small, insignificant. The egg wouldn't have to be from a woman anyway," Erik proclaimed.

"It wouldn't? Well, where would it come from, starship galactica?"

"It could come from a bovine, or an ovine. It wouldn't matter. It's just cytoplasm."

"Erik. What were we just saying a while ago about the cell environment making all the difference in the world in the genes' expression? First, you're talking about cloning Robby. Now, you've gone beyond that, making him into a chimera, with a cow or a ewe in a Petri dish!"

Erik was lol. "Nah, man. That's not what I said."

"Whatever, Erik. Hey man, I've got to go. We can figure this stuff out later."

"Yeah, me too, I'm supposed to meet Theseus in a little while for some special project ."

"Oh yeah? What's that?"

"I don't know. He said we'd be going out to the lab on River Road."

"I bet I know what it is."

"What?"

"You'll see. Hey, I gotta go. See ya."

hddq://theclone.dsh

Three hours later:

"Freedom!" yelled Bo.

"Yeah! Freedom!" echoed Willie, as one bovine blastomere to another. "We're outta here! Whoaoaoaoa!" Irresistable, rapturous suction was transporting them—Bo, and Willie and several hundred more of their companions beyond the confines of the bovine blastoceol they'd been languishing in for several days now. It felt like a great whooshing reversal of gravity, as they were, without warning, being sucked straight up into the great glass micropipette that had descended from the sky under the careful manipulation of Dr. William Theseus.

"There now, Erik. I've gotten most of them, I think," said the doc.

Whirring and whirling and splishing and splashing, the totipotent stemmy blastomeres of Elsie the cloned cow were being gathered, levitated, and translated to a gleaming glass dish that had been specially prepared for them. In that idealized, carefully concocted environment, they would be destined to grow perpetually in the assisted bliss of bovine stem cell culture. It was an uplifting experience for sure.

Bo's nucleus felt like it was spinning. "Awesome! That was better than Thunder Mountain Railway."

"You can say that again. Buzz Lightyear must have arranged for that one."

"Now, then. Here's the handoff. It's fourth and goal on the two. Take this pipette, Be careful not to break the plane of the laminar flow. Position it just above the Petri."

Erik was following instructions, while carefully observing sanitary protocols along the way. He was trying not to breathe, but allowed himself some liberty in that endeavor so as not to swoon onto the blastomeres.

Dr. Theseus resumed his direction, in a low, clear voice. "Lower the pipette carefully into the dish and, when you're ready, simply release the cells into the medium. That's right. Good job." They watched for a few seconds as Elsie's progeny stem cells were turned out to graze in their Petri dish pasture.

"Whooohooo!" shouted Bo. "Slip and slide!"

Willie challenged his buddy: "I'll race you to the other side,".

"Set the Petri into that incubator. Double-check the temperature setting. It should be set at 37° C. Be careful not to touch anything unnecessarily, When you're done, wipe everything down again with the alcohol. Now we'll give them a few days to see what the little buggers can come up with."

"What's in this medium, Dr. Theseus?"

This medium is a portion of a batch they made at LSU yesterday. They sold me a little bit. It's a solution of inorganic salts that the cells will need for metabolism. It's chemically balanced to duplicate osmotic pressure that the cell would have if it were actually in a cow uterus. It also contains amino acids and vitamins, for nutrition, and a pH indicator, and some alkaline buffers to keep the pH up where it ought to be—around 7.3."

"And how many stem cells do you think we transferred?" asked Erik.

"If we got, oh, a couple hundred from this week-old morula, we're doing good. We'll be checking them every day. Sam will do most of that since he lives here."

"It's too bad Robby's not around to get in on the action. I know he likes this sort of thing."

"Robby actually did the cloning procedure last week."

"That's funny. Sam and I were talking earlier today about cloning him."

"Cloning Robby?"

"Just joking around. We were talking about cloning one of Robby's cells so that we could grow a Robby embryo and then culture his stem cells and then direct some of them into being neurons for his spinal cord repair."

"If you could pull all that off, I'd nominate you for the Nobel. Maybe one day. Maybe one day you'll be on a team that can put all that together."

"I'd like that, and maybe working with Robby on it. He told us this morning that he's sure now. He absolutely wants to do spinal cord regeneration research."

"Hmm. Why am I not surprised. He certainly has a powerful incentive to move in that direction now."

hddq://robbysdream.sam

Robby had a dream.

It was the hammer and sickle thing. Freedom verses Slavery: Embryos crying out for personhood, but being herded instead into chimeric concentration camps under glass, their chromatic hammers swinging with molecular blacksmithery, forging the plasmidic implements of a bogus new world.

Eggs of Women crying out for fertility and progeny, but instead being scythed into Auschwitzian abyss.

And he heard their singing:

Hmphh ... Ah ...Hmphh ... Ah ...
That's the sound of the men working on the chain
gang.
That's the sound of the men working on the chain
gang.

And he knew the grunts of thousands of men a-groanin'; he heard the songs of millions of women a-moanin', giving birth. He heard the cries of their wounds, the pangs of their wombs. Slaves, they were. He heard them singing. *Don't ya hear Jerusalem moan? Don't ya hear Jerusalem moan?* No, it weren't all voluntary. No, Virginia, it weren't all voluntary. Hmphh ... Ah ...

Hmphh .. . Ah .. . *Pull that barge. Tote that bale.* He saw the burlap cotton sacks dragged upon the ground. Hmphh .. . Ah .. . Hmphh .. . Ah .. . He heard Moses demanding of the pharaoh, *Let my people go.* He heard Moses demanding of the pharaoh, *Let my people go.* He heard America singing, *follow the drinking gourd, follow the drinking gourd.*

He saw the strong brown arm of Washington Jones pull his great grandfather from the flood that swirled about a faltering riverboat. He felt the loss of footing as the boat careened upon raging waters, felt the lurch as the boat hit the mama oak and came to a sloshing, creaking crashing halt.

He saw, beyond the torrential horizon, the sod ripped from prairies by oxen teams, and he heard their bellowing, the cracking of the whips as Herculean animals strained and primordial prairie grasses became torn, the black earth turning up its wormy, smarmy loam to be kissed by the sun and drenched by the spring rains, the winter snows, the corn's roots, the wheat's shoots. He heard America singing, strains of music born of the resolve of freedmen, homesteaders, pioneers, farmers, Scandinavians, Scotch, Irish, African, indentured to the soil, and to their hopes for promised land.

Oklahoma! He heard Oklahoma, thousands of homesteaders spread in expectation across the dawning prairie horizon, buckboard wagons, horses, mules in anticipation of that great sounding signal from Uncle Sam, brought forth beneath the billowing skirts of fertile farming women, freckle-faced children in the shaded wagons, oxen in the sun, horses on the run.

Freedom? Yes, some were free, but 't'weren't all that sweat dripping into from free brows, Virginia. Much of it had come slitherin' in wet slavery drops of toil and blood and tears.

He heard low, slow, insidious munching of the dreaded boll weevil, chomping into oblivion acres upon millions of acres of lily-white wads of forced servitude.

He heard, like God, innocent blood crying out from the ground.

He heard the clanking of chains, the clashing of cultures and civilizations. *Can you hear the Cherokee moan? Can you hear the Chickasaw moan?.* He felt the tearing of their platted cords, the stomping of their ancestral hordes. It was a mournful cry heard round the world.

He heard the low, slow voice of Willie's embryonic call, *Freedom!*

He heard the high, spry response of Bo's ironic refrain, *Freedom!* blasting forth in totipotent nuclear song. The strains were there, ringing in his dream, clear as a splitting bell, bringing forth the clarion knell. He knew he heard the song; then it was gone.

He heard Elsie's low bovine moan. *Where Bo is now?*

hddq://theseusmed.loc

"Oh!" blurted Mick, bellowing like Balaam's ass. "For chrissake! Not you again."

Ophelia had violated Mick's personal space by poking her head into his hospital room. "Hey, I need to talk to you. I won't hurt you. You look like a man who needs a little feminine perspective."

"Say what?"

"Can I come in for a minute?" asked Ophelia, adding an element of the feminine mystique to her voice.

"Yeah, whatever." Mick dropped his head back on the pillow. There was something he liked about this woman, even though her age was a little older than he was accustomed to appreciating.

"So how are you doing, Mick?" said Ophelia, flippantly, as if they'd been raised together near a duck pond.

"I'm good," he answered, sassily. He looked out the window; his voice dropped. "This place is like a f....g prison."

"That's a bad word. You don't wanta be uttering it," cracked Ophelia.

"What?"

"Prison. It's a bad word."

"Sheez. Hey, what's a classy lady like you doing hanging around a hospital? Don't you have anything better to do?"

"I'm visiting you, for one thing. Isn't it nice to have someone who cares?"

"Like hell. You don't know me from Adam."

She looked at him steadily. "True enough, Mick. So what are you gonna do about it? Kick me out?"

"No. Your visit is convenient. Maybe you can help me spring this joint."

"Maybe. Aren't you being detained? Aren't there charges pending against you?"

"My lawyer has taken care of that. I'm out on bail now."

"Oh, is that so? How convenient."

"Yeah. This knife thing happened in my kitchen."

"Right."

"In my home, you know. It was self-defense. I was acting in self-defense."

Ophelia studied Mick's face. She had interviewed men of similar attitude before, men whose lines of distinction between deluded thoughts and thoughtless deeds were blurred by inebriants. "So, did, uh, did Robby have a weapon that he was about to use against you?"

"No, but Simon did. How do you think I got this?" Mick pointed to his bandaged thigh.

"Who struck first?"

"They entered my domicile."

Ophelia was lol. "Your *domicile!*"

"I'm serious, lady!"

"The jury will decide. What about the gold?"

"What gold?"

"The gold that was out at Theseus plantation, but now it's not because someone took it."

"Why are you asking me?"

"You're the only one who knew where it was."

"Who told you that? I've got nothing to do with it."

"You lie like a rug, boy."

"Are you crazy, woman? Just who are you to come snooping around, all the way from Ohio or wherever the hell you came from. You oughta go back there."

"North Carolina. I'm the person who got the other half of this stash."

"Third," said Mick, carelessly.

"What?"

"Never mind."

"I heard what you said. You know there were twice as many of the gold pieces here in Louisiana as there were where I come from."

"How did *you* get in on of this alleged gold?"

Ophelia was lol again. "*Alleged* gold? Who taught you that word, your lawyer?" She saw his face change. "Never mind. If you can get out of here, why don't we go find it? I have an idea where it might be."

"Where's that?"

"Uh, there are actually a couple of places. One of them is really close to the Theseus place. There's a country road bordering the property that I think might have been really attractive to the thief when he was trying to get away."

"You've been out there?"

"Oh yeah. Theseus dragged me out there at one in the morning the same night it happened."

"What did you see there?"

"Ha! A big hole in the ground!"

"How do you know it wasn't a setup? How do you know he didn't dig the hole himself and then bring an unsuspecting person like you out there to make it look like somebody else had done the job?"

Oh, now this is interesting. Ophelia put on her best perplexity. "Well, now, I *don't* know that, now that you mention it."

"He never owned that gold, you know. It's University property. He would have had to finagle some kind of scheme like this to recover it for himself."

Oh, the twisted ingenuity of a criminal mind that happens to be part banker. Ophelia was leaning hard into her thinking cap. "Hmm. Imagine that." She knit her eyebrows

A nurse walked in. "Is everything okay, Mr. Basker?" She had a thick Mexican accent.

"When will Dr. Richelieu be in here? He's going to release me today."

"He's just down the hall, sir, making rounds. He'll be here in a few minutes. Is there anything I can do for you while I'm here?"

"Just ask those nurses, please, to get my papers ready for checking me out of here."

"That would be a doctor's order, sir."

"Whatever. Tell him to get his ass down here." The nurse left the room. "He's been my doctor ever since I can remember," he said to Ophelia.

Mick looked at her and paused for a few seconds, as if he were seeing her for the first time. "Would you help me get out of bed?"

"Sure." And she did. He hobbled over to the bathroom, wincing along the way, and stepped inside the door. She heard the deadbolt turn. He was in there for ten minutes. Ophelia was whistling Dixie.

Dr. Richelieu walked in. He was tall, and bore a strong resemblance to Charles DeGaulle. "Bonjour," said Ophelia, and laughed. "I mean, hello."

He smiled at her and pointed at the bathroom door. "What are you doing in there, Mick? I don't have all day."

"I'll be out in just a second. Are you gonna let me out of here?"

"Come on out and we'll talk about it."

The deadbolt turned. Mick hobbled out of the restroom and leaned against the bed. "Thanks for dropping in, doc. As you can see, I'm getting around pretty good for someone who was just shot a couple days ago. I'm ready to leave now."

"You need to keep that wound clean, and wrapped up for the next week. If it starts to hurt any more than it does now, call me. You can unwrap it to take a shower after tomorrow. Be sure and bandage it back up good, and use the Neosporin on it. I want to see you next Monday in my office. Any questions?"

"You got a prescription?"

"I called them in already—two of them, one for the antibiotic, and the other for pain."

"That's what I'm talking about, doc." Mick raised his hand in mock salute. "See ya!"

"You behave yourself, Mick."

"Right. I'm all over it."

The doctor walked out. "Can you give me a ride home?" he asked.

"I don't have a car here."

"We can take mine. It's in the parking lot. It'll take a few minutes to get this shit together, if you don't mind."

"That's fine, Mick. Take your time. Do you want to get in the wheelchair? It might save some time getting down to the car."

"Yeah. Hey, could you pick up that book, please?"

Ophelia reached to the floor and retrieved the book that had fallen behind the bed. It was a book on card tricks. She watched the young man struggle to gather everything, which included a very slick pair of pinstriped chartreuse designer pajamas, into a duffel bag and a briefcase. There wasn't much to it. He sat in the wheel chair. She handed him a floral pot that had been on the window sill. The card was said, *Get Well Soon, Mom and Dad.* She set it gingerly atop the duffel bag on his lap. The briefcase was also on his lap. The other flowers, from Josephine, she took with her left hand, and rolled him out of the room.

Two nurses offered a polite goodbye as Ophelia wheeled him past the nurses' station. When they reached the elevator, she said, "Do you want to go up to Robby's room?"

"Why would I want to do that?"

"I just thought you might want to." There were many life principles that Ophelia would like to have imparted to the young desperado, but she had a more important mission in mind. For now, she'd keep the verbiage to a minimum. She had heard somewhere that if you give a thief enough rope, he'd hang himself. Mick seemed to have a teratoma noosed around his soul.

Coils

26

"Turn right out of here. Take this street to Carrollton. Then turn right again." He slid the seat back as far as it would go, and stretched his right leg out. It was obvious Mick was dealing with some pain.

"You might have rushed it a bit, checking out of the hospital so soon," said Opelia. Mick didn't say anything. Driving the Jaguar was a new experience for Ophelia. *I could get used to this.* When they reached Carrollton Avenue, she turned right.

"Go up to the expressway, and turn right onto it." They rode in silence for a few minutes. Mick was nervous. And so was Ophelia, not knowing what she had gotten herself into. She had entered his room on an impulse about an hour and a half ago. Now she was breezing along in control of a Jaguar on a concrete ribbon that stretched eastward, just a little higher than the funky city below. It was about four in the afternoon. The city was hazy, like the unclear sort of agenda that seemed to hang over their expedition. Or maybe the unclear agenda was in her mind. Ophelia had no idea where they were headed. Over to the right were the brown and grey, dated, middle of the pack skyscraping obelisks of an old city whose glory days had checked out about 1965 or so, leaving generous tips for the bellmen and the cab drivers and the dancers and the jazzmen on the street and providing suitable gratuities for the artists and fortune tellers on Jackson Square, but no guaranteed income for those citizens born into the metropolis where every man is a king, and the queen of hearts trumps spades with the everpresent half-empty glass in her hand and a gaggle of Mardi Gras beads coiled around her neck while the jack of diamonds stands outside a strip club on Bourbon Street summoning desperate souls.

But it wasn't entirely dicey. New Orleans' irresistible character and native nobility was—in spite of the worn-out rehearsals of a painted lady personsa whose playbill was perpetually posted on that old streetcar named desire—despite all that hurley-burley girly exploitation, its future hung upon, still, the solid hopes and noble dreams of a million creole souls whose thin checkbooks and postage stamp domiciles sheltered them from the same deluge of disaster that lapped upon the levees or bridges or subways or suburbs or cul-de-sacs of any city in the wounded, wound-up world. Furthermore, there was still a place there where you could hear old colored men and young, hopeful white guys and gals who had a thing or two to learn about authentic music sing *Just a Closer Walk with Thee*. There's always hope. There's always hope for a great city. *And I told him that.*

"Take this exit," said Mick.

A few minutes later, "Turn here,". He pointed to a short driveway on the left.

Ophelia disembarked from the Jaguar chariot, walked around to the other side, feeling as if she were now a personal chauffeur for a debilitated criminal. She opened the door, retrieved from the back seat the crutches that the medical people had provided, and handed them to the whippersnappin' young banker whose fortunes were now somehow unexplainedly linked to hers, as if *some consequence yet hanging in the stars shall bitterly begin with this night's revels..*

Slowly, Mick righted himself from the chariot's passenger seat, closed its door, hobbled to the door of his funky little warehouse kingdom. She handed his keys to him. He found the right one, inserted it into the deadbolt, let himself in. His wary companion followed.

Mick promptly sat down at his antique, water-stained wooden desk, opened the bottom drawer, withdrew a stumpy glass tumbler and a half-empty whisky bottle, poured himself a drink, and took a swig. "You want a drink?" said he.

"Uh, yeah, I could, uh, sure."

From the low drawer, he produced another stumpy glass. He poured some whisky into it.

"Do you have any water? I like mine with, uh, a little water."

He pointed to a small refrigerator on a table to his left. "Over there, and there's ice too, if you want it."

She could see the relief in his eyes as he poured another one. *What now?* And she noticed that, as he leaned back in the chair, it rolled back slightly away from the desk, and he was relaxing. He had been released from the sterile, unfamiliar environment of a hospital room, and now was returned to the kingdom of his own roost, the intoxication of his own mind. He looked around the large garage-room with satisfaction. It was stacked high with boxes and odd items from, apparently, all over the world. *He must be running an import business.* Scattered and stacked in crannies between crates, bolts of colorful fabric and an odd menagerie of animal sculptures, were an eclectic hodgepodge of brass vessels, glass vases, kettles, pottery, jars and painted dishes, gauche adornments hung like curtains, paper flowers of red and yellow, smallish knickknacks. Mick's eyes surveyed the scene with self-congratulatory glee and palpable relief, until at last they rested upon a certain spot, at which point the contentment within him devolved into a kind of unexpected alarm. Setting his good leg awkwardly on the floor, he leaned forward attentively and announced:

"Someone has been in here."

Then he was struggling to right himself. She walked to where he was, extended a hand to him, so that he could get to his feet. Having accomplished this, he shuffled toward the spot that had caught his attention, where stood an open cardboard box. He opened the flaps, peered inside, reached into it and moved its contents around, as if looking for something he knew not what. Then she saw in his hand a large book, coffee-table book, on Mayan art. Setting it aside, he withdrew a primitive clay figure, and set it aside. As he turned slightly in her direction to resume the inventory of his stuff, a puzzled look crossed his face. Mick was trying to remember something. Encountering a wrought-iron glass-topped table in the middle of the room, he negotiated himself around it, using its convenient height for support. Moving steadily away from her toward the far wall, which was lined with shelves full of more stuff, he said it again:

"Someone has been in here."

Then it became evident to Ophelia that he was progressing toward a specific object, which, when he had reached it, he studied carefully. It was an art figure of a burro. She thought it must be a Mexican piece. With its back about one meter high, it stood straight and dumb, expressionless, as a burro would. The large ears, neck, back, sides, legs, all parts of it except face and tail, were artfully covered with small multi-colored, one-square-centimeter tiles, laid in thin white grout that surrounded every piece. The tail was different. Made of natural fiber, probably hemp, it hung limply, about half as long as a person's arm.   Mick ceased his labored movements and stood inspecting it, his right hand resting on its back. Ophelia had a bizarre thought that the colorful donkey might somehow turn its head aside and speak to the man. But of course this did not happen. Instead, he spoke to it: "Don't tell me. . ."

There was an old wooden chair nearby. Pulling it to his side, he managed, with some difficulty, to seat himself in it with the injured leg straight out in front of him. In this awkward position, he was directly behind the lifeless animal, his face level with the tail. He lifted its tail, as if he were about to do some kind of veterinary examination. His face was very close to the rump, and it almost seemed for a moment that he was about to kiss the ass. *What a ridiculous thought! Oh, but he is s a strange man, a lonely man.*

Then Mick reached between the statue's legs, where the gonads would be on a real donkey, and grabbed something. Ophelia heard a low scraping sound that sounded as if it were coming from a hollow space. Then there was a chunk of the body in Mick's hand. He set it gently on the floor, at the same time lowering his head to get a direct view into the donkey's backside, where the large intestines would be. And then his head was upright again, now with an expression of absolute horror. Hurriedly, he inserted his arm, and it went all the way into the ass' vacant interior. Ophelia could hear Mick's hand thrashing inside of it, grasping for some prize or object that was not there. Exasperated, he quickly withdrew his arm, pushed the object away from himself as if attempting to overturn it. But it did not turn over; it simply stood there, as a stubborn mule might do in the presence of an invasive man.

Mick's sudden wrath alarmed Ophelia. She was, after all, a doctor of anthropology, accustomed to the quiet decorum of tamed, academic men whose studious comments such as *I think therefore I am,* and *on the other hand,* filled numerous echoing cupolas with polite conversation, and complemented many a rotunda of civilized, evolving society. But this guy was a horse of a different color. He was crazy! And he manifested that dysfunction by thrashing, throwing objects about the room, cursing profusely, screaming in purgatorian agony until at last he toppled from the little chair and landed on the cluttered concrete floor. After the chaotic minute of acting out, Mick's consequent position was sprawled helplessly between the donkey and a garish antique brass winged gargoyle with its tongue stuck out. He lay there with tears in his eyes and the debilitating awareness that some absent person had nefariously betrayed him.

The professor wanted to just check out, because she was scared of what this man might do, but instead she managed to collect her internal reserves of kindness and corrective inclinations, and so she said:

"Mick?"

He didn't say anything.

"Mick?"

"Could you please just leave?" was his response.

"How are you going to. . .you can't—"

"Just don't you worry your pretty head about it. I can take care of myself. Thanks for the ride. See ya."

She walked back to the chair where she had been sitting before; she sat in it.

"Is there something wrong?"

"Look, lady—"

"Is there something missing?"

"Shit! woman!"

"Is it the gold?"

"Dammit! Get out of here. You're trespassing. I'll call the cops on you.

"Ha! Fat chance." There was a phone handset on the desk beside her. Opheliia grabbed it and tossed it in his direction. "Go ahead." The phone hit the burro's side and landed with a thud on his injured leg.

"Oh, shit!" He reeled in pain.

"Oh, I'm sorry, Mick. I didn't mean to hit you with it." She really had not meant to hurt him.

"Are you going to leave, or not?"

Now there was a resolve in his voice that indicated a return to some semblance of rationality. She had alienated him, or he had alienated himself, or there was some secret that he still had a presence of mind to conceal. She re-evaluated her position, decided to concede it. She had, after all, learned something about him, and now she had his address—his second address.

"Very well then, Mick. Have it your way. Have a nice day." Without further ado, she was outta there. She slammed the door behind her. Its rattling finality was the conclusion to an unanticipated, freaky encounter between two individuals whose paths would never have crossed had it not been for the impulsive knocking of an anthropologist's delicate hand upon a hospital room door in mid-afternoon.

Now it was time for the anthropologist to conduct some unstructured field observation. She was wandering through a clamorous creole dusk, making olfactory notes about the power of simmerin' mustard greens on one block and red beans on another to startle her appetite. The wily Mick was left behind to stew in his own juices. *Br'er fox, he was laid low.*

Soeur *rabbit, she done bolted.* She be skedaddlin', wide-eyed, down Esplanade, toward the River, and wondering what to do about it.

hddq://genesis4.loc

Then Mick, having very little strength left to right himself, just laid his head upon the concrete floor. This life had propelled him beyond the anal end of his own striven, driven strength. Now all was still, but not by his choice, and behold. He had a dream.

He was standing at the stern of a boat as it sped upon the River. The wind was cold and damp and whipping in his ears. The ship's wake went out and away from him, churning symmetrically white and muddy brown in frothy, powerful frenzy. Distant banks of the river seemed to be moving away, converging far behind him as they slid toward some small or vast finitude at the horizon. It was the very present sliding into its inevitable past. He could see what was to the west, and what was to the east, and what was behind him to the south, to a point. But beyond that horizon speck and line, he could not see.

There was a point in time and space at which his own perception failed him. Beyond that line he must accept some other rendition than his own.

Then he saw the face of one whom he had stabbed. And Robby opened his mouth to speak, and when he had opened it, Mick saw within it a deep darkness, a deep dark abyss of human vulnerability and frailty, which he himself, Mick, had cut asunder. And he saw Robby's life hanging by a cord. And he saw himself, Mick, reach into a sheath and withdraw a sword, with which he would sever Robby's silver cord. But then Robby opened the mouth of darkness and spoke, as if he were speaking from the dead, and he said:

"I am crouching at your door. Your own hand has cut my cord, and nearly put me in the River, where I may yet perish beneath the wake of your ship. But whether I sink beneath that wake or not, I will still come crouching at your door. My silver cord will wrap around you, and I will pull you in here with me, Mick. In the end, the River and the cord and the darkness will have you as well." And he heard Robby's spectre crouching at his door.

Oh yes, there **was** a knock at the door. Mick turned his head. *Where am I? I am...I am in my warehouse.* There was another knock at the door. Then another, and another, a loud one. "What--?" He wanted to open his mouth to speak to the door, to speak to the person at the door, but his mouth would not move, his soul could not speak. "Wha--?"

The door opened. "Mick?"

"Wha--?"

"Yo, Mick. It's Vinnie. You in here?"

"Wha--?"

hddq://theseusmed.loc

"Dad, what do you think is the difference between an embryo in a woman's womb and one that is frozen after being fertilized *in vitro?*"

"Growth," replied Noah. "If we could look at them both right now, and then look at them both one week from now, the embryo *in utero* would have grown, would have added more cells, progressed to a new stage of development. The one that is frozen would have, of course, shown no change whatsoever. Isn't it amazing? A person's life can be totally suspended like that, and then renewed at a later point in time."

"If it *is* a person," said Erik, who was visiting.

"Of course it's a person," said Noah. "If it's a human egg that's been fertilized by a human sperm, it's a person."

"That figures," said Sam. "The female egg, which has 23 chromosomes, is half a person. When the sperm, which also has 23 chromosomes, unites with it, then it becomes something else entirely—a *person*, with a complete set of 46 chromosomes."

"Is personhood defined, then, by the number of chromosomes?" asked Robby. "Someone with Down's Syndrome has an extra 21st chromosome, making a total of 47. Is he, or she, a person?"

"He has more than enough chromosomes to be classified as a person," said Sam, smiling

"He's overqualified," quipped Erik, facetiously.

"Right, but still a person," said Sam.

"Yeah," agreed Robby. "But I'm wondering about something else. For thousands of years, each *person* that has been born had to survive a difficult journey—you might even think of it as a kind of trial—in which, as a brand-new zygote, they had to complete a sojourn up the fallopian tube and then implant in the uterus. Nowadays, with *in vitro* fertilization and freezing, the process for attaining embryonic status—you might say the ordeal that must be endured in order to reach *personhood*—becomes something fundamentally different from what it was before. It requires, not *natural selection*, but rather a scientific selection that's made by a third party, a scientist. The scientist takes the place of the historical third party, God, or perhaps chance (if that's the way you view it). I'm just wondering if this definitive change in the selection mode affects the embryo's status as a person. Is the *in vitro* person who gets laid into a deep freeze for several years human in the same sense as someone who is conceived naturally in a woman's womb?"

"Absolutely," said Noah to his son. "Think about the big picture, and the potential *growth* within that big picture. Imagine what each embryo would look like ten years from now. Each one would be a ten-year old child, a real person. The conception process would not have made any difference."

"Unless one of them is put into a freezer. Then it remains a speck for however many years while the other becomes a person—a ten-year old child," said Robby.

"Even if one was put on ice," said Sam. "if you took it out of the freezer after ten years, and implanted it in a woman's uterus, it would still become a person."

"It would *become* a person?" asked Robby. "What was it while it was in the freezer? I mean, isn't a **person** someone who breathes, or at least processes oxygen in some way, feels, responds to stimuli, moves around a little bit? Isn't that what establishes personhood? That they are able to somehow *respond to* the conditions around them."

"You're switching definitions on us," said Erik. "We already said it was a person when it was conceived with the total chromosome package of 46."

"But here's what I'm getting at," said Robby. "If the mother, or any other woman for that matter, requests that the frozen embryo be taken out of the freezer, implanted in her womb, and allowed to grow as a fetus and eventually a baby—that's one thing."

" It's perfectly natural," said Erik, "that she would want that for her baby."

"It's not exactly *natural*," said Robby, " It's pretty high-tech, actually, but, it *does* work. Sure. I got no problem with it. We could say it's a legitimate way to bring a person into the world—if the process is allowed to progress to its full fruition and purpose."

"That's the birth of a child," added Noah, "and the personhood that accompanies each child's entrance into this world."

"You guys think too much," said Erik.

"It's not really because of thinking that we arrive at this conclusion, Erik. It really comes down to what we believe. Believing is not the same as thinking, and it doesn't necessarily interfere with scientific method or enquiry. But hey, you're right about one thing. I am thinking a lot here. I'm trying to figure a few things out . I've just been stabbed in the back, and I'm thinking about life a little differently. Is that okay?"

"Sure, Robby. I didn't mean to ruffle your feathers. But it's all really just molecules and cells interacting with each other. I think you're making too much of it."

"Maybe so, Erik. But think about this. What if one embryo gets implanted in mama's uterus—one little baby Huey, and it grows up just fine, no problem, a perfectly normal person. I'm not saying that can't happen. But the other zygotes that were formed at the same time when Joe Scientist released daddy's sperm into mama's eggs *in vitro*. What about, after ten years, or twenty years, that embryo is still sitting there, on a shelf in a dark, lifeless place, 196 degrees Celsius below zero. Maybe the donor parents are dead, or divorced. Or maybe there is an interruption in the supply of liquid nitrogen. Could be any number of things. What about the little *person* then, huh? That's a helluva long time to wait for a bus, or a stork or whatever. After twenty years, let's say, nobody wants the embryo any more, and maybe it's not practical to maintain its frozen condition. So here comes the medical researcher, with the best of intentions of course, to the lab and tells the lab technician that he'll take the embryo and use it for research to help find a cure for Parkinsons or Muscular Dystrophy or hemophilia or some other genetic disease."

"Sure," said Erik. "Makes perfect sense."

"But I thought we said it was a person, because it had 46 chromosomes, way back when, twenty years ago when it was fertilized."

"How would the embryo be used in medical research?" asked Noah.

"Good question, dad," said Robby. "And that's really what I'm wondering about, because most likely what they would do in the lab would be this—remove the inner cell mass, and then culture the embryo's totipotent cells for research purposes."

"So that would kill the embryo, wouldn't it?" asked Noah.

"Yes." said Robby.

"But ten or twenty years from now things could be totally different," offered Sam. "By that time, maybe they could peel a few stem cells out and then release the embryo, unharmed, back to a mother for implantation," Sam said.

"What mother, though," asked Erik, "would want to take a chance on an embryo that had been robbed of some of its cells? It might be damaged, And chances are there'd be a whole bunch of other frozen embryos (they call them 'snowflakes' by the way) that hadn't been manipulated in that way, to choose from. No prospective parents would want to take a chance on a kid—a 'snowflake'—that may be damaged, when there is a plentiful supply of untouched embryos around to choose from."

"So the one that has been tampered with might as well be turned over to science," declared Erik.

"Like a cadaver," remarked Sam.

"But a cadaver has already had a shot at life," said Noah.

"Right, dad." A cadaver has already acquired and released a *soul*," agreed Robby. "Not only that, but it probably agreed to, while it was still a living person, donating its leftover parts to science."

"It was pro-choice," cracked Sam.

Hahaha.

"What we're really talking about, then, is sacrificing the little embryo person so that some other person can be cured of a disease," remarked Noah.

"That's the only function that it has," said Erik. "Nobody else has use for it."

"Well, this is what I'm *wondering* about, you see," said Robby, holding up his hand. " Because what if the person who might receive the benefit of this embryo's involuntary sacrifice is *me?*"

"You betcha," said Erik. "There are surplus embryos whose ICM stem cells are being harvested right now, as we speak, so that the medical profession can devise a procedure to regenerate *your* spinal cord."

"Sacrificed," said Robby, grimly.

"You're worth it," Becky interjected, looking at her son."

"I appreciate that mother," said Robby, "but what I'm worth is not the issue. What are *they* worth, as persons, or as potential persons? That's the issue."

"It might be a moot point anyway," said Sam.

"How's that?" asked Robby.

"The treatments for spinal cord injury will most likely be built upon the work of *neural* stem cells, not embryonic stem cells."

" You mean adult stem cells?" asked Robby.

"Yeah, everybody has them," answered Sam. "They're in your body, any adult body, in various locations. That's how our bodies replace damaged skin or muscle tissue, or broken bones, or lost blood. It's all about adult stem cells."

"But, Sam, I don't think neural cells in the spinal cord operate regeneratively. They don't have those capabilities like other stems in other types of tissues."

"True," agreed Sam, "but the neurons in your *peripheral* nervous system can regenerate. The nerve cells in your limbs, skin, most any place in your body can replace themselves. They have resident adult stem cells that can take on the renewal functions."

"And that is what the researchers are attempting to do, I think. They're trying to find a way to enable those neurons in the spinal column and brain to have that same capability," said Robby.

"That's where the embryonic stem cells come in, Robby," said Erik. "The researchers need massive numbers of pluripotent stem cells to carry out the experiments in the labs. It's just like any science. There's a lot of hypothesizing, a lot of trial and error. They need a lot of raw material to work with. So they need large numbers of undifferentiated cells in culture. Once thay have a bunch of them proliferating, they can split the colonies up and tweak them in various ways to specialize as whatever type of cell they're working on. Certain ones of them can be manipulated into becoming neurons."

"So they sacrifice little person embryos so they can do their experiments," said Noah.

"I suppose so," Sam agreed warily, "if you want to look at it that way."

"It's like primitive men sacrificing animals so they can have food and clothing," continued Noah. "Except for this fact: these are humans, they are *persons*." .

"Right," agreed Robby. "We did say they were 'persons.' Remember?"

"If you want to look at it that way," added Erik.

"Well, that's what I'm wondering about. That's why I brought it up. If I'm now considered to be a 'victim' who can benefit from this type of research, I'm, uh, just trying to decide how I feel about it."

"Don't think too hard about it," advised Erik. "If they make a breakthrough in the next few years, you may have a chance to walk again. Then you'll have something to celebrate."

"True, Erik. and that's why I find myself, in this debilitated condition, *really* wanting to be a part of whatever research is underway to solve this problem."

"The choices look pretty clear to me," said Erik. "They're doing the research, probably making steady progress. You either jump on the bandwagon or you don't."

"I've got plenty of time to consider the options, Erik. So I'm going to take a close look at them. There's more than one bandwagon out there on the research train."

"That's right, son," agreed Noah. "One thing you'll definitely have in the foreseeable future is time to think."

Breaks

27

"Johnny told us there were cops all over the place at your house."

"Help me up here,, will ya?" demanded Mick.

Vinnie and Tony each got on one side of Mick's fallen stature. Vinnie was anxious to offer his explanation of the ass' missing payload, so he spoke hurriedly as they lifted Mick up to a standing position. "We figured they might come here looking for the gold. With you strung up in the hospital, somebody had to get over here and get the stuff out so they wouldn't find it. So we did."

"Where is it now?"

"It's at my brother's apartment."

"Where's that?"

"Canal Street."

Slowly, they escorted their crippled mentor to his desk, where he plopped into a chair. "Damn. This is starting to hurt again." Wincing, Mick pulled a prescription bottle from his pocket, opened it and extracted a pill. "Vinnie, pour me a drink, will ya?" Vinnie responded obediently. Leaning his head back, Mick tossed the pill in his mouth, took a slug from the stumpy glass. "Does your brother know there's a fool's ransom of gold in his apartment?"

"No. I've got it tucked away."

"Who is your brother?"

"Julian, you know. He works at Louie's Restaurant."

"Oh yeah. Why'd you take it there?

"His place is closer than any other good place I could think of. And he wasn't home at the time, so that made it pretty easy to get it hidden away."

Mick sat back in his chair, feeling the effect of his whiskey, and comforted in the knowledge that soon the pain pill would kick in. "We need to go over there and get it."

"No problem, boss."

"You think you can drive my car?"

"Yes, sir!"

"Let's do it then."

A few minutes later, Mick was installed in the back seat of his BMW, with Vinnie at the wheel, Tony riding shotgun. Vinnie gingerly backed the chariot onto Esplanade, eased it into Drive and got on down the road. They turned onto Royal Street, which would be a straight shot all the way to Canal Street, where Julian's apartment was.

"Julian's place is on the second floor, and it's right on the corner above the drug store. But there's no elevator. How do you want to do this?"

"Is your brother home?"

"No. He's at work now."

"Good, except there's no way I can get up those stairs with you without a whole lot of hassle."

"Yeah. But there's a loading zone right outside. If you want me to park there, Tony can go up and get the bag."

"Is that on the Canal Street side, or the Royal Street side?"

"That loading spot is on Canal. The stairway door is on Royal."

"When we get there, take it slow, and I'll tell you what to do."

They went the full distance of Royal Street. Darkness had descended. Now they were less than a block from the place. The apartment door would be coming up on the right. Mick was slumped in the back seat, his neck extended like a turtle's, scoping out the logistics of the situation. Sidewalks on both sides of Royal Steet were crowded with the Quarter's inevitable evening curiosity-seekers and chronic revelers.

"Tony, do you know where the gold is inside the apartment?" asked Mick.

"I know exactly where it is. Vinnie put it in the cabinet behind Julian's old record collection."

"You think you can get in there and bring the stuff out here without screwing up?"

"Oh yeah."

Vinnie handed his young companion a key ring. "It's that key with the round head. Put everything back *exactly* the way it was, so Julian won't know anything, and so he won't bitch about us messing up the place. Don't forget to turn out the light when you leave."

As they approached the apartment door, Vinnie said," No place to park. You wanna go around the corner and hang at the loading zone and wait for him there?" Vinnie turned his head, looked at Mick, so as to get direct instruction.

"No. Tony you get out here. We'll circle the block and come back for you." Vinnie stopped the Beemer. He felt like he was driving Cinderella's carriage. At any moment it could turn into a pumpkin.

Tony opened the passenger door, leaped out, closed the door a little harder than necessary, darted like a bat between parked cars and strollers on the sidewalk. As Vinnie eased the car up to the line to wait for the Canal Street traffic light and the pedestrians to clear, Mick watched as Tony let himself into the apartment door, without a hitch. Vinnie spun the power steering like a ballerina to make a right onto Canal. They rode down Canal Street one block, turned right, went around the block completely and came back to the apartment door again. No sign of Tony. He was still inside taking care of business, so they made another round.

On the sidewalk, just outside Julian's apartment door, this is how it happened:

"What is that smell, honey? asked Gertrude Twain, calling to her husband, Jim. Gertrude, a large woman, stopped in her tracks. "Omigod, Jim! I can't stand it. Where is that aroma coming from?"

Jim, who had been rolling along ahead of her in his motorized wheelchair, responded, "What smell, dear? I don't smell anything."

"Come back here for a minute and catch a whiff of it. Whatever it is, I want to find wherever its coming from and have dinner there."

Jim halted the wheelchair abruptly. Just to his right, an easel had been inconveniently placed on the sidewalk with this message painted on it: *For the benefit of Mr. Kite, there will be a show tonight . . .Shears'*

Lounge, 357 Canal. Unable to make a proper turn, he dropped his machine into reverse to sniff out whatever it was that Gertrude was discovering.

At that moment, Tony was locking the apartment door. Having accomplished his upstairs mission, he pivoted toward the street, where he would rejoin his mentors with the long-awaited precious cargo, which he carried in a large fabric bag with a wooden handle.

"I know what it is, Jim. It's crawfish etouffee, " said Gertrude.

Tony turned around.

"I wanna get a cookbook, and when we get back to Cairo—"

Without warning, Tony was suddenly spread-eagled on Jim and his wheelchair. And the angels were singing.

Excuse me. They were not singing. The ringing sounds that harmonized near the corner of Royal and Canal were not angels. They were the pinging of gold florins—dozens of them—cascading onto grody, cigarette-butted pavement. In the air for one slow-motion moment, they ascended and descended, sparkling beneath the streetlights, glinting amid the neon haloes and the headlights, announcing their rare metallic presence to the city of New Orleans. They wobbled to a rest, some of them, beside old chewing gum wads, rolling across the feet of fortunate strollers, leaping gloriously over the dingy curb, miraculously landing in the expectant hands of Harry the handout king who sat strategically nearby, even bumping the steel-belted sidewalls of rolling Firestones and Uniroyals out on Rue Royale. And when all had settled into momentous occasionality, there lay the empty fabric bag beside Jim's wheelchair, it's logo emblazoned upward for all to appreciate: *Bull's Run, Las Vegas, Nevada.* In spite of Tony's small stature hung clumsily over his hurting right shoulder, Jim could see three gold florins on his lap.

"Doubloons!" somebody yelped. "It's Mardi Gras!" Then, as if a flock of pigeons were their progenitors, the ravenous passersby made their eager visitation, groping the dark sidewalk.

"That's mine!" Tony shouted, to no avail.

Back at the other end of the block, Vinnie was turning the Beemer from Iberville Street onto Royal, but couldn't move beyond the corner. Traffic was backed up. Mick strained his neck out the window. Vinnie knew this was cause for worry, especially since his careless sidekick was in the vicinity of the unknown delay. He said," I can't see what it is, but there's something going on up there."

Something snapped in Mickey's soul. He opened the back car door. "Vinnie, come over here and help me get out, will ya?"

They were stuck in the traffic anyway. Vinnie set the Beemer into Park, opened the driver door, got out, walked around to the rear passenger side where Mick was struggling to upright himself. With just enough room between the curb and the car to step onto the street, Vinnie put his foot down next to a beer can, reached down, grabbed Mick's upraised hand, and gently pulled him out of the car. Mick slowly negotiated himself over the curb and onto the sidewalk. Vinnie shut the door behind him. "Okay," said Mick. "Thanks. I'm going to walk up here and see what's happening. How 'bout you find a place to park somewhere whenever this loosens up."

"Okay, Mick."

With that suggestion, Mick winced, and set out traipsing toward the apartment at the far end of the block. He dragged his shot leg, assuming an awkward rhythm that approached the speed of a racing snail. He couldn't see what was happening up ahead, except that he knew there were people crouched on the sidewalk, or kneeling on it. A sizable crowd had gathered; they impaired his view. It made no sense that a dozen strangers were groveling on the sidewalk. He thought for a moment they were praying. Somebody somewhere was praying.

When he reached the lowered crowd, he saw what occupied their busy, grasping hands; they were gathering golden spots from the concrete. And he knew that all was lost. They seemed like a flock of chickens pecking away at his fortune. Mick searched within himself for some resolve to stop them—to assert his claim to the gold. And then he knew, for the truth flooded his mind, that he had no claim to the gold. It never was his, never would be.

Tony was there, looking like the lost kid that he was, and when he caught sight of Mick, he stepped gingerly through the gang of scrappers, now dispersing. In his hand was the Las Vegas bag, which he sheepishly handed over to Mick. Peering into it, Mick could see some coins in the bottom. Tony started to speak: "I was turning around and—"

Mick raised his hand to signal silence. "Later," he said. Now he was watching the crowd evaporate, their pockets no doubt heavier than before.

They had done a thorough job of clearing the ground. There was not a stray coin in sight, only the flat darkness of city sidewalk grunge remained. All was as it had been before Tony collided with Jim Twain. Busy people had resumed their passings on a busy street, like nothing had happened.

Then out of the darkness one man stepped directly in front of Mick. His dark hair and beard were long. An enigmatic hint of a smile brightened his face. He seemed familiar. The man's large hands were cupped together, and he positioned them directly over the bag that was now in Mick's hands. "Hold on tight," said he. Releasing his hands slowly from the cupped position. the stranger produced a torrent of gold florins, plummeting directly into Mick's bag. Mick could hear them individually striking the gathered horde below. Their increasing weight required that he place one hand underneath the bag to prevent its ripping. Then Mick saw the man's empty, upturned hands, and the bag had become heavy. Mick looked directly into the stranger's eyes. "Thank you," said Mick.

The stranger offered only the veiled smile, then slid to Mick's right side and walked away, headed in the direction from which they had approached. Mick pivoted clumsily to witness his departure, and saw nothing more than a long-haired man walking away through a crowd of people in the streetlight-neon glow of city night.

Tony was looking at the guy too. Then he looked up at Mick with something between dread and wonder in his young face. Mick rolled the fabric bag into a bundled lump, handed it to Tony and asked, "Can you hold this for me?"

Tony said nothing, only hung his head sheepishly. Mick gently placed his right hand on the back of the kid's neck. Tony thought Mick was going to shake the hell out of him. But Mick didn't. He squeezed the kid's neck affectionately, like an older brother would do. Mick smiled. "No problem. Come on, let's go." They headed back toward the Beemer, which had just begun to move.

When they had managed to get back in Mick's car, Vinnie asked, "You wanna go back to Esplanade?"

"Nah," answered Mick. "Go to the Med Center at Theseus."

hddq://makeitright.msg

Mick walked into Robby' hospital room. "Hello, Robby," said he.

"Hello, Mick."

"I owe you something."

"What's that, Mick?"

"An apology. I'm sorry I stabbed you in the back."

"Hey, man, forgiven," said Robby.

Their eyes met. Water under the bridge, Spilt milk. Straw that broke the camel's back. Two broken lives. What else is new?

Mick saw Dr. Theseus standing at the foot of the bed. "I owe you something, too." With that admission, he held out the rolled-up fabric bag, heavy with some precious contents. William accepted it, then unfurled it, garish Las Vegas logo and all. He glanced inside the bag; his eyes expressed no surprise. " Thank you for finding this for us, Mick. This is the seed of the Robby Davis Foundation for Spinal Cord Regeneration Research." Plato Zupoff's earthen deposit had at last found its appropriate best use.

And so had Mick.

There were two other people in the room. They stood directly opposite him on the other side of the bed. "And I owe you an apology as well," he said to Noah. "I'm sorry I stabbed your son in the back. I was wrong."

"How did you arrive at that conclusion?" asked Noah.

"I, uh," Mick hesitated, with tears—pain, repentance, deliverance, joy, whatever. It was a chimera of emotions. "I, uh, I got tired of kissing ass, or kicking against the pricks, or. . ." He raised his head, with a kind of relief suddenly illuminating his demeanor. "Mr. Davis, you owe me something."

"What's that?"

"An explanation."

Made in the USA
Charleston, SC
30 August 2010